WHITE LIES

CHRISTOPHER HYDE

WHITE LIES

SIMON & SCHUSTER

LONDON·SYDNEY·NEW YORK·TOKYO·SINGAPORE·TORONTO

First published in Great Britain by
Simon & Schuster Ltd in 1990
A Paramount Communications Company

Copyright © Christopher Hyde, 1990

Simon & Schuster Ltd
West Garden Place
Kendal Street
London W2 2AQ

Simon & Schuster of Australia Pty Ltd
Sydney

A CIP catalogue record for this book is
available from the British Library
ISBN 0–671–71710–3

Typeset in Ehrhardt 11/13 by Selectmove
Printed and bound in Great Britain by
Richard Clay Ltd, Bungay, Suffolk

AUTHOR'S NOTE

The research in *White Lies* is accurate, as is all the information relating to the history, structure and day to day routines within the White House. In the interests of public safety a small number of technical details have been altered slightly.

Christopher Hyde

In loving memory of
Little M.
Too short a life,
but lived with utmost joy.

PROLOGUE

Hotel Washington
Washington DC
10 April 1945

The two men occupying the opulently decorated sitting room of the suite in the Hotel Washington were dressed in civilian clothes, but it was clear from the way the older man stood and moved that he was uncomfortable out of uniform.

While the younger man read, his companion, dark-haired and heavyset, stood by the window, teeth clamped around the end of his long, fuming cigar. It had been dull and overcast all day, and the fading of light into darkness was a barely perceptible exchange of one shade of grey for another, shadows for night. Below him he could still see the classic roof line of the Treasury Building, and beyond it, surrounded by trees, the White House itself.

Roosevelt wasn't there, of course; he'd been absent since the last days of March, travelling to the 'Little White House' in Warm Springs, Georgia, for three weeks of recuperation after Yalta. The First Lady was there, as were dozens of other people, but without 'The Boss' in residence, the grace and power of the famous building was somehow diminished.

The younger man, thin-faced, balding and wearing rimless spectacles, tossed the report onto the coffee table in front of him. He lit a Murad cigarette from the pack in his suit jacket, then leaned back against the flowered cushions of the chesterfield.

'Is it true?' the young man asked.

'Yes,' the older man answered, turning away from the window and speaking around the end of his cigar. 'He's reversed his position entirely.'

'It's unbelievable, General.'

'He wants to show them films after we test.'

'It won't be enough,' said the younger man, shaking his head. He took off his glasses and began polishing them with a handkerchief from the breast pocket of his suit jacket. 'The entire committee was in agreement about that.

Stimson, Vannever Bush, Fermi . . . my God, even Oppenheimer said the only thing that would do it would be a full scale military operation.'

'Does he really think Hirohito is going to give up just because we show him some pictures?' The general bit down hard on his cigar.

'It goes beyond that,' said the younger man, replacing his glasses, using pinched fingers to seat them neatly on the bridge of his long, patrician nose. 'There's Stalin to consider, for one thing. He'll swallow Europe whole if we let him; this atom bomb might be just the thing to make the son-of-a-bitch stop and think for a minute or two.'

'What about Truman?' the general asked. 'Would he use it?'

'He's not even supposed to know about it,' the younger man replied. 'But yes, we have his word on that.' There was a long, thoughtful pause. The general went back to the window and stared out into the gathering darkness.

'We'll have to act quickly,' the general said finally, his back to the younger man. 'A month or two ago it wasn't as important. The test wasn't going to be until August. We thought perhaps . . .'

'You thought that Roosevelt would be dead by then,' the younger man said bluntly. 'According to the reports we're getting from Warm Springs it looks like he's getting better.'

'What does the Admiral say?' the general asked.

'He's guarded, so is Dr Bruenn.' The younger man shrugged. 'But he's gaining weight, eating more, swimming in the pool. On the other hand, he could die tomorrow.'

'We knew that when we convinced him to run for a fourth term. That's why Harry Truman is Vice-President, and not Henry Wallace,' the general growled, turning. His cigar had gone out long ago, but he appeared not to notice. The younger man lit another Murad. With a faint smile on his face he reached into the inside pocket of his elegantly cut jacket and took out a plain leather cigarette case and a pack of Camels. He laid them on the coffee table, then sat back.

'What the hell is that?' the general asked, frowning.

The younger man sighed. 'You and I have known each other for some time, General. You know who my family is, and you know what we believe in. That's why you brought me into this in the first place. I assumed you were serious.'

'I am,' the general snapped. 'We all are.'

'Good,' the younger man said, nodding. 'I'm glad to hear it.' He took a long draw on his cigarette and let the smoke slowly out through his nostrils in twin plumes. 'The cigarette case is an exact duplicate of the one used by Mr Roosevelt. The cigarettes are exactly what they appear to be: Camels, the President's brand, if you recall.'

'I've never noticed,' the general said.

'Believe me, he smokes Camels. Exactly six a day, according to Dr Bruenn's new regimen. Our information is that he actually smokes almost twice that number, although this is down considerably from his previous two and three packages.'

'All right, so you and your friends on E Street created a replica of the President's cigarette case. I appreciate dramatics as much as the next man, but perhaps you could get to the point.'

'Certainly. The cigarettes in this package have been doctored, if you'll pardon the pun.'

'Go on,' the general said.

'The material in the cigarettes is a byproduct of work being done for us by the people at DuPont. A fibre. I'm not entirely sure of the chemical makeup, but when you ignite the substance it gives off a poison gas. The effect is much the same as a cerebral haemorrhage.'

'Sounds like something out of a dime novel,' the general grunted.

'Perhaps,' said the younger man. 'It does work, however, and it leaves no trace behind.'

'What are you suggesting?' the general said finally.

'That we substitute our cigarette case, along with one of our cigarettes in among some perfectly normal ones.'

'And who performs the dastardly deed?' the general scoffed. 'One of Donovan's Daredevils?'

'No. Someone from outside. Someone with a reason to be in Warm Springs.'

'Who?'

'A friend of mine. His name is Hollis Macintyre.'

'Any relation to the Admiral?' the general asked, stiffening.

'No. None at all. He was assistant to Roosevelt's Senior Military Advisor. Now he's working as a courier, bringing the White House bag back and forth.'

'He says he'll do it?'

'Yes.'

'Why?' the general asked coolly.

'Because he's a patriot, for one thing. Roosevelt is dying, it's simply a matter of time. Hollis is as aware as you or I that the President is in no condition to negotiate a peace in Europe with Stalin, and if we don't use the atom bomb in Japan we'll be committing a million men to an invasion. If blood is going to be spilled, Hollis would rather it was Jap blood than American.'

'I don't suppose your Mr Macintyre sees any personal benefit for himself?' the general asked wryly.

'Our grateful thanks will suffice,' the younger man replied, looking directly into the general's eyes.

'When does he leave for Warm Springs?' the general said, looking down at the familiar pack of cigarettes on the table.

'Tomorrow afternoon,' the younger man answered quickly. 'He flies to Fort Benning and then a Secret Service detail drives him to Warm Springs.'

'Call him,' said the general after a moment. 'Call your patriot. Tell him to come to the hotel.'

'Of course.' The younger man nodded. The general went back to the window and looked down. The Treasury Building was dark and there were only a few lights on at the White House.

'He's dying anyway,' the general said softly, speaking to his own reflection in the dark glass of the window. 'It's not as though it's murder.'

'Excuse me?' said the younger man. He was standing at the desk on the far side of the room, the telephone receiver in his hand. 'Did you say something, General?'

'No,' he answered, shaking his head slowly. 'I didn't say anything at all.'

The Little White House
Warm Springs, Georgia

On 12 April 1945 at 3:35 p.m., central time, Dr Howard J Bruenn pronounced Franklin Delano Roosevelt dead. According to Dr Bruenn, the cause of death was a massive cerebral haemorrhage. No autopsy was done, however, and therefore the diagnosis was never proven to be accurate. Furthermore, within twenty-four hours of the President's death, all medical records relating to Mr Roosevelt vanished from the Bethesda Naval Hospital. There is also no trace of any records for the more than twenty-nine pseudonyms used by Roosevelt over the course of his years at the White House. Neither the Navy Medical Center nor the federal Office of Personnel Management has any explanation for this occurrence.

On 16 July, in Potsdam, Germany, President Harry Truman was informed of the successful test of the atomic bomb. On 6 August, while journeying home from the Potsdam Conference on board the heavy cruiser, USS *Augusta*, President Truman was notified that the atomic bomb had been dropped on Hiroshima, Japan, the previous day at 7:15 p.m., Washington time.

On 9 August 1945, Hollis Macintyre, now working as a Special Advisor to the War Department, completed a 22-page report describing his role in the events leading up to the death of Franklin D Roosevelt, including the code name for the operation: Romulus. It also listed the names of all other people involved in the conspiracy, including their functions. When the report was completed he placed it in a small, sealed document case which was then consigned to the fireproof safe hidden under the floor of his bedroom at Stoneacres Farm, Virginia.

PART ONE

'We were sure that ours was a nation of the ballot, not the bullet, until the murders of John Kennedy, Robert Kennedy and Martin Luther King.'

Jimmy Carter, Speech at the White House

CHAPTER ONE

The August sun glowed like a hot coal on the Maryland horizon, hazed by the stunning waves of heat rising up from the city, and stained a bruised orange-green by a thousand different airborne pollutants. Sinking slowly it cast a long, rippling trace across the Potomac, briefly glancing across the hull of a sleek rowing shell making its way downriver like a graceful, multi-legged insect.

Except for the shifting blade of light across the water Washington had given itself up to the night; Roosevelt Island was a dark mass of shadow on the river and the ghost-blue landing beacons at Washington National were already shimmering in the distance.

Hudson Haines Cooper, dressed in an ornate, blue and yellow dressing gown and with a lead crystal glass of scotch in his hand, stared out through the living room window of his Watergate apartment. He was alone, the ten-room luxury suite was dark behind him, and the only sound was the low hum of the central air conditioning. Cooper swirled the ice cubes in his glass and shook his large, bald head. The view was perfect, but like most things in Washington, the surface only served to shroud the lie beneath. The Potomac was a sewer, Roosevelt Island at this time of night was a rapist's haven and National was a pilot's nightmare.

> When you defile the pleasant streams,
> And the wild bird's abiding place,
> You massacre a million dreams
> And cast your spittle in God's face.

The verse from the John Drinkwater poem had come unbidden into his mind, but it was apt enough. He shook his head again and turned away from the window. Apt perhaps, but ironic coming from his lips. He sipped his scotch and stared into the shadows of the apartment. Shadows and lies, his stock in trade.

He was sixty, tall and gaunt, the skin on his skull and across his cheeks taut and seamed like parchment, his neck above the fine silk of the robe a twist of ropy tendons. Sixty years and every one showing. Forty of them spent with Central Intelligence, twenty as Deputy Director of Operations, ten here at the Watergate, without Miriam, alone, a widower, childless. *Shadows and Lies*. The perfect title for his autobiography, but wasted, of course, because DD Operations didn't write their autobiographies – it was against the law.

The doorbell chimed and Cooper crossed the long, broad living room and went down the short hall to the entrance. He put his eye to the peephole. Barron, in civilian clothes, looking very nervous. Cooper threw the locks and opened the door. Barron stepped inside. He was wearing a winter suit and his pudgy face was sheened with perspiration. He looked like he'd been drinking.

'The living room,' Cooper said, pointing the way. He locked the door and followed Barron into the large room. Cooper sat down behind the gate-legged table he used as a desk and switched on the green-shaded lamp. He indicated a chair and Barron sat down. The chair and table, like everything else in the apartment, was early American; Miriam's choice, not his, but something Cooper had never bothered to change.

Barron squirmed on the hard pine seat, a thin leather case in his lap. The lamplight made him look sickly. Behind him, Cooper could see the last slice of sunlight vanish. Full night.

'I was surprised when you called,' said Cooper. He flipped open a small wooden box on the table and took out a cigarette. He lit it with a dull grey Cartier lighter that had been Miriam's and sat back in his chair, waiting.

'I thought it was important,' Barron answered. 'I thought you'd want to know as soon as possible.'

'Presumably this has something to do with President Tucker's physical.'

'Yes.' Barron nodded. 'I'm afraid it does.' He opened the case in his lap, fumbling with the zipper. He was still sweating, even in the air conditioned apartment. He pulled a folder out of the case and handed it across the desk, but Cooper waved it away.

'I'm not a doctor,' he said quietly. 'You are. You're the President's doctor. Tell me in your own words.'

Dr John Barron was Senior Resident Medical Officer at Walter Reed Hospital, a full colonel in the army, and the man in charge of the president's bi-annual medical check-ups. He was also one knot on the string of Washington 'contacts' personally run by Cooper as DDO.

'The President checked in with us three days ago,' said Barron hesitantly. 'I ordered up all the regular tests, but Mrs Tucker had previously told me, in confidence, that the President had been having headaches and the odd memory lapse. Nothing extreme, but enough to worry her. President Tucker made no mention of it himself.' Barron paused, blinking.

'Go on,' said Cooper.

'I added several other tests to the series. CAT scan, PET scan, full blood and endocrine work up . . .'

'Yes.'

'The PET scan showed some atrophic shrinking. There were anomalies in the blood serum and the endocrine. I still wasn't entirely sure, so I asked the President if he'd help me with one of my research projects while he was waiting for the test results. I told him I was doing a paper on stress. He agreed and I put him through the Wechsler Adult Intelligence Scale. There are eleven subtests, each one scored separately. The Wechsler is given to gauge memory function primarily, and also simple logic. Why are dark clothes warmer than light clothes, in what way are an egg and a seed alike? Repeating a series of digits in order, that kind of thing.'

'And?'

'He has definite aphasia, the inability to find the correct word; ataxia, short term memory loss . . . a number of other symptoms.'

'Symptoms of what, exactly?' asked Cooper gently. Barron tried to see beyond the light, blinking again.

'I think the President has Creuzfeldt-Jacob disease. There was no sign of anything like this in the tests I ran just after the inauguration. The differential in the PET scan is marked. There's no other dementia with an onset that rapid.'

'Dementia?'

'CJD is a primary undifferentiated dementia. Very much like Alzheimer's,' Barron answered, taking refuge in the language of his profession. 'If I had a sample of his brain tissue it would almost certainly show the classic plaques and tangles associated with the disease. I'm not an expert, but I pulled everything I could out of the research library and it matches up with all the information I have on the President.'

'The prognosis?' asked Cooper.

'Poor. The Alzheimer-type symptoms will become more pronounced. There is a possibility of violent behaviour, hypersexuality, even incontinence.'

'Over what period of time?'

'Six months. Certainly less than a year.'

'Until the dementia is fully formed?'

'Until he's dead,' said Barron bluntly.

Cooper stubbed out his cigarette in a bronze shell ashtray on the desk. There was an economic summit in four months and a trip to China in five.

'How long can the symptoms be disguised? Surely there must be drugs . . .'

'According to what I read there's only one. Nalaxone. It's experimental. At best it only dampens the symptoms briefly.' The young man paused, fingers twisting in his lap like fat little worms.

Cooper looked beyond the glare of the light, trying to read Barron's expression. The doctor was in his early thirties, playing out a family tradition of military service before opening up his own practice in Boston, and that itself would be no more than a jumping off point for a political career. If he played the game and drank scotch in the right parlours he'd be Surgeon General in ten or fifteen years. A flabby, pale and frightened fool suddenly charged with the responsibility for a deadly secret.

'How many people know about this?' Cooper asked quietly.

'No one,' said Barron, trying to make his voice firm, and failing. 'Everything is in this file.' He handed the folder across to Cooper, visibly relaxing as it left his hands. Cooper took it, but left the file unopened in front of him.

'What about Mrs Tucker? What has she been told?'

'Nothing.'

'No explanations for her husband's headaches, the memory losses?'

'Normal stress reactions for a man in his position. I suggested she have him take more vitamins with breakfast.'

Cooper could see a vein twitching on Barron's temple. The burden was too much; he wouldn't last long. A born confessor.

'My god! Mr Cooper, what are we going to do?'

'Nothing,' the DDO replied. 'At least for now.' He paused. 'Do you have any leave due?'

'Yes. Two weeks. I was going to take my boat down to Cape Cod and visit my parents.' The doctor frowned. 'Why?'

'Take the leave. Starting tomorrow. Call in sick if you have to. I want you at home, close to the telephone for the next few days.' The tone was firm and paternal, but they were orders, not suggestions.

'All right.'

'Tell no one about this, do you understand? No one.' Cooper leaned forward slightly, letting the puddle of light on his desk etch his cheekbones and eye sockets with shadow. 'For your own sake,' he added, after an almost imperceptible pause.

'Pardon?' Barron blinked.

'You're a cardiologist, Dr Barron, not a neurologist. What if your diagnosis is incorrect? We need time to get another opinion on this.' Cooper tapped the file on the desk in front of him with a long bony finger.

'The diagnosis is accurate,' answered Barron.

'Are you willing to stake your reputation on that?' asked Cooper. 'Willing to stake your career on it, perhaps?'

'I . . .'

'Go home,' said Cooper, standing up. He tightened the knot on his robe and stepped out from behind the desk. 'Try not to think about any of this. If you have a problem, call me and no one else, all right, Doctor?'

'Yes.' The voice was still frightened, but it was meek now; Cooper had him under control for the time being. Barron stood and Cooper led him to the door. They shook hands briefly and then the doctor left.

Cooper went back to the desk, picked up the file and carried it to one of a group of high-backed upholstered chairs arranged close to the big picture window. Then he went into the kitchen, made himself a small plate of sliced, raw vegetables and carried it back to the living room.

Eating slowly, pausing occasionally to sprinkle a few grains of salt on a slice of cucumber, he read through the file twice, then set it aside. He took his empty plate back to the kitchen, poured himself a cup of decaffeinated coffee from the Braun percolator and returned to the desk. He lit a cigarette, then switched off the desk lamp, darkening the room completely. Since Miriam's death he'd rarely had more than one or two lights on at a time in the entire apartment.

Through the picture window, Maryland was nothing more than a tangle of suburban light, breached in the centre by the huge cauldron of black marking Arlington National Cemetery. Over there a hundred thousand men were sleeping, some of them his friends, all of them past the time for secrets. Frowning at the the thought, Cooper sipped his coffee and smoked, his mind playing over the problem Barron had given him like a pianist's fingers on a keyboard, trying to coax an answer out of dissonance.

He *would* get a second opinion, of course, that was easy enough, but he knew intuitively that Barron's diagnosis was correct. Geoffrey James Tucker, the youngest President of the United States since Jack Kennedy, was going to become clinically insane by Christmas. The corollary to that appalling fact was the consequent ascension of Vice-President Vincent Teresi to the Chief Executive Office.

He reached out in the darkness, picked up the telephone receiver and punched out a number in Burning Tree, Maryland. It was answered on the third ring.

'Macintyre?'

'Yes?' A voice like ragged thunder. Power in a single word.

'Cooper.'

'Yes.'

'Do you recall our conversation some time ago concerning crossword puzzles?'

'I do.'

'I have a clue.'

'Go on.'

'Seven letters. Raised by a wolf on seven hills, wanders until he finds eternity.' There was a long silence on the other end of the line. Finally Macintyre responded.

'Romulus.'

And so it began.

CHAPTER TWO

Stephen Padgett Stone woke at 7 a.m. to the tinny sounds of the Beach Boys on his clock radio. They were singing 'California Girls' and instead of making him feel eighteen again it made him feel exactly what he was, a forty-year-old sentimental fool who could still quote from Desiderata. He snorted angrily at himself and sat up in bed, peeling the sweaty sheets away from his body. He'd come a long way in twenty-odd years; closet hippy at USC to FBI counterintelligence specialist. On the way there'd been a tour in Vietnam, Quantico, endless postings to field offices in places like Sioux City, Iowa, and a failed marriage without children.

He made a small groaning sound, trying to ignore the taste in his mouth and the humid air in the apartment. Scratching at the thick trail of salt and pepper hair that curled up his still-flat belly, Stone headed for the bathroom, wondering when the condominium committee in his building would get around to fixing the central air conditioning system.

Reaching the bathroom he flipped on the light, squinting in the sudden glare. He washed and shaved quickly, avoiding the face that stared back at him from the medicine chest mirror. He was already on intimate terms with every crack, crevice and cranny, thank you very much, and while women once commented that he looked like a dark-haired Robert Redford, the best he got now was comparisons to a weathered Alan Bates.

Stone went back to the bedroom, threw on his dressing gown and went to the kitchen for phase two of the morning routine. He fired up the coffee machine, put a couple of eggs on to boil, and wandered around the apartment, picking up after himself, ending up back in the bedroom where he dressed.

Breakfast ready, he carried eggs, coffee and cigarettes out onto the balcony. The view was one of the best things about the apartment. The building was on Foxhall Road between Georgetown University and the reservoir and from where he sat Stone could look out over the Potomac to Theodore Roosevelt Island, and beyond, to the Lincoln Memorial.

Humming an off-key medley of Beach Boy tunes he worked his way through the eggs quickly, then sat back with his coffee, lit a Camel Light and allowed himself twenty minutes of peace before he pole-vaulted himself back into the arcane realities of being a modern day G-man. He shook his head and took a long drag on his cigarette. Debbie, his ex-wife and still occasional lover, liked to tease him with the G-man label.

He hardly fitted the mould of the classic Hoover FBI agent. His degree was in engineering, not law, he wasn't much with a gun, and worst of all, he couldn't bear wearing a hat. The truth was he'd never even thought about the FBI until coming back from Vietnam.

In country he'd been assigned to an intelligence unit and he'd spent most of his time working the back streets of Saigon, following hookers and hotel busboys suspected of being VC agents. After a year he finally realised that virtually everyone in the country was potentially a Victor Charlie, but by then he'd been bitten by the intelligence bug and the Bureau seemed like the logical place to go. Slightly less than fifteen years later that decision had taken him to the Deputy Director's slot in a Bureau counterintelligence programme called REDNET.

REDNET's job was to track, monitor, and hopefully snare any and all Soviet Military Intelligence – GRU – agents working out of the DC area. It was a tall order, considering that the GRU operated twenty-five active, registered agents out of the Soviet Military Office on Belmont Road as well as an unknown number of 'illegals' and paid contacts. On top of that the GRU also 'owned' Aeroflot, the Soviet state airline, and Stone and his people had to keep an eye on that operation as well. It was an exhausting job, and most of it consisted of boring routine, but Stone loved every minute of it.

It was that very love for his work that had cost him his marriage. Debbie, his ex, was a go-getter with half a dozen degrees to her credit, most of them to do with European and specifically Russian history. She worked as an analyst for ESI, the European Studies Institute, which they both knew was a discreet arm of the Central Intelligence Agency.

Right from the beginning of their relationship, Debbie recognised that Stone was in a dead end as far as promotions were concerned. His boss, William Ruppelt, was in for the duration, and Stephen's only hope was a lateral transfer to a different division with more chance of advancement. Debbie had argued for the transfer, but Stone had been adamant: he liked the work he did and wouldn't trade it for a promotion to work he enjoyed less. His apparent lack of ambition had been a wedge between them, and as Debbie Rosen Stone rose through the ranks at ESI while Stephen languished, their relationship began to fall apart. Last year after almost a decade of marriage, they ended it formally. Oddly, or perhaps inevitably, their sex life together flourished after they severed the legal bonds and they now saw each other regularly. Neither of them really had time for a full commitment and their arm's length 'friendship' seemed to suit them both.

Stone refilled his coffee cup and lit another cigarette. Ten more minutes and he'd start the day. He grimaced, remembering some of the arguments he'd had with Debbie; right up until the end he'd taken most of the blame on himself, but it finally occurred to him that although his lack of ambition might have been part of the problem, her jealousy about his job was an equally important factor. He didn't just like his work, he loved it and that was something Debbie simply couldn't understand.

Travkin had been the straw that broke the camel's back.

Eighteen months ago, Dimitri Alexandyr Travkin had been no more than a name on a file. Up until then the GRU major had been working out of the Soviet legation in New York and came to Washington rarely. Then the Deputy Resident at the Soviet Military Office in Belmont Road had died of a heart attack and Travkin had taken on the job, thinly disguised as a member of the Soviet Trade Mission.

Almost immediately Stone and his REDNET operatives saw that Travkin wasn't the lackadaisical Deputy Resident his predecessor had been. Within a few weeks he'd re-established connections with the previous man's agents and informers as well as cultivating his own. Unlike his KGB colleagues, Travkin seldom trolled the bars and bistros looking for disaffected civil servants whose information rarely justified the expense of gathering it. Instead, the young, good-looking Russian dressed himself in clothes right out of *Gentlemen's Quarterly* and searched out his quarry at gallery openings, diplomatic receptions of every stripe, and as many blue ribbon social events as he could crowd into his overloaded diary.

Early on, Stone had manufactured a meeting with Travkin at a Corcoran Art Gallery cocktail party. Stone introduced himself as a patron of the arts, and Travkin countered by calling himself a director of Soveca SA, a computer corporation based in Paris. Soveca was a real company, with real offices and a real interest in computer technology, but the name stood for Soviet Economic Agency, and the technology they traded in was of questionable origin.

Both men were entirely aware of each other's identity, but enough titbits of positive and negative information passed between them to make continuing their relationship worthwhile. From that point on both Stone and Travkin made a point of going to the same parties and events, and once or twice the two men had actually played raquetball together, using Travkin's membership at the Westin Fitness Centre.

Stone had devoted enormous amounts of time to Travkin, with the eventual hope of turning him, or co-opting him as an agent-in-place. Debbie had called it an exercise in futility. Whatever the case, Stone became fascinated with his Soviet alter ego, and that fascination, and the mental energy it required, had been too much for his wife.

Now, after a year and a half, it was obvious that either Stone or Travkin would have to make a real move towards recruitment or co-option. Ruppelt was beginning to make noises in that direction, and Stone assumed that Major-General Gennaddi Koslov, Ruppelt's opposite number at GRU, was becoming equally impatient.

If Travkin moved first and made some kind of overture to Stone, REDNET would have just cause to request an expulsion order from the State Department, and Travkin's whole network would collapse. On the other hand, if Stone made the first move and Travkin didn't bite, their covers would be blown irretrievably and the operation would collapse.

Stone wasn't looking forward to either eventuality. He'd grown to like and respect Travkin over the past months, and he also knew that it was unlikely that he'd ever find himself pitted against such an intelligent and resourceful opponent again. The FBI man stubbed out his cigarette, stood up, and slipped on his sports jacket. By definition two intelligence operatives on opposite sides could not be friends; on that score both GRU and FBI agreed. Friendships, even strange and distant ones like his relationship with Travkin, were essentially dangerous, if for no other reason than the fact that they weakened judgement.

'To hell with it,' Stone grunted. He swilled down the last few sips of cold coffee and left the apartment.

By eight-thirty he was parking his overworked Rabbit convertible in a slot behind the REDNET offices overlooking Folger Park. The building had once been a mansion belonging to a US senator and as far as Stone was concerned, it was one of the major blessings of his job at REDNET.

Because the programme was not quite 'official' by Bureau standards it had been exiled from the J Edgar Hoover Building on Pennsylvania Avenue, and Stone couldn't have been happier. The old mansion had none of the crisp, bureaucratic efficiency of headquarters, but by the same token it also didn't have any of the Bureau's well-known empire building and political infighting. Counterintelligence had always attracted oddballs, and REDNET seemed to attract the weirdest of the lot, with the exception of William Ruppelt. As the REDNET senior administrator Ruppelt had to attend regular weekly meetings at the J Edgar, but Stone rarely set foot in the place at all any more. For the most part CI-Q was allowed to do its job in peace.

Stone locked his car, crossed the small lot and ducked under the awning that shrouded the rear entrance to the building. He showed his ID to the security guard behind a scarred old wooden desk, then rode the creaking old cage elevator up to the third floor operations centre, a rabbit warren of offices, narrow wood-floored corridors and a single, monstrous blower beside the stairway that was supposed to provide air conditioning in the summer and heat in the winter. In reality all it did was make an incredible amount of noise.

At that hour of the morning Operations was almost empty except for a couple of bleary-eyed Night Watch Special Agents in Communications. He poked his head in, picked up the log from one of the yawning men and continued on to his own office which stood across from Ruppelt's at the end of the corridor. He glanced out of the tall, recessed window and caught a glimpse of the Capitol dome rising over the trees around the park. He began going over the night log, checking on the movements of visitors, guests and clients. In CI-Q terminology a visitor was a registered agent of a foreign nation. A guest was a Soviet intelligence operative, and a client was one of those operatives' known clandestine agents.

Every visitor, guest and client had a file and code name and each of the Special Agents attached to REDNET had his own 'patch', or group of files to maintain. Operations was divided into thirteen sub-sections, one for each 'Red Zone', or area of concern, each sub-section with a Special Agent In Charge, usually an Inspector, who reported to Stone. Stone, as Deputy Director, then reported to Ruppelt and he in turn reported to Headquarters.

To an outsider it might have seemed like an overly complex system, but in fact it was necessary. There are eight Soviet establishments within Washington. In addition there are the Tass News Agency, *Pravda* and *Izvestia* in Chevy Chase, and the Soviet 'dacha' or country place, a forty-five acre estate at Pioneer Point in Maryland. In all there are slightly more than a thousand Eastern Bloc employees in the DC area, and approximately one third of these are visitors and guests.

And that didn't include the clients.

Thankfully, it had been a good night, at least according to the log. No major activity at any of the main Soviet installations, nothing special at any of half-dozen ongoing special surveillance projects and, best of all, no car rentals. By federal law no Soviet diplomat or agent was allowed to travel more than twenty-five miles out of the capital area without a special permit and they weren't allowed to drive any vehicle other than one with the special red white and blue DFC licence plates. D for Diplomatic Corps and FC for Fucking Communists, according to local mythology. When a Soviet agent wanted to make a drop or contact, in and out of Washington, they regularly rented vehicles, usually from the Avis booth at the Visitor Information Centre. Just as regularly they were watched, followed and photographed.

By the time Ramona, the girl in the cafeteria, had brought him the coffee he'd buzzed for it was almost nine o'clock and his perusal of the night log was nearly complete. The Russians might all be atheists, but it seemed that they took Sundays off just like everyone else.

'You really are going to have to get this place decorated.' At the sound of the voice Stone looked up. Mort Kessler was standing in the doorway, glancing around his office with a mock frown on his face. Kessler was on the short side for Bureau material, muscular with a shock of red hair and eyebrows so pale they were almost nonexistent. Quirky, given to fits of temper when frustrated, he was also a natural bloodhound and he had a photographic memory for faces.

He was also right about the office. Except for a map of Washington pinned up on one wall the room was bare. The only furniture was a desk, office chair, a wooden armchair for visitors and a wood-veneered credenza behind the desk loaded with books Stone hadn't opened in years.

Kessler dropped down into the armchair, reached out and snagged Stone's coffee cup and sat back with it cradled in his hands as though for warmth. He lifted the cup, took a sip and frowned.

'Jesus, Stef, how can you drink this shit?' Kessler put the cup back on Stone's desk.

'It's espresso.' Stone grinned, lighting a cigarette. 'Ramona makes it specially for me every morning.'

'Ramona has a crush on you.'

'She's a woman of taste,' countered Stone blithely.

'She's at least sixty, she barely speaks English, she has a moustache and she probably works for DGI,' replied Kessler. DGI was Direccion Generale de Inteligencia – Cuban Intelligence.

'Tell me what's going on out at the airport,' asked Stone, changing the subject. Kessler, with his phenomenal memory, was a 'floater' within CI-Q, attached to no particular patch, going where he was needed, but paying special attention to Washington National and the Baltimore Airport. The red-haired man could watch two or three hundred people get off an international flight and pick out the one face he'd glanced at in a file six months before.

'Nada.' Kessler shrugged. 'But I followed up on that advisory we had yesterday on your friend Travkin.'

'And?' said Stone.

'He landed at Gander, went on to Ottawa and spent the night at the embassy there. He's booked in on an American Airlines flight that gets in at ten this morning. You want a team on him?'

'No. He's holding the bag; that means he'll go straight to the SMO. We can pick him up there.'

'Okay.' Kessler glanced at his watch and then bounced up out of the chair. 'Five past nine. God's on his way up.' God was Bill Ruppelt, the Most Punctual Man in the World. Using a stopwatch Kessler had once timed the CI-Q boss through his daily routine over a week-long period and Ruppelt hadn't deviated by more than a minute throughout the five-day test. Arrival at 9:05, park car, enter building, into elevator at 9:07, arrival in office 9:08. Meeting with Stone from 9:15 to 9:35, bathroom 9:40 (morning edition *USA Today* indicates bowel movement), return to office 9:55.

Laughing, Stone waved Kessler out of his office and picked up the night log again. In three minutes Ruppelt would pass the open doorway and it wouldn't do to be seen gazing out of the window. Trying to look as studious as possible he stared down at the pages of the log, waiting for God to reach the third floor.

As Deputy Director of Central Intelligence Hudson Cooper was allowed office space in all of the CIA's buildings, including the headquarters building behind the wire in the Langley compound and the laboratories at Curry Hall. The offices he liked best, however, were in the original OSS building at 25th and E Street, both for the historical significance of occupying the same suite of rooms once used by Wild Bill Donovan, and also because 2430 E Street was a lot closer to downtown Washington than the brooding pile of marble and steel squatting in the middle of a forest on the other side of the Potomac. Few of his predecessors had liked the Langley compound, insisting that it had been obsolete before it was finished in 1963, and Cooper showed his disdain for the campus-style complex by rarely going there.

Like most of the senior executive offices within the CIA the DDO's suite was expansive, oak-panelled and furnished with a men's club combination of dark wood and old leather. The suite consisted of an antechamber, main office, full, four-piece bathroom, private dining room and kitchen. Five high windows looked out over the landscaped grounds and down to the head-high chain link fence surrounding the property.

Cooper, dressed in a dark, three piece suit, sat behind the desk in the main office and went over Barron's file yet again. He'd slept poorly the night before, plagued by the information the file contained, and furious that he could see no realistic solution to the problem. Even so, there were steps to be taken, and he'd arrived at the office before seven, getting as much work done as possible before the official day began.

Finishing Barron's report, he slipped the file into the centre drawer of his desk, locking it with the key he kept on his watch chain. He turned to the computer terminal, cleared the screen, then pressed the intercom button on the telephone, calling for his assistant. A few moments later the door to the main office opened and a tall, middle-aged man with glasses and thinning, sandy hair stepped into the room, a thick, buff-coloured file envelope in one hand. There was a diagonal blue stripe across the envelope, marking it as a CIA 'Soft File' which meant that it had no circulation beyond the DDO's

office and did not even exist in any official sense. Paul Mallory crossed the room and sat down in one of the visitors' chairs, the file in his lap.

'You've found something, I see,' said Cooper, lighting a cigarette and nodding at the file.

'Yes, sir.'

'Quick work,' Cooper murmured; there was a note of disapproval in his voice.

'I came across the subject while I was in Threat Analysis several years ago,' Mallory explained. 'He seemed to be what you were looking for so I went and found the jacket on him.' The bookish man seated across from Cooper had been a Project Threat Analyst before coming to the Deputy-Director's office. His work had involved taking project plans from Operations and running them through a variety of computer generated 'Threat Evaluations' to see if the plans were feasible.

'Your opinion?' Cooper asked.

'The subject is completely non-judgemental. Emotionless, practical, straightforward. Follows orders to the letter. On the surface you'd probably say he was sociopathic, but there's nothing to indicate that in his psych profile.'

'Let me see his summary.'

Mallory opened the file, slid out the top sheet and handed it across. Cooper found himself staring at a four by five colour photograph clipped to the top of the page. The face was was tanned and intelligent, square-jawed, lean, with deep-set grey eyes and a thick mass of black hair tinged with grey at the temples. He appeared to be in his late thirties or early forties.

'His Agency acronym is QJ/RAIL,' said Mallory, pulling the file out of its envelope. 'He operates under the name of Eric Rhinelander.'

'His real name is Phelps?' asked Cooper, reading from the summary sheet.

'Hard to say,' answered Mallory, poking his glasses up onto the bridge of his nose. He hunched over the main file, peeling back the pages. 'He was an orphan, picked up in Germany in 1945. He appeared to be no more than a month or two old. He'd been given to a local priest just prior to the Allied advance.'

'Who adopted him?'

'A British signals officer. He married a German girl during the occupation. Couldn't have children because of measles, so they adopted and settled down on the wife's family farm outside Frankfurt.'

'How did he get here?'

'Parents died when he was ten. Phelps had a brother who'd immigrated here before the war. They took the kid in. New York. He went to school there, dropped out of Columbia and enlisted in the air force. They sent him back to Germany because he spoke the language, and he wound up flying Special Operations with the Ravens into Laos and Cambodia. That's how we found him.'

'Did we train him?'

'Yes, sir. The full curriculum. The Farm, Quantico and Lake Mead. He was good when we picked him up and just about the best when we finished with him. That was in '73. He worked on contract from then on.'

Cooper nodded. QJ/RAIL had been trained as an assassin, a job description denied by every president since Ford had signed an Executive Order stating that no employee of the federal government would have any involvement in any political assassination. By signing annual contracts QJ/RAIL skirted the ruling in its strictly legal sense.

'Where is he now?' Cooper asked.

'Jamaica,' answered Mallory. 'At least he has a house there. He hasn't worked for us in five years now.'

'Who does he work for?'

'Anyone who'll hire him. People who know him by reputation. Most of them appear to be Southeast Asians involved in the drug trade. He made a lot of connections in the Triangle during the late sixties and early seventies. So far he's avoided anything "red white and blue". According to our records he hasn't set foot in the States in years, let alone worked here.'

'Then he has no record?'

'No, sir.' Mallory shook his head. 'Nothing except this file. When he was with the Ravens they wiped all his military notations and since he was contract for us, the Agency has no hard file. He's clean, just as you requested.'

'Do we have anything on his recent movements?'

'No, sir.' Mallory smiled; he'd anticipated the question. 'I did run a check on drug-related killings over the past few months.' He let it dangle.

'And?'

'Three days ago five Cambodians were assassinated in an Amsterdam loft, all of them big in the Khmer Rouge. Pol Pot's inner circle, including his sister-in-law. There was a sixth corpse as well, a man named Charles Yang. Heavyweight in the opium business.'

'You think it was this man Rhinelander?'

'It's a good bet, sir. The killing was done with a Carl Gustav rocket launcher from across the street; no fooling around with sniper rifles or anything like that. The description of the man in the rented room across from the loft fits QJ/RAIL well enough.'

'Where does that lead us, if anywhere?' asked Cooper.

'Yang's main competition in Europe is a French-German named Phillipe Groman,' Mallory replied. 'According to our information Groman has been handling all the opium and heroin base the Khmer use to finance their weapons purchasing on the Continent. If Yang was cutting him off Groman might have hired our man to snuff the opposition.'

'Where is Groman?'

'Paris.'

'You think Rhinelander might be there as well?'

'It's possible.' Mallory shrugged his narrow shoulders. 'If he was going back to Groman for the payoff.'

'I see.' Cooper swung around in his chair, turning to the giant globe that stood on his right. He spun it slowly. It was old and showed a world that had vanished long ago. Belgian Congo, Siam, French Equatorial Africa, Dutch Guyana, British Honduras. Back then, the greatest instrument of foreign policy had been a gunboat, now it was surveillance satellites and Star Wars. He found Paris, covering it with the tip of his index finger. He smiled wanly. If only it were that easy. He turned back in his chair and faced Mallory.

'Find him,' he ordered. 'Go to Paris. Today. Tell him I wish to speak to him on a matter of urgent business and give him the number for my white telephone. If he is not in Paris, go to Jamaica and wait for him to return. I want to speak to him as soon as possible. I want you to get back to me on this within twelve hours.'

'Yes, sir.' Mallory waited for a moment, but Cooper was obviously finished with him. He stood up finally and left the office. The DDO turned in his chair and stared out the window. Another blistering day. He glanced at the old fashioned Hamilton on his wrist. An anniversary present from Miriam. It was almost noon and by now the Barron operation he'd initiated last night would be under way; there were no answers yet, but at least the tracks were being covered.

In his personal and professional life fear was something which Colonel John Barron had rarely encountered. Since he was too young and far too well connected for Vietnam, his adolescence and early adulthood had followed a comfortable pattern of proper schools, proper friends and proper women. His success as a doctor was assured and his position as Senior Resident Medical Officer at Walter Reed had been decided over lunch at the Jockey Club. The fact that he was a reasonably good doctor with a definite talent as a diagnostician was irrelevant; if he'd been Sweeney Todd the course of his life would have been unchanged.

A year before when Hudson Cooper had quietly taken him aside and asked him to be his eyes and ears at Walter Reed, Barron had been flattered. For someone used to a life of utter predictability, the thought of working for the CIA had been seductively appealing. It never occurred to him that Cooper had wanted nothing more than a monitor on the new President's general health, or that he had half a dozen other informers at Walter Reed and Bethesda, each one paid to keep him up to date on the medical status of the Joint Chiefs and anyone else of note at the Pentagon. Not that it would have mattered; Barron enjoyed his secret cloak and dagger life, occasionally meeting Mallory, the DDO's assistant, and passing on some titbit he thought might be of interest.

But that had changed in an instant. It wasn't a game any more, and after his meeting with Cooper the night before, the full implications of what he'd done had struck him like a hammerblow. Not only had he violated his oath as a doctor by divulging patient information, he'd prejudiced his future and put his own reputation and that of his entire family into the hands of a total stranger.

By dawn, bleary-eyed from lack of sleep, hands shaking from a dozen cups of coffee, he'd come to the only decision possible. Morally he had no choice, he was going to have to blow the whistle on the whole affair, no matter what the consequences. But first he'd have to clear it with his family.

By nine he'd managed to clean himself up a little and he'd put on a clean uniform, more for the sake of his own morale than for any official reason. He booked himself onto a Boston flight, called in sick at the hospital and left his McPherson Square apartment, taking the elevator down to the garage beneath the building. He reached the basement, took out his keys and walked along the echoing concrete, heading for his reserved space at the rear of the first level.

Barron reached his car, a black Thunderbird, and opened the door. As he did so he heard a crashing sound and turned in time to see two men slam open the sliding door of the dark blue van in the spot beside him. Before he could utter a sound the two men had dragged him into the interior of the van while a third dropped down to the ground, slid the panel closed and took the keys out of the Thunderbird's lock. The third man climbed into Barron's vehicle and drove off slowly, heading out of the garage. A few moments later, a fourth man, behind the wheel of the van, followed the Thunderbird.

Inside the van Barron struggled desperately but it was no use. The larger of the two men holding him had one hand clamped over his mouth while the other arm snaked around his neck. Using a roll of nylon reinforced fabric tape the smaller man bound Barron's legs together and then his arms. Together, rocking jerkily with the movement of the van, they dragged Barron over to a fifty-gallon plastic drum. The drum had been lashed to a pair of cleats welded to the side wall and each time the van turned or changed lanes water sloshed out onto the bare metal floor.

Staggering, the two men upended Barron's bound body, the big man taking his hand away from the doctor's mouth just before it was forced under water. They held him there, grunting with effort as the body whiplashed back and forth, dousing them both. When the movement stopped the smaller man went to the front of the van and opened a large vinyl overnight bag. He began removing a selection of casual clothing they'd taken from Barron's boat earlier that morning.

The larger man stayed beside the drum, supporting the doctor's lax, overturned form. Barron was probably already dead, but it was absolutely necessary for the lungs to be filled. The water in the barrel had been taken from the Potomac and when the autopsy was performed on Barron the findings would be consistent with accidental death by drowning. Sometime within the next twenty-four hours the doctor's body would be found close to the *Tarantella*, dressed in appropriate clothing, right down to the Topsiders on his feet. His car would be found in the Buzzard Point Marina parking lot.

The van, complete with the fifty gallon drum, would be taken to a wrecking yard in Alexandria, Virginia, and burned down to the axles. When the vehicle had been completely 'sanitised' it would be put through a crusher and turned into a four foot square cube of scrap metal.

The four men, hired out of Miami through a series of cut-outs, would return to Florida that evening and rendezvous to receive their fee at a house south off the Calle Ocho in Little Havana. When it was certain that all four men were in the house a second, independently hired two-man team would detonate the seven charges of C-4 explosive strategically placed under the floorboards of the house, instantly vaporising the structure and its occupants.

By midnight any connection between Colonel John Barron, Hudson Cooper and the mental health of the President of the United States would have vanished.

CHAPTER THREE

After twenty years as a professional soldier, twelve of them spent in Soviet Military Intelligence, Dimitri Travkin was positive that he had discovered the essential flaw in the philosophy of Marxist-Leninism.

Humour, or more precisely, the lack of it, was the key. The Russian people were funny enough, but after two weeks of leave in Moscow the GRU colonel was convinced that to become a card carrying member of the Communist Party involved compulsory surgery to remove that part of the brain responsible for laughter.

Jokes gained you nothing but blank stares, a funny anecdote was enough to have you brought up on charges and a Politburo pun was probably good for a one-way ticket to the gulag of your choice. It was too bad; a couple of dirty stories told at a summit conference would do more for world peace than dismantling a few dozen obsolete missiles.

Comedy was what he liked most about Americans; even Reagan had managed a few good lines during his presidency and Ford had an act worthy of the Marx Brothers. It was also rumoured that Nixon had a personal collection of utterly obscene jokes that made Richard Pryor look like an amateur. Of course the essence of the best American humour was satire, a word which simply didn't exist within the Kremlin walls. The rules of the game had changed since the Eastern Bloc upheavals of 1989–90, but for the most part, at least in the intelligence field, the players had remained the same, and if anything, their dour, humourless outlook on the world had only intensified with the looming spectre of democracy on the horizon. For the twentieth-century spy or counterspy, peace was a nightmare.

Travkin was reasonably sure that his enjoyment of American comedy had been noted on some file deep within the bowels of the Mount Alto Complex on Wisconsin Avenue, and there was probably some grimy little KGB shithead who kept track of his record purchases, right down to his latest Howie Mandel album. It didn't bother him; after two years as GRU Deputy Resident he'd established his reputation more than adequately, with a score of well-placed informants and illegals sprinkled all over the District of Columbia and beyond. At thirty-eight he was the youngest Deputy Resident in the Second Directorate and in a year or two he was virtually guaranteed a full residency or a posting back to Moscow Centre.

Travkin glanced at his watch and frowned. Three o'clock. He wouldn't be posted anywhere if he was late for his meeting with Koslov. The Deputy Resident yawned, and made his way to the bathroom of the small apartment. The living quarters were on the fourth floor of the Soviet Military Office on Belmont Road. Travkin had his own apartment closer to downtown, but he'd arrived on a late flight the night before, doubling as a courier and carrying the military pouch from Moscow Centre. He'd come directly to the SMO on Koslov's orders, sleeping off his jet-lag before the afternoon briefing.

He stared at the reflection of his narrow, almost feline face in the mirror, pushing back an unruly strand of the blonde hair he'd inherited from his mother's side of the family. The deep-set hazel eyes and the patrician nose came from his father, god rest his soul. Now *there* was a man who knew how to laugh! Travkin grinned, remembering his father's great booming laugh, knee slapped, head thrown back as he roared at some joke.

'Faith and begorrah, but you're a handsome boyo!' he crooned, the accent a bizarre blend of Russian and Irish. He brushed a spot of lint from the shoulder of his Joseph Wilner silk made-to-measure and left the apartment, taking the rear stairs down to Koslov's second-floor office.

From the outside the SMO is a handsome, redbrick Georgian building surrounded by a discreet wrought iron fence. Inside it is a maze of small offices and narrow hallways with low lighting that gives the place and its occupants a pale, sickly look. The furniture is utilitarian, the floors are bare wood and there is not a single piece of artwork in the entire building. During the summer months the central air conditioning is permanently set on cold, and in winter the furnace keeps the building boiling hot. The windows are allowed to accumulate soot, making surveillance photography difficult. To Dimitri Travkin's delicate nose, the place always seemed to smell faintly of damp wool socks.

The Major General was reading at his desk when Travkin entered the room. The desk was metal, the swivel chair behind it was wooden, there was one wooden office chair directly in front of the desk and half a dozen dark-brown filing cabinets against the far wall.

Travkin seated himself on the wooden chair and waited patiently. He could see Koslov's scalp beneath a thin covering of nicotine-coloured hair. The scalp was pink and smooth, like a baby's. Then Koslov lifted his head and the image vanished. The heavy, dark-jowled face was anything but babyish. Thin, colourless lips, permanently crimped around the soggy end of a foul-smelling Opal cigarette, large, coal-black eyes set deeply above the sagging cheeks and topped by shaggy, yellow-white brows, a nose that made Travkin's look tiny by comparison, nostrils flared, thick with curling hair. The voice, when he spoke, was the rasping product of fifty years of smoking and a quart of vodka every day for almost as long.

'Dimitri Alexandyrevich. You are looking well after your leave.'

'Thank you, General.'

'Your family is well?'

'Yes thank you, General. My mother sends her best wishes and greatly appreciated the box of chocolates you sent.'

'One should not forget old friends,' said Koslov. He and Travkin's father had fought together in the Great Patriotic War. According to his mother, Koslov and his father had competed for her favours and his father had been the successful suitor.

Travkin blinked, trying to erase the absurd image of Koslov on bended knee in front of his mother with a bunch of flowers in his hand. Fits of laughter in front of one's superior officer were not wise, especially when the officer was Major General Gennaddi Mikailovitch Koslov of the GRU.

'Thankfully things were quiet during your absence,' the old man grunted. He pushed a sheaf of papers across the desk; transcriptions of coded messages from his source agents. Travkin left them where they were for the moment. 'Little of interest,' said Koslov, tapping the sheets with a nicotine-stained index finger. 'Borovsky handled the drops.'

'Yes, sir.' Borovsky was an idiot who could barely tie his shoelaces but even he was capable of emptying a few "letterboxes".

'Your relationship with this man Stone,' said Koslov, after a momentary pause while he relit his Opal. 'It concerns me.'

'Sir?'

'We know he is an agent of CI-Q, the FBI's REDNET programme. By the same token he is certainly aware that you are not a member of our Trade Mission.'

'Yes sir.'

'I see no productivity from the relationship. His intent is clear; he has hopes of turning you.'

'I am aware of that, General.'

'Then why continue the charade?' Koslov asked, the wide brow furrowing into a dozen bulldog creases.

'Better an enemy one knows than one who is hidden.' Travkin shrugged. 'I am the passive partner. I expend no energy or manpower maintaining a casual friendship. On the other hand I've counted as many as six of his men keeping me under surveillance. When I wish to avoid them, I do so and go about my business. The product is their wasted expenditure of time and personnel.'

'I see.' Travkin knew that he didn't see at all. Koslov was old guard, capable of little in the way of subtlety. As far as he was concerned the general population of the United States was a bubbling pool of corruption, and any individual was capable of co-option for a price. If you couldn't appeal to a potential source's greed, you trapped him with sex or drugs or a combination of all three. It was true up to a point, but people like Stephen Stone were the hounds in this particular fox hunt, and Travkin wanted them in plain sight at all times.

If his friendship with Stone and their once a week raquetball game deflected REDNET's attention away from Travkin's real work then it was worthwhile. There were other, more complex reasons for continuing the friendship, but Travkin knew enough about the politics of the Soviet military not to reveal all his sources, to his boss or anyone else.

'All right, Dimitri, continue the liaison for the time being, but be advised that Older Brother has been sniffing at your tail.' Older Brother was the GRU term for the KGB. 'Perhaps it is your expensive clothing, Dimitri Alexandyrivich.'

'Of course,' Travkin replied, his expression serious. 'I will be the first Soviet Intelligence Officer to defect to the west over a question of wardrobe. My God, sir, don't they have anything better to do?'

'Perhaps not, Dimitri, but I beg you to take their interest seriously. Gurenko would like nothing better than to see me with egg on my face.' Vladimir Gurenko was the KGB station chief in Washington and Koslov's opposite number.

'I'll try to be careful.' Travkin stood up and gathered the pile of messages from Koslov's desk.

'Do that,' said the old man. He waved a hand; it was a dismissal.

Walking softly over the creaking floorboards, Dimitri Travkin left the office. Forty minutes later he was back in his apartment, soaking in a hot tub and listening to Bill Cosby moan and groan about his childhood while he went through the stack of messages Koslov had given him. He was halfway through an Old Weird Harold skit when he reached the brief note from his source in the file room at Walter Reed Hospital.

In Paris, night had fallen, bringing darkness to the city but no relief from the oppressive heat which had left its occupants stunned for the last three days. The August *fermeture annuelle* was in full swing and any Parisian who could afford it had fled to cooler climes, leaving the sweltering city to the tourists.

Unlike most major cities, Paris, arrogant to the point of martyrdom, refused to believe that pollution existed. Factories belched smoke, automobiles went without emission control and they still used diesel fuel in large parts of the Metro system. Because of this the effect of the heat wave was multiplied a thousand fold and the city choked under a colossal bell jar of umber-coloured air.

Eric Rhinelander, naked, lay on his narrow bed in the Pension Lipp and tried not to breathe too deeply. He was hot, tired and angry. If it hadn't been for Groman's stupid attempt to double-cross him he would have been back at Goldeneye on Jamaica's north coast, enjoying the evening breeze as it swept across the cliffs of Oracabessa.

He had completed the assignment in Amsterdam exactly as Groman had requested, extracting Yang and the others with the precision of a dentist pulling half a dozen rotting teeth. He'd taken the train to Paris that same night, expecting the final portion of Groman's promised payment. It had not been forthcoming and the pig-eyed whoremaster refused to answer any of his calls.

The money was of less concern to Rhinelander than his reputation. Groman was too well connected to be ignored. If Rhinelander allowed himself to be cheated by the man, others would make the same attempt. It was an irritating waste of time, but Groman had to be taught a lesson that would be heeded by anyone else who came along after him.

The assassin sat up, swinging his legs off the bed, skimming the film of sweat from his broad chest with the palm of one hand. He picked up the old, stainless steel Rolex from the bedside table and glanced at the time. Nine-fifteen. Groman wasn't expected at the Cardinal's Cap for another three quarters of an hour and the flight to Montreal didn't leave until midnight. There was plenty of time.

He padded across to the small porcelain sink on the other side of the room and sponged himself down. He had the body of a much younger man, shoulders, back and chest knotted with muscle, thighs hard, the hair over his groin thick, curly and dark. The only real clues to his age were the faint grey wings of hair at his temples and the fanning web of tiny lines at the corner of each eye.

He dressed; white, open-necked shirt, dark, slightly pleated trousers, cream-coloured linen jacket and a pair of soft, well-used English loafers. The rest of his clothing was already at Charles de Gaulle and would be put onto his flight automatically.

He strapped the small, eight-shot Sauer Automatic pistol to his ankle, using two thick rubber bands. He walked across the room and back, adjusting to the weight and feeling for slippage. He added a third rubber band for insurance, then gathered up his wallet, airline ticket, keys and small change. The last item, a chrome-plated ball-point pen, he clipped to the breast pocket of his shirt.

Rhinelander left the room and went down the narrow stairs to the main floor of the pension. He paid his bill and was given his passport in return, a

Canadian one in the name of John Duncan. Business completed he stepped out into the narrow confines of the Rue Des Anglais. The street was dark, empty and smelled of cats. He turned left, making his way quickly to the Boulevard St Germain, and picked up a taxi. After a ten minute run through the almost empty streets the taxi began to climb the hill towards Sacre Coeur, following the twisting maze of one way streets and alleys until it reached Impasse Souris in Montmartre.

His passenger delivered, the driver took his fare and drove off quickly. Rhinelander watched him go, then turned and entered the deeply shadowed recesses of the narrow, dead-end alleyway.

The end of the street was blocked by a tottering four-storey building, its walls grime-encrusted, the main floor windows bricked up, and the entrance secured by a heavy wooden door, strapped and studded with iron. Once upon a time the building had probably been the home of a well to do merchant, but now it looked like exactly what it was – a whorehouse.

He stepped up to the door and knocked once. After a moment a small peephole opened at shoulder height.

'*Was?*' asked a tired voice, speaking in German. The eye peering dimly out at Rhinelander was small, wary and ringed with greying skin.

'*Ich suche Fräulein Harriet,*' Rhinelander answered, slipping easily into his mother tongue. '*Beeilen sie sich bitte, es ist dringend.*'

'*Ja, ja,*' muttered the voice wearily. 'Of course it is urgent. For you men it is *always* urgent. You think only with your balls.' The peephole slammed shut and Rhinelander heard the sound of a bolt being drawn back. The door opened and he stepped inside quickly. The grey-haired drudge who'd answered his knock locked the door again and shuffled away without a backward glance. Rhinelander kept his jacket on, ignoring the empty row of metal coathooks in the foyer. From the looks of it business at the Cardinal's Cap was slow.

He went down the short passage to the main hall and looked around in the dim light. There was a faintly stylish aura about the broad vestibule with its high, ornately worked plaster ceiling and the big, wrought iron spiral staircase that led to the upper levels. But time had passed, taking the grandeur of the house with it. There were holes in the plaster and stains of mildew and rot. There was the dull odour of sour cabbage in the air, mixed with the reek of linen left too long between changes.

Ranged around the oval room were several tables and half a dozen mismatched chairs. A few velvet-shaded lamps threw pale smudges of light across the faces of the women in the room, most of whom were playing cards or simply staring into space, their features blank.

Rhinelander looked away, trying not to breathe too deeply; the room was like something out of Breugel, and far too reminiscent of his dreams. A moment later a middle-aged woman appeared on the stairs. She was dressed in a long, blue and orange kimono, her dark hair knotted casually at her neck. At first glance she seemed as false and desolate as the others, but there was a hint of intelligence in her grey-green eyes and the lines around her painted, cupid's-kiss lips were from laughter, not despair. Reaching the bottom of the stairs she held out a thin, long-boned hand. Rhinelander took it briefly, nodding.

'Herr Duncan,' she said softly, her voice a practised croon. 'How nice to see you at the Kardinalen Kap again. What can we do for you tonight?' The woman's German was stiff and formal, the accent forced. She was French, but Groman wanted authenticity and the Cardinal's Cap was supposedly a recreation of a prewar brothel in Berlin of the same name. The woman had a good memory; he'd only been at the whorehouse once before, for his original meeting with Groman.

'I need your help,' said Rhinelander, holding the woman's eyes. 'Can we go upstairs?'

'You want me?' asked Fraulein Harriet archly, cocking one hip, the bone standing out like a blade beneath the thin synthetic silk of her robe. 'You realise that it will cost you more, Herr Duncan?'

'Money is not a consideration,' he answered, still speaking German. 'I want your time, not your body, *meine Dame*.'

'Ah, so I'm a lady now!' she laughed. 'Hear that, girls?' she said, speaking French. 'A slut no more!' The other women paid no attention.

'I can go elsewhere,' Rhinelander said quietly.

'*Nein, nein, teuer Knabe*! If it is Harriet you want, then Harriet you shall have. Come along.'

She led him up the staircase to the narrow corridor that ran the length of the second floor, each cell-like room blocked by a plain, anonymous door.

'How do the women know which room is theirs?' Rhinelander enquired.

'If the room is not locked, it belongs to them.' Harriet laughed. 'Only the special rooms are marked, and my own room, of course.' She winked at Rhinelander and grinned. 'Rank hath its privileges, even here, Herr Duncan.'

She stopped in front of a blue-painted door and drew a key ring out of the pocket of her robe. She led Rhinelander inside, closed the door and then went to the centre of the room, standing on a small square of oriental carpeting, its design almost completely worn away. There was a metal bed and a small bedside table on one side of the room and a fabric-covered folding screen on the other, presumably hiding the chamberpot and other toilet facilities.

The woman kept her smile fixed and her eyes on Rhinelander as she undid the belt of her kimono and let it fall to the floor with a shrug. She was fit enough for a woman her age, the breasts full and sagging only slightly, the belly a single curve, the pale patch of her sex unobtrusive.

'So, what shall it be, Herr Duncan?' she asked, her eyes flickering to the narrow iron bed and the thin mattress.

'I want you to get down on your knees,' he instructed.

She nodded, at ease with the familiar request, and did as he asked, then stared up at him, arms outstretched, hands beckoning.

'Come on then,' She murmured. He moved closer until he was standing directly above her.

'Close your eyes,' he said.

'Shy?' she asked, laughing.

'Just do it.'

'*Jawohl, mein Herr*!' She grinned, obeying. Her lips parted expectantly, waiting for him to begin.

Rhinelander bent slightly and reached down, pulling the pistol away from its rubber band holster. He placed his left hand on the top of Harriet's head, then slipped the barrel of the gun between her lips and teeth. Her eyes flew open at the cold metallic touch and she blinked up at him, terrified. He pushed the barrel more deeply into her mouth.

'Don't move, not even an inch,' he said quietly. He took his hand away from her head and pushed back the slide, cocking the weapon. 'The slightest pressure and your teeth will be blown out the back of your head along with your brains,' he whispered. 'I will ask you questions, you will answer. Lie and you are dead. If you understand, blink your eyes.'

She did so, rapidly. He slid the barrel out of her mouth, the metal wet with saliva. He backed away, keeping the pistol trained on her. 'When Groman comes here, who does he fuck?'

'Me. Usually.'

'This room?'

'No,' she answered, her voice quavering. 'The special room. The furniture there is nicer.'

'That is the room with the peephole, yes?'

'Yes.'

'What about Max, the bodyguard?'

'Herr Groman doesn't let him come in. He stays with the car.'

'Where does he park?'

'Rue Poulbot.'

'Good.' Rhinelander nodded. 'You're doing well. Now then, when Groman visits, how long does he stay?'

'An hour, sometimes two or three if he takes cocaine.'

'Does he take it often?'

'Often enough.'

'Is there a rear exit from here?' Rhinelander already knew there was but he wanted to know if she'd tell him the truth.

'Yes,' she nodded. 'There is an alley. Follow it and you come to the stairs at Rue Drevet.'

'Good. Stand up and put on your robe.' The woman did so, her eyes never leaving the pistol in Rhinelander's hand. 'Take me to the room. Not the bedroom, the one with the peephole.'

He followed her out of the room and along the corridor. They made several turns until she reached a door close to a narrow flight of stairs.

'The stairs lead to the back kitchen,' she offered, following his glance.

'Fine. Show me the room.'

She nodded and took out the key ring again. She opened the door and stepped aside, gesturing into a tiny, cupboard-sized space. In the weak light from the corridor he could see that it contained nothing but a high stool and a single coat hook. Rhinelander eased into the room and sat down on the stool. By crouching slightly he brought his eye to a hole in the wall about the size of an American dime.

The room on the other side of the wall was clean, with freshly painted white walls and a bland selection of modern furniture. There were a few landscape prints on the walls and the floor was covered in subdued green carpeting. It looked like something out of a Holiday Inn.

'The hole is covered by the shadow of a wall sconce,' explained Harriet nervously, standing in the corridor. 'You can see everything that goes on.' She paused. 'Some people like that.'

'So I've heard.' Rhinelander climbed down from the stool. He stepped out into the hallway and stared at the woman silently. Finally he spoke. 'It is almost ten o'clock. Groman will be here any moment.'

'Yes.'

'Bring him here. Do whatever is neccessary to distract him. I want him between your legs and thinking of nothing else, understand?'

'Yes . . . yes.'

'Tell him anything, warn him, and I will know. And I will kill you.'

'You will be watching?'

'Yes.' Rhinelander pushed her gently. 'Go. Be downstairs to greet him.'

The woman gave him a brief, frightened look and then retreated down the hallway. Rhinelander returned to the cubbyhole and closed the door, leaving it slightly ajar. Without hurry he slipped off his shoes and socks and hung up his jacket on the hook behind him. Then he settled down on the stool to wait.

Less than five minutes later he heard the muffled sound of voices coming from the corridor. He leaned over and put his eye to the peephole again. The door to the bedroom opened and Harriet appeared, followed by the heavyset figure of Groman. Once the drug dealer had taken pride in his longshoreman's body, but too many years of indulgence had taken their toll. Even in his expensive suit and hand-made shirt the man's belly bulged far over his belt, and the big, peasant's face was stained on cheek and nose with blossoms of broken blood vessels.

Without a word Harriet began working at Groman's zipper, then dropped down in front of him. She slipped the brown worm of his limp organ into her mouth and began to suck noisily. Within a few moments the worm had become a hooded snake, thick and long, standing out absurdly from his trousers, the head a slick glistening purple in the bright light from the ceiling fixture.

'The bed,' Groman ordered, his voice hoarse. By the time he'd stripped off his clothes, Harriet was already on the mattress, one leg raised, waiting for him. He climbed into bed with her, pushing her legs apart, and she spat into her hand, wetting herself. Without any preliminaries he lowered his large body over hers, plunging himself deeply inside. She grunted, wincing with pain, and then gripped his pale, furry shoulders as he began a jerking, angry rhythm, buttocks clenching with effort, toes digging into the bedding.

Rhinelander stepped gingerly off the stool and out into the corridor. It was empty. From somewhere below he could hear the faint sounds of a stereo playing Charles Aznavour. There were no voices, just the music and the sound of cards being dealt. He stepped along to the door of the peephole room and paused, standing on the balls of his feet, his ear an inch from the thin wooden partition. Groman was grunting loudly with each stroke now, counterpoint to the squeaking of the bedsprings.

Silently, Rhinelander reeached into his pocket and removed the ballpoint. It was actually a metal, telescopic pointer of the kind used by university lecturers and Rhinelander had altered it by removing the plastic tip and replacing it with the last half inch of a tungsten steel leatherworker's awl. He clicked the knurled button on the top of the pointer, unlocking it, then pulled it out to its full, eighteen-inch length and twisted the end in a half turn, locking it in place again.

He opened the door carefully, the steel tube of his weapon held lightly between the thumb and forefinger of his right hand. He slipped noiselessly into the room on bare feet, crossing the carpeted floor in three quick steps. Groman had his face buried in Harriet's right shoulder, powerful hands clutching her upraised buttocks as he pounded into her, his large, sagging testicles slapping at the puckered bud of her anus with each stroke.

Almost without pause, Rhinelander found his point and moved, thrusting forward with the pointer, driving the awl-tip into the vulnerable four-inch target of Groman's perineum. The long weapon sliced neatly up into the big man's bladder, intestine, stomach, liver and heart. With a grimace, Rhinelander pressed his thumb against the end of the device, pushing the last inch into Groman's writhing, steel-skewered body. The drug dealer made a choked, mewling sound as every organ in his body ceased functioning simultaneously and then his head dropped down onto Harriet's chest, a smothering deadweight.

Rhinelander grabbed the hair at the back of the corpse's head and pulled it back. Harriet stared up at him, white-faced and paralysed with fear, Groman's dead penis slithering out between her legs.

'Remember this,' Rhinelander hissed, bringing his face down to within an inch of the woman. 'Remember how he died and tell anyone who wants to know.' He pulled harder on Groman's hair, dragging him off Harriet and rolling him over onto the mattress beside her. Mouth working soundlessly she crabbed off the bed, staring at the corpse. There was a damp stain on the sheet and Rhinelander smelled urine. The woman had wet herself with fear.

'Who are you?' she managed, her voice stuttering.

'A ghost,' he answered. 'Someone who never existed.'

'Are you going to kill me as well?'

'Of course not,' Rhinelander answered. 'You didn't cheat me, he did.' He smiled at her, his expression almost gentle. 'Stay here for at least thirty minutes,' he commanded, his voice quiet. 'That way there will be no trouble.'

'Yes . . . yes, of course,' she said. He turned and left the room, returning to the cubbyhole for his jacket, socks and shoes. He put them on quickly, then took the rear stairs down to the back kitchen. Fifteen minutes later he took a taxi to the Aerogare station at Porte Maillot and from there he boarded the shuttle bus for Charles de Gaulle. At midnight exactly his Air Canada 747 took off en route to Mirabel Airport, Montreal.

CHAPTER FOUR

The fat man sat in the conference room of the Georgetown safe house, the nib of his heavy Mont Blanc fountain pen gliding easily over the surface of the yellow legal pad on the table in front of him. The hand holding the expensive pen was small and very pink, the skin smooth and hairless, the nails perfectly manicured.

At the other end of the long table, Hudson Cooper watched the hand and the pen, mesmerised by the smooth movement of the glittering solid gold nib and the soft, almost feminine fingers wrapped around the thick, black-laquered barrel. The delicate hand was completely at odds with the rest of the fat man's body and had a life of its own, giving no hint of the immense power it could wield with a single stroke of that same black pen.

The fat man was Hollis W Macintyre and with the exception of the President he was probably the most important man in Washington, if not the entire United States. Physically, he was either dramatically imposing or repulsive, depending on your point of view. At eighty he still had all his hair, a crowning glory of thick pure white atop a massive, leonine head. Cheeks and jaws were draped in Churchillian jowls, the eyes were large, dark and hawk-hooded and the short, tree-trunk neck was wedged between massive shoulders and arms. He dressed impeccably, custom-cut white silk three-piece suits from Hong Kong in the summer, dark pinstripes in the autumn and winter, and always with his trademark red white and blue polka-dot bow tie.

Macintyre's formal occupation was the chairmanship of the President's political party but that was really nothing more than a flag for him to fly under. After almost half a century in the shifting sands of federal politics he had innumerable allies in both Houses of Congress, sat on the boards of a score of institutions and multinational corporations and was owed favours by virtually every important figure in Washington from bureaucrats in the Budget Office to the Joint Chiefs. In addition, he was chairman pro tem of the Romulus Committee, a position not noted in any biography, official or otherwise.

'I believe I have the salient points,' he said, capping the pen. Macintyre's voice was rich and deep with the rolling timbre of a natural orator. The large, hooded eyes stared blandly down the table at Cooper. 'I presume Colonel Barron's diagnosis has been verified?'

'Certainly,' Cooper nodded, 'by one of the best neurologists in the country. He had no idea who the patient was, of course.'

'What about this Barron fellow? How far can he be trusted?' asked Macintyre.

'The question is irrelevant,' Cooper answered, smiling briefly. 'Colonel Barron had a boating accident today. A fatal one.'

'I see,' Macintyre answered. 'This was necessary?'

'By my estimation there was no alternative. To have taken him any further would have involved Romulus. I felt it was better to forestall any possible complications.'

'Yes. You're probably right.' The fat man leaned back in his chair, the small hands clasped together over his enormous belly. He glanced briefly at the trays of hors d'oeuvres and wine on the sideboard to his left. The refreshments had been brought in by stewards from Cooper's own staff who had long since left the building. They would return in the morning to clean up the remains. 'How much have you told the others?' he asked finally.

'Nothing,' Cooper answered, shaking his head. 'I wanted the chance to confer with you first.' He paused. 'Romulus has never dealt with anything of this magnitude before.'

'True,' agreed Macintyre. 'And like your Colonel Barron, some of them are not altogether trustworthy, at least in this instance.' The 'others' included the Deputy Chairman of the Joint Chiefs of Staff, the Secretary of State, the Assistant Secretary of the Treasury and the Attorney General. In all, Romulus was made up of ten people who between them covered most major elements of the federal government and the armed forces.

'So what do we tell them?' Cooper asked. He checked his watch. 'They'll start coming within the next half hour or so.'

'We tell them the truth,' said Macintyre, shrugging his massive shoulders. 'Or at leat a part of it. The President is ill, but at this point we're not certain how ill. We do know that the illness could well become disabling in a short period of time. That should cover things for the moment.'

'Fair enough, but what about Teresi?' Cooper asked, referring to the Vice-President, Vincent Salvatore Teresi.

'Our Italian friend bullied his way into the Vice-Presidency,' Macintyre responded, a note of anger in his voice. 'If I hadn't outmanoeuvred him at the convention and offered him the position on the ticket he would have split the party in half.'

'Or become President,' said Cooper dryly.

'Indeed,' said Macintyre. 'In which case we would all be out of work, believe me.'

'Romulus wasn't created to deal with questions of partisan politics,' said Cooper, an edge to his voice. 'It was devised to deal with a potentially disasterous oversight within the Constitution. Our employment or lack of it is hardly a consideration.'

'Don't be naive, Hudson. The Romulus Committee was created because Franklin Delano Roosevelt was dying of heart disease and had a fellow traveller as Vice-President. If he, or Eleanor, or any of his close friends had known how sick he was, he would never have run for a third term and Wallace would have become President. We needed the third term and we needed Harry Truman.'

'This is hardly the same situation,' said Cooper.

'I disagree,' replied Macintyre, shaking his large head slowly. 'I think the situation is almost identical. In less than six months we're going to be hosting a major summit. In terms of world politics that summit is even more important than Potsdam. There they were cutting up Europe – this time the entire world is at stake. Beyond that you know as well as I do that with the democratisation of the Eastern Bloc we've got billions of dollars in military appropriations riding on this, not to mention the fate of NATO, Star Wars and our relationship with the Third World countries when Central and South America get on the band wagon. Those bastards in the Kremlin have taken away all our enemies, Hudson. All we have left is that idiot Qaddafi. That summit is the single most important political event of the past seventy-five years. It will set the standard of international relations well into the twenty-first century. Do you want Vincent Teresi representing our interests? He'd give the Soviets Central America on a platter. Among other shortcomings, the man is a sentimental fool. Simply in terms of national security I think the question of his assumption of executive power certainly falls within the mandate of this committee.' Macintyre paused and sat forward, hands splayed on the surface of the conference table. 'Consider this, Hudson. The Romulus Committee has only been convened seven times since the death of FDR.' He lifted his hands and began counting off each instance on his fingers. 'Eisenhower's heart attack, the Marilyn Monroe affair, Oswald, Ruby, twice during Watergate and once following the Hinkley attempt on Reagan. Of the seven meetings only two resulted in direct action, but partisan politics was a part of every one.'

'What exactly are you suggesting?' asked Cooper. He knew the answer, since there was only one, but it would come from Macintyre's lips, not his.

'I'm not entirely sure at this point,' the fat man said thoughtfully. He stroked the underside of his fleshy chin with the thumb of one hand. 'I do know one thing, though: under no circumstances can Vincent Teresi be allowed to assume the Presidency of the United States.'

There was a soft buzzing sound from the foyer behind Cooper. The first of the other committee members had arrived. Macintyre rose ponderously to his feet. As chairman he would act as host and greet his guests. 'I think we should delay discussion of the details until after the meeting,' he warned quietly. 'I'm afraid some members of the committee might be a trifle squeamish about that sort of thing.'

'As you wish.' Cooper remained seated while Macintyre walked heavily past him and left the room. He stared at the empty chair at the other end of the table, remembering the pink soft hands. '"Who is there then, would rid me of this troublesome priest?"' he quoted, whispering softly.

CHAPTER FIVE

After the standard, 45-minute ritual of meandering metro rides, double-backs on foot and switched cabs, Dimitri Travkin arrived at the main entrance to the Smithsonian. He was well aware that the paranoid arabesque he'd just gone through was normal operating procedure, but he found it all more than just physically tiring. He lived in a world of nagging fears and doubts, where everything and everyone was suspect.

Sighing, Travkin jammed his hands into the pockets of his sports jacket, jogged up the steps and went into the Great Hall. How did you keep your sanity in a business where nothing was as it seemed? No wonder so many of his colleagues were alcoholics. He skirted the crowd of tourists around the Washington planning exhibit and headed for the Mall exit. Give it another couple of years and he'd be ready for that job at the Soviet Military Academy Koslov had been hinting about. A normal life, or something close to it. Perhaps even a wife, children?

Travkin snorted at his fantasy and pushed out through the doors and into the sunlight. He slipped on his sunglasses, then followed the main footpath through the neatly planted elms to the Mall proper. A good place to meet. The greensward was more than four hundred feet across, stretching from Madison Drive to Jefferson, and two miles long, going from the Washington Monument to Capitol Hill. If anyone was following either him or his contact they'd be clearly visible from a long way off. He walked east along Jefferson, taking his time, pausing at the sunken sculpture garden behind the drum-shaped Hirshorn Museum.

He lit a cigarette and glanced around. No sign of any REDNET people, and no sign of Scanlon either. Travkin dragged deeply on the cigarette and exhaled, frowning. He'd give the man two minutes, no more; it was very bad manners to keep a Deputy Resident waiting, especially when you expected to get money from him.

Scanlon, a clerk in the Library at Walter Reed, had been one of Travkin's first enlistments, and still rated as the easiest. The man was a racist, white supremacist pig, and representing himself as an anti-gun-control lobbyist Travkin had explained that he wanted access to health information at Walter Reed to keep track of their enemies in Congress. Scanlon had taken the bait and the money that went with it, something Travkin could prove with photographic evidence if the man ever became a problem.

Travkin dropped the butt of his cigarette onto the gravel path and ground it out with the toe of his shoe. In any other circumstances he would have ignored Scanlon's request for a meeting, but coming so soon after the death of Barron, the President's doctor, Travkin had been intrigued. President goes into Walter Reed for a physical, President's physician has a fatal accident on his boat, then the summons from Scanlon.

'Mr Smith?' Travkin turned at the sound of the low-pitched voice. It was Scanlon, white shirt billowing over a fat gut, dark wet patches under the arms, a wrinkled seersucker jacket hooked on one finger and draped over his shoulder. Sweat was beaded in the short man's curly hair and he was breathing in short hard gasps.

'Let's walk,' said Travkin. Without waiting for an answer he struck out across the Mall, heading for the Museum of Natural History. He could hear Scanlon panting behind him, trotting to keep up. On the far side of the open space Travkin found an empty park bench and seated himself. Scanlon dropped down beside him with a grateful sigh. Travkin lit another cigarette and waited for the man to catch his breath.

'Jesus, it's hot,' the clerk muttered, his breath still coming in harsh little gasps.

'Why did you ask for the meeting?' Travkin asked bluntly. It *was* hot, and he didn't like the idea of spending any more time with Scanlon than he had to, intrigued or not.

'Barron.'

'The President's doctor. The one who died.'

'Right.' Scanlon pulled a crumpled handkerchief out of his pants pocket and wiped his face.

'What about him?'

'I'm not sure if it means anything, but I switched to the morning shift the same day Dr Barron drowned.'

'Yes?'

'Well,' Scanlon said, wiping his face again, 'one of the things you do first thing in the library is go over the request log.'

'Explain,' Travkin interrupted.

'The request log. It's all on computer. It's got all the requests for material on it from the previous shift. It shows what material was sent up to which doctor so the guys on the next shift can make sure they get back to the library.'

'What does this have to do with Dr Barron?'

'I'm getting to that,' said Scanlon. 'I mean I didn't know Barron was dead so I didn't think too much of it at the time, but it clicked later on.'

'What clicked?' Travkin asked, annoyance creeping into his voice.

'The night before, Dr Barron called in a request for anything the library had on something called . . . shit.' The fat man dragged his jacket into his lap and fumbled in one of the inside pockets. He brought out a folded sheet of paper and opened it. 'Here it is. He wanted information on Creuzfeldt-Jacob disease.'

'Spell it,' Travkin instructed. Scanlon did so. Travkin stubbed out his cigarette and looked up and down the Mall. He checked his watch. Another fifteen minutes and the lunchtime crowds would begin to appear. 'What is this illness?' he asked.

'Beats me.' Scanlon shrugged. 'He asked for some stuff on Alzheimer's at the same time, if that means anything. Anyway, that's not what I thought was so interesting.'

'Oh?'

'Yeah.' Scanlon nodded. 'What got me was that when I put in a call to Barron's office the next day to ask for the material back, I got told he'd never asked for the stuff in the first place. They said it must be a computer glitch. So I checked.' Scanlon paused and wiped his face a third time.

'And?'

'I went back through the log, and by Christ if there wasn't any sign of a request from Dr Barron. I even went back into the stacks and checked out the material he was supposed to have asked for. It was all there, filed just the way it's supposed to be. Damndest thing.'

'What do you think it means?' Travkin asked, already forming his own opinion.

'Obvious,' Scanlon grunted. 'Barron died. He was asking about something somebody didn't want anyone else to know about. So they cleaned the slate and put everything back nice and tidy.'

'*They* cleaned the slate?' Travkin asked. 'Who do you think "they" might be?'

'Dunno.' Scanlon shrugged. 'Have to be somebody pretty high up to start fiddling with the computers that way.'

'You have access to personnel files, don't you?' Travkin asked suddenly.

'Sure.' Scanlon nodded, frowning. 'Why?'

'I want Barron's.'

'All of it?'

'Yes.' Travkin bit his lip thoughtfully. 'Right back to his medical school days. You can call me at the usual number when you're ready to hand it over.'

'I'll see what I can do.'

'One more things,' Travkin said slowly. 'How do they keep track of telephone calls at Walter Reed?'

'Computer,' Scanlon answered. 'They've got a call-accounting system tied into the central control unit.'

'Can you get into it?'

'Sure.'

'I want to know if Barron made any outside calls around the time he called down to the library.'

'Okay,' Scanlon warned, 'but it's going to cost extra.' He dabbed at his upper lip with the handkerchief.

'I'm aware of that,' Travkin answered, nodding curtly. 'There will be another five hundred in the envelope this month.'

'Fine,' beamed Scanlon.

'I want the information quickly,' said Travkin, standing. He turned and headed back down the Mall towards the Washington Monument. Scanlon watched him go and then stood up himself and walked away in the opposite direction.

Stephen Stone sat in the dark basement screening room and stared at the grainy telephoto image on the large-screen television. He worked the remote control in his hand, moving the picture back and forth. Mort Kessler sat on his left, while the lip-reader sat on his right. The lip-reader was Norman Traynor, a bullet-headed Bureau man of the old school who'd gone deaf ten years before. He'd avoided being put out to pasture by learning how to lip-read for long range surveillance operations like this one.

'"I want the information" . . . something,' Traynor said as Stone ran the last few seconds of the tape again. 'I can't make out the last little bit. Your target turned away at the end.'

'Sorry about that,' said Kessler. 'Your boy is pretty cautious. We couldn't risk getting much closer. We were up in the tower at the Smithsonian for this. That's maybe four, five hundred yards.'

'That's all right.' Stone shrugged. He turned to Traynor. 'You get all of it?' he asked. The heavyset, grey-haired man nodded, snapping the cassette out of the small tape machine in his lap. With the videotape running he'd transcribed directly onto the cassette.

'I'll take it up to technical and match audio to the picture. You should be able to see the mix in a couple of hours. I'll let you know.'

'Great,' Stone said. 'Thanks, Norm.'

'My pleasure.' The lip reader stood up and left the screening room.

'Well?' asked Stone.

Kessler clambered to his feet, found the light switch on the far wall and turned it on. He began to pace back and forth in front of him and described the surveillance. 'From the Mall he went up to the Library of Congress, on foot mind you, and went through the card indexes for about half an hour. After that he took a cab to an antiquarian bookstore on M Street. McCanns. They specialise in medical and technical reference books. He bought two books on dementia and a general text on brain diseases. From there he went to three more bookstores. Same thing. Books on Alzheimer's, dementia, mental illness and brain diseases. Then he went back to his apartment. Paid cash at the antiquarian store and at the other three as well.'

'Smart,' Stone grunted. 'You have to give your name and provide ID to get stuff out of the stacks at the Library of Congress. He probably used their card index to get an idea of some titles to go after, then hit the stores working off that list.'

'I wonder what he's up to,' said Kessler.

'Dunno,' Stone muttered, watching the thin line of smoke from his cigarette trail up to the low ceiling of the screening room. 'But we're one step ahead of him.' He pulled himself up in the seat. 'Let's see if we can come up with some material on Barron's practice outside of the President. Find out who he's been treating lately and if we can find some connection between a patient and this Creuzfeldt-Jacob thing.'

'Do we pull in Scanlon?'

'No, not yet. Let him run a little longer.'

'Anything else?' Kessler offered.

Stone tapped his fingers on the arm of the chair. 'The pathologist,' he said finally, staring at the blank television screen a few feet in front of him.

'Who?' asked Kessler.

'The pathologist. Whoever it was at the Coroner's Office who did the autopsy on Barron. See if you can get me his name, would you?'

'You sound like you're on to something.'

'Not really,' Stone said thoughtfully. 'But if Dimitri is interested in the dead Dr Barron, then so am I.'

Rhinelander moved easily through the pale green water, fins pumping in strong rhythmic strokes as he cruised above the reef. He swam in a long-established pattern, pausing at each float on the grid to take another set of photographs. The bright yellow plastic spheres bobbed at the end of ten foot long nylon cords anchored to the reef, providing him with a standard position from which to shoot so that the same portion of the reef's surface could be documented each time he made a run.

He paused at the outermost marker and lifted the Data Scan console dangling from his waist to check the readout. This was his second dive of the day and he'd been down seventy minutes. According to the display on the console he had eleven minutes bottom-time left. Not enough time to make another pass, and with the sun almost directly overhead the usual shoals of brilliantly coloured reef fish were absent. Another time. Turning away he let his arms dangle at his side, following his bubbles towards the surface, and the bobbing spearhead shadow marking his 30-foot Boston Whaler, the *Whisperland.*

Reaching the stern of the high-sided sport cruiser he spat out his mouthpiece and stripped off his mask. Slipping off his flippers he tossed them into the boat and boosted himself up onto the metal dive step bolted to the transom. He flipped inboard and began to strip down, beginning with the Nikonos camera, and ending with the dark green wetsuit he'd been using for the past six years. He ducked into the lower cabin, pulled a bottle of Red Stripe out of the little refrigerator in the galley and took it back on deck. He climbed into the cockpit seat and settled back against the sun-hot leather. Squinting through the lightly tinted windscreen he could make out the steep green hills above Discovery Bay, almost four miles away.

He sipped the cold beer, savouring the crisp bite as it struck his tongue. The sun felt good on his bare skin and he was already beginning to feel the tensions of the last few days begin to recede. If there was any security to his life, any sense of belonging in a real world, it was here, on the reef, feeling the gentle swell lapping at the *Whisperland*'s hull. Before Jamaica, the boat, and the house at Oracabessa his life had been little more than reactions to events. Born with no real identity of his own, he adopted masks to suit his needs and the requirements of his work; trained to kill, he killed, elevating the assassin's trade to the level of art.

Rhinelander smiled, reached out and took a cigarette from the pack of Senior Service on the cockpit shelf. Setting his beer down he lit the cigarette, then plucked a few shreds of tobacco from the tip of his tongue. On the pages of some secret file deep in the vaults at Langley he was probably listed as a psychopath, but he knew the psychiatrists on staff at the Agency only used the word to comfort themselves and rationalise the insanity of their own positions.

Not that it mattered. Some years before he had finally come to see the truth of his life; unlike most people, he lived on two planes of existence, call them overworld and underworld. Overworld was his life here, the life which the general population would see as 'normal'. Underworld was an existence populated with the Breugel nightmares of people like Phillipe Groman and the snakepit politics of Pol Pot's grisly henchmen. Both worlds had their own natural laws and constants, both had their own loyalties and lies, both had their separate sets of rules which had to be obeyed, and with care, both worlds could be lived in, feeding on each other in an endless, delicately balanced cycle. Rhinelander took a long swallow of the warming beer. If that was madness, then so be it. He closed his eyes and let his head fall back against the seat. An hour in the sun, another cigarette or two and another beer. After that he'd weigh anchor, head for the dock at Ocho Rios, then home to Breakers.

Paul Mallory, Special Assistant to CIA Deputy Director Hudson Cooper, reached Jamaica aboard the noon American Airlines flight landing at Montego Bay's Sir Donald Sangster Airport. Already wilting in the wet heat, he endured the tooth-rattling electrified steel band on the main concourse and threaded his way through the scattered, off-season crowds to the Budget booth. Half an hour later, after confirming his reservation at the Ocho Rios Americana, he piloted the bruised Toyota he'd rented out onto The Queens Drive, took A-3 west and began the fifty-mile drive to Oracabessa.

The narrow switchback road along the coast was an odd combination of bright modern resort hotels and tumbledown shacks, mangrove swamps and blue and silver beaches. Gigantic ferns choked flaking billboards advertising Red Stripe Brewery Fresh Beer and Tropigaz. There were cane fields and coconut palms, stone-hut villages, long abandoned, broken windows like dark, staring eyes. Mallory ignored all of it, concentrating on the road; for him, Jamaica was no island paradise, it was a trap waiting to be sprung.

Mallory had been recruited into the CIA during his last year at MIT and joined the Agency six months after Richard Nixon became President and Richard Helms took over as Director of CIA. Already comfortable with the fledgling field of computers he was assigned to the Threat Analysis and Plans division, spending most of his time gathering information about countries in Central and South America. During his tenure with the TAP group he went on occasional fact-finding missions to the countries in question, but those trips bore no resemblance to his recent journey to Paris, and now Jamaica.

In the past Mallory had never found his work difficult to justify, and he'd certainly never felt himself to be in any personal danger. He thought of himself as a statistician who happened to work in the field of intelligence, nothing more; a demi-scientist in a secure job, with all the best computer toys in the world at his disposal.

This was different. Hudson Cooper had a broad mandate within the CIA, but it was clear that this operation had been conceived and put into effect well outside the normal protocols. Cooper's interest in the QJ/RAIL file was more than casual, and Rhinelander was much more than your average ex-Company man. He was an assassin who'd never come close to being caught or implicated in a political killing. If Cooper was fishing around for a man like Rhinelander, it could mean only one thing – he wanted someone dead. Mallory also knew that you didn't hire someone of QJ/RAIL's quality for a bit of minor housecleaning. The target of Cooper's interest had to be big league.

Mallory frowned and pushed his glasses back onto the bridge of his nose with a practised finger. Big league, but who? Ever since Cooper had shown interest in the QJ/RAIL file, Mallory had been going through his mental Rolodex trying to figure it out. The most likely target was someone high in a foreign intelligence operation, but there had been nothing in the wind recently except for yet another mole turning up in the UK.

One thing was certain, if Rhinelander was being used, the prospective victim had to be a so-called hard target; a person, or persons, surrounded by a lot of protective security, or situated in a difficult location – the Kremlin, for instance. Mallory sucked air through his clenched teeth and tapped his fingers on the sticky plastic of the steering wheel. Being involved in some clandestine and possibly unsanctioned operation of Cooper's made him very nervous, especially when it involved assassination, which, by Mallory's expert estimation, was an outmoded and statistically ineffectual instrument of foreign policy.

Passing through the tiny village of Salt Gut, Mallory eased off on the gas and began paying attention to the directions he'd been given at the airport in Montego Bay. A few miles down the narrow highway he spotted the abandoned remains of the Shell station blasted by the '88 hurricane, and turned off onto an even narrower dirt road leading towards the coast. As promised, he came to a pair of overgrown gateposts, each one topped with a large, carved, black-painted falcon.

There was no gate blocking the entrance so Mallory turned the small sedan down the jungle-choked trail. After a hundred yards the canopied track ended in a small clearing facing the ocean. There was a modest, cement-walled bungalow in the centre of the open space, angled slightly away from the gleaming water and the low cliffs above the beach: Breakers, built next door to the summer house once owned by Ian Fleming, creator of James Bond, and now occupied by Eric Rhinelander, a man who possessed the real-life version of that fictional character's licence to kill.

Mallory parked the Toyota and stepped out into the bright sunshine. Squinting, he adjusted his glasses again and took a deep breath. An odd combination of smells: the rich scent of the screening foliage mixed with the salt-bitter breath of the onshore breeze. He turned and, shading his eyes with one uplifted hand, examined the house. Single-storied, deep-set window openings blocked by fat-slat venetian blinds. Jalousies; that's what he remembered his deep-south grandmother calling them; like something you'd expect to see on the windows of a plantation home in Georgia.

The roof was covered in worn shingles, whole sections looking much newer than others. The hurricane? Mallory did a full circuit, his shoes crunching on the crumbling patio-stones around the house. All the windows were shuttered against the early afternoon heat. The building was constructed in a thick L-shape with two entrances – one through a set of shuttered French doors that faced the sunken, overgrown garden on the ocean side, the other through a narrow wooden door on the side of the house near where Mallory had parked the Toyota. The French doors were locked. Completing his circuit he knocked hesitantly on the narrow door and waited. He looked around, but there were no vehicles other than his own. Mallory knocked again, harder this time, then tried the old-fashioned, thumb-latch handle. The door swung open, revealing a cool, dark vestibule. Wishing it had been locked, he stepped inside, carefully closing the door behind him.

The bare walls were roughly plastered, the floor concrete, painted a dark blue and partially covered by a scattering of thin, plaited rush mats. Directly in front of Mallory a narrow hall ran down the length of the house while to his left a doorway led into a small galley kitchen. Beside it an archway opened onto the large, low-ceilinged living room. Ignoring the kitchen Mallory stepped into the living room, peering into the gloom. The only light came from the cracks between the shutter slats creating knife-blade beams alive with eddying motes of dust.

Again the walls were bare, rough plaster. The furniture was sparse and nondescript. The room said nothing about Rhinelander at all.

Mallory returned to the vestibule and paused for a moment, listening hard. Slight rattle of the shutters, distant surf, birds, the hard, echoing beating of his heart ... get out, get out, get out. Rational thought told him that invading the privacy of a professional assassin was not a good idea, but his own curiosity led him down the short hall to the other rooms. If Rhinelander came back to the house he'd hear the car pull up in plenty of time.

The first door led into a cramped bathroom. The second room was no more than a spartan sleeping cell. Single bed on a metal frame, freestanding closet. There was a book on the table, *Caribbean Reef Fishes* by John Randall. Mallory picked it up and flipped to the title page. Rhinelander was still a cipher; so far the house was about as interesting as a Holiday Inn. He turned towards the door. Cooper wanted an edge, but it didn't look as though he was going to get it. Mallory went into the last room at the end of the hall. Dark as a tomb. Fumbling, he found a light switch beside the door and flipped it on.

'Jesus Christ.'

All four walls of the twelve by fifteen room were covered in bookshelves from floor to ceiling. A long, counter-style work station was ranged along one of the book walls, fitted with a Compaq 386/25 computer, Hewlett Packard laser printer, scanner, plotter, the works. All of it was right up

Mallory's alley and he knew he was looking at a good fifty Ks' worth of hardware. Resisting the temptation to sit down at the keyboard and boot up Rhinelander's hard drive, he turned his attention towards the books.

The wall behind the work station was given over to a wide-reaching array of books on oceanography, marine biology, marine technology and naval history. The wall opposite was a library of travel books: Fodors', Fielding's and Baedeker's guides, both modern and old, shelves full of neatly filed maps, one whole shelf devoted to European rail-guides and a score of Kodak Carousel boxes, each one marked with the name of a different country or city. The bulk of the travel books concentrated on Southeast Asia and Europe, but there were also a number of them covering the Caribbean, Central America, South America and the Orient.

The bookcases facing the door were the most telling. The upper shelves contained rows of *Jane's Weapon System* yearbooks going back to the middle sixties, books on Soviet and American weaponry, various US Army handbooks on unconventional warfare and ring-bound catalogues from every major arms manufacturer in the world. Below the ordnance books were dozens of titles relating to intelligence, both domestic and foreign: *CIA in Central America, Agency, Rise and Decline of the CIA, The Puzzle Palace, Soviet Military Intelligence, Deep Black, The President's Secret Wars, Society and the Assassin, The Assassin's Art, Low Intensity Warfare* . . . the list went on and on. Below that, filling out the lower shelves, were titles dealing with the drug trade: Alvin Moscow's *Merchants of Heroin, Trail of the Triads, Inside the Golden Triangle.*

Except for the books on the sea, the library made sense in a macabre fashion. The average fictional assassin was a bullet-headed sadist like Nash in *From Russia with Love*, or a faceless, slightly effete nemesis figure like the killer in *The Day of the Jackal.*

Rhinelander, on the other hand, his psychotic character profile aside, was a professional killer who took his job seriously. The books on ordnance kept him up to date on available weaponry, travel guides told him what to expect in various airports and hotels, and books on the intelligence community and the drug underworld gave him some basic research on what to expect from both enemies and possible employers. Neat and tidy, very businesslike. Still . . .

Mallory pursed his lips, eyes blinking behind the lenses of his glasses. He felt a dull twisting in the pit of his stomach and for a moment he tasted bile in his throat, remembering. In Paris, Henri Faligot of the Directorate for Surveillance of the Territory – DST – had shown him coroner's photographs of Phillipe Groman's corpse, in situ at the Cardinal's Cap brothel in Montmartre. *That* was Rhinelander's profession, and no well-ordered room like this could change the reality of those stark, obscenely clinical black and white images.

He thought of leaving then, simply turning tail and fleeing. He could report back to Cooper that he hadn't been able to locate QJ/RAIL and that would be the end of it. He'd probably wind up being dumped back down to Threat Analysis or worse for his failure, but at least he'd be in a world he understood.

Mallory eased his glasses back up onto his nose and made a little snorting sound. Melodrama. All he had to do was make contact with the man, arrange a meeting and that would be that. Part of his mandate from Cooper was to find out as much as he could about Rhinelander before the meeting, and that was precisely what he was doing now.

Ignoring the cramping sensation in his gut he sat down in front of the computer and began booting it up, enjoying the familiar routines. He pulled up the main menu for the hard drive and stared at the screen. Rhinelander was running a variety of software: word processing, filing, bookkeeping and telecommunications as well as a computer assisted design program.

According to the screen about a third of the hard drive's eighty-megabyte memory was given over to a series of files referred to in the main menu as RAC. Poking at the keys, Mallory opened the main file and saw that it was sub-indexed with dated, smaller files. They were chronological, going back three years in seven, fourteen and twenty-one day intervals. He tapped open a file from a year before and was instantly rewarded with a three dimensional grid, the lines in glowing amber on a dark blue ground. It looked like a radar screen. The title in the top left corner gave the date and then the name: Reef Analysis Chart.

It took him a few minutes, but Mallory figured out the codes and deciphered the screen. The grid was a representation of a section of reef and by keying in different commands he could include temperature, currents, tide levels, schooling fish . . . anything. Mallory sat back in the chair and poked at his glasses. This explained the books on oceanography. Rhinelander's hobby?

'Enjoying yourself?' The voice came from behind and Mallory whirled, heart smashing at his ribs, glasses almost flying off his nose. He could smell himself, the acid sweat of fear, and his mouth was cotton-dry, all in a split second. Rhinelander stood in the doorway wearing a dark blue shortsleeved knit shirt and tight, pale grey shorts. His feet were bare and he held a small, flat, automatic pistol in his right hand. He held the pistol loosely, barrel aimed at the floor.

'Uh. . . .' It was all Mallory could manage.

'Get up,' Rhinelander ordered. Mallory did as he was told, legs rubbery, barely able to support him. Rhinelander stepped aside, motioning with the pistol. 'The living room.'

Mallory nodded weakly and began to walk, the sensation of his shoes on the hard floor numb and distant. Rhinelander followed him down the hall and through the arch. He motioned Mallory to the couch and then sat down himself, easing down onto one of the club chairs, the pistol held in his lap, honey bars of sunlight striping his face and chest.

'What's your name?' asked Rhinelander. The tone was even, the voice unaccented. Not American, not British, not anything. Mallory stared at the gun hand, unwilling and unable to look into the man's dark, dead eyes.

'Mallory, Paul Mallory.'

'Washington.' It wasn't a question. There was no point in lying.

'Yes.'

'CIA?'

'Yes.'

'Who?'

'Cooper.'

'How can I know that?'

'I have ID,' Mallory answered. His eyes flickered to Rhinelander's face for an instant. The expression hadn't changed. Neutral, uninterested, as though Mallory was nothing more than a crawling insect on the floor.

'Anyone can have ID. Do better.'

'Your file designation is QJ/RAIL. Your operating name for the Company was Eric Rhinelander. You were. . . .' Mallory hesitated, frightened.

'Yes?'

'You were recently in Paris.' Mallory swallowed hard, wondering how much he'd have to say.

'Yes.'

No change in expression, the gun hand motionless. Mallory saw the eight-by-tens of Groman, sprawled on the whorehouse bed, the seeping, perfect puncture, like a blood-oozed second anus. It would take Rhinelander less than a second to lift the automatic, aim and fire. In his mind's eye he could see the spray of blood and brains, caught for an instant in the light slatting through the shutters.

'You . . . you were responsible for the death of a drug dealer named Phillipe Groman.'

'He cheated me,' Rhinelander replied calmly, explaining a simple fact of life. 'He was responsible for his own death. He knew the rules.'

'I see,' muttered Mallory, wondering what the rules said about entering Rhinelander's home uninvited.

'No, you don't see at all.' The automatic shifted slightly in Rhinelander's lap. There was a long pause and then he spoke again. 'Why are you here?'

'Mr Cooper would like to speak with you.'

'Speak with me?'

'See you.'

'Why?'

'I have no idea.'

'What are you to Cooper?'

'I don't understand.'

'What do you do for him?'

'I'm his special assistant.'

'Before you worked for him, what department were you in?'

'Threat Analysis and Plans.'

'No operational experience? Field work?'

'No.'

'Were you given any instructions about setting up a meeting?'

'No. He said you wouldn't trust anything he set up.'

'He was right.' There was another long silence. Mallory could hear the surf pounding somewhere in the distance. Rhinelander seemed to be looking past him, lost in thought. The wings of grey at his temples looked pure white against the darkness of his tan and the lines around the eyes and the deep caliper creases around the mouth made his face look too old for the hard athletic body.

'Do you have a number for him?' Rhinelander asked finally. Startled, Mallory gave a quick nod.

'On a card,' he answered. 'In my wallet.'

'Take it out.'

'Yes,' Mallory answered, head bobbing. His glasses had slipped again but he made no move to reposition them. He reached into his jacket slowly, took out his wallet and extracted the printed card with Hudson Cooper's telephone, teletype and fax numbers printed on it.

'Leave it on the coffee table.'

'Yes.' Mallory leaned forward and placed the card gently on the table.

'Now get out of my house,' Rhinelander ordered. Mallory stood up, sweat running down his jawline. Fright sweat, cool and oily. A terrible spasming cramp in his bowels. Knowing how lucky he was to be alive.

'What do I tell Mr Cooper?' he asked. 'About the meeting?'

'Tell him anything you want,' Rhinelander answered. 'Anything at all.' He made a small, flicking gesture with the pistol in his lap. 'Go.'

Mallory went.

CHAPTER SIX

Stoneacres, ancestral home of the Macintyre family, was located on the Virginia bank of the Potomac, thirty miles southeast of Washington, halfway between the town of Woodbridge and the FBI National Academy at Quantico. It was neither stony nor particularly ancestral. The 400-acre estate was a mixture of natural woods and rolling meadows. The twelve-bedroom colonial mansion had been built in 1910 by Charles Macintyre, Hollis Macintyre's father. Macintyre senior, a naturalised American born in Glasgow, had been trained as a dental technician. In 1901 he invented and patented a process to make cheap amalgam for fillings and within five years he was a millionaire.

After tripling his money by investing in the fledgling Ford Motor Company he married the daughter of an influential congressman and retired to live the life of a respectable country gentleman, his days spent polishing porcelain dentures discreetly forgotten. Within a very few years, through the good graces of Macintyre's father-in-law and wife, Stoneacres had become an accepted part of genteel Washington society, its lofty halls and oak-beamed chambers playing host to an endless array of princes, politicians and presidents.

Hollis Crandall Macintyre was born on 6 February 1911, sharing his birthday with the man who would eventually become the fortieth President of the United States, Ronald Reagan. As the first of five children and the only male heir, Hollis Macintyre found his early life was a well-ordered series of events designed to groom him for a position among the nation's powermongers: a private education at Lockhart Academy, a degree in business from the University of Virginia and then a commission in the army.

Returning to civilian life in 1933 Macintyre immediately went to work as assistant to General Edwin M Watson, President Roosevelt's senior military aide. A number of the Macintyre family's Republican friends were infuriated by what they perceived as a treasonous betrayal of upper-class values, but Hollis Macintyre had been born a realist, and even as a young man he was acutely aware of power and its usefulness.

Franklin Delano Roosevelt had been elected by a landslide, and for all its welfare-state overtones Hollis Macintyre saw that the New Deal centralised power in the federal government and particularly in the hands of the President. The White House was the perfect place for a man like Hollis Macintyre to learn the savagery and subtlety of life in the nation's capital and by the time of Pearl Harbor, he was known throughout the bureaucratic offices of Foggy Bottom and the corridors of Congress as the Detail Man, always willing to give a favour in the present, for the promise of two in the future. By the time of Roosevelt's death in 1945 he was one of the least liked and most respected men in Washington.

Macintyre's career from that point on had been given over to consolidating the gains he made in those early years, building a ziggurat of favours and foibles, secrets and lies. His titles and job descriptions within the political and governmental structures of Washington were irrelevant; he took power where he found it and dispensed favours without prejudice.

The only constant through all those years was his membership of Romulus. An accident of fate had made him instrumental in the group's creation, thus making him privy to all its secrets, a cachet he shared with no one else. Through the nine presidential administrations since Roosevelt it had been Hollis Macintyre who vetted each new member of the Committee, and Hollis Macintyre who ensured that retiring members maintained their pledges of secrecy. It was a measure of his abilities that in almost fifty years, none of the 111 members, past and present, had ever mentioned the Romulus Committee in public, and with the exception of a few vague rumours which surfaced from time to time, virtually nothing was known of its existence.

On the fifth day following the initial meeting of the Romulus Committee regarding the Barron diagnosis, Hollis Macintyre awoke at 6:30 a.m. At 7:00, with breakfast over, he took his last cup of coffee into the bedroom, seated himself in a silk-upholstered chair beside the four-poster bed and began to work his way through the morning papers. Normally his reading would have taken place in the limousine on his way into the city, but today was Sunday and his only meeting for the day would take place here, at Stoneacres.

Flipping open the bulky parcel of the Sunday *New York Times* he pulled out the magazine section. The cover story was a profile of Vincent Teresi, Vice-President of the United States. Macintyre felt his breakfast sour within the confines of his enormous belly and he frowned, staring at the smiling, cap-toothed face on the cover. A modern version of Frank Sinatra with thick black hair, twinkling dark eyes and his patented 'trust me' grin. At forty-four he was the media's darling, and since the death of his wife in childbirth three years before, Washington's most eligible bachelor.

With a grunting sigh, Macintyre pushed the stack of newspapers off his lap and onto the floor. He didn't have to read the article to know what it said; he'd had the 'sheet' on Teresi ever since he'd come out of nowhere to claim the Vice-Presidential ticket. Macintyre glanced around the large, richly decorated room, which reflected a life given over to the serenity of order, position and wealth – icons of power which appeared to be anathema to the Vice-President.

Born in New York and raised in California, Vincenzo Salvatore Michael-angelo Teresi came out of the classic immigrant stewpot of brickworkers, fruit vendors and dockworkers that made up the Brooklyn of the late forties. Vincent's father was a skilled mechanic and moved to San Diego in the early fifties, taking advantage of the growing aerospace industry. Somewhere between New York and the west coast, Vincenzo became Vincent. By the time he graduated from high school, any trace of Brooklyn was gone and Vince Teresi was the quintessential Californian.

He was also smart enough to know that he had neither the academic qualifications nor the money for university, so he enlisted in the air force, qualified for both officer training and flight school and wound up spending the next two years flying high altitude reconnaissance missions over North Vietnam. His tour over, he returned Stateside and re-upped, accepting a posting to the Air Force Directorate of Operational Intelligence at the Pentagon. The work wasn't particularly demanding and he put his free time in Washington to good use, managing to obtain a basic law degree from Georgetown University.

After almost six years in the military he left Washington and returned to California, working for a number of law firms as well as dabbling in local, municipal, and finally state politics. With hindsight Hollis Macintyre could see a familiar thread running through the Vice-President's political history, reminiscent of his own studied climb to power. Teresi was willing to do favours for just about anyone and volunteered for everything, one favour leading to another, methodically propelling the young man from the Los Angeles District Attorney's office to the State Legislature, and finally to the Governor's Office as a low-profile member of the Reagan palace guard.

Instead of following Reagan and his cohorts to the White House in 1980 Teresi decided to follow his own path, remaining in California, where he specialised in environmental law and began building a position within the party's National Committee. By the end of the Reagan administration he'd managed to quietly consolidate the less conservative, younger factions within the party. The day before the convention to nominate Tucker for President he made his move. A succession of problems including the last Quayle scandal had convinced Bush not to run for another term, leaving the field wide open.

During his brief meeting with Macintyre Teresi had been friendly, but firm. Either he rode the ticket as Tucker's running mate, or he'd start a

fight on the convention floor to split the vote. Teresi didn't have enough
delegates to carry the nomination, but a weak win for Tucker at the
convention would be the kiss of death for his chances at the Presidency.

Macintyre knew that his failure to spot Teresi's end run marked the
beginning of the end for his own career, but he had no choice. Teresi
got the nod and became Geoffrey Tucker's running mate. Ironically, after
the election most of the media credited Teresi's good looks and oratory as
being the factors which boosted Tucker over the top, giving him the narrow
margin over his opponent needed to win.

The end result for Hollis Macintyre had been inevitable. After slightly
more than a year in office, the Tucker administration was in good shape
and Teresi's image was getting bigger and better by the minute. In three
years, Tucker would run again and win, and four years after that Vincent
Teresi would take the nomination.

By that time, if he was still alive, Hollis Macintyre would be almost
ninety and long since relegated to elder statesman status. The king had
his heir, succession was assured, so there was no longer any need for
the kingmaker. On inauguration day, Hollis Macintyre's invitation was
overlooked, and from then on he had been slowly but surely cut out of
'the Loop' of protocol and communication giving access to the White
House.

Macintyre smiled thinly and turned in his chair, lifting the porcelain cup
and saucer from the table at his side. He took a small sip of the cooling,
aromatic coffee and nodded to himself. At eighty he was perfectly willing
to give up the reins of power and take his place in the history books, but
it would be on his own terms, not those of the upstart son of a Brooklyn
tool-and-die maker.

There was a faint knock and the bedroom door was opened. Benjamin,
Macintyre's butler, chauffeur and bodyguard, stepped into the room. The
stooped, grey-haired black man had been in service at Stoneacres his entire
life. Like Hollis Macintyre, Benjamin had never married. He lived in his
own three-room apartment in the east wing of the house and was in charge
of the housekeeper, cook, two maids and the gardener who made up the
staff of the estate.

'Good morning, sir.' The aging servant's voice was a harsh whisper.

'Good morning, Benjamin,' said Macintyre. 'Have our guests arrived?'

'Mr Cooper called to say he'd be a few minutes late,' said Benjamin.
'Mr Swanbridge is waiting in the sun room, sir.'

'All right, Benjamin.' With a groaning sigh, Macintyre levered himself up
out of the chair, leaning heavily on the arms for support. 'Coffee and orange
juice in the library when Mr Cooper arrives,' he ordered. 'Tea with lemon
for Secretary Swanbridge and ask Mary if the scones are ready yet.'

'Yes, sir' Benjamin answered, nodding again. 'Will there be anything else?'

'No thank you, Benjamin. Just see to it that we aren't disturbed. No telephone calls or other interruptions.'

'Of course, Mr Macintyre.' Benjamin withdrew and after straightening his bow tie in front of the circular Tiffany mirror beside the door, Macintyre followed.

He went down the broad, carpeted staircase, crossed the main hall and went into the large sun room. Its far wall was made up entirely of floor-to-ceiling windows. French doors looked out onto the sloping lawn and the river, a hundred yards away. The furniture, a scattering of wicker and white wrought iron, was part of the original decor.

'Joseph,' said Macintyre, entering the sun-bright room. 'Good of you to come.'

Cigar held slackly between thin lips, Geoffrey Tucker's tall, bald and professorial-looking Secretary of State turned away from the French doors and crossed the room to greet Macintyre with an extended hand. Joseph Swanbridge did not wear his sixty-eight years well. The eyes behind his old-fashioned wire-rim spectacles were deeply inset and bagged, his skin had an unhealthy pallor and the man's brown-spotted hands were twisted with arthritis. He drank too much, smoked too much and worked too hard, but the brain behind the watery blue eyes was one of the best in the country. Swanbridge was the only other member of Romulus who had been told the extent of the President's illness.

'Hudson's not here yet, I gather,' said Swanbridge, his voice wheezing slightly around the cigar.

'Not yet,' said Macintyre. He took Swanbridge by the elbow and guided him towards the doors leading back into the hall. 'You can have tea in the library while we wait for him.'

The library was a large chamber sheathed in books of all descriptions, many of them leather-bound. A delicate Hepplewhite writing desk stood in one corner, a large, glass globe beside it. The floors were pegged oak covered by a scattering of oriental carpets.

Macintyre sank into one of the upholstered chairs and watched as Swanbridge, an inveterate pacer, moved slowly around the room, examining the spines of books with a close eye and occasionally picking up knick-knacks from the small tables set here and there. Eventually, like some gangly, bald-headed insect, Swanbridge settled.

A few minutes later Benjamin appeared, wheeling a trolley. He laid out scones, preserves, butter, a tall, frosted beaker of orange juice, crystal goblets, coffee and tea, cups and saucers. He nodded silently to Macintyre and retired. Before he was out of the room Swanbridge had poured himself a cup of tea and was busily buttering one of the scones. Macintyre smiled briefly as the Secretary of State spilled crumbs down the front of his rumpled suit. Except for state occasions when he was forced into formality, Swanbridge was an archetypical slob.

'You've had several days now to assimilate the information regarding the President's condition,' Macintyre began, as Swanbridge smoothed butter onto his second scone. 'Have you formulated an opinion?'

'An opinion regarding what?' asked Swanbridge. He popped half of the second scone into his mouth and began to chew, staring blandly across the table. He took a swallow of tea, then set the cup down again. 'According to your information the President is suffering from a degenerative brain disease, so what is there to opine? He either has the disease or he does not.'

'You're being tediously academic, Joseph,' Macintyre sighed. 'And you're evading the question. Geoffrey Tucker has Creuzfeldt-Jacob disease. He will die from it. Before he dies from it he is potentially capable of a number of demented acts. It behoves us to do something about the situation.'

'Now you're the one being tedious,' Swanbridge answered, his voice cold. 'You've known about this for a week. Your information came from Hudson Cooper. In the meantime the President's attending physician at Walter Reed dies in a boating accident. You inform me of the President's condition, and then you call this meeting.'

Swanbridge dropped the remains of his scone back onto the plate and sat back, reaching into the pocket of his jacket for a fresh cigar. He puffed it into life, staring at Macintyre through a billowing haze of smoke. 'You don't want my opinion, Hollis,' he said finally. 'You want my complicity in whatever scheme you and Hudson have cooked up between you.'

Macintyre smiled and let out a small, coughing laugh. Swanbridge's Secret Service designation was 'Nutcracker' and he'd been given the code name with good reason. He might have crumbs on his lapels and gravy stains on his tie, but he also had the shrewdest political sense Hollis Macintyre had ever known.

'I prefer to think of it as a contingency plan,' the fat man replied. 'We are facing a serious political crisis of which you, by neccessity, are a part.'

'If the President is unable to function Section Four can be invoked,' Swanbridge responded, referring to the paragraph within the 25th Amendment covering Presidential incapacity.

'It would tear the country apart,' Macintyre said flatly. 'Section Four is a panacea, Joseph, and you know it. The words sound good on paper, but putting them into effect is virtually impossible.'

'I'm aware of the problems.' Swanbridge tapped ash into his saucer. 'Teresi would have to get a consensus from Cabinet, then apply to the

Speaker of the House and the President pro tempore of the Senate. If Tucker took it into his mind to fight he could ask for a vote in both houses of Congress.'

'He has forty-eight hours to call the vote if Congress is in session,' said Macintyre. 'Twenty-one days if it is not. As you are aware, the summer recess.'

'Indeed,' Swanbridge replied. 'Even without a vote, invoking Section Four could well be a long-drawn-out affair, and that presumes Mr Teresi's co-operation.'

'Something we're not likely to get,' Macintyre grumbled. 'And even if we did, we'd wind up with him as President.'

'Quite so.' Swanbridge puffed on his cigar. He rubbed a free hand thoughtfully over his bald scalp, as though polishing it. 'Regardless of what effect Section Four might have, Mr Teresi assuming the Presidency would have catastrophic results, I'm afraid.'

'The media love him but he's made a lot of enemies on Wall Street,' said Macintyre. 'And he has every military contractor along the Beltway biting his nails.'

'If Vincent Teresi became President we certainly would lose a great many friends,' Swanbridge agreed.

We'd lose more than friends, Joseph,' Macintyre warned. 'We'd lose everything.'

'Which brings us back to your so called "contingency plan",' said Swanbridge. 'Presumably you've come up with a number of options.'

'Certainly.' Macintyre nodded. 'Several.' He cleared his throat, waving a discreet hand at the smoke generated by Swanbridge's cigar. 'The most obvious is the least attractive: we simply do nothing and let nature take its course, in which case the transition of power becomes a simple one – Teresi becomes President and chooses someone to fill his position as Vice-President, much the same way as Ford took over from Nixon.'

'And I'd be out of a job within twenty-four hours,' interrupted Swanbridge.

'Along with the rest of the Tucker cabinet,' Macintyre agreed. 'We'd go from a relatively conservative and even-handed administration to progressive chaos overnight.'

'That's not the point,' said Swanbridge, shaking his head. 'The real problem is that Vincent Teresi thinks he's Jack Kennedy reborn, and he's not. He's a babe in the woods when it comes to foreign policy and he doesn't have the strategic smarts of a gnat. Lots of charm and elan, but not much depth. He has too many weaknesses. Fatal flaws, you might call them. So we rule out option one. What's next?'

'We dirty Teresi's diaper, find a Chappaquiddick, real or otherwise,' said

Macintyre. 'Hudson has worked up a few scenarios.'

'From the tone of your voice I gather the scenarios weren't sufficiently workable,' said Swanbridge.

Macintyre shrugged. 'The scenarios weren't the problem, it was their net effect. First Tucker dies of a degenerative brain disease, then the Vice-President is scandalised into resigning. The Dow-Jones would go through the floor. You wouldn't be able to elect one of our people to the White House for a hundred years after that. It would be political suicide for the party.'

'The third option?' asked Swanbridge.

'The final one,' said Macintyre. 'The simultaneous death of both President Tucker and Vincent Teresi.'

'An accident?' queried Swanbridge, no sense of surprise in either his expression or voice.

'We considered it,' Macintyre said. 'The most realistic plan would involve Air Force One. Hudson feels the logistics and possibility of discovery rule it out.'

'So?'

'Assassination,' Macintyre replied, biting hard on the word.

'An ugly term.' Swanbridge's cigar had gone out. He tapped off the cold ash directly into his teacup and relit the butt with another match. 'An ugly act as well, even when considered hypothetically.'

'Agreed,' said Macintyre. 'Nevertheless, its results can sometimes be justified.'

'In a banana republic, perhaps,' Swanbridge answered, lifting his shoulders in a shrug. 'In this country it has done nothing but lead to tragedy and confusion.'

'Granted,' Macintyre replied. 'There have been eleven assassinations and assassination attempts from Andrew Jackson to Ronald Reagan. The man who tried to kill Jackson was a mentally disturbed house-painter and John Hinkley Jr. got off on an insanity defence. Even the two Puerto Ricans who tried to kill Truman were mentally disturbed.'

'Make your point, Hollis,' Swanbridge sighed.

'The point is, Joseph, the reasons for a madman to assassinate a President are usually only clear to the madman. The act itself serves no positive function, it only disrupts.'

'You're saying that your plan is somehow different?' asked Swanbridge, the scepticism clear in his voice.

'Not my plan so much as Hudson Cooper's,' Macintyre answered.

The Secretary of State let out a braying laugh. 'Good lord, Hollis! There's no need to cover yourself quite so soon! This mysterious scenario is still in cloud-cuckoo land as far as I'm concerned.'

'I'm afraid it's already gone beyond that,' said Macintyre. 'And like it or not, you *are* involved. Jack Reynolds is Speaker of the House; he's seventy-three and he has a pacemaker. Charles Whittaker is President pro tempore of the Senate. He's had cancer twice already. They would almost certainly disqualify themselves as Presidential material.'

'You're saying the office would devolve to me?'

'According to the Succession Act of 1955, you would be next in line.'

'I see.' Swanbridge paused, rolling the cigar between his lips. 'You said the scenario was already operative. I presume you mean the supposedly accidental death of Dr Barron?'

'Yes.'

'Hudson's work?'

'Yes.'

'I have doubts concerning Hudson's judgement,' said Swanbridge slowly. He dropped the last half-inch of the cigar into the dregs of his tea. 'Recently he's shown what I would term an unhealthy obsession with his wife.'

'His wife is dead, Joseph,' responded Macintyre.

'My point exactly,' Swanbridge murmured. Macintyre shrugged off the comment.

'He'll be here in a moment, Joseph. I'll let him tell you the details of his plan and you can judge for yourself. Personally, I find the man's idea rather cunning.'

Swanbridge made a small snorting sound and reached into the pocket of his jacket.

'Too much cunning undoes,' he said, pulling out another cigar and stripping off the plastic wrap.

'Good Lord, Joseph!' Macintyre laughed. 'A proverb?'

'A warning,' Swanbridge answered flatly, then popped the cigar into his mouth.

CHAPTER SEVEN

General Vladimir Gurenko, Senior KGB Resident in North America, stood at the picture window of his penthouse office in the Mount Alto complex of the Soviet Embassy and stared out at central Washington spread out below him. Directly in front of him and less than half a mile away he could see the rooftop of the Vice-President's house in the Naval Observatory grounds and to his right, in the distance, he could easily make out the White House and the Capitol Building a mile beyond it.

Gurenko, a lean, dark-haired man in his early fifties, had risen through the ranks in the KGB, forging his career on the basis of productivity rather than the more common route of bribery and the secret lists of the 'nomenklatura'. Opting for the most onerous and dangerous assignments, and serving in places like Cambodia, Cuba and Afghanistan, Gurenko had leapfrogged over less ambitious colleagues, working his way up through the system and finally capturing the plum: Chief of the Washington Residency. With much of Central Europe in a state of political and economic flux since the housecleaning in 1989, the Washington Residency was more important than ever before. Like it or not the Americans were having to make some serious adjustments of their own, especially in terms of military spending. Gorbachev's upheavals had led to massive problems within the USSR, but his foreign policy had left the US holding the bag, and it was clearly labelled 'warmonger'. Running the KGB in Washington had become an even more sensitive posting now, and Gurenko knew it required some very careful footwork; the lines between enemy and ally had blurred, which made everyone's life more difficult.

Wisely, since taking over the position after the retirement of his predecessor a year and a half before, Gurenko had not practised the classic KGB pattern of reassigning and firing. Instead he'd done his best to forge new alliances and relationships, while getting the job done as efficiently as possible. It seemed to have worked, and the reports that Valentin Ivashutin, his deputy, was sending back to Moscow Centre were mostly favourable.

Gurenko himself reported to only one man – Sergei Kuryokhin, Chief of the First Department of the First Chief Directorate. This was the division of the KGB responsible for residencies in Washington, New York, San Francisco and Ottawa, as well as co-ordinating the operations of East European and Cuban intelligence services against the United States. The First Department had been on extremely shaky ground politically and so far it appeared that Kuryokhin appreciated Gurenko's efforts to keep things on a smooth and even keel in Washington. Gurenko intended to keep it that way, which was why he had been so disturbed by the memo he'd received that morning from Yuri Sidorov, Director of Technical Support.

'Well?' he asked, turning away from the window. 'What do you think?' Seated on a couch at the other end of the sparsely furnished room, Valentin Ivashutin, Gurenko's deputy, went over the memo from Technical. It was almost thirty pages long and included transcripts of several different telephone conversations.

'It would appear that Comrade Travkin is overstepping the bounds of his authority,' answered Ivashutin. He was as lean as his superior, but taller, with black hair thinned into a widow's peak. He was known as 'The Weasel', a nickname that suited him perfectly.

Gurenko crossed the room and sank into a chair across from Ivashutin. A low, highly polished birchwood table sat between them, resting on a brightly coloured Afghani 'war' rug, Gurenko's most prized possession, purchased during his two years in Kabul. The rug's motif was repeating series of tanks, anti-aircraft guns, helicopters and soldiers. The red-faced soldiers were Soviets, the yellow ones Afghani partisans. Inevitably, the Afghanis were shown killing the Soviets, complete with lines of bullets flying from the barrels of the Afghani rifles.

'Is it worth pursuing?' Gurenko asked, gesturing at the report in Ivashutin's hands.

'As an officer in GRU Colonel Travkin should be addressing matters of military intelligence. Instead he has now met twice with this clerk from Walter Reed Hospital. As you know we only had Comrade Travkin under light surveillance prior to that, standard procedure for a Deputy Resident. The second time we were able to get better information.'

'The telephone number reference?' said Gurenko.

'Yes.'

'Which you then traced to Hudson Cooper?'

'Yes. The number was unlisted but not difficult to obtain.'

'Presumably Comrade Travkin has done the same thing.'

'Certainly,' said Ivashutin. 'His contacts in the telephone company are probably as good as ours.'

'If not better,' Gurenko said.

Ivashutin smiled at the oblique reference to the GRU's propensity for lavishing money on their informers and hired field agents. 'An interesting puzzle,' he said, dropping the report onto the table between them. He let the observation dangle, allowing Gurenko to come to the obvious conclusion.

'Does Cooper have his medical checkups done at Walter Reed?' asked the KGB Resident.

His deputy nodded. 'Yes. His doctor is a man named Weinstein.'

'Then we may conclude that Comrade Travkin knows something about Mr Cooper's medical condition which we do not,' mused Gurenko. It opened up a number of intriguing possibilities. With only a few notable exceptions the position of Director of Central Intelligence was political and not based on any real experience within the intelligence community. The last DCI with an intelligence background had been William Colby. The various deputy directorships, on the other hand, were truly powerful positions and as DD Operations, Hudson Cooper's was the most powerful of all.

'I wonder . . .' Gurenko murmured.

'*Osin?*' asked Ivashutin, using the Russian word for autumn.

'It occurred to me, yes.' Gurenko stood up and went back to the window overlooking the city, hands clasped behind his back. Autumn was the code name for the near mythic KGB 'tapeworm', or mole, buried within the Central Intelligence Agency.

The Senior Resident knew virtually nothing about the agent, other than the presumption that he was highly placed within the agency. Gurenko didn't even know who Autumn's handler was. Twice during his tenure in Washington, Gurenko had played brief host to a courier sent from Moscow by Kuryokhin. On both occasions the courier had arrived without warning, carrying the diplomatic pouch from Moscow. After presenting Kuryokhin's respects, the courier had vanished for twenty-four hours, then reappeared in time to carry the return pouch back to the Soviet Union.

Six months before, on a short leave to attend his mother's funeral, Gurenko had had his suspicions borne out when Kuryokhin, in the privacy of his dacha and under the influence of a considerable amount of vodka, had congratulated him on handling the Autumn courier with such discretion. The very fact that his superior had mentioned the tapeworm's codename to him was a compliment and a sign of trust and now Gurenko had a way to return the favour.

If Autumn was as valuable as he seemed it was likely that he was highly placed in a sensitive division of the CIA. The most sensitive, and certainly most useful division from the KGB's point of view, would be the Directorate of Operations, which included covert action, foreign espionage and counterintelligence and counterespionage, making it the exact equivalent of his own First Chief Directorate.

Based on the assumption that Autumn was somewhere in the CIA Directorate of Operations, any information regarding the health of the man in command of that directorate could be vitally important. As he stared out over the heat-hazed city Gurenko suddenly realised that Autumn could conceivably be in line for Hudson Cooper's job. He turned from the window again, trying to keep his expression as blank as possible. Ivashutin was *osnovnoi*, high in the ranks of the elite nomenklatura, and god only knew whom the man was reporting to other than Moscow Centre. Gurenko knew he had to walk a fine political line as well as cover himself in case things went wrong.

'We should look over the file on Hudson Cooper,' Gurenko said finally. Ivashutin nodded and reached into the breast pocket of his jacket. He took out a small notebook and scribbled a reminder.

'What about Travkin?' Ivashutin murmured, ballpoint poised.

'Full surveillance. Tap his phone, follow his car. Complete documentation and at least two men on him at all times.'

'Will you be reporting to Centre?' asked Ivashutin calmly. It was the key question. Autumn was Kuryokhin's asset and to interfere with him was potentially dangerous. Even the use of his code name in a communication was a risk. On the other hand, Hudson Cooper's medical condition might well have a vital bearing on Autumn's continued safety. Gurenko cursed silently; it was another example of how politics within the KGB interfered with the real work at hand.

'I want you to complete the report,' Gurenko said finally, making the best of the situation. 'Sign your name under my authority.'

'Of course,' Ivashutin said. 'What kind of encryption and transmission?'

'Use your own code,' Gurenko replied. 'I don't want it going anywhere near the U-3 people.' U-3 referred to the third level below ground where signals were coded and then transmitted. Logging a transmission through Sidorov's people was like shouting over a party line. 'When you have the report coded, send it by pouch,' Gurenko added. Using the diplomatic courier meant that Kuryokhin wouldn't have it for at least thirty-six hours, but there was no other way of keeping Autumn secure.

'Will that be all?' asked Ivashutin. He climbed to his feet, snapped the notebook closed and returned it to his pocket.

'I'll want to read the report before you send it off, of course,' Gurenko warned.

'Of course.'

'And I want you to destroy every copy of the memo report from Sidorov with the exception of the one you just read,' Gurenko went on. 'Append that to your own report.'

Ivashutin left the office silently, leaving Gurenko alone with his thoughts. He turned back to the window, looking out again over the sun-baked city.

In KGB parlance Washington DC was symbol and centre of 'The Main Enemy'. It sounded silly, of course, as infantile as Reagan's infamous description of the USSR as 'The Evil Empire'. But the average American *was* fundamentally suspicious of the Soviet Union, assuming its citizenry was made up of mindless, bullet-headed robots, just as the average Muscovite *did* see the United States as a pernicious wasteland of corruption, immorality and nauseating overindulgence. Neither description was accurate, but both contained grains of truth. Tearing down the Berlin Wall, firing corrupt politicians and changing governments all over Eastern Europe hadn't done very much to change any of those opinions. It was ironic, really, since both Soviets and Americans prided themselves on patriotism, and both nations had been born out of armed rebellion. At its simplest level the antagonism between the two superpowers was easy enough to understand – it was just an old fashioned, deeply rooted fear of strangers. Shoot first and ask questions later. Gurenko shook his head. He was no better than the rest: children playing games with incredibly dangerous toys.

Autumn was a case in point. A tapeworm lodged deep in the belly of the Central Intelligence Agency and a secret symbol of its ineptness and inadequacy, the phantom asset was also capable of pointing out the paranoias and internal politicking of the KGB with embarrassing accuracy. Gurenko sighed; none of it was going to change, at least not in his lifetime. He, like every other intelligence officer, Soviet, French, British or American, lived in a world of lies that went from purest white to deepest black.

Idly, Gurenko picked up the high-powered Meade binoculars and focused them on the roof of the White House, three miles away to the southeast. During the Carter and Reagan administrations, extensive renovations had been done on the third, or attic floor of the executive mansion, and on warm days, using the binoculars, Gurenko had occasionally seen people sunbathing on the roof of the solarium. Today the roof was empty except for a shirtsleeved Secret Service agent, sweating away his shift in a lawn chair set up below the limply hanging Stars and Stripes.

Gurenko put the binoculars gently back on the windowsill. Pointless voyeurism was counterproductive to the cause of Soviet Intelligence, and he, for one, had work to do. Turning his back to the view he buzzed his secretary for coffee and then settled down to examine the pile of weekly expense reports in front of him. Within a few moments he was totally immersed in the columns of figures and he had completely forgotten about Dimitri Travkin.

While Vladimir Gurenko of the KGB tried to decipher the inevitably inflated expense reports of his junior officers, Dimitri Travkin of the GRU was seated in front of a computer terminal in his cubicle at the Soviet Military Office on Belmont Street trying to unscramble a puzzle of his own.

The terminal he was using, like all the others in the SMO, was an out of date Zenith hooked into an equally archaic mainframe in the basement. Both mainframe and terminals were bug-checked regularly and protected from electronic eavesdropping by copper sheathing in the walls, but Travkin still got twitchy when he worked classified information on the screen.

Not that anyone ghosting his data would get much for their trouble; with the few facts he was trying to stitch together he might just as well have been trying to spin straw into gold. Grumbling under his breath he straightened up in his chair, stretched and then lit a cigarette. He glanced around the room, squinting through the haze of cigarette smoke and frowning. His office was no more than a twelve by twelve box, most of it filled with filing cabinets and archive boxes piled to the ceiling. At least it had a small window, almost opaque with dirt and soot, but still admitting enough light to let him know if it was night or day.

'Shit,' he muttered, looking back at the screen. For the last three days he'd been devoting almost all his time to the Scanlon material and Koslov was badgering him to get back to more productive work. As Deputy Resident Travkin was responsible for management of all the operational officers both in Washington and New York, specialist officers and the material they were preparing for transmission to Moscow and the monitoring of the various 'illegals' and their controlling operational officers.

Travkin cursed again, scrolling through the meagre dossier he had assembled. Perhaps Koslov was right; what he had didn't amount to very much. At first it had seemed as though he was on to something, but the more he looked the less he saw.

Barron, for instance. After doing some very basic research Travkin had learned that Barron hadn't been the President's personal physician at all, merely the attending physician who oversaw the Chief Executive's bi-annual checkups. The real presidential doctor was a man with the faintly sinister name of Hacker. Hacker and a support staff of sixteen had a full-scale clinic in the basement of the White House itself. According to Travkin's information Jim Hacker was an old high school friend of the President's and was a general practitioner with no speciality.

Travkin's initial reaction had been to connect Barron, the President and the library request but now he wasn't so sure of that either. As far as he could tell Barron really had died in a boating accident and as it turned out, his uncle had Alzheimer's. Everything could be explained away easily enough except for Scanlon's photocopy of the printout from the Walter Reed telephone log. According to the log, Dr Barron had only placed one outside call, and that was to Hudson Cooper, Deputy Director of Operations for the CIA. A simple check revealed that Barron was not Cooper's physician at Walter Reed.

Digging a little deeper, Travkin had followed up by meeting one of his contacts in the telephone company. The contact, a systems engineer named Zaritski, thought that Travkin was an alcoholic West German journalist with more money than brains; the GRU Deputy Resident had done nothing to change the man's mind, paying him well on the few occasions he'd been used.

At Travkin's request, backed up by five hundred-dollar bills in an envelope, Zaritski had spent a few off-duty hours tracing Hudson Cooper's Watergate number through the telephone company's labyrinthine computer billing system and he came up with a number, this one in Virginia. Zaritski, reporting back to Travkin, said that the number, although unlisted, was traceable through the billing office. According to the engineer the number was billed to someone named Hollis Macintyre of Woodbridge, Virginia. The name obviously meant nothing to Zaritski, which was probably just as well, but it put another wrinkle of confusion onto Travkin's brow. What was the connection between an army doctor at Walter Reed, the DDO for the CIA and a cranky old bulldog politico like Macintyre? None of it made any sense but there obviously *was* a connection.

Barron had called for the information relating to Creuzfeldt-Jacob disease and associated dementia at 6:15 p.m. At 8:30 p.m. he placed his call to Hudson Cooper. At 10:15 p.m. Cooper in turn called Hollis Macintyre in Woodbridge. Within twenty-four hours of Cooper's call, Dr John Barron was dead.

Travkin sighed. Every instinct told him there was some sort of elusive relationship between the three men, but coming up with real proof was something else again and real proof was what Koslow was calling for if he wanted to continue with the project.

Barron's call for information on Creuzfeldt-Jacob disease might have been for a paper he was writing. The call to Cooper could have been a social one, as could the call from Cooper to Macintyre. None of it was even mildly suspicious except for Scanlon's assertion that the request logs at the Walter Reed Hospital had been tampered with, and Scanlon's testimony could hardly be called fact.

The telephone beside the computer terminal buzzed and Travkin picked up the receiver. It was Gregor Savin, the Operational Officer Travkin had assigned to keep an eye on Hudson Cooper. So far Cooper had done nothing out of the ordinary.

'Yes, Savin?'

'I have a transmission.'

'Just a moment,' Travkin answered. Like every other intelligence organisation operating in Washington, the GRU had a variety of ways to ensure that radio, telephone and microwave transmissions remained secure. With Koslov's tacit approval Travkin had outfitted his Operations people with a Swedish-made encrypting device called a Transfertex SR22. The machine, attached to a normal telephone, had a nine-digit numerical pad and the random numbers for both transmitter and receiver were changed once a week. Travkin connected his base unit receiver, set the nine numbers, then picked up the telephone again.

'Savin?'

'Yes. Connected.'

'Good. Go ahead,' Travkin urged.

'Hudson Cooper and his assistant . . .'

'Mallory?'

'Yes. They arrived at Dulles about half an hour ago. Cooper went to the VIP lounge for international flights and Mallory went to the American Airlines desk. I sent Lovchikov to join the line behind him. He came back and told me that Mallory picked up two first class tickets to Barbados. The flight leaves in ten minutes. Lovchikov is watching the gate to make sure they actually get on that flight.'

'Are they using their own names?' Travkin queried.

'No,' Savin answered crisply. 'Cooper is travelling as a Mr John Barnes. Mallory is using the name Akroyd. Thomas Akroyd.'

'All right, Savin. Good work,' Travkin said. 'Stay there until the flight takes off, then get back here as fast as you can.'

'Fine.' There was a burst of electronic noise as Lovchikov ended the transmission from his end. Travkin unhooked the Transfertex device and hung up the telephone. He sat back in his chair, scratching his chin thoughtfully. Another anomaly and something to tweak Koslov's imagination at last. Travelling with Mallory and using false names it was unlikely that Cooper was going to Barbados for pleasure, and it was unheard of for a man at Cooper's level to appear in the field on an operation. Ergo: something very strange was going on, strange like the phone call from Barron to Cooper. Nodding to himself he picked up the telephone again and dialled a three digit internal number.

'Documents, Lieutenant Kapalkin speaking.'

'This is Colonel Travkin.'

'Yes, Colonel, what can I do for you?'

'I need cover.' Travkin rubbed a clammy palm against the fabric of his trousers. Pray that Koslov sees this the way I do, he thought.

'Of course, Colonel, anything in mind?'

'Swiss?' Travkin suggested. His English was good, but accented enough to mark him as a foreigner. 'Visas for the United States and Great Britain. A few credit cards, some pocket litter.'

'Do the cards have to work?' asked Kapalkin.

'No,' Travkin answered. 'I'll be using cash.'

'Good. That will speed things up considerably, Colonel.'

'I want it all by four,' Travkin warned, glancing at his watch. It was already one-thirty.

'Fine,' breezed Kapalkin. 'We have your photos on file. Give me an hour or so.'

The Documents Section had instant access to a gigantic data base of information relating to passport regulations, identity cards, driving licences, passes, military documents, police documents and air, sea and rail tickets.

At any time of the day or night, using a secure satellite link, Kapalkin could find out the entry requirements and documentation for any given control or passport point in the world, including the types of questions likely to be asked and what stamps should be on the passports or other travel documents. Kapalkin had access to a variety of blank passports, identity cards and driver's licences.

Travkin shut off the computer terminal. He had an overnight bag already packed in the courier's apartment on the top floor. If he could convince Koslov of his suspicions he could be on his way to Barbados while the trail was still warm.

Stephen Stone pulled the nondescript car pool Chevy into a No Parking Zone on H Street, killed the engine and pulled down the passenger side visor to display the regulation FBI 'On Duty' sticker. Already dressed in a DC Public Works coverall, he picked up the hard hat from the seat beside him and put it on, completing the image. Scooping up an official looking clipboard from on top of the dashboard he climbed out of the car, locking the door behind him.

It was another hazy, humid day in the capital and he could already feel the sweat trickling down his ribs. Feeling a little idiotic in his disguise he walked quickly down H Street, then turned right on Jackson Place. Across the street on his left was the parched, brown-edged grass of Lafayette Square. Pennsylvania Avenue and the northern perimeter of the White House grounds was less than a hundred yards away to the south.

Stone shook his head, still not quite sure how a top Soviet agent like Travkin had managed to swing an apartment within spitting distance of the

President of the United States. It was especially ironic considering the sinful amount of money he paid in rent for his own high-rise hole in the wall on 16th Street, a mile to the north.

The FBI man glanced down the street. Jackson Place allowed parking on the west side and as far as Stone could see, every spot was taken. He slowed, spotting the surveillance vehicle, a light green, high-sided van with DC Public Works stencils all over it. Kessler had managed to put it into perfect position, just south of Travkin's building.

The narrow townhouses on Jackson Place had been erected in the mid 1800s. Anachronistic, newer buildings, such as the small apartment building Travkin occupied, had been remodelled to conform to the nineteenth-century ambience of the little street.

Stone went around to the rear of the truck and gave the proper coded knock. He waited for a few seconds, then pulled open the rear door and stepped inside. His nose wrinkled as he was hit by a wall of hot, soup-thick air tinged with the scent of male perspiration and old socks. Mort Kessler and a Communications Division jock named Dofney were seated at a bank of electronic equipment bolted to the side wall of the truck. Both men were stripped to the waist with headphones clamped over their ears. The van was lit dimly by a single fluorescent light in the ceiling.

Seeing Stone, Kessler pulled off the headphones and tossed them onto the console in front of him. He swivelled around in his chair, face almost as red as his hair and a nasty look in his eyes. Stone took off the hard hat and dropped down onto a bench seat opposite the electronic console. He found himself staring at a quartet of video monitors providing exterior coverage of the van.

'This is a surveillance vehicle, right?' said Kessler, his voice sour.

'Right,' Stone nodded, trying to keep a straight face.

'More precisely it's a fucking surveillance vehicle for use in Washington goddamn DC, am I correct?'

'Right as rain.'

'Got all the best equipment,' Kessler snarled, waving a hand at the stacked electronic equipment. 'We got Cougarnet here, we got Comsec Speech Security, Scanlok for radios, Voicelok for phones, fibre-optic video capabilities . . . shit, we've even got your basic Microwave Resonating Cavity bug. *BUT*, by God, we don't have fucking air-conditioning.'

'I'll take it up with Director Ruppelt.' Stone grinned.

'Sure you will, and Mr God will tell you all about his budget problems,' snorted Kessler. The red-haired man lit a Kool, adding to the already foggy atmosphere within the truck. 'Did you get it?' he asked finally. 'It' referred to wiretap authorisation from the Foreign Intelligence Surveillance Court. The court, undoubtedly the least known division of the American judicial system, was supposed to judge the relevance and legality of submissions by the FBI and other federal agencies for the electronic surveillance of suspected foreign agents. Not once in the court's history had it ever turned down such a submission.

'Of course I got it.' Stone answered. He reached into the bib pocket of the coveralls and pulled out a thick, cream-coloured document.

'Good. Especially since we've already done the work.' Kessler looked expectantly at Stone.

'What do you mean you've already done the work?'

'Just that,' Kessler answered blandly. He hooked a thumb at Dofney. 'Chuck planted 'em and I kept a lookout.' He nodded towards the video screens. The tiny, fibre-optic lenses were mounted high on the van body, giving a 360 degree view from four cameras, all connected to a VCR and an effects panel in front of Kessler.

Dofney looked like a college football player: overmuscled with an out of date crew-cut, and no more than twenty-five years old. He turned in his chair and gave Stone a broad, collegiate grin. 'Radio bug in each room,' he said proudly. 'And an RF flooder on the main junction box. Already got it tuned in. This guy Travkin does have air-conditioning, by the way – his apartment was nice and cool.'

'Did you find any tell-tales?' Stone asked.

'You mean, like, hairs on door cracks, talcum powder on briefcase locks?' Dofney asked, surprised. 'James Bond shit?'

'Something like that.' Stone nodded, sighing. The young agent was looking at him as though he'd just been released from an old folks home.

'Uh, no,' Dofney said finally. 'You mean people still do things like that?' he added.

'Sometimes,' Stone replied. He decided it was time to change the subject. 'Tell me about his apartment. Describe it.'

'Do better than that.' Dofney grinned. He tossed Stone a thick packet of Polaroids bound with a rubber band. 'Old Mort here said you'd want them.'

'Old Mort was right,' said Stone. He flipped through the photographs, eager for a more intimate view of his quarry.

A large, one-bedroom apartment with a bay window looking out over the statues in Lafayette Square. White walls, highly polished hardwood floors and lots of small oriental rugs. The bedroom was sparse, furnished with a lot of modern plastic.

Kitchen hi-tech, complete with Cuisinart and all the bells and whistles: espresso machine, pasta maker, Braun coffee maker. Living room: fireplace with a pot of dried flowers in the grate, collection of vaguely antique stringed instruments on one wall, Bang and Olufsen stereo, complete with a CD player, television and one whole wall filled with books.

Dofney wasn't quite as brainless as he looked – he'd taken more than a dozen close-ups of the book titles. A lot of American military history, biographies of a number of conservative politicians and a huge collection of books on Hollywood, especially on comedy and comedians. Taking up a whole shelf above it were at least a hundred joke books, some of them apparently quite old. Except for a small section of murder mysteries and thrillers there didn't seem to be much in the way of fiction.

'Interesting,' he said, slipping the rubber band around the pictures again.

'I'd say Comrade Travkin was taking full advantage of his tour of duty in the decadent west.' Kessler grinned. 'According to Chuck here, your boy has got about fifty different kinds of condom in his bedside table.'

'All colours and flavours,' snorted Dofney. 'That guy's no spy, he's a pussyhound.'

'Don't underestimate him, he's a spy all right,' Stone answered. 'Just remember, this man is a GRU Deputy Resident for DC and he's not even forty yet. He's working at least a dozen people we know about and probably a whole lot more besides.' Stone paused and wiped sweat off his forehead with the sleeve of his boilersuit.

'You went through his apartment, Dofney, and I'll bet you didn't find one thing in it with any kind of personal connotation. No address books, no letters, not even a postcard from home. You can bet your ass he empties his pockets every day before he leaves work, just to make sure he doesn't bring back any incriminating pocket litter. Don't kid yourself, Agent Dofney; Dimitri Travkin is a professional, and he's dangerous.'

Dofney opened his mouth to reply but Kessler's voice cut him off. 'Company,' the red-haired man said sharply.

'Where?' Stone asked, leaning forward, his eyes scanning the video monitors.

'Camera 1, north,' Kessler answered crisply. He stabbed the record button with his left index finger and the auto-zoom with his right. Stone watched as the image on camera 1 tightened, showing the street and a few cars. 'The dark blue Ford,' said Kessler. 'Dip plates. DFC 677.' Kessler squeezed his eyes shut for a fraction of a second, thinking. 'She's out of the Mount Alto Complex, not the SMO. I'd say she's KGB.'

'What do we do now?' asked Dofney, his voice nervous.

'Nothing,' Stone answered, keeping his eye on the screen.

'They're sniffing,' explained Kessler. 'They'll make a pass and go around the block.'

'I don't get it.' Dofney frowned. 'If they're KGB what are they doing here?'

'They don't teach you much in ComDiv, do they?' Kessler asked rhetorically. They all watched as the Ford slid off the Camera 1 screen, then reappeared on Camera 2, moving away towards Pennsylvania Avenue. 'It's Big Brother, Little Brother,' the red-haired agent explained. 'There's no love lost between the KGB and the GRU so they watch each other. These guys are probably just making a routine run on the building. GRU has a lot of its people housed outside the Mount Alto Complex and the Killer Bs are jealous.'

'It sounds stupid to me,' Dofney said.

'You think it's any different here?' Kessler asked. The Ford turned right onto Pennsylvania Avenue and vanished. 'The CIA watches the DIA and NSA watches them right back. It's the same thing, except we dress better than they do.'

'I think it goes a little deeper than that,' Stone laughed. Kessler lifted a single, expressive eyebrow and turned back to the video monitors. He punched up the zoom on camera 1, waiting for the Ford to reappear. Less than a minute later, it did.

'Here she comes,' Kessler murmured. He hit the time counter, the display running in the lower right hand corner of all four screens. The car was definitely going slower the second time around. It slid past the van's position and Kessler went to camera 2 again.

'They're stopping,' Stone whispered, watching the screen and ignoring the puddling sweat under his eyes. The body heat from the three men and the heat of the equipment had turned the truck's interior into a jungle.

The rear door of the Ford opened and two men appeared, both carrying small black bags. The tall one was dressed in shorts, Hawaiian shirt and a straw hat while his shorter companion was wearing a jogging suit. 'Two doctors going to a costume party,' Kessler grunted. The KGB men reached the sidewalk and Kessler punched up camera 3, giving them a view of the sidewalk and Travkin's front door. On the camera 2 screen the Ford was pulling away. The two men appeared on screen, walking towards Travkin's building. 'Straw Hat is a Line KR boy named Stefan Gontar,' said Kessler as the two men entered the building and disappeared from view. 'I've never seen the other one.' Line KR stood for the KGB counterintelligence section.

'Technical support?' Stone offered.

Kessler nodded. 'Could be.' He turned to Dofney. 'Give us some sounds, kid.'

'Sure,' Dofney answered. He hit several switches and there was a faint hum as the recorders began to turn. The technician turned to Stone, obviously worried. 'You think they're sweeping the place for our bugs?' he asked. Stone shook his head.

'Too much of a coincidence,' he said. 'I think we just stepped into some interagency shit here.'

'You mean they're bugging his place too?' said Dofney.

'Probably,' Stone said. 'Are they likely to trip over your stuff?'

Dofney thought for a moment, then lifted his broad shoulders. 'They might, but I doubt it. The RF flooder is two blocks away.'

'What about the other bugs?'

'C-Comm's,' Dofney answered. 'We get them custom made to look like Duracells. I took the real batteries out of his smoke alarms.' He laughed. 'Mind you, we're shit out of luck if he has a fire.'

Stone heard a faint crackling sound from the speaker. Kessler slipped on his headphones and Dofney boosted the volume. Stone could hear the creaking of a door, then footsteps – metal clips on hardwood.

'They're in,' Kessler murmured. Stone joined the two agents at the electronics console, crouching down between them and listening. There were more footsteps, sniffing noises, as though one of the intruders had a cold, and then voices.

'*Sveyarlo* . . . something about a drill,' said Stone, straining to hear. He'd spent four months on a Russian language course after joining REDNET, but he was far from fluent. A few seconds later he heard a high-pitched whining sound.

'Portable drill,' Kessler said. 'Probably taking a chunk out of the baseboard.'

'Radio bug?' asked Stone, glancing up at Dofney.

'No, sir,' the technician answered. 'We can service ours from any building around here, They don't have that kind of access.' Dofney paused, thinking. 'Probably an MRC at some inaudible frequency, real high, say 330 megaHertz.' An MRC was a Microwave Resonating Cavity bug of the type used by the Soviets to monitor conversations in the US embassy in Moscow. In that case the bug, less than three inches long, was secreted inside the carved seal of the United States which hung behind the Ambassador's desk.

'It won't interfere with our signals?' asked Stone.

'Nope,' Dofney answered, shaking his head. 'They'll run a tight beam off the roof at Mount Alto to pick it up.'

'One of them is leaving,' said Kessler. The men in the van watched the video monitor but after two long minutes, no one appeared. There were more drilling sounds from Travkin's apartment.

'The other guy is probably tracing the phone line,' suggested Dofney. 'Tapping the junction box.'

'All of a sudden your boy is a very hot item,' said Kessler, giving Stone a meaningful glance. He returned it silently; there was nothing about the situation they could discuss in front of Dofney.

A strident electronic buzz filled the interior of the van and Kessler picked up the scrambled radiophone handset from the console in front of him. He listened for a few seconds, nodded once and then turned to face Stone.

'What?'

'It's Midbrook,' Kessler answered. 'He's got the service watch at SMO. He says Travkin just got into an airport limo, carrying an overnight bag. He wants to know if he should follow.'

'Yes,' Stone responded quickly. 'But only until he figures out which airport they're going to. Once he's done that tell him to get one of our people there before the limo, if that's possible, but for Christ sake be discreet!'

'Right.' Kessler turned back to the radiophone.

Stone stood up and went back to the bench seat on the other side of the van. He sat down heavily and lit a cigarette. If Travkin was acting as a courier again he would have used a vehicle from the SMO or Mount Alto car pool. The fact that he was carrying an overnight bag and hadn't come back to his own apartment to pack meant that he was in a hurry. But why, and for what? Stone shook his head. 'What the hell is the little bastard up to?' he whispered.

CHAPTER EIGHT

As the name implies, Garrison Savannah, home track of the Barbados Turf Club, is close to the old British Garrison. The eighty-year-old facility is a mile or so from the centre of Bridgetown, capital of the island, and operates two full seasons of regular six- and seven-race cards.

For off-island aficionados, used to modern track facilities, Garrison Savannah is an archaic eyesore. The rickety old grandstand is made of wood, and with the exception of a few private box seats for Turf Club members, hard bench seats are the rule. Smoking is allowed, so there is the constant threat of fire, the overhead canopy leaks when it rains, and during each race the entire grandstand shakes as the horses thunder past.

Outside the track, parking is haphazard with no real lots, the stables to the north of the field are a slum, and the inside rail around the paddock is decorated with scores of garish, brightly coloured billboard advertisements for everything from Chez Monique's to Willie's Watersports.

Eyesore or not, the track is one of the most popular attractions on the island, and on the regular Saturday race days, or for special stake races, the grandstand is filled to capacity with fans from all over Barbados, as well as hordes of tourists from the nearby Hilton and the other hotels along the Highway 7 coastal route to Grantley Adams International Airport.

Seated deep in the shadows on the top bench under the grandstand canopy, Eric Rhinelander watched as the horses assembled for the last race on the card – the Concorde Stakes. The race, underwritten by British Airways, had been sponsored to celebrate the fifth year of Concorde service to Barbados and with a £10,000 stake it had attracted every thoroughbred racing enthusiast on the island.

Rhinelander, appropriately dressed in sneakers, jeans and a Barbados Wildlife Trust T-shirt, sipped at his large cup of Banks Beer, occasionally lifting his Tasco binoculars to look down at the track. The bench beside him was filled with a boisterous party of Bajan locals, hooting and yelling to friends below them. Rhinelander ignored them, and each time he lifted the binoculars to scan the track he allowed himself a few seconds to focus on the lowest box in the private Turf Club section at the north end of the grandstand.

There were five people in the booth, two couples and a single man. The two couples were dressed casually, the men in jackets and open necked shirts, the women in skirts and blouses. The single man was dressed nautically in blazer, white ducks and an officer's cap. Once upon a time the man had obviously been quite good-looking but through the binoculars Rhinelander could see the fine strawberry booze marks on his cheeks and nose. He was fiftyish and jowled, thick through the middle and when he took off his cap to wipe the sweat from his forehead Rhinelander could see a broad patch of hairless, tanned scalp. What hair remained, once blond, was now a nicotine-coloured white. His name was William Harper and he was CIA Station Chief for Barbados.

Deeming that the island was neither economically nor strategically important, the State Department had seen fit to assign a chargé d'affaires rather than an ambassador to the small Caribbean nation. The tiny diplomatic staff was housed in a suite of offices in the Canadian Imperial Bank building on Broad Street in Bridgetown. Visiting the offices shortly after his arrival, Rhinelander made a quick reconnaissance, picked up a few pamphlets and left.

Based on what he had seen, and the information contained in the pamphlets, Rhinelander came to some quick conclusions. According to the brochure describing the office of the chargé d'affaires and its services, there were eight people employed: the chargé d'affaires himself, a man named Howard Sawyer, his assistant, two secretaries, a receptionist, an immigration officer, an information officer and a public affairs officer.

From past experience with CIA stations abroad, Rhinelander suspected that Harper, the information officer, was the man he was after. His office was almost the same size as the chargé d'affaires', and it was obvious that he had more money than his boss. He drove a two-year-old Volvo, dressed expensively and lived aboard $60,000 worth of motor sailer moored on the Waterfront Arcade at the foot of Bay Street. By contrast Sawyer, the chargé d'affaires, drove a five-year-old Izuzu sedan and lived with his wife and two children in a relatively modest bungalow.

Renting a canvas roofed, open-sided Mini-Moke Rhinelander spent two days keeping tabs on Harper, and by the end of the second day he was positive that the man was CIA. He worked no more than an hour or two a day at the office, spending most of his time aboard his boat and doing the rounds of Bridgetown clubs and bars in the evening.

Not that he wasn't working; if Barbados was like other small CIA stations, Harper's mandate from the people at Langley was probably to cultivate, emulate and infiltrate the upper echelons of Barbadian society. The long term results of his hobnobbing would be a good selection of dossiers of both locals and their visitors, some of which might be useful to the Agency.

In CIA parlance, Harper was 'trolling', with the car, boat and Turf Club private box as both bait and cover.

During the Grenada invasion and the CIA destabilisation efforts which had preceded it, Barbados had proven its strategic value as an intelligence and military staging base and Harper's continued presence insured that other nations, especially those in the Caribbean and Central America, recognised that the long arm of the US military was never far away.

Somewhere along the line, however, Harper had developed a private sideline. Focusing on the box again, Rhinelander took another look at the two couples seated with the station chief. They weren't really couples at all, of course; the women were imports, tall and blonde, probably from Miami or Nassau, and the two men were both employed by the government of Colombia. The older of the two, a short, bearded man named Torres, was assistant to the Colombian chargé d'affaires, and his younger, taller and clean-shaven companion was supposedly a chauffeur. If Rhinelander was reading the signs correctly, the Colombians and Harper had some sort of drug scam going, probably involving the 'Special', a regularly scheduled diplomatic pouch used only by the CIA, and utterly taboo.

Since putting Harper under loose surveillance, the station chief had spent a great deal of time with Torres and the chauffeur, most of it on the boat. That morning, prior to leaving for the track, Harper and the two Colombians had spent a couple of hours loading food, liquor and water onto the boat as well as topping up her fuel tanks. It was two hundred miles from Bridgetown to the Venezuelan coast, half that to a mid-point rendevous with a drug ship; all in all at least a twenty-four-hour round trip on a boat the size of Harper's.

Rhinelander couldn't have cared less about Harper's involvement in the drug trade; he wouldn't be the first CIA employee to use his position for personal gain, nor would he be the last. What did matter was that Harper's interests were elsewhere for the moment. If the red-faced station chief was en route to a cocaine rendezvous he wouldn't be interfering in Rhinelander's affairs.

The grandstand crowd, noisy to begin with, let out an exuberant, blossoming roar of appreciation as the starting gate yawned open and the horses broke into the first straight. All around Rhinelander spectators had leapt to their feet, waving their arms, screaming for their favourites, betting slips clutched in their hands. Ignoring the race and the frenzied crowd, Rhinelander began to move, pushing his way along the aisle until he reached the main stairs leading to the track.

By the time the horses thundered into the second turn, Rhinelander had made his way down to the base of the grandstand. A commentator was calling the race order incoherently over the public address system and all he could make out was the name of the favourite, a three-year-old named Charlie Muffin. According to the race programme the horse was owned by a syndicate headed by William Harper.

Ducking into the cool shadows, Rhinelander headed down the broad, dark passage that led back under the grandstand, pushed through the turnstile and stepped out into the sunlight. Behind him he could still hear the roaring crowd, but the parking lot in front of him was silent. Just outside the chain link fence a group of luridly painted private buses were waiting for the last race to end, hoping to steal away passengers from the public bus line.

He found his rented Mini-Moke, and a few moments later he pulled out onto the highway, heading north into Bridgetown. Even with the racing programme well under way the traffic was still horrendous and it took Rhinelander almost fifteen minutes to navigate the mile or so of road back to Trafalgar Square and the yacht basin by Chamberlain Bridge.

Guiding the Moke over the bridge separating the Careenage from the Inner Basin, he turned left around the statue of Lord Nelson and threaded his way along the wharf until he reached the car park at the far end of the harbour. Lifting the binoculars again he panned down the forest of ship masts and tightly clustered buildings along the pier until he picked out Harper's boat, *Sandpiper*, the name clearly visible on her transom. The boat identified, he sat back against the seat, and closed his eyes.

Forty minutes later, on his fourth check with the binoculars, Rhinelander spotted movement aboard *Sandpiper*. Harper, Torres and the driver were making ready for sea. There was no sign of the two women. Rhinelander assumed that they were either below in the cabin, or hadn't been invited along on the covert journey. If Harper had any sense, it would be the latter.

At almost exactly four p.m. *Sandpiper* came puttering along the Careenage, sails partly unfurled and ready to be hoisted once they reached open water. Keeping well back in the shadows of the Moke's canopy Rhinelander watched as the motor-sailer went by. Harper, officer's cap firmly down over his forehead, was at the wheel, while the Colombian chauffeur, now stripped to a pair of skimpy shorts, was scrambling around the foredeck, making a show of gathering up tackle for the benefit of the two blondes lounging in their bikinis against the cabin bulkhead. Rhinelander shook his head. Not smart.

He waited until *Sandpiper* cleared the harbour entrance, then started up the Moke again. If things went according to schedule Mallory and Cooper would be arriving at Grantley Adams on the seven-thirty flight from Dulles. That gave him a little more than three hours, and there was still a lot to do.

*

The Tropicana Court Hotel was located on the beach off Highway 7 just beyond the village of Hastings and about three miles from the centre of Bridgetown. The hotel, isolated from its more luxurious neighbours by several hundred yards of rocky cliff on either side, consisted of a three-storey main building, pool, open air restaurant and a modest stretch of pleasant, shallow-water beach.

The main building comprised eighteen units on three floors with a pair of exterior staircases at the rear of the building leading up to motel-style open-air walkways. The units were identical, with kitchen, bathroom and bedroom-living area. A sliding glass door led out to the balcony, with a view of the pool and restaurant as well as the ocean beyond. The balconies were separated by full-height walls of roughly stuccoed concrete, each one fitted with a bolted connecting door.

On his arrival in Barbados, Rhinelander had chosen the Tropicana Court both for its isolation and the straightforward access to the units. He'd rented two adjoining rooms, number thirteen and fourteen, located on the third floor at the eastern end of the building. He told the manager that he was expecting friends from the States and was renting the second room on their behalf. He took the units for a week and paid cash in advance. Watching as the manager tapped the requisite information into his computer, Rhinelander could see that rooms fifteen to eighteen were not booked for that period. He would have the top floor to himself.

Following the departure of Harper and his companions Rhinelander piloted the Moke back to Garrison Savannah and beyond it to the hotel. He parked the car in the lot, then climbed the stairs to the third floor. After removing the tell-tale sliver of cellophane from the lock he inserted his key and opened the door. Remaining in the open-air walkway he listened carefully and sniffed the air. Everything seemed in order. He entered the room, closed and locked the door, then checked bathroom, kitchen, living area and balcony. Empty.

Standing on the balcony Rhinelander lit a cigarette and glanced down at the pool. A middle-aged man with a sunburn on his fleshy shoulders was doing slow laps, while two women in bikinis lay tanning in a pair of green, webbed plastic chairs. They were paying no attention to the man in the pool. Rhinelander sat down at the balcony table, tipping his ashes into a butt-filled saucer. Through the screening line of trees between the pool and the sea, he noted that the beach was almost empty as well. Things were quiet at the Tropicana Court.

He sat on the balcony for a few minutes longer, smoking his cigarette and listening to the shrill sound of crickets and the muttering of the ocean. When the cigarette was finished he butted it into the saucer and went back to the living area. Squatting down he reached under the overhanging coverlet of the bed nearest the balcony and withdrew a well-used, pale blue vinyl flight bag emblazoned with the Pan Am symbol. He unzipped the bag and began removing the contents: hand-drill, a package of hacksaw blades, electrical tape, eyeglass screwdriver, a roll of speaker wire, a tube of liquid solder, insulated wire-cutters, and a package of plumber's putty.

Also in the flight bag was a shoebox containing a Panasonic voice-activated memo-corder, one 120 minute BASF micro audio tape, a package of Duracell AAA batteries, and a large, fifties vintage Bel-Tone hearing aid. Rhinelander had purchased all of this, including the flight bag, at a number of stores in Bridgetown over the previous three days.

Using the eyeglass screwdriver Rhinelander carefully removed the flesh-tone cover of the hearing aid and examined the device closely. As he had expected, the mechanism consisted of a miniature transistorised receiver connected to a microphone and battery. Using the screwdriver as a lever, Rhinelander delicately removed the microphone from the earpiece, then separated it completely from the rest of the unit by snipping the wires leading to the receiver. He then clipped a six foot length of speaker wire and rebuilt the hearing aid circuit with it, bonding the new length of wire with a minuscule amount of the liquid solder.

Leaving the solder to harden he went back to the bed, picked up the drill and the hacksaw blades, then carried them to the party wall between his room and the one next door. Sitting cross-legged on the floor he chose a spot directly over a wall socket and quickly drilled two pairs of parallel holes about eight inches apart directly above the outlet. Using one of the hacksaw blades he joined the four holes, then pried out the square of plasterboard. Sliding down, he peered into the opening; his measurements the day before had been accurate – the electrical box and wall socket on the other wall matched the one on his side.

He boosted himself up, went back to the bed, picked up the batteries, memo-corder and the electrical tape, then carried them to the table. The liquid solder had set nicely, making a solid connection. Rhinelander tore off two six-inch strips of electrical tape, then gently picked up the receiver end of the hearing aid. He butted the receiver end to the condensor microphone in the memo-corder, attaching it with the two strips of tape. The end result of his labours was an unsophisticated, but perfectly workable bugging device.

Replacing the tape machine's batteries with the new Duracells, Rhinelander loaded the tape, then ran a quick check, setting the tape machine on record and whispering into the microphone end of the hearing aid, his eyes on the voice-level needle on the recorder. It worked perfectly. He rewound the tape, then carried the electronic package to his newly opened hole in the wall.

Picking up the drill again he reached into the hole, running his finger under the cast steel box covering the outlet in the other room. Using his finger as a guide he drilled a small hole through the plasterboard just under the box. That done, he withdrew the drill and set it aside. Taking the package of putty he kneaded it for a few seconds, then tore it open. Balling a wad of the grey compound between thumb and forefinger, he made a thick collar around the microphone from the hearing aid. He reached into the hole again, found the tiny hole below the electrical box, then used his other hand to carefully place the microphone, pressing firmly to ensure that it would hold. With the microphone in position he eased the memo-corder into the hole, letting it rest on the wooden framing joist between the two panels of plasterboard. He replaced the square he'd removed, securing it with more putty, then cleaned up after himself, using the flight bag as a catch all.

Ten minutes later he was finished, satisfied that any evidence of his modest renovations had been removed. Finally, he pushed the bureau a foot to the left, hiding the scored area of wallboard above the electrical outlet. He looked around the room again, then checked his watch. The whole procedure had taken less than an hour; there was plenty of time left.

Rhinelander went out onto the balcony, pulled back the heavy bolt on the connecting door and stepped across onto the adjoining balcony. He slid open the glass door and entered the living room. The unit was the mirror image of his own, the furniture and decor duplicated exactly. He crossed the room to the electrical outlet beside the bureau and got down onto his hands and knees. There was a tiny dribble of plaster dust on the skirtingboard. Rhinelander licked the tip of his finger and dabbed it over the offending area. The plaster dust vanished. Bending even lower he checked the drill hole. The opening was completely invisible, a pinhole lost in the shadows of the socket and the skirtingboard.

A thorough search by a team of trained debuggers from the Agency would be able to spot it eventually, but Rhinelander wasn't giving Hudson Cooper the luxury, or the time for that. Returning to the balcony, Rhinelander bolted the adjoining door, then left the unit through the regular door, locking it behind him. He returned to his own room, dropped the key to number 13 into a Tropicana Court envelope and sat down at the desk to write a brief set of instructions for Cooper.

Five minutes later he was back outside and climbing into the Mini-Moke. Two minutes after that he was on his way to Grantley Adams International Airport.

*

According to established CIA tradecraft, Hudson Cooper and Paul Mallory should have travelled separately from Washington, but Cooper had decided to forgo procedure. Since they were both flying on diplomatic passports, with Mallory handcuffed to the Central Intelligence 'special' diplomatic bag, it seemed absurd to sit apart during the flight and go through customs and immigration singly.

The flight came in exactly on time and the sun was only just lowering on the horizon as the two men reached the bottom of the steps and began walking across the tarmac to the terminal with the rest of the passengers.

'What on earth is that noise?' asked Cooper. The air was filled with a continuous, creaking whine, like thousands of tiny, squeaking wooden wheels in need of grease.

'Crickets,' Mallory responded. While Cooper had spent the four and a half hour flight staring blankly out the window, his assistant had passed the time by reading three hundred pages of the *Insight Guide to Barbados*. 'They have a plague of crickets in Barbados. They're everywhere.'

'Oh,' Cooper answered, not even mildly interested, his thoughts focused on Rhinelander and their meeting.

They ducked under the concrete canopy over the main entrance doors and stepped inside the terminal. Sidestepping the main line of passengers winding its way through customs and immigration they flashed their red-covered passports and were given priority treatment. Within ten minutes they reached the main concourse.

'The message said we should go to the American Express kiosk,' Cooper said, obviously uncomfortable. The whirling currents of humanity that eddied through the concourse were dressed in a wild assortment of brightly coloured tourist clothes while Cooper wore a dark grey business suit complete with white shirt, striped tie and black wingtips.

'That way,' Mallory said, pointing down the concourse to the familiar blue and white sign. Cooper's assistant was dressed more appropriately in an open necked shirt and a cream-coloured, summer weight sports jacket. The large, metal-sided attaché case handcuffed to his left wrist was a dead giveaway, however, and for anyone who cared to notice, the two men were clearly not tourists.

With Mallory in the lead they made their way through the dense traffic on the concourse and eventually reached the small Amex booth. A pleasant, smiling woman greeted them and Cooper asked if their were any messages for him. The woman checked a bank of pigeonholes on her left, then handed him an envelope. Cooper thanked her, then moved to one side with Mallory.

'A key,' he said, tearing open the envelope. He read the message on the

Tropicana Court letterhead, then handed it to Mallory. The instructions were simple and clear. They were to take a taxi from Grantley Adams to the Tropicana Court and use the key to get into room 13. Rhinelander would meet them there and after their meeting Mallory and Cooper would then return to Grantley Adams for the midnight British West Indies Airline flight to Miami, connecting to an Eastern flight to Washington DC. The BWIA tickets would be found on the desk in their room. The note reiterated what they had been told previously: if Rhinelander became aware of any surveillance of himself or the room at the Tropicana Court, he would not appear for the meeting.

'Fair enough.' Mallory nodded. It wasn't fair at all, of course, at least not as far as he was concerned. He was becoming more and more deeply involved with Cooper's sub-rosa escapade and he liked it less and less with each passing day. Being party to some sort of clandestine operation involving the Deputy Director of Operations was bad enough without the complication of involving an assassin like Rhinelander. He'd seen the photographs in Paris, and he'd seen the cold, dead eyes of the man in Jamaica. Mallory had the sinking feeling that if he made it through this alive he'd wind up explaining his actions in front of a Congressional Investigating Committee.

Thus far the only positive note was the fact that Cooper had offered no information about the nature of the project, and Mallory, of course, had asked no questions. Still, he wasn't a fool and all those years in Threat Analysis had jaded him severely when it came to field operations. Back then of course it had never occurred to him that he would one day be taking an active part in one.

They found a taxi and gave the driver the address. Like all of the cabs in Barbados, theirs was unmetered, but neither Cooper nor Mallory was interested in haggling and they agreed to the first price mentioned by the driver. Muttering under his breath about 'assified' American tourists the driver flung the car into the stream of traffic heading for the highway.

By the time they reached the Tropicana Court night was falling and the sun was no more than a narrow slash of colour on the western horizon. The driver, still talking to himself, sped off towards Bridgetown, leaving Cooper and Mallory at the foot of the winding stairs leading up to room 13. Cooper gave Mallory the key. The implication was clear. If Rhinelander was waiting up there to spring some sort of trap, it would be sprung on Mallory. He started up, Cooper trailing a few steps behind.

Slightly out of breath and heart beating hard from more than simple exertion, Mallory reached the top of the stairs and walked a few paces to number thirteen. Glancing over his shoulder he saw that Cooper was waiting at the head of the stairs. He gave his boss a brief nod, inserted the key in the lock and stepped inside. He reappeared a few moments later, poking his head around the doorframe.

'Clear,' he called out softly. Cooper joined him at the door and both men went into the unit, Mallory standing aside and closing the door after Cooper had entered.

'Sweep it,' Cooper ordered. He switched on the lights in the main room and looked around carefully. Inspection complete he went to the balcony door, slid it back and stepped outside. In the meantime Mallory unlocked the handcuff on his wrist and set the metal case down on the bed. Taking a ring of keys out of his pocket he opened the case and flipped back the lid. Inside was a second, slightly smaller case which he also opened.

The second case contained an ISA countermeasures receiver and a separate chart/screen scanner. The receiver scanned all radio frequencies from 20 kiloHertz, which was just beyond the range of human hearing, up to 1 gigaHertz, which was the end of television and the beginning of microwave. The scanner, once connected to the receiver, offered a panoramic display of any and all radio signals in that range, detecting any evidence of 'snuggling', a common bugging practice where the surveillance device uses a frequency close to that of a major radio or television station and hides in its shadow. On both chart and screen, major carriers such as a radio station would show up as a sharp peak, with any bugs showing up as minor peaks close to the major signal.

Mallory connected the receiver to the scanner, carried both across the room to the desk, then plugged the receiver into the wall. Because of the harsh, overhead lighting and his own lack of experience, he failed to notice the tiny pinhole just beneath the plastic socket cover.

Returning to the desk he toggled the power switch and checked the display lights. A flat carrier signal appeared on the dark green monitor screen and there was a sharp buzzing sound as a blank tongue of paper slid out of the slot at the bottom of the control panel. He adjusted the controls, then put the machine into scan mode.

The curved line on the screen instantly jumped into a series of peaks and valleys, and the chart paper began to stream out of the machine. Mallory carefully examined both, then reached into his jacket for the *Insight* guide book.

'Anything?' asked Cooper, stepping back into the room and closing the sliding glass door.

'Spikes at 790 and 900. Three FM and one television.' He gestured with the guide book. 'It fits in with local radio and TV.'

'Any snuggling?'

'No.'

'Then the room is clean.' Cooper nodded to himself and sat down at the table between the bed and the balcony door. The director relaxed visibly, satisfied that they weren't under any kind of audio surveillance. His assumption was wrong, of course, since the ISA unit was capable of digging out sophisticated radio devices but was blind, deaf and dumb to the basic wire and microphone bug Rhinelander had used.

'Now what?' Mallory asked, packing up the equipment.

'Presumably our man will show up when he's satisfied that we're alone,' Cooper answered. 'Until then we wait.'

Eric Rhinelander sat at one of the umbrella-topped tables between the bar and the pool of the Tropicana Court. He sipped his bottle of Banks Beer slowly, his eyes on the square of light that marked room 13 in the main building. A few minutes previously he'd seen the silhouetted figure of a man on the balcony. Cooper, or perhaps his assistant, Mallory.

He lit a cigarette, careful to keep his face turned away from the window, even though he was shielded by the umbrella. He took a drag on the cigarette and exhaled slowly, the smoke dribbling between his parted lips and pluming from his nostrils as he considered his situation. His instincts told him not to meet the two men in room 13. Mallory finding him in Jamaica had been a warning: his ex-employers knew where he was and what he was doing. That was bad enough, but the fact that Cooper wanted to meet him personally was worse. The Deputy Director of Operations for the Central Intelligence Agency did not meet with a 'wet affairs' operative unless he was putting together something even the CIA didn't want to be involved in.

Rhinelander took another long drag on the cigarette, eyes drifting up to the lit window of room 13 again. He'd gone over all the permutations a hundred times, and he still hadn't come up with any clear answer. In the final analysis, though, there were only two real possibilities; either Cooper wanted to hire him, or, for some obscure reason, Cooper wanted to kill him.

Not that it mattered very much; one way or the other his days in Jamaica were over, and one way or another he'd have to confront Cooper, so it might as well be now. He checked his watch, took a final sip of beer, then butted the cigarette into the plastic ashtray on the table. It was time.

He made his way around the pool, the rubber soles of his sneakers making small hissing noises on the water-stained concrete. He kept close to the wall, out of room 13's line of sight, then went around the side of the building, heading for the stairs at the rear. In the darkness, the only sounds came from the crickets, the sea and the gentle wind that whispered through the leafy branches of the nearby trees.

Rhinelander reached the stairs and climbed them, two steps at a time. He reached the third floor and without hesitation went to the door of number 13 and knocked. He hadn't risked bringing a firearm into Barbados, and it was equally unlikely that Cooper or Mallory had tried either.

The door opened. It was Mallory. He was dressed in an open necked shirt and trousers. To the left Rhinelander could see a jacket hanging on a hook. Wise move; by taking off his jacket the CIA man was showing that he was unarmed. Looking over Mallory's shoulder he could see a slim, balding man seated in a chair by the balcony door. Hudson Cooper, jacket still on and tie neatly knotted. Mallory extended a hand which Rhinelander ignored. He closed and locked the door, then gestured to Mallory, indicating that he precede him down the short hallway between the kitchen and bathroom of the unit. Mallory did so.

As they came into the main room, Cooper rose from his seat and extended his own hand. This time Rhinelander took it. The grip was warm, firm and dry. If the DDO was nervous or frightened he was hiding it well.

'Hudson Cooper,' he said, letting go of Rhinelander's hand. 'We did everything you asked.'

'Good,' Rhinelander said. 'We should get down to business, you don't have much time.'

'No,' Cooper agreed. 'You've put us in quite a tight schedule, I'm afraid.'

'It was necessary,' Rhinelander replied. 'Especially after the violation of my privacy a few days ago.' He looked pointedly at Mallory.

'I'm sorry about that,' Cooper answered. He cleared his throat and gestured to his assistant. Mallory crossed the room and leaned down as Cooper whispered something. Mallory nodded, then went out onto the balcony, shutting the sliding glass door firmly.

'You don't trust him?' Rhinelander asked.

'Of course I trust him,' Cooper said. 'But this is need to know.'

'I see,' Rhinelander said. 'What he doesn't know won't hurt him.'

'Something like that,' Cooper answered. He cleared his throat again, nervously. There was a short silence. Rhinelander frowned, his expression irritated.

'The whole process of arranging this meeting has taken up a lot of my time,' he said quietly. 'Let's not waste any more of it. Why don't you tell me what you want?'

'We want to employ your services.'

'Who is "we"?' Rhinelander asked. 'The Agency?'

'Not exactly,' Cooper replied. 'Let us simply say that "we" is a group of highly placed and influential people.'

'I was trained by several organisations, including yours, Mr Cooper. You know what I am and what I do. Let's get to the point. You want me to kill someone. Who?'

The Deputy Director hesitated for a moment. After this there would be no turning back: he and the other members of the Romulus Committee would be committed. He gritted his teeth, silently cursing the twists of fate and circumstance that had brought him to this moment. Finally he spoke. 'Geoffrey James Tucker, the President of the United States.' He kept his eyes on Rhinelander, waiting for some clue to his emotions. There was none. He simply nodded, then lit a cigarette.

'Why?' he asked a moment later, blowing out a long tail of smoke.

'He's dying,' Cooper explained. 'A degenerative brain disease. He'll be dead in less than a year. The disease takes the form of a progressive dementia which might prove to be . . . embarrassing, given his position as Chief Executive.'

'I see,' Rhinelander said, his face still a mask. 'Does President Tucker know that he has this disease?'

'No.'

'But you do. And several others, I presume?'

'Yes.'

'If Tucker dies Vincent Teresi becomes President. I can't believe you'd want that.'

'No,' Cooper answered.

There was a brief moment of silence as Rhinelander digested that piece of information. He nodded to himself. 'You want me to kill them both,' he said finally. He reached out and stubbed his cigarette into the ashtray on the table between them. He didn't light another.

'Yes.'

'You have something in mind,' Rhinelander said thoughtfully. 'Something else you want to accomplish.'

'Yes,' Cooper agreed. 'We thought of having Teresi die "accidentally", but that still left us with the problem of Tucker's progressive dementia. A Vice-President dying accidentally, a new Vice-President chosen by a President whose health is ailing, and then a presidential resignation or death in office . . . it would be too much.' The Deputy Director hesitated for a moment, then went on. 'But we came up with another idea.' He hesitated again, almost as though unwilling to say what had to be said.

'Go on,' Rhinelander said. He glanced over Cooper's shoulder. Mallory was outside on the balcony, leaning on the railing and studiously presenting his back to the proceedings within the room.

Cooper spoke again. 'Two months ago we were advised by our Station Chief in Beirut that a new terrorist group was being organised by a senior member of the Abu Nidal group. The man's name is Nezar Assad. The focus of the group was to be the United States. We put Assad under surveillance and ten days ago we caught him trying to enter the country illegally at the Niagara Falls border crossing. We now have Assad under protective custody. Learning of the President's tragic disability we knew that drastic measures had to be taken, and it occurred to us that perhaps Mr Assad could be of some assistance.'

'You want to use him as an Oswald,' Rhinelander said, following Cooper's line of thought. 'I do the work and he takes the fall. In the end, Libya gets the blame.'

'Precisely,' Cooper answered. 'If we had absolute proof that both the President and the Vice-President had been assassinated by a Qaddafi-sponsored killer we could write our own ticket in the Middle East. Everyone would be on our side.'

'When?' Rhinelander asked.

'Soon. Six to eight weeks at the most. It has to be done before the President's symptoms become more noticeable.'

'Where?'

Cooper hesitated again. He and Macintyre had put the scenario together. A terrorist strike at the heart of America. An act so fundamentally violent and obscene that any form of retaliation would seem justified. It seemed like madness, sitting here with this man, but perhaps that was the object of the exercise.

'The White House,' Cooper said bluntly. 'For maximum effect, the Oval Office.'

Rhinelander thought for a moment and then shook his head. 'It may not be possible,' he responded finally. 'At best it would be a very, very difficult proposition.'

'We concede that,' Cooper agreed, 'but as a symbolic target it's unquestionably ideal. Second best would be Camp David, third and fourth would be Air Force One or the *Sequoia*.'

'I'd need to do some research before I agreed to proceed with it,' Rhinelander warned. 'Presidential assassins have a poor record of escaping intact.'

'I can understand your hesitation.'

'I'd also like a question answered,' Rhinelander said.

'Certainly.'

'Why me? I can think of half a dozen people with my . . . qualifications.'

'Anonymity,' Cooper answered. 'As you say, there are a number of highly qualified people in your field. None of them are as invisible as you, however. As far as we can tell, the Soft File held by our office is the only documentation of your existence on this planet. You vanished officially when you joined the Phoenix programme. Since then everything about your identity has been manufactured. It's as much an asset to us as it is to you.'

'Especially if the project goes wrong and I have to be erased,' Rhinelander put in.

'Far more to the point is the fact that if you ran into difficulty and were captured or killed, nothing would lead back to us,' Cooper responded. 'Anything else?'

'Terms.'

'Go on,' Cooper said.

'First, understand that I haven't agreed to anything at this point. I'll do some research to see if it's feasible. If it is, I'll let you know.'

'How long?' Cooper asked.

'A week, ten days at the most.'

'Agreed.'

'For that I want two hundred thousand dollars, up front and non-refundable, plus the non-traceable ID I'll need to make use of it.'

'Agreed.'

'Any hint of surveillance by any of your people and I disappear. I need the anonymity as much as you do.'

'Certainly, that's clear enough.'

'Mallory, your assistant.'

'What about him?'

'I deal with him only. After this he's the only one I see or have any contact with. He supplies me with anything I want.'

'He's not a fool, in fact he's already nervous,' said Cooper. 'To tell him any more about this is the same as signing his death warrant. He'll know that.'

'He knows you want someone killed, he doesn't know who,' Rhinelander answered. 'Tell him something he'll believe.'

'All right.'

'Another thing. The final payment is going to be heavy.'

'How much?' Cooper asked.

'As much as you can afford,' Rhinelander answered, showing a brief, flashing smile. 'I'll want it all in uncut gemstones. No diamonds, they're too hard to sell and too easy to trace. Emeralds only and nothing over a carat.'

'That can be arranged,' agreed Cooper. 'Anything else?'

'Yes,' Rhinelander said, his voice calm. 'Cross me, make any attempt to set me up or throw me to the wolves and I'll kill you . . . all of you.'

'I understand. You have no reason for concern.'

'Good,' Rhinelander said. 'Then our meeting is finished.' He lit a cigarette and leaned back in his chair. Cooper checked his watch, then went to the balcony door and rapped lightly on the glass with one knuckle.

Startled, Paul Mallory turned, a surprised look on his face. Cooper crooked a finger, ordering him inside. Mallory obeyed.

'The meeting is over,' Cooper said. 'We should be getting back to the airport.'

'Yes,' Mallory said. He skirted the table where Rhinelander sat smoking and picked up the polished metal case containing the ISA equipment.

'Find anything with that?' Rhinelander asked. Mallory shook his head. 'Nothing,' he said.

'I didn't think so.' Rhinelander turned to Cooper. 'Before you leave Barbados, try the seafood platter at the Voyager Restaurant in the airport. It's quite good and there's no meal on the flight to Miami.'

'Thanks for the advice, we'll do that,' Cooper answered. He extended his hand to Rhinelander; it was ignored. 'We'll be in touch,' he said lamely.

A few moments later the two men had gone, leaving Rhinelander sitting alone in the room. He waited, smoking quietly, giving them time to call for a taxi from the manager's office on the main floor. After two cigarettes and a quarter of an hour he stood, turned off the lights and left room 13, locking the door behind him.

Entering number 14 he retrieved the tape machine and pulled off the hearing aid attachment. He rewound the tape and listened for a moment. The bugging device had picked up everything clearly; he had his insurance policy.

Slipping the tape into the pocket of his jeans he went to the balcony and stepped outside. Three floors below, the pool was a shimmering blue rectangle, glowing eerily, empty at this hour of the night. Faint sounds of laughter and conversation wafted up from the restaurant, and in the distance he could hear the faint pummelling echo of the waves as they struck the beach.

The tape had been essential, the covert insurance vitally important, especially now, knowing about the operation Cooper was planning. There was no way in the world a man like that would leave anything to chance. Somewhere out there Cooper had a back-up, blind to the operation itself, hired to clean up loose ends when it was done, win or lose.

Rhinelander stared down at the pool, thinking about the reef. That was over now; Cooper had discovered it, destroyed it for him. So he really had no choice now. He'd see if the operation was feasible and if it was he'd do it. If he survived, then he'd become someone else again, go somewhere else again, and this time he'd go forever.

CHAPTER NINE

Sergei Kuryokhin tightened the knot of his tie around his thin, wrinkled throat, idly glancing out the third floor window of his apartment on Moscow's Zhdanova Street. A bright sun was pouring down from a clear sky, and it was warm too, judging by the light summer clothes worn by the few pedestrians on the street below. It was after nine and the early morning crowds heading for the Metro station on Dzerzhinski Square had long since thinned and vanished. Taking a deep breath the white-haired, slightly stooped old man smiled happily. The apartment he had occupied for the better part of forty years was above the Sardine Café, and today, by the succulent odours wafting through the vents, it appeared that they were making *pyelmeni*, spiced, meat-filled dumplings usually served in a vegetable broth. Before going to work he would place an order to be set aside for his dinner that evening. He shrugged on the jacket of his Bond Street tailored three-piece suit, decades out of date, and examined himself in the mirror hanging from his closet door. An old man, certainly, there was no escaping that, but a dapper old man, by god!

Kuryokhin twisted a Lucky Strike into his old fashioned amber holder and lit it with the Strategic Air Command Zippo lighter he'd confiscated from the U-2 pilot, Francis Gary Powers, in 1960. The elderly man took a long indulgent drag and smiled. *Pyelmeni*. A good omen for the day.

Leaving his attic-like apartment Kuryokhin placed his order with the café owner, then crossed the narrow street and went in through the main entrance of the five-storey Hotel Berlin. It was another benefit of his apartment's location; the Berlin was a hotel for foreign tourists and he could buy his Lucky Strikes at the kiosk there, using hard currency.

Cigarettes purchased, Kuryokhin went back out into the sunshine, blinking behind the thick lenses of his spectacles. Humming a tuneless melody he walked the short block to Dzerzhinski Square and the Metro.

As Chief of the KGB First Department of the First Chief Directorate Kuryokhin certainly rated one of the big Chaika sedans with the MOC licence plates and a driver to go with it, but he preferred public transportation. Any KGB driver he used would probably be spying for someone else, automobiles could be bugged, and anyway, he enjoyed the fifteen-minute ride beneath the River Moskva and Leninsky Prospekt.

His train was almost empty except for a few ancient *babushki*, their thick gnarled fingers gripping the handles of innumerable *sumka*, the inevitable paper and plastic shopping bags carried by the well-prepared Muscovite consumer. As the train headed deeper into the southern suburbs, it emptied even more and by the time Kuryokhin reached the Belyaevo station he had the car to himself.

He left the subway at the next stop, Tyeply Shtan, the blandly named 'Warm Field' which the First Chief Directorate had adopted as its headquarters. The Tyeply Shtan Metro station above ground was a small, modern, glass and steel edifice just inside the K Ring Road on Trade Union Street. There was no other building within five hundred yards. As usual, one of the dark-green minibuses was waiting just outside the station, its sole purpose to ferry First Chief Directorate personnel to and from the Metro station.

Flashing his pass, Kuryokhin boarded the bus and a moment later they were in motion. A narrow road led west into what appeared to be an isolated pine forest. Ignoring the no smoking sign Kuryokhin lit another Lucky Strike, enjoying the pastoral scenery, knowing that it would soon vanish. Abruptly the bus entered a huge clearing. In its centre, rising above the trees like some alien artifact, was the real Tyeply Shtan, a nine-storeyed building constructed in three wings. There were a further six storeys underground, including the hardened bomb shelter, and the flat roofs of all three wings sprouted a forest of telecommunication antennae. The building had space for fifteen thousand employees.

The minibus stopped at the bleak main entrance to the building. Kuryokhin thanked the driver pleasantly.

Once inside the building, Kuryokhin headed for the lift and his meeting with Baklinov, his man on the Washington Desk, in the 'Egg'.

The Egg, like its counterparts in most major embassies and intelligence installations, was a room-sized capsule invulnerable to any and all surveillance procedures. As well as being insulated, both physically and electronically, the interior of the chamber was also swept prior to each meeting, as were all those people in attendance. The Tyeply Shtan capsule was located ninety-two feet underground, next to the bomb shelter.

The elevator doors opened on the B-6 level and Kuryokhin stepped out into a small vestibule manned by a uniformed officer. He showed his pass, then turned right, following a narrow corridor to the large, copper-lined room housing the Egg. There was a guard in civilian clothes. He ushered Kuryokhin through a heavy, rubber-edged door, then shut it, confining the First Department Chief in a small, steel-walled airlock. A few seconds later the door at the other end of the tiny room opened and he stepped into the Egg.

The chamber was twenty feet long and twelve wide, just big enough to accommodate the oak conference table and a dozen chairs. The walls were made of a black plastic substance, the floors were thickly carpeted in dark blue and the only light came from four recessed panels in the ceiling. In addition to the basic furniture there was a portable paper shredder and a water cooler. The overall effect was sombre and slightly claustrophobic. Each time he entered the secured area Kuryokhin felt as though he were being buried alive.

Baklinov was waiting for him, seated to one side of the armchair at the head of the table. The man was of medium height and broad-shouldered, his dark hair receding on both sides to form a long widow's peak. At forty-two the jowled, thick-browed man looked more like a wrestler than an intelligence officer with an academic background.

Kuryokhin sat down at the head of the table, pulling a large, cut glass ashtray closer to him. He glanced at his wristwatch. Ten-thirty and he'd only had three cigarettes since awakening; the indomitable Dr Trepov would be pleased. He rewarded himself by plunging a fourth Lucky Strike into his holder and lighting it.

'Well?' he asked, turning to Baklinov.

'It concerns the report from General Gurenko,' replied the Washington Desk Controller. 'There have been developments.'

'Go on.'

'Travkin, the GRU Deputy Resident, was seen boarding a flight to Barbados in the Caribbean. He returned some twenty-four hours later.'

'A brief vacation,' Kuryokhin murmured, puffing on his cigarette.

'When it was discovered that he'd gone Gurenko had a watch put on the airport. There was a late night flight from Barbados and there was a possibility Travkin might be returning on it. As it turned out he wasn't, but according to Gurenko's surveillance team Hudson Cooper was on board the flight, along with his executive assistant, a man named Mallory.'

'Interesting.' Kuryokhin nodded. He slouched down in the chair, eyes half closed, the cigarette in its holder pointing up to the ceiling. 'The presumption, I suppose, is that Travkin had a meeting with Cooper in Barbados.'

'I can't think of anything else.' Baklinov shrugged. 'I'd say he was being turned.'

'With a man of Cooper's stature as case officer?' Kuryokhin scoffed. 'Possible, perhaps, but highly unlikely.'

'What if Travkin specifically asked for Cooper?' Baklinov suggested.

'Why would he do that?' Kuryokhin asked, sitting forward. 'And more importantly, once asked, why would Cooper respond?' The question hung in the air for a long moment.

Finally, frowning, Baklinov spoke up hesitantly. 'Because he had something to offer?' the husky man suggested.

'Indeed.' Kuryokhin nodded. One-handed, he pinched the cigarette out of its holder, stubbing out the remains in the ashtray. 'I wonder what?' The old man pursed his lips thoughtfully. 'We need links. Puzzle pieces.'

'In his initial report comrade General Gurenko brought up the possibility of *Osin*,' Baklinov said delicately. Kuryokhin shook his head.

'Autumn is not a factor in this,' he said slowly. 'There is no way that Travkin could know anything about him.' Without thinking the old man took out another cigarette and placed it in the holder. Bringing up the subject of the tapeworm was undoubtedly the reason behind Baklinov's request for a meeting in the Egg. Only a dozen people within the KGB knew about the deep cover agent, and fewer than half that number knew the code name.

Autumn had been Kuryokhin's asset from the beginning, going back to his days as KGB Resident in Budapest. Since then he had nurtured the agent's rise to prominence within the United States intelligence community. The old man lit his cigarette, clamping down on the worn amber holder with his teeth. Autumn was his insurance policy, the jewel in the crown of his achievements, and any thought that he might have been compromised was deeply disturbing.

'What about Travkin's interest in this man from the military hospital?' Baklinov suggested. 'Could there be a connection?'

'Perhaps.' Kuryokhin nodded. 'But we need to know more. A list of patients treated by this man Barron, for example.'

'That should be easy enough,' Baklinov responded. He paused, then spoke again. 'I assume that the surveillance on comrade Colonel Travkin should be maintained.'

'Certainly,' said Kuryokhin, smiling thinly, grey eyes pale behind his spectacles. 'But suggest to Gurenko that he try his best to keep from stepping on the toes of Gennaddi Koslov. We have troubles enough without rousing that old bear.'

'Of course,' Baklinov answered, inclining his head slightly. He stood up, aware that the meeting was over, and left.

'Interesting,' the old man said quietly to himself. 'But why Barbados?' He sat for a few minutes, thinking hard, digging into his recent memory. Something he'd heard, or read about in a monthly status report. Finally he had it. He rose from his chair and headed for the airlock door. To confirm his suspicion he'd have to see Lemesh, his opposite number in the Second Department, handling Central America.

William Arnold Ruppelt, Director of the FBI's REDNET programme, sat behind his desk and listened attentively as Stephen Stone and Mort Kessler brought him up to date on the Travkin surveillance. Ruppelt was the ideal Bureau man; happily married with three children and a rancher-split in McLean, Virginia, he'd worked his way methodically up through the FBI bureaucracy, going from one Field Office to the next, slowly building up brownie points, taking night courses, attending special seminars and reading all the right books. He even looked like an FBI man; slim, tall, invariably dressed in a navy or dark grey suit, wingtip shoes, conservatively cut hair in salt and pepper and bifocals for the *Washington Post*.

Behind Ruppelt an air-conditioner wheezed noisily in the high, narrow window. Outside the July sun streamed mercilessly down out of a hazy blue sky. Stone grimaced; no wonder Congress began winding down as the first cherry blossoms began to fall. The city really was unfit for human habitation between mid-June and late August.

'I'm not sure I see where all of this is going,' Ruppelt said as Stone finished his briefing. 'Is this man Travkin going over to the Company?'

'Appearances would seem to suggest that.' Stone nodded. He shifted uncomfortably in his seat. Ruppelt's wife Connie had done the decorating in his office and it was full of low, leather and chrome furniture that suited neither the high-ceilinged nineteenth-century architecture of the building, nor the 1950s personality of her husband.

'But why Barbados?' Ruppelt asked, frowning.

'We think we've got that figured,' put in Kessler. 'Central Intelligence has no mandate to operate within the United States; Barbados makes the whole thing kosher.'

'But it's still poaching,' Stone insisted hotly. 'Travkin's no walk-in. He's GRU Deputy Resident for Washington and New York – that's our turf and Cooper knows it; we advise the Agency of our activities through the Interagency Committee, that's by Presidential Directive. He knows Travkin is ours.'

'Perhaps Travkin came to him,' Ruppelt said placatingly. 'We have no control over that. The question we should be addressing is why.'

'It has to be the Cabrera thing,' said Kessler, glancing over at Stone.

'Cabrera?' Ruppelt asked. 'Francisco Cabrera, the President of Costa Rica?'

'That's right,' Stone said. He hadn't wanted to bring the subject up until he was sure, but Mort was right to mention it now; another five minutes and Ruppelt would have thrown in the towel and given Travkin up without a fight.

'I'm not sure I understand,' Ruppelt said. 'What does Costa Rica have to do with this?'

'Costa Rica is just about bankrupt,' Stone explained. 'For the past year or so Cabrera has been playing footsies with the Soviets. Rumour has it he's offering them a Pacific port in exchange for all sorts of aid. State knows about it and they've been backing someone named Juan José Morazan. He's Chief of the Policia Nacional. Five thousand men, American trained and armed. It's what passes for an army in Costa Rica.'

'I still don't see,' Ruppelt said.

'We found something interesting when we went after Dr Barron's patient list,' Stone continued. 'Three days before Dr Barron died Morazan was at Walter Reed for some fairly serious abdominal surgery. State brought him up from San José as a courtesy; I think Morazan is a West Point graduate, or something. It was kept pretty hush-hush: nothing in the papers. Anyway, as Senior Resident Medical Officer, Barron was given overall control of the case, even though he wasn't doing the surgery or anything else.' Stone let it hang, hoping that Ruppelt would make the association on his own. He didn't.

'Go on.'

'Morazan is seventy-one. From what I've been able to find out that makes him a prime candidate for this Creuzfeldt-Jacob's disease Travkin was so interested in. If Morazan is on the verge of going into some sort of Alzheimer's state that makes it a whole new ball game for State, and for any kind of covert action Cooper might have had planned to install him as the new Presidente.'

'It also throws a new light on Barbados,' added Kessler, sitting foward in his chair. 'There's a good chance of a third party being present at the meeting. Someone from Costa Rica.'

'Do Dr Barron's records show any sign of the disease being present in Morazan?' Ruppelt asked.

'Impossible to say one way or the other.' Stone shrugged. 'Walter Reed won't tell us a thing, and we can't get any kind of court order because officially it's a Military Reservation.'

'Maybe we should ask Travkin,' Kessler put in, his voice sour. The red-headed agent was clearly frustrated by the whole thing. 'He seems to have better connections at Walter Reed than we do.'

'I think we should back off the whole operation for a while,' Ruppelt said calmly. 'We don't want to tread on the Company's toes.'

'Why not?' Stone shot back. 'Cooper's treading on ours.'

'That remains to be seen,' said Ruppelt. He stood up, planting his palms flat on the desk in front of him, signalling the end of the meeting. 'For the time being I'd like you to leave it alone. I'll bring the case up privately with Cooper at the next Interagency meeting.'

'When is that?' Stone asked. Ruppelt leaned forward and flipped through the large, leather-covered diary on his desk.

'Two weeks today,' he said finally, looking up.

'Wonderful,' Stone sighed, standing. 'So what are we supposed to do for the next fourteen days?'

'At last count there were several hundred Soviet registered aliens in Washington,' Ruppelt answered blandly. 'Perhaps they might deserve some of your attention?'

'Come on, Stef,' Kessler said, knowing when they were beaten and heading for the door. 'Let's go catch some commies.'

A few minutes later the two men regrouped in Stephen Stone's office. Mort Kessler had taken a brief sidetrip down to the canteen, returning with a plate of microwaved Danish and two big mugs of coffee. Ignoring the hot, soggy rounds of jam-smeared pastry, Stone lit a Camel Light and sipped at his coffee.

'So now what do we do?' he asked, glancing at Kessler, seated on the other side of the desk.

The red-haired agent lifted his shoulders wearily. 'I hate to say it, but the Roop is right. Dimitri Alexandyr isn't the only game in town. We've got at least a dozen of Gurenko's boys and girls trolling for goodies in every bar around the Beltway, and we still haven't finished up with the list of known illegals working for Travkin and Koslov. Just tagging the new fish from the last Embassy rollover in January could keep us going all summer.'

'Statistical work,' Stone grunted. 'Glorified filing.'

'That's the kind of thing Ruppelt likes,' Kessler answered. 'He's a slogger. Does things by the book.' The agent made a snorting sound and took a bite out of his strawberry Danish, then spoke around the mouthful. 'The last thing he wants is some kind of glitz and glamour operation. He'd crap if he ever saw his name in *Time* magazine.'

'There are eighty-six people working out of this place,' Stone answered. 'They follow people, take pictures of people and listen to people. I'm supposed to co-ordinate all that and report to Ruppelt. That's what the book says.'

'So?' Kessler asked.

'So that's what I do most of the time,' Stone said bitterly. 'You know as well as I do that we're a watchdog operation, and we do it pretty damn well, but every once in a while we get a Dimitri Alexandyr Travkin.'

'A player.'

'Exactly,' Stone said, poking the air with his cigarette. 'Someone who's playing the game. A challenge. And he's on to something, Mort, I can smell it from a mile off. He's on to something and we're going to miss it.'

'You think the Roop is going to hand off Dimitri to Cooper?' Kessler asked.

'Of course.' Stone nodded. 'It avoids a confrontation and gives him a few brownie points.'

'So what do we do about it?' asked Kessler. 'Buck the system?'

Stone sat back in his chair, the mechanism squeaking. Eight agencies and thirteen committees of the National Foreign Intelligence Board handled counterintelligence procedures in the United States and abroad. Like everything else in Washington, the question of counterintelligence was a political and logistical maze that seemed made for professional bureaucrats like William Ruppelt. It had not, however, been created for Stephen Stone.

He knew exactly where he stood within the Bureau; his only promotional opportunity was to take over from Ruppelt, a position he neither wanted nor would be given. At forty he knew his career was blocked, so when push came to shove he had very little to lose. The choice was clear: play Ruppelt's game and back off, or be the cop he wanted to be and go after Travkin. Stone sat forward in his chair again.

'It would be risky,' he said at last. 'Cooper is Deputy Director of Operations. That's a nice euphemism for covert action. He wouldn't be handling Travkin personally unless the stakes were very high. The whole thing smells really political to me.'

'You think it's more than Cabrera?' Kessler said, filching one of Stone's cigarettes.

'I think if we dig much deeper we're going to find ourselves up to our necks in stuff we might not want to know about,' Stone warned. 'If we keep going we're going to have to do it very, very quietly.'

'That can be arranged.' Kessler grinned. 'You're the Deputy Director. Come up with an operation, give it a code name for the file jacket and make me Special Agent in Charge. I'll put a group of people together who can keep their mouths shut. The Roop knows I'm a floater so he won't notice if I'm not around for a while.'

'This could get us into trouble,' Stone said quietly. 'A lot of trouble.'

'Is that an out you're offering?' Kessler asked.

'I suppose so.'

'Screw it,' answered the red-haired agent with a broad smile. 'Anything beats counting Eastern Bloc heads coming off the Aeroflots at Dulles.' He butted his cigarette and took another from Stone's pack. 'So what are we going to call this operation anyway? It should be something nice and bland for the Roop.'

'I'll check,' Stone said, turning in his chair and booting up his computer terminal. Like every other division of the FBI, REDNET used a book of file code names selected randomly by computer, then arranged in alphabetical order. As a name was used the file name was removed from the book.

'What is it?' asked Kessler, watching as Stone jotted down a name from the screen.

'Couldn't be better,' Stone answered, keying off the machine. 'The title for the file is BACK DOOR.'

On the other side of the city Dimitri Travkin was seated at an umbrella-topped table in the courtyard café of the Georgetown Four Seasons, enjoying a frosty, mid-afternoon glass of iced tea. The open area was almost empty except for a few late lunchers, most of the hotel's guests preferring the air-conditioned confines of Aux Beaux Champs, or high tea in the plushly decorated lobby. Dressed in a lightweight, off-white Armani suit and wearing his favourite pair of Serengeti Driver sunglasses Travkin was the quintessential Four Seasons type and with proper Washingtonian politesse, no one paid him the slightest attention except the waiter, hoping for a better than average tip.

Sipping his iced tea the GRU Colonel tried to concentrate on the sheet of notes in front of him, making a vain attempt at giving his thoughts some kind of order before he went back to the SMO on Belmont Road to brief Koslov on the Barbados trip, something he'd managed to avoid for the past twenty-four hours. He sighed, then lit a cigarette. On top of everything else he was being followed and that was worrying him.

The surveillance itself wasn't the problem, he was used to Stone's REDNET squads tracking him, and he knew that Gurenko's people sometimes had him on watch as well, but Stone's FBI and Gurenko's KGB followed set patterns and routines that were as recognisable as they were easy to shrug off. Neither Stone nor Gurenko made any real attempt to keep their tracking covert. They knew Travkin was a player in the game and let it go at that, their surveillance nothing more than flag-waving, a method of letting him know that he wasn't the only wolf in Washington walking around in sheep's clothing.

This was different. The team working his movements today had been top-flight professionals and if it hadn't been for a few very minor errors, Travkin never would have noticed he was being tailed. Even so, it was almost noon before he realised, and it took him another hour to identify his watchers. By the time he'd made his way to the Four Seasons he was positive that the men were neither FBI or KGB. The cars were wrong, the clothes were wrong, and so were the routines and patterns.

So who were they, and why the sudden interest? The average American, when he thought about it at all, might be able to name four or five intelligence organisations but Travkin knew better. At last count there were twenty-four *American* intelligence organisations operating in Washington. On top of that there were at least fifty-seven foreign intelligence groups operating within the DC area, from the United Kingdom's SIS to Japan's Naicho and the Italians' SISMI. Travkin knew that any one of these groups might be on his tail, but why?

Washington was a dead issue during the summer months, it was a time for staff rotations, holidays and make-work projects. Except for the regular servicing of his sources and agents the only thing he was working on that was of any interest was the Walter Reed information. Could that be it? He frowned, drawing hard on his cigarette, then glanced down at the list again. Just what did he have?

According to Scanlon, his file-clerk source at the Military Hospital, Barron had requested information relating to Creuzfeldt-Jacob disease two night before his 'accidental' death. Late the following day the telephone billing computer at Walter Reed listed a Maryland to DC call. The number turned out to be that of Hudson Cooper, DDO for the CIA. Digging a little deeper Travkin had used another source, this one in the telephone company, to get him a print-out of any calls made from Cooper's regularly listed number at the Watergate for that same evening.

There were four outgoing calls that could be traced; two were made to 703–482–1100, the main number for the Central Intelligence Agency, one to Cooper's office number in DC and the fourth to Hollis Macintyre, an old guard pork barrel politician who'd been edged out of the Tucker administration. There was clearly a direct connection between Barron and Cooper, but that seemed to be as far as it went.

The oddest piece in the puzzle was Cooper's sudden trip to Barbados with his assistant, Paul Mallory. Unless he was having some sort of oddball gay affair with his assistant, Cooper had gone to the Caribbean island on Agency business, and had done so clandestinely, travelling on a bogus diplomatic passport.

There was nothing evidential to tie the Barron telephone call to the brief Barbados sortie, but Travkin had acted on instinct and followed them. The trip had turned out to be almost a total loss which was one of the reasons he'd been avoiding Koslov's wrath; justifying an overnight flight to the Caribbean on the monthly expense lists sent back to Moscow wasn't going to be easy.

He'd arrived in Barbados less than ninety minutes after Cooper and Mallory, catching a direct BWIA flight from Dulles. After discreetly spreading around some hard currency and a few plausible lies he managed to discover that Cooper and Mallory had arrived in Barbados, then taken a taxi to a mid-priced apartment hotel called the Tropicana Court. The taxi-driver, a middle-aged Bajan named Leon Blaize, remembered his 'assified' passengers, although the night manager at the Tropicana did not.

After some delicate prodding about whom the two men might have been visiting, the manager came up with a name and a description: John Duncan, a Canadian. The man had rented two apartments side by side, but apparently had made no use of either. According to the manager Duncan was dark-haired, tanned like someone who'd spent a lot of time in the tropics, in good shape and probably in his early or mid forties. He'd paid for both rooms in cash.

More money changed hands and Travkin was given the keys to rooms 13 and 14. Thirteen was sterile but its next door neighbour was a little more interesting. Travkin discovered the neatly cut hole in the party wall almost immediately and matched it to the pinhole under the electrical outlet next door. Thirteen had been bugged, probably by the anonymous Mr Duncan. After six hours of dozing in a plastic seat at Grantley Adams and another four on the flight back to Washington, Dimitri Travkin still hadn't come up with an answer that made any sense.

On the other hand, the list he'd picked up from Scanlon's dead-drop earlier that day appeared to provide a clue. Travkin stared at the piece of paper on the table in front of him. One name jumped out: Juan José Morazan, Chief of Costa Rica's Policia Nacional, a 5,000 man elite force that combined army, federal police and secret police in one tidy package.

According to the most recent intelligence reports he'd read, Morazan was the chief threat to the semi-secret, open port negotiations the Costa Rican government was having with Moscow, and the likely figurehead for a CIA- backed coup. According to Scanlon's list, Morazan had been brought to Walter Reed for abdominal surgery and Barron had been the doctor of record.

Travkin lifted his glass, draining the last of the iced tea. He sucked an ice cube from the glass and cracked it thoughtfully between his teeth. Morazan was old, a good candidate for Creuzfeldt-Jacob disease. With their figurehead gone, how could the CIA control the Policia Nacional? A potential problem with a major Central American coup attempt was certainly enough to bring a man like Cooper out of the woodwork, and the Costa Rica connection made Barbados a little easier to understand. But where did the 'Canadian', John Duncan, fit in, and why had he seen fit to secretly record his meeting with Cooper and Mallory? The GRU Colonel checked his watch: three-fifteen; time to play the game.

He stood, reaching into the breast pocket of his jacket, and took out his wallet. He dropped a five-dollar bill on the table, then began threading his way through the maze of empty tables. Out of the corner of his eye he spotted one of his tails beginning to move. Medium height, well-groomed and wearing a neatly tailored grey suit. Mirrored sunglasses and highly polished black dress shoes. Definitely not KGB and too short for the FBI. Travkin had mentally tagged him as 'Brooks Brother'. If things were going true to form, 'Seersucker' and 'Moustache' would be waiting in the lobby. The two in the lobby had been driving a dark blue late model Thunderbird. If he walked, 'Brooks Brother' would follow, aided by another two-man team outside. Good, but not good enough.

Dimitri Travkin hadn't chosen the Four Seasons randomly. With parking at a premium in the Georgetown area, the hotel offered valet service for those who could afford it, bringing the cars up from their underground lot. Arriving at the lobby entrance an hour or so before, Travkin had slipped the driver ten dollars above the parking fee, promising another ten if he brought the car up to the entrance at exactly three-fifteen. Even if Seersucker and Moustache were right on his heels it would take at least three or four minutes to bring their car up, and by then he'd be long gone. The stunt wouldn't do much in the long run, but at least it would flush the watchers, announcing that he knew they were there.

The valet parking attendant had been true to his word and Travkin's dark green embassy Chevrolet was waiting at the curb, engine running. He palmed a folded ten dollar bill into the young man's hand, slid behind the wheel and took off, wheeling the car around the brick clock tower in front of the hotel and cutting into the traffic on M Street. A few seconds later he bullied his way through the intersection at 29th Avenue and headed north, making for Q Street and the Dumbarton Bridge over Rock Creek Parkway. He'd lost them, for now, anyway.

PART TWO

'I have no enemies. Why should I fear?'

William McKinley

CHAPTER TEN

Eric Rhinelander arrived at Miami International Airport on an Eastern Airlines flight from Kingston, Jamaica. He wore a plain, dark blue suit, carried two rust-coloured, canvas-sided suitcases and used a Canadian passport identifying him as John Duncan. According to the passport he had been born in Toronto, Ontario, 22 March 1943 and his profession was listed as 'freelance journalist'. The passport had been originally issued in November of 1967 and first renewed in May of 1972. Since that time, conforming to Canadian immigration law, the passport had been renewed every five years. The passport and the documents that went with it were authentic. Duncan really had been a freelance journalist, working out of Saigon. The young man had been killed along with eight other innocent bystanders in a bicycle bomb explosion at a sidewalk café.

Following the established practice of those days, Duncan's hotel room had been cleaned out by professional thieves within a few hours of his death and his personal effects, including clothes, wallet, a Nikon camera, an Olivetti Lettera 22 typewriter and a passport, had been put on the black market.

Normally, bureaucratic process rendered personal documentation useless after a relatively short period of time, but in Duncan's case he had neither next of kin nor a full time employer, so the passport was never cancelled by the Canadian government. Rhinelander had purchased the passport and wallet while in Cambodia in 1971, then renewed the passport at the Canadian Embassy in Bangkok, Thailand, in 1972, using the birth certificate from Duncan's wallet as proof of identity and providing a new set of passport photographs, these ones showing him with a full beard.

Since then he had renewed the passport within six months of its expiry date, always providing new photographs. Rhinelander used the passport only for travel, preferring to develop separate identities while working on a project, keeping the Duncan name in abeyance until it was time to leave, or in case of an emergency.

Given the present situation, Rhinelander knew that the value of the Duncan persona was just about finished. Mallory had broken his cover in Paris and managed to reach him in Jamaica. Beyond that, the project at hand made the adoption of a new personality imperative. John Duncan,

vaporised on a Saigon sidewalk more than twenty years before, was about to
vanish again.

After using a hospitality phone to book himself a room at the Fountainbleu, Rhinelander eventually extricated himself from the steady current of
people that ebbed and flowed throughout the enormous concourse and
reached a cab stand. Fifteen minutes later he was on his way into Miami
in air-conditioned comfort. When the driver, a Cubano from Little Havana,
tried to start up a conversation, Rhinelander answered in German and the
trip was completed in silence.

The Fountainbleu, an enormous beachfront hotel with 1200 rooms, was
exactly what Rhinelander wanted: complete anonymity at a hundred and
fifty dollars a night.

He crossed the monumental lobby with its trademark chandeliers, checked
in, arranged for a rented car and went up to his room. It was small, plain and
ordinary, with a view of the Atlantic Ocean and the sunlit beach eighteen
floors down. He ordered coffee and a copy of the *Miami Herald* from room
service and spent a few minutes unpacking. Most of the clothes had been
purchased in Jamaica, and although Rhinelander had long ago taken care
to have any identifying tags removed, the clothes, like Duncan's passport,
would soon vanish.

The coffee and newspaper arrived as Rhinelander was unpacking the last
of his things. He took both to the small table beside the window, lit a cigarette
and got down to work. Turning to the birth and death announcements he
began going through the obituaries.

In Frederick Forsyth's *The Day of the Jackal*, the nameless assassin
manufactured a new identity by applying for a passport in the name of a
person who had died in infancy. The plot further depended on a variety
of bureaucratic oversights as well as some simplistic security measures at
a variety of international airports and border crossings. Rhinelander, who
had enjoyed the bestseller enormously when it was published, realised that
the Jackal's days, if they had ever existed at all, were long gone.

To follow Forsyth's scenario for creating a new identity now would be an
invitation to disaster; computerisation and centralisation of records had seen
to that. The scenario was also unnecessarily complicated; there were easier
and less time-consuming ways of providing yourself with a brand new name,
rank and serial number.

Rhinelander found three likely candidates in the death notices. The most
promising was the obituary of a man named Holt.

> HOLT, GAVIN. Suddenly, at the age of forty-three in Miami. Only
> child of George and Elvira Gavin of Valdosta, Wisconsin, who
> predeceased him. Friends may call at Baxter and Styles Funeral Home,

3205 NW 11th Avenue. Funeral Service at 2 p.m. 17 July, cremation and interment to follow at Southern Memorial Park Cemetery, 151 St. NE, North Miami. In lieu of flowers donations to the American Heart Association will be gratefully accepted.

Checking the Miami telephone directory Rhinelander saw only one G Holt, with an address on Biscayne Boulevard. He dialled the number and let it ring fifteen times without an answer. Mr Holt was definitely not at home. He turned to the yellow pages, found the number for the Southern Memorial Park Cemetery and called. According to their directions the cemetery was a good fifteen miles from the downtown core, almost on the borders of Dade and Broward counties.

Rhinelander glanced at his watch and saw that it was just past 1 p.m. The funeral service would take the better part of an hour, and the slow-moving procession would take almost that long to reach the cemetery. He had a minimum safety margin of three hours and a maximum of five. Good enough. Using the phone once again he called down to the lobby and asked for his car to be brought around, then quickly put on new clothes, dressing in a pair of jeans, sneakers, a white shirt and a lightweight, brown leather bomber jacket.

Change completed, Rhinelander stripped the cases from all four pillows on the queen size bed and packed them into a bright yellow, nylon athletic bag he'd carried in his luggage. He added his Nikon F2 camera, a 250 to 500 mm zoom lens and a pair of thin driving gloves.

Carrying the bag he left the room, locking it carefully behind him, then took the elevator down to the lobby. Pausing briefly he purchased a street atlas for Miami, then stopped again in the flower shop, where he bought a dozen long-stemmed tea roses. Then he picked up his rented car, an air-conditioned, dark blue Pontiac Tempest.

He drove off, pulling to a stop in the parking lot at Indian Beach only a few hundred feet away from the hotel. Turning the air-conditioning up against the blistering heat outside, Rhinelander spent ten minutes examining the detailed street atlas, trying to orient himself.

According to the map, which showed street numbers block by block, Holt's address put him just slightly south of the Dolphin Expressway, facing Bicentennial Park. Use a felt marker, Rhinelander marked the spot. Without haste he undid the ribbon around the box of roses, then emptied the bright red flowers into the trunk. He peeled back the mat over the spare tire, lifted out the jack and put it into the box. Opening the athletic bag he removed the pillowcases and put them into the flower box with the jack.

Holt's address turned out to be a white brick condominium called the Foxfire. The building was rectangular, sixteen storeys high, with both above and below ground parking. Toting the Nikon with its long lens, Rhinelander crossed Biscayne Boulevard and stepped into Bicentennial Park. The large area of grass and trees sloping down to the water was being well used, the pathways filled with mothers pushing strollers and men and women in business clothes on their lunch hours. Among the adults, like brightly coloured fish darting back and forth, kids in bandanas and electric-hued satin shorts skimmed by on roller skates or twisted through the meandering crowds on skateboards.

In the distance Rhinelander could see the jutting masts of boats at the marina adjoining the park. Making his way slowly along one of the pathways he found a park bench and sat down. He spent a few minutes clicking off half a dozen random exposures with the empty Nikon, then turned slightly so that he was facing Biscayne Boulevard and the Foxfire. Bringing a high-powered telescope or binoculars to the park might have excited some interest, but no one paid any attention to a man with a camera.

Squinting through the lens he adjusted the zoom until it was tight on the main door of the building. He panned back and forth slightly, as though looking for a shot, then hit the shutter release. The Foxfire had no doorman, unless he was on a break. The entrance foyer was a blank space between two sets of glass doors with the buzzer-board and mailboxes on the left hand wall. Press half a dozen buttons and someone would probably open up, but if anybody asked questions later, they'd remember.

Rhinelander stood up casually and strolled back up the pathway to the street. He crossed Biscayne, turned left and went through the main doors. Checking the buzzer board he found Gavin Holt's name: 1116. Eleventh floor. Turning away from the inner doors, Rhinelander went back out into the stunning heat, feeling the sweat begin to ooze out of every pore. In Jamaica the heat had been dry, offset by the cooling winds from the sea; here the heat was morbidly oppressive, any breath of air leaving the faint smell of rot in your nostrils. Rhinelander frowned: the sooner he was out of Miami the better.

Returning to the car, he put the camera into the trunk and picked up the beribboned box of 'roses'. He turned onto 10th Street, and again onto NE 1st Avenue, finally reaching the wide alleyway that provided access to the rear of the Foxfire. The back of the property was a mess, overflowing dumpsters waiting to be emptied, the asphalt on the parking lot cracked and repaired a thousand times. There was a dual ramp, one section leading up to the above-ground lot, and one leading down to a battered, chocolate brown metal rolling door. A sign over the garage door warned people to use their key even if the door was open. To the left, halfway down the ramp, there was a pole with a key box jutting out.

Rhinelander walked up the ramp to the above-ground lot, put the flower-box down on the ground and lit a cigarette. Leaning on the guard rail he smoked and waited. Less than five minutes later a car came down the alley, turned onto the down ramp and stopped at the key box. The driver rolled down his window, inserted his key, and a few seconds later there was a creaking, rumbling noise as the garage door rolled up.

As the car moved forward again Rhinelander glanced at his watch and leaned over the railing. The car disappeared into the underground lot and after a short pause, the door began to close. The whole process took twenty-one seconds; plenty of time.

Ten minutes later another car turned down the alley and headed for the ramp. Rhinelander bent down, picked up the flower box and began strolling down the upper ramp. By the time he reached the alleyway, the driver of the second car had already keyed the box. Rhinelander turned and began walking down the alley, listening to the sounds of the door cranking upwards. He did a slow count to ten, giving the vehicle enough time to get into the garage, then turned on his heel and sprinted for the lower ramp. He reached it with time to spare and ducked under the closing door. Squinting in the sudden darkness he saw the tail lights of the car he'd followed.

He waited in the shadows of a concrete pillar, watching as the driver parked, then left his car. The man crossed the lot to a bank of elevators, lit brightly from above by a sulphurous, high intensity spotlight. The security light was a joke since the main illumination for the lot was provided by strips of fluorescents, most of which had burned out.

Rhinelander watched as the elevator arrived and the driver disappeared. He waited another few seconds, then walked forward casually. Anyone coming into the garage now, either from outside or via the elevators, would assume he'd just parked his car. He reached the elevators, punched the up button and waited. A few moments later the light went off, a bell chimed and the doors of the elevator on his right opened. He stepped into the empty cage, tapped the eleventh floor button and adjusted the weight of the flower box.

He rode up without anyone else entering the elevator, then stepped out into the eleventh floor corridor.

Holt's apartment was at the end of the hall, directly opposite the stairwell door. Good, Rhinelander thought, nodding to himself, only one adjoining wall. Without hesitation he pulled the ribbon off the box, opened it and took out the automobile jack and the pillowcases. Forming the pillowcases into two thick pads he lifted the jack, placing it horizontally across the door, the butt end facing the doorframe just above the knob, slipping the folded pillowcases into position between the jack ends and the metal frame. Holding everything in place with one hand he worked the crank on the handle until the jack was firmly wedged against the doorframe. Checking the hallway he began to crank again, grunting with effort as the pressure built.

The technique utilised by the assassin was well known by the security and insurance industries, but rarely mentioned to prospective new home buyers. As Rhinelander knew, modern construction methods leave a lot to be desired. To avoid complications and facilitate volume buying of door and frame combinations, the buck, or hole cut for a door, is often made well oversized, usually by one or two inches.

When the frame and door are installed the space between the edge of the buckhole and the frame is filled with wooden wedges at two or three points, then plastered over. Over a relatively short period of time the wedges loosen after repeated opening and closing of the door, and the frame begins to 'float' in the resulting airspace.

With a jack the frame can be bent outwards into the airspace, and in the case of Holt's door, only three-quarters of an inch was necessary. The Shlage Series B locking unit was quite a good one, with a five pin tumbler and a deadbolt, but its qualities were irrelevant. Forty-two seconds after inserting the jack, Gavin Holt's door literally yawned open all by itself.

With another check down the hall, Rhinelander used the side of his foot to sweep the flower box into the apartment, then hit the jack-release with the heel of his hand. He pulled the jack out of the frame, threw the wadded pillowcases after the flower box and stepped into the apartment himself. He closed the door, holding it shut until the frame settled back into its normal position. He was in. He picked up the jack, pillowcases and flower-box, set them on a low wooden table beside the doorway, then began to explore.

The apartment was large and brightly lit by windows on two sides. To the left of the front door was a narrow, galley-style kitchen and there was a bathroom on the right. Beyond the foyer, directly ahead, was the living room, complete with a balcony looking out over Biscayne Boulevard to the park beyond. There was a master bedroom with an en-suite four piece bathroom between the living room and the dining room with a short hall leading to the wood-panelled den at the corner of the building.

Except for the bathrooms and kitchen the floors throughout the apartment were covered in short-pile dark grey carpeting. The walls were bright white except for the bedroom, which was a deep, almost institutional green. The furniture was industrial-style; black-enamelled pole lamps, leather and chrome chairs and couches, a slab of marble resting on a pastel-painted sonotube. The kitchen was done in deep blue Formica, outfitted with half a dozen high-tech appliances and a gigantic double-doored, jet black refrigerator.

To Rhinelander, the most telling of the rooms was the den. Two walls were taken up by floor to ceiling bookcases, a third held a computer table, pen-plotter drafting table and filing cabinets, while the fourth was mostly window. A quick check of the files and the book titles gave him Gavin Holt's occupation: he was an architect, specialising in medium size and small medical institutions like clinics, rest homes and walk-in dental suites. Flipping through some of the files Rhinelander saw that Holt had an office address in the CenTrust Tower. From the quality of the furnishings and the sophisticated at-home computer array it was clear that he had been doing well.

In a folder tabbed 'personal banking' he found a neatly typed list of code numbers for half a dozen credit and cash cards as well as bank statements and credit card receipts. According to the receipts all the cards were up to date. Rhinelander copied the code numbers down on a sheet of paper from a scratch pad on the desk and slipped it into his pocket. There was also a file marked 'legal', but there was no evidence of a will. If Holt had died intestate his affairs would be handled by a Dade County Public Trustee, turning the resolution of the dead man's estate into a lengthy bureaucratic process that could take weeks or even months. Rhinelander nodded to himself, pleased.

Holt's attache case was stowed neatly between the drafting table and filing cabinets. Opening it, Rhinelander discovered trade magazines, an address book, several pens and, in a rear pocket, Holt's passport. Turning to the first page Rhinelander stared at the dead man's photograph. Thin-faced with a narrow moustache and balding; no resemblance, but the description was reasonably close: hair – dark brown, eyes – blue, height – 6'1". With a new photograph carefully removed from the Duncan passport it would do well enough. Rhinelander put the passport back in the pocket of the attache case, added a few random pages from the filing cabinet and some books from the shelves on the far wall, then closed the case, taking it with him to the bedroom.

Rhinelander went through the room slowly and methodically, his methods based on long experience. The bedroom cupboard, half the length of the room, with mirrored doors, revealed a dozen tailor made suits and half that many sports jackets. Shelves above held shirts, folded and wrapped in plastic, printed with the name of a local dry cleaner. Below the hanging suits and jackets was a row of shoes from Florsheim wingtips to tennis shoes. The cupboard also held a bagged set of golf clubs, a pair of dumb bells and a leather racket bag. The racket bag held a Slazenger squash racket, a can of balls and a pair of expensive looking protective goggles. There was no sign of wear on the racket handgrip, and the can of balls was still sealed. On the other hand, the golf clubs had obviously seen long use.

He began going through the inner and outer pockets of the suit jackets, hitting paydirt on the second one in from the left. A ring of keys and Gavin Holt's wallet complete with credit cards, driver's licence, social security card, library card from the main branch at the Metro-Dade Cultural Center and the pink slip for a 1957 Austin Healey sports car. Wallet in hand, Rhinelander turned and looked around the room, remembering the obituary.

Donations to the Heart Association. Holt had probably died in the apartment, victim of a heart attack. Friend, neighbour or co-worker had discovered the body and made the funeral arrangements. You don't need ID to check into a funeral home and as far as Rhinelander knew, people weren't buried carrying their wallets. The same was true of the passport. The chances were good that the wallet and its contents wouldn't be missed for some time, if at all.

He shoved the billfold into the hip pocket of his jeans and continued his search. Gold Dunhill lighter with the initials GH, matchbook from Joe's Stone Crab in Miami Beach, half a roll of spearmint Lifesavers and a Cross ballpoint done in brushed steel. Rhinelander took it all. Search complete he pulled out the golf bag and a large, black, hard-bodied suitcase from the interior of the cupboard.

Rhinelander snapped open the Samsonite and flipped it onto the bed. He dumped the contents of Holt's other pockets into the suitcase, then went back to the cupboard. Checking the sizes on the shirt collars he saw that they'd fit and tossed half a dozen into the suitcase. He then went through the man's chest of drawers and added jockeys, dark socks, two pairs of cufflinks and several folded handkerchiefs. Both handkerchiefs and cufflinks were initialled like the lighter.

With his foraging done Rhinelander closed the suitcase and took a last look around the room. Everything was as it had been. Satisfied, he picked up the suitcase and hefted the golf bag, taking them both to the foyer. He glanced at his watch. Two-thirty: he'd been in the apartment for slightly more than half an hour; still plenty of time. He went back to the den, sat down at Holt's desk, and rummaged through the drawers until he found a Miami-Dade telephone directory.

According to the phone book the Florida Department of Motor Vehicles office was located in the Metro-Dade Center on NE 1st Street. He punched out the number and after three different referrals he had the information he wanted. In the case of a lost driver's licence, a replacement could be provided on the spot as long as you had a birth certificate, Social Security number and the original number of the driver's licence that had been lost. Pleased, Rhinelander hung up the telephone and stood up. If things continued to go smoothly he'd have usable photo-ID before the day was out.

Fifteen minutes later, after another check to make sure that the apartment was in order, Rhinelander left the Foxfire, this time using the front door. He had the suitcase in one hand and the golf bag over his shoulder – just another upscale Miamian starting out on a golf vacation. Reaching the car, he opened the trunk, removed the automobile jack from the golf bag and put it back in its proper niche. He put the suitcase and golf bag in the trunk, closed it, then climbed into the car, starting the engine and the air conditioning.

An hour later, his new driver's licence replacing Holt's old one, Rhinelander headed back to Miami Beach and the Fontainbleu Hotel.

The following morning Rhinelander returned the rented Tempest, checked out of the hotel and took the airport shuttle to Miami International. Using one of the pay toilet booths on the arrivals level he carefully destroyed all his John Duncan ID, including the passport, then flushed the remnants into oblivion.

He returned to the crowded concourse and went to the Citibank cash machine where he inserted Holt's Mastercard. He tapped out the code from the list he'd copied and waited. A few moments later two hundred dollars' spat obediently out of the slot. Rhinelander put the cash and the card back into Holt's wallet. If the Mastercard hadn't been cancelled, the other credit cards were probably serviceable as well.

From the cash machine Rhinelander continued down the concourse to the American Express travel booth and purchased three thousand dollars' worth of traveller's cheques – half the maximum allowed on Holt's Gold Card. The transaction went off without any problems. With the traveller's cheques in his wallet he doubled back to the Hertz counter and rented a black, air-conditioned Lincoln Continental.

While he waited for the car to be brought up from the garage Rhinelander jotted down a detailed set of directions given to him by the reservations clerk, along with a complimentary road map of Florida. Five minutes later he was driving east on the Airport Expressway, and fifteen minutes after that he reached the Highway 95 interchange and went north, heading for the next stop on his itinerary: Palm Beach and the Breakers Hotel.

CHAPTER ELEVEN

Washington's Au Pied de Cochon is an authentic French bistro on Wisconsin Avenue between Dumbarton and N Street. There are half a dozen 'authentic' restaurants of one kind or another in the same area, including Aux Fruits de Mer next door and the Georgetown Bar and Grill across the street, but Au Pied is the only one open twenty-four hours a day. The food is cheap and reasonably good, the service is adequate and the quasi-French atmosphere comes complete with a sidewalk patio, zinc bar, checked tablecloths and *café-crème* served up in enormous bowls. It has also been the site of a number of Soviet defections over the years, that fact commemorated by a brass plaque beside the unassuming front entrance.

'The CIA are children,' commented Major-General Gennaddi Koslov. The GRU Resident tore off a piece of his croissant, popped it into his mouth and washed it down with a long swallow of coffee. Squinting in the bright sunlight he watched the early morning tourists parading by a few feet away on the sidewalk side of the patio. He shook his head. 'Yurchenko and his Central Intelligence escort were having dinner here after his so-called defection and the escort just let him walk away.' Koslov laughed heartily and popped another piece of croissant into his mouth. 'He actually walked back to Mount Alto!'

Vitaly Yurchenko, Sergei Kuryokhin's deputy in the First Chief Directorate, had 'defected' in Rome in August 1985. Three months later he redefected, giving a Washington press conference at which he insisted he'd been kidnapped and drugged by the Americans. The incident had been horribly embarrassing to both the CIA and the FBI and a major 'disinformation' coup for Kuryokhin and the KGB.

'I think you underestimate the Agency,' said Travkin, lighting a cigarette and ignoring the bowl of coffee on the table in front of him. 'They simply play by a different set of rules. Yurchenko was supposedly a defector, not a prisoner. The only way his babysitter could have stopped him was by main force.'

'They were fools!' growled Travkin's bull-necked superior. 'The whole thing was an exercise in triple-think. The CIA had spent years trying to track down Kuryokhin's mythical asset within their midst and had come to the conclusion that there was no tapeworm or mole at all. Yurchenko defects, then tells them that they are right. Soon after, Yurchenko returns to the fold, thus negating any information he gave to the CIA. Central Intelligence therefore assumes that Yurchenko was lying and that there really is a tapeworm in their midst. The myth is maintained, the CIA's paranoia increases, and more time, money and effort is wasted trying to track down the nonexistent agent of influence. Absurd!'

'You give comrade Kuryokhin a great deal of credit,' Travkin said.

'Unlimited credit,' Koslov replied. 'Our friend Sergei has taken the fine art of bullshit to new heights.' He shrugged wearily. 'And why not? Considering the fact that with the Central Intelligence Agency and the FBI he has an audience willing to accept any sort of simple-minded twaddle he produces.'

'What about Cooper?' Travkin asked, bringing the conversation back to the subject at hand.

'You give me nothing but a few unconnected facts and suppositions, Dimitri Dimitrovitch,' Koslov answered. 'I'll need more if you expect me to act.' The old man's bushy eyebrows arched and he rubbed a white-whiskered jowl with a thick-fingered hand. 'And frankly, Dimitri, your recent escapade in Barbados does little for your credibility.'

'It was necessary and useful,' Travkin insisted. He pushed his coffee aside and leaned over the table. 'Recent information bears that out.'

'Really?' Koslov replied, acid in his tone. 'Is it information I can use on a budget report to explain your little holiday?'

'Cooper and Mallory went to Barbados where they met with a man named Duncan. The fact that Cooper was personally involved in such a rendezvous is suspect in itself. The operation with Duncan is an important one.'

'Who is this man Duncan?' Koslov asked. 'Do we know anything?'

'According to his passport he is Canadian, a journalist.'

'What does Ottawa have to say about him?'

'I cabled Kamenev, he has illegals in the passport office there as well as their National Revenue department. John Duncan was a freelance journalist who went to Vietnam during the early part of the war. He has renewed the passport several times since then but has never spent any time in the country.'

'So?'

'So this "John Duncan" has not filed an income tax return since 1969.'

'Black market documents?' Koslov asked.

'Presumably. Whatever the case, the man who met with Cooper and Mallory was no freelance journalist.'

'And where is he now?'

'Here,' Travkin answered. 'Or Miami, at any rate. I checked with Intourist; he came in on an Eastern Airlines flight from Kingston, Jamaica, the day before yesterday.'

Tracking Duncan hadn't been difficult: Intourist, the state travel authority, operated like any other travel agency and used Pegasus, the International Association of Travel Agents' reservation computer program. Using Duncan's name and the Caribbean as point of origin, Intourist had come up with the Miami arrival almost instantly. A separate, clandestine program ran behind Pegasus – a 'worm' which effectively blanked out the original request for information.

'So tell me,' said Koslov, leaning back in his chair and lighting an Opal. 'What is your theory about this man?'

'I think Duncan is a killer, an assassin hired by Cooper. My information from Walter Reed points to Juan José Morazan having a degenerative brain disorder. We already have information regarding Morazan's connection to the CIA. A coup has been expected for some time now. We are presently in the midst of negotiations with Francisco Cabrera, President of Costa Rica. If the negotiations are successful, we will have an open port in Pacific Central America. Such a port will increase our presence in Central America greatly, consequently lowering United States prestige in the same area. Since the European shift Central America has become more strategically important. Highly sensitive. The United States will do whatever it can to delay our intrusion. It could well be another Cuba, or even a Vietnam. Such a confrontational situation could be disastrous for everyone.'

'There is sense in what you say,' Koslov agreed, nodding. 'Go on.'

'Cabrera comes to Washington in a month for talks with President Tucker; a state visit with all the trimmings. I think this man Duncan will attempt an assassination.'

'You think Cooper has planned this?' Koslov asked.

'Yes,' Travkin said firmly.

'No.' Koslov shook his large head. 'It would be counterproductive. Cabrera is a leftist; he would be transformed into a martyr overnight.'

'That worried me too,' Travkin replied, 'until I did some research into Cabrera's past. As a martyr he would be somewhat flawed.'

'Why?'

'There is a definite link between Cabrera and a man named George Morales, a Colombian drug dealer convicted in Miami. There is also a connection between Cabrera and the Nugan Hand bank. It would take very little to turn Cabrera the leftist into Cabrera the drug kingpin. Costa Rica's wealth, what there is left of it, is controlled by no more than twenty old guard families, and half of them are involved in the drug trade; Cabrera's murder could reasonably be laid at the doorstep of any one of them. With Cabrera dead, Morazan could justifiably declare martial law and that would be the end of our Pacific port.'

'And you assume such a plot is imminent?'

'Speed is of the essence. Morazan is dying. With Cabrera out of the country there will be no better opportunity. With martial law declared Morazan could step down, or be made to step down, and a puppet installed in his place. It wouldn't be the first time the CIA has been involved in such an action. There is even a historical precedent – Cooper was part of the operations group to destabilise the Figueres regime in 1955. He knows the territory.'

'It would seem that you've done your homework, Dimitri Dimitrovitch,' Koslov murmured.

'It fits,' Travkin insisted. 'It all fits.'

'Perhaps,' Koslov answered. He stubbed his cigarette out in the buttery remains of his croissant. 'But it is not our concern.'

'What?'

'It is not our concern,' the general repeated. 'You are Deputy Resident for the GRU in Washington. Your job, and mine, is to collect intelligence information of a technical nature which might be of value to the military. Your flight of fancy regarding Señor Morazan and Señor Cabrera does not fall within our mandate. If anything it is a job for Elder Brother.'

'The KGB has had cold feet about Central America since the Cuban Missile Crisis,' Travkin snorted. 'Gurenko wouldn't touch this information with a ten-foot pole.'

'Nor will I,' Koslov replied dryly. 'Consider this. Assuming for the moment that you are right, what should we do? The Central Intelligence Agency hires a killer to assassinate the Presidente of Costa Rica. The chances are good that they would fail, but fail or succeed, there would be an investigation. What would happen when such an investigation revealed that we were involved, no matter how innocently? You're not describing a potentially valuable GRU operation, Dimitri, you are laying the groundwork for a trip to the incinerator at Khodinka.'

'Then what do we do?' Travkin asked.

'Nothing.' Koslov answered. *'Pravda ne isvestia i isvestia ne pravda.'* The white-haired man laughed, quoting the old joke, a pun on the names of the two state newspapers. 'Truth isn't news and news isn't truth.' He wagged a thick, nicotine-stained finger at Travkin. 'But true or not, I don't want to see my name in an American newspaper; I am looking forward to an easy death, pickled in vodka at my dacha in Podolsk.'

'There is one other thing,' said Travkin. 'I'm under surveillance.'

'So?' Koslov shrugged. 'We watch Gurenko, Gurenko watches us and the FBI watches everybody.'

'It's not the KGB and it's not Stone's people either.'

'Really?' Koslov asked, interested. 'Who then?'

'I'm not sure, but at a guess I'd say they're CIA,' Travkin responded.

'*Yeb moy!*' said the General, cursing under his breath. 'How long?'

'Since I returned from Barbados.'

'A caboose?' Koslov asked, using the Russian term.

'Perhaps,' Travkin answered weakly. A caboose was an agent who kept a colleague under surveillance from a distance in an effort to see if the man he was watching was being followed by an enemy.

'Of course it was,' Koslov said, scorn in his voice. 'They set him at the airport there and he saw you follow Cooper in. Damn it, Dimitri! You should have been watching for something like that!'

'I was in a hurry,' Travkin answered, knowing the excuse was laughably weak. As Deputy Resident part of his job was training GRU staff to recognise just that kind of procedure. Koslov was right; it was inexcusable.

'Do they know you've flushed them?'

'I believe so, General.' Travkin said stiffly, retreating into formality.

'What about your apartment?' asked the grim-faced Resident.

'Sir?'

'Has it been bugged?'

'I don't know,' Travkin answered, shaking his head. Koslov sighed.

'I want you out of there and into Belmont Road by this evening,' said the old man. 'You can use the courier's quarters.'

'It is only surveillance, General,' Travkin countered. 'I don't think I'm in any present danger.' The thought of camping out in the dingy attic apartment at the Soviet Military Office was enough to make his skin crawl. Dustballs under the bed and battery acid disguised as coffee from the cafeteria.

'To hell with present danger!' Koslov snapped. 'This is a question of security. If Cooper is staging some sort of assassination plot we must be completely removed from it. If I had any sense I'd insist that you take two weeks' leave at home, just to get you out of the way.'

'For how long?' Travkin asked.

'For as long as it takes!' Koslov answered. 'At least until this man Cabrera has returned home.'

'*If* he returns home,' Travkin warned.

'The fate of a banana republic head of state is no longer a question which should interest you,' Koslov said. 'Put your time to good use and prepare that report on the New York illegals you've been promising me for the last month.'

'Yes, General,' Travkin replied, trying to inject a humble note into his voice. The General was letting him off easy and he knew it; a week or so in

Belmont Road was a mild punishment compared to what Koslov could have done. On the other hand, there were some unresolved questions Travkin still wanted answered. He banished the thought from his mind and stood up. Koslov might be an old friend of the family, but first and foremost he was a general in the GRU and not someone to cross. If he continued his investigations after being directly ordered not to the frog-faced old man was capable of inflicting serious damage to his career.

Jamming one hand into his pocket Travkin made a mildly obscene gesture with his balled fist and bowed tightly to his superior. 'I'll pack some things and bring them to Belmont Road immediately,' he said.

'Good.' Koslov frowned. 'And I'll have none of your impudence, Dimitri,' he added. 'I was making *"figa v. karmane"* to my superiors before you were born.' Travkin's fist opened in his pocket as though he'd been clutching a hot coal. 'If you wish to say something to me,' Koslov continued, 'say it to my face and not from your trousers; it is most definitely *ne kulturney.*'

'Yes, sir.' Travkin answered.

'All right,' the General said. 'Enough indigestion for one day.' He lit another Opal and made a dismissing gesture with one hand. 'Leave me in peace now; I'll see you this afternoon in my office.'

'As you wish, General,' Travkin answered stiffly. He turned on his heel, threading his way through the maze of tables to the street. He decided against taking a taxi back to his apartment and turned south; there was still an early morning freshness in the air and the walk would do him good. At the very least it might serve to work off some of his frustration.

Seen through the tinted glass of the limousine's windows, the streets of downtown Washington slipped soundlessly by like a smoked grey dream. In the sealed rear passenger compartment of the bulletproof Lincoln, Hollis Macintyre listened to Hudson Cooper's report as he relaxed in air-conditioned comfort, oblivious to the heat and humidity being endured by the capital's less fortunate citizenry. The vehicle, complete with driver, was nominally attached to the executive garage, but Joseph Swanbridge, using his authority as Secretary of State, had had the car assigned to Macintyre on permanent loan, listing the aging politician as a 'senior advisor'.

'From what you say it would appear that there are cracks in your security,' the enormously fat man said quietly. Seated across from him, a glass of mineral water in his hands, Hudson Cooper shrugged.

'An unfortunate coincidence. We had no idea that the GRU had an asset at Walter Reed.'

'Or that the GRU man in question was part of an ongoing watch programme by the REDNET group,' Macintyre added, irritation in his voice. 'The skein we've been weaving seems to be unravelling, Hudson.'

'It can be gathered in again,' Cooper said. He sipped from his glass. The limousine was whispering across the Arlington Memorial Bridge, the distant bulk of the Pentagon squatting like a gigantic bunker to the south. Glancing through the window Cooper found himself wondering what the massive building would look like in a thousand years; a brooding, dangerous ruin, its history clouded in myth? Or a museum filled with dusty icons from an angrier time?

'How much does this man Travkin actually know?' Macintyre asked. The Lincoln came off the bridge and turned north onto the George Washington Parkway.

'Very little in terms of verifiable fact,' Cooper replied. 'He clearly assumes that one of Dr Barron's patients at Walter Reed has Creuzfeldt-Jacob disease. He knows that Barron telephoned you, and presumably he also knows that you telephoned me. He was serious enough to follow myself and Mallory to Barbados, so *we* can assume that he has some information about our man Rhinelander.'

'And Stone, the FBI man?' Macintyre queried.

'Ruppelt was very quick to hand off the information,' Cooper said slowly. 'He's a bureaucrat willing to do anything to keep his job. The last thing he wants to do is stick his face into an Agency operation. He didn't come right out and ask, but I'm fairly sure he thinks we're about to catch Travkin.'

'A defection?' Macintyre asked.

'Yes,' Cooper said. 'And I didn't say anything to make him think any differently. According to Ruppelt, Stone thinks all of this activity has something to do with Francisco Cabrera.'

'The Costa Rican? Why?'

'We've got an ongoing situation with Juan José Morazan, Cabrera's Jefe of the Policia Nacional. Morazan was in Walter Reed at the same time the President was in for his check-up.'

'Morazan was one of Barron's patients?' Macintyre asked, eyes widening.

'Not directly, but as Senior Resident Medical Officer, Barron was officially in charge of admitting him.'

'So Stone thinks that Morazan has the disease?'

'It seems that way.' Cooper nodded. 'Hopefully Travkin thinks the same as well.'

'What *is* wrong with Morazan?' asked Macintyre.

Cooper laughed briefly. 'That's the irony,' he said. 'Stone and Travkin aren't too far off the mark. There's nothing wrong with Morazan at all. We had him up here for a briefing, and the medical cover seemed like a good idea. From what Ruppelt told me, Stone thinks Morazan has the disease, which is throwing a wrench into our plan to get rid of Cabrera because of his upcoming deal with the Soviets.'

'So you think the Russians have the same idea?'

'Probably,' Cooper answered. 'In which case they'll back off completely.'

'You think so?' Macintyre asked, one eyebrow lifting.

'Absolutely,' Cooper said firmly. 'The Central American situation is far too fragile for them to prejudice by involving themselves in a CIA wet operation. They'll stand back and wait to see what happens.'

The limousine reached the Fairfax County line. In a few minutes they'd reach the Chain Bridge turnoff to Langley. Macintyre stroked the side of his nose with one delicate forefinger and looked thoughtfully out the window. 'The Russian has the wrong idea but he's too close. He has to be taken out,' the fat man said at last, hand returning to nest with its mate on the broad expanse of gaberdine-enclosed gut.

'I agree,' Cooper said.

'Can it be done safely, without undue exposure?'

'I believe so,' Cooper answered. 'Ruppelt is expecting a defection. I think we should give it to him.'

'What about Travkin's people?'

'We can make it play,' said Cooper. 'Travkin's an oddball – expensive dresser, very Westernised. Koslov at the GRU might have his doubts, but the KGB will buy it.'

'You have a procedure?' Macintyre asked.

Cooper nodded. 'It's already in progress.'

'Any other problems?'

'None that I can see. Ruppelt has already taken his people off Travkin and with the Russian out of the picture Stone won't be able to do anything with the little bit of information he has on hand.' The Lincoln reached the Chain Bridge interchange and drifted onto the exit ramp. A large green sign announced that the 123 exit led to the Federal Highway Administration and the Central Intelligence Agency.

'What about your assistant, Mallory?' Macintyre asked.

'I gave him the Cabrera/Morazan scenario along with a few extras,' replied Cooper. 'A drug-related situation that connects the Station Chief in Barbados to Costa Rica and the Nugan Hand bank scandal.' The CIA man drained the last of his mineral water, then continued. 'It's thin but it should hold up while he's staging Rhinelander.'

'And then?'

'And then he retires,' Cooper replied, his voice cold. 'Permanently.' The Deputy Director of Operations stared at the man seated across from him. 'Don't worry, Hollis. Everything is covered.'

'I hope so,' said Macintyre, his lips pursed, 'for all our sakes.'

*

Paul Mallory, coffee in hand and still wearing dressing gown and slippers, watched the passing traffic on Alexandria's King Street from his second-floor apartment. Even before he'd become Hudson Cooper's assistant Mallory had been able to afford better than the one-bedroom apartment above a store on the narrow, bustling street, but it had been his first home after leaving MIT and moving had always seemed more trouble than it was worth.

To some people at the Agency, Mallory's single status so late in life might have been cause for suspicion, but a full-scale investigation by the Human Resources Division prior to the Cooper job had come up with nothing. The search revealed that Mallory had never been particularly good with women and in point of fact had little real interest in them. He didn't appear to have any gay leanings either and the investigators finally came to the conclusion that Paul Mallory was exactly what he seemed to be – a highly intelligent man who was a genius with computers and whose only quirk was collecting paperback murder mysteries and thrillers.

The balding, slightly stooped man turned away from the high bay window and shuffled along beside the floor to ceiling brick and board bookcases that filled the entire side wall of his living room. Sipping at the cooling coffee in his mug he glanced at the titles on the shelves, enjoying their familiarity.

True to his methodical nature, Mallory's collection was arranged first by genre, then by subject matter, and finally by author, alphabetically. Ludlum and Littell were classed as Espionage Thrillers/US, Fleming as Espionage/UK, John D Macdonald as Action/Adventure/US and Christie, P D James and Ruth Rendell as Murder Mystery/UK. There were a dozen other categories represented in the 5000-volume collection, each book carefully logged onto a catalogue program of his own invention and stored in the custom-built 386-megabyte IBM system set up on the opposite side of the room.

In addition to simply cataloguing the books, Mallory had also broken each volume down, listing accurate and inaccurate terminology used, interesting technology and procedure and any other information he thought might be useful. He'd begun 'editing' his books shortly after reading *Six Days of the Condor* in which a foundation supposedly funded by the CIA actually did go through books for information. The novel was eventually made into a film starring Robert Redford.

At first Mallory's breakdowns of the books he purchased had been done out of curiosity, but shortly after he'd begun he discovered that there were a number of groups involved in role-playing games via computer. Five years ago there had been only a few hundred, and none devoted to spies or mysteries. Now there were more than 10,000 electronic role-playing 'bulletin boards' nationwide, with several hundred falling into the mystery/espionage category. Each member of a group had his own password to log onto the 'bulletin board' and his own role to play in an ongoing game. In the beginning Mallory had logged onto every bulletin board he could find, but now he'd cut himself back to fewer than ten, all of them very sophisticated and with some of the games lasting for months.

Frowning, Mallory turned and crossed the room to his work station. The computer was on, the cursor on the amber screen blinking impatiently. Using his free hand the CIA man pushed his glasses back up on his nose and sighed. He had to confront it and deal with the situation – that's why he'd called in sick after all. But not quite yet.

'One more cup of coffee,' he muttered. He left the living room and went down the narrow hall to the galley kitchen. After rinsing out his mug he poured a fresh dose from the Braun and added cream. Carrying the mug with him he went into his bedroom.

It was small, barely more than a cell, with a small window facing the littered alleyway behind the building. Mallory dressed quickly, slipping on a worn MIT sweatshirt and an ancient pair of blue nylon track pants dating back to his high school days. He let out a brief ironic chuckle. What would Mr Colfax say now? From failed jock to Super Agent Six.

An ex-fighter pilot in Korea, the slab-muscled physical education teacher had laughed at the spindle-legged kid trying out for the track team, calling him a variety of things ranging from four-eyed wimp to needle-shanked nerd. He'd been right, of course, and Mallory didn't make it beyond the first cut, but he'd never forgiven Colfax for judging him before he'd had a chance to prove himself.

Mallory snorted, pulling the drawstring tight around the waist. He picked up his coffee and headed back to the living room. To hell with the past and people like Ernie Colfax. This was beyond name-calling and the stakes were a lot higher than a place on the team and a letter on his sweater. But the anger was the same: Hudson Haines Cooper had judged him a fool and had done so unwisely.

He sat down in front of his computer, booted up the disk he'd copied from the Langley mainframe and reviewed the information. Idiotically, as he watched the material scroll by on the amber screen, Mallory wished that he'd taken up smoking when he was a kid; at least them he'd have something to ease the tension. He sipped the scalding coffee and bit his lips instead.

According to Cooper's story, the clandestine employment of QJ/RAIL, aka Eric Rhinelander, was an Agency housecleaning operation. The scenario was artfully simple. The Barbados Station Chief, a man named William Harper, was deeply involved in cocaine traffic from Colombia to the United States via Costa Rica, Jamaica and Bimini, just off the Florida coast. Harper's Costa Rican connection was a man named Carl Alphonso

Hoffman, heir to the Hoffman-Ramirez coffee fortune and also adjutant to Juan José Morazan, head of the powerful Policia Nacional.

The way Cooper told the story, Hoffman was providing safe haven for the aircraft used by Harper and his people, as well as security for transshipment of the cocaine from an airstrip outside San José to the Atlantic port of Limón. It also appeared that Morazan knew about the drug trade and Hoffman's involvement, but was turning a blind eye to it for certain 'considerations', which included the political and financial backing of the Hoffman-Ramirez consortium.

Since Morazan was also CIA-backed and the State Department's choice to run Costa Rica after Cabrera, Hoffman, and particularly his involvement with a CIA Station Chief, was cause for alarm. Rhinelander's job was to 'clean house', a bland euphemism for assassinating William Harper and Carl Alphonso Hoffman if it was deemed necessary. The unspoken presumption was that the Agency was getting ready to make a move in Costa Rica and Cooper didn't want to leave any dirty laundry where the *Washington Post* could find it.

At first glance it seemed to fit into established Agency protocols, but Mallory had spent too long in Threat Analysis to take such things at face value. He also found Cooper's personal involvement suspect. In a situation such as the one the DDO had described, Cooper's first priority would be to distance himself and any other Agency people from the project. Hiring a man like Rhinelander was odd as well. 'Soft file' or not, he had been employed by the Agency and, God forbid, with enough digging a Senate Investigating Committee would be able to make a connection. Far easier to co-opt one of Hoffman's own people, or at least hire someone out of Costa Rica.

Mallory sat back in his chair, eyes on the screen, the palm of one hand rubbing back and forth across his broad forehead. The story Cooper had given him didn't fit, ergo, Cooper was lying to him and the story was a cover. Query: why would Cooper lie to him? Answer: because the real operation was too sensitive even for the DDO's Special Assistant.

He poked his glasses up onto the bridge of his nose and nodded thoughtfully. That fitted at least. The real operation was ultrasensitive, so much so that Cooper was handling it himself, taking on the function of Rhinelander's case officer, using his own assistant as a conduit. As Deputy Director of Operations Cooper had enormous power, and releasing money from the various 'special' accounts used by the CIA would present no problem. Covering his trail would be equally simple.

And that was the bottom line, and Mallory's real reason for calling in sick. The Rhinelander operation, whatever it entailed, and whether it succeeded or failed, was going to need a complete sterilising procedure.

Special accounts would be fiddled, any and all files destroyed, and finally, a double blind team would be hired to remove Rhinelander once and for all. After that there would only be one connection between Hudson Haines Cooper and the operation: Paul Mallory.

Worked up as a cold-blooded assessment for a Threat Analysis the conclusion would have been obvious: as the liaison between Rhinelander and Cooper he represented the only remaining link between the operation and the Agency, and on that basis his life was in jeopardy: if he represented any threat, real or imagined, Cooper would squash him like a bug.

Leaning forward, Mallory tapped out a command and the scrolling stopped. He sat back, pulling at his lip, examining the screen. It was a detailed description of the Grenada situation in October of 1983, showing beyond a shadow of a doubt that there was no strategic reason for the invasion. It also showed clearly that the planning of 'Urgent Fury' had been a disaster, with no co-operation between the various armed services. The report went on to list the real casualties of the operation, including a team of Delta Force Commandos who died because no one had thought to check the fuel level of their helicopter. It was damaging material, and compared to some of the other data he'd pulled out of the Langley computers, it was small potatoes.

With his high-level security classification and his computer expertise, downloading the information had been relatively easy, and it would take someone a long time to trace the data-theft back to him. The real difficulty lay in a method of squirrelling the documents away where no one from the Agency could find them.

The whole idea of using computerised data to hold over the Agency's head had come from Robert Littell's novel *The Amateur*. In both the book and the movie which followed, the lead character, Charlie Heller, had stolen data and used it to force his superiors to allow him to track down and kill the terrorists who had murdered his girlfriend. Heller secreted the data in the memory of an electronic horoscope machine located in a restaurant close to the house owned by his girlfriend's father.

A cute gimmick, but even when he'd first read the novel several years before, the question of the horoscope machine had offended his statistician's sensibility. Heller was a computer code specialist, so encrypting the documents presented no problem, but even with the documents ARCed, or compressed, the tiny memory of the horoscope machine wouldn't have been able to hold more than a small portion of the data, much less be able to pump it out onto the machine's video-screen. Worse than that was the physical vulnerability of the horoscope machine. What if it was taken back to the shop for maintenance? Or simply removed because it wasn't making enough money at the restaurant?

Mallory was sure he'd come up with a better idea. Seated in front of the computer he began working his way through a set of procedures that would hopefully offer him an escape hatch if the Rhinelander project began to turn sour.

First he used an ARC program in his hard drive to compress the data he'd stolen. The program removed all the spaces between letters and words, allowing the data to take up a smaller electronic 'footprint'. It was a common program for games and other material being downloaded or uploaded into electronic bulletin boards.

With the data compressed Mallory then ran an encryption program, turning the compressed data into an incomprehensible clutter of letters and numbers. Following that he added a clock facility tagged with three commands, one to decrypt, and another to alert the bulletin board system operator, or SysOp. The third command set the time – in this case 4:15 a.m. Eastern Standard Time.

When everything was ready on his own computer, Mallory switched on his modem, pulled his terminal program up out of the hard drive and then went looking for an appropriate board. It took him the better part of an hour, consulting a print-out of active bulletin boards, then dialling them, but he eventually found what he wanted.

The board was called Sherlock's Home, a 24-hour detective role-playing game operated by someone named David Prados. The address was in District Heights, not too far from Andrews Air Force base. According to the message board Prados was off in Europe somewhere for an indefinite time, but Sherlock's Home was on automatic, able to take messages and also remain on the LODIS WEB.

It was the WEB information that interested Mallory. LODIS stood for Long Distance and WEB was a networking of bulletin boards allowing messages to be transferred over huge distances without incurring line charges. As in an old fashioned station-to-station telephone exchange, data was bounced from one bulletin board to another close by, which in turn passed it along to the next board on the access route. Messages could be uploaded into the bulletin board, then sent automatically when the WEB went into operation, usually between 3:30 and 4:30 a.m. Eastern Time.

The way Mallory had set up his commands, his message, fully decoded, would go out over the WEB, bouncing from terminal node to terminal node, downloading into each bulletin board as it went along. There were thousands of boards on the WEB network, and each one of them would receive the message, flashing with an urgent command for the Systems Operator.

To stop the message from going out over the WEB, Mallory would have to boot up the Sherlock's Home board and reset the clock function every day, sometime before 4:15 in the morning. If he didn't reset the clock each day before that time, the damning message would automatically begin showing up on thousands of computers across the country.

Satisfied that he'd done everything possible to safeguard himself, Mallory called up the Sherlock's Home message function, then tapped out the send command. The bulletin board asked for a password and, grinning sourly, Mallory logged himself on as Moriarty. The screen cleared, then demanded a file name for his message. He typed in Baskerville, then the letters ARC, indicating that it was a compressed program. The bulletin board accepted the file name and the data began to upload.

Letting out a long breath Mallory stood up and carried his coffee cup back to the kitchen. When the data had uploaded and the floppies were destroyed he'd be able to relax. For a little while at least. He tipped out the cold brown brew into the sink, poured himself another cup and found himself thinking about school days again, wondering if his life might have been different if he'd made the track team after all. Mallory shook his head slowly. It wouldn't have made the slightest difference and he knew it.

Top Secret, Bob Burton's glossary of espionage terminology, defines 'safe house' as a '*residence that is used as a meeting place, refuge or network headquarters for intelligence purposes. It is generally deeded to or registered to a "cleared" person who has no trace.*' What the book does not mention is the huge volume of such places used by the intelligence community, friend and foe, especially in the Washington area. The twelve major intelligence organisations, which included the FBI, operated almost two hundred accommodation addresses, while foreign embassies and agencies such as the KGB, the GRU and the Chinese SAD made use of another hundred.

The safe house chosen by Stephen Stone as operating headquarters for his BACK DOOR surveillance operation on Dimitri Travkin was a unit in a small condominium complex below the Naval Observatory. The two-storey apartment was accessible from an underground parking garage, providing a certain level of security and anonymity, and had been purchased by a fictitious corporation for use by visiting executives. The corporation was actually an element of the FBI witness protection programme, and the apartment was occasionally used to interrogate potential customers.

Rather than going through the standard requisition procedures to log out the apartment for official use, Stone simply went down to the Administration Services Division at the Hoover Building, waited until the clerk in the crowded office left her post, then reached over the counter and snagged the keys off their pegboard hook. The chances of anyone else asking for the apartment over the next few weeks were slim, and if someone did requisition the safe house, Stone could cite a paperwork mixup and bow out gracefully.

Equipping the apartment had been equally straightforward. With the dummy BACK DOOR file as backup, Mort Kessler had stroked Tech Services for everything they needed, including a voice encryption unit, radios, a PC terminal connected to the National Crime Information computer at the Hoover Building, and night surveillance equipment.

Using BACK DOOR as his authority once again, Kessler had seconded four men he trusted from the Baltimore and DC field offices, telling their superiors to contact Stone for the transfer verifications. As Deputy Director of REDNET, Stone had enough authority to satisfy the field office inspectors and he was careful to remove the related paperwork from the inter-office memo circuit before it reached Ruppelt. BACK DOOR had become a ghost project, a Flying Dutchman sailing the bureaucratic seas of the FBI, invisible to everyone except Stone, Kessler and their little group of agents.

The object of the exercise, at least as far as Stone was concerned, was to maintain a loose surveillance of Travkin and see what they could catch in the net. Stone was interested in seeing whom the GRU Deputy Resident was contacting on his own, but he was equally curious about anyone else showing an interest in the man.

Since Stone was supposedly off the Travkin assignment and devoting his energies to more mundane matters at the CI-Q offices in Folger Square he could only get to the safe house sporadically, but so far Mort Kessler had identified two sets of watchers on Travkin. According to Kessler the first set was obviously KGB, running a surveillance almost as loose as their own. He had yet to officially identify the second group, although he had ruled out another FBI operation. Long range photography showed a rotation of eight men, two women and at least six cars and they were keeping Travkin on a short leash. To Kessler it had all the earmarks of a CIA babysitting job, which fitted the defection scenario.

Stone wasn't so sure. If Travkin was going to defect, why hadn't he already done so, and if it was a babysitting surveillance, why was it going on for so long? On the other hand it was equally possible that Travkin was KGB bait and Gurenko was working some kind of sting, playing the GRU man the way the KGB had conned the Agency into accepting Vitaly Yurchenko, then pulling the rug out from under them. It was a game of paranoia playing off paranoia, and from the looks of things, no one wanted to make the first move.

At two that afternoon Stone booked out of Folger Square, telling the pool receptionist on the operations floor that he was taking the rest of the day off. After spending ten minutes wrestling with the rag top on the Rabbit he drove across town, his mood as oppressive as the muggy, cloying atmosphere.

By the time he reached Union Station and the traffic circle around the Columbus Memorial he had it neatly wrapped up in three words: anger, frustration and stupidity. Anger because of Ruppelt's kiss-ass the Company attitude, frustration because the Travkin thing was suffering from chronic gridlock, and stupidity because he should have known better. Once upon a time he really believed he was doing some kind of tangible good for his country but that had vanished a few years back along with his marriage. His loss of faith and his separation from Debbie were linked, of course. Over time he'd had less and less in common with his wife, and concurrently he'd grown to doubt the goals and objectives of the Bureau, particularly where he was concerned. Like his occasional passionate interludes with Debbie there had been a few times when he felt good about his work in counterintelligence, but it wasn't enough. In both cases, the commitment just wasn't there any more.

Lighting a cigarette he worked his way through the heavy traffic heading west on Massachusetts Avenue. Maybe he could add self-destructive to his list of words. Mounting the BACK DOOR operation was an invitation to disaster and he wondered if he hadn't subconsciously pushed himself out on a limb on purpose. Every instinct told him that there was a connection between Barron's death, Hudson Cooper and Dimitri Travkin. He wasn't buying the Morazan/Costa Rica connection either. It was bigger than that and Stone had a sinking feeling that it was about to blow up in his face. If it did, and Ruppelt discovered BACK DOOR, that would be the end of his career or maybe worse.

Stone turned into the small residential enclave below the Naval Observatory. Driving into the dark maw of the underground lot he parked the Rabbit, then walked the two short flights up to the interior hallway that ran along the base of the complex. He found the door to the apartment and let himself in with a duplicate key Mort Kessler had given him.

Entering the safe house Stone saw that the red-haired agent was at his control station in the living room, radio equipment piled up on the table in front of him, a pair of oversized headphones hanging around his neck like a horse-collar. The agent was chewing his way through an enormous, complicated-looking sandwich and there was a long-necked Budweiser sitting on top of the frequency scanner. Kessler nodded to his superior, then went on with his sandwich.

Stone took off his jacket, enjoying the chilled air circulating through the air-conditioned apartment. He went to the kitchen, found a can of Pepsi in the refrigerator and snapped it open. He lit another cigarette, then took the open can of pop back to the living room.

The apartment was beige, bland and anonymous. The bookshelves were empty, there was nothing on the mantel of the gas fireplace. On the walls were framed posters from art galleries no one had ever heard of. The main floor was made up of living room, kitchen, powder room and den, while the second floor contained three bedrooms and a full bathroom. The only interesting thing about the place was the view from the living room. The apartment complex was located at the end of a cul de sac, and you could see down into Rock Creek ravine and beyond to the parklands.

'What gives?' Stone asked, sinking down into an upholstered chair, balancing an ashtray on one arm and the Pepsi on the other. Kessler shrugged and picked up the Budweiser. After a long swallow he put the bottle down, belched lightly and shrugged again.

'Not much. He had breakfast this morning with Koslov at Au Pied de Cochon. From there he took a walk back to his apartment. He's been there ever since.'

'Anybody watching him?'

'The KGB boys seem to have booked off for lunch,' Kessler answered. 'Probably depending on the bugs they installed to keep tabs on him.'

'Ours are still in place?' Stone asked.

'Sure.' Kessler reached out and flipped a toggle on one of the pieces of radio equipment. A steady, hollow hiss began to crackle out of the external speaker set up beside Kessler's Budweiser. 'That's the open mike on his phone.' Kessler hit the toggle again and the sound vanished. 'He's been pretty quiet since he got back from breakfast. Little bit of slamming and banging, drawers being opened, that kind of thing, but not much else. Oh, he had a shower.'

'Exciting stuff,' Stone grunted. He took a sip of his drink. 'What about our people?'

'Tobias is feeding the pigeons in Lafayette Square; he'll take him if he goes out on foot again. Copeland is parked around the corner.' The red-haired agent sat forward suddenly, pulling the headphones up and clamping them around his ears. 'Hang on a minute,' he muttered, fiddling with the dials in front of him. 'He's on his way out and it sounds like he's carrying something.'

'Like what?' Stone asked, leaning forward in his chair.

'Box, suitcase maybe. It's heavy.' There was a pause, then Kessler nodded. 'That's it, he's out. Locked the door behind him.' The agent pulled the large, base station microphone in front of him, then switched on the big Motorola transceiver, leaving the speaker open. 'Compass One, this is Compass Zero, how do you read?'

'This is Compass One. I read you fine.' Compass One was George Tobias, the agent in Lafayette Square. Compass Two was Bob Copeland, waiting in an unmarked car on H Street in front of the Metropolitan Club.

'Little Fox is moving,' Kessler instructed. There was a long pause and then Compass One responded.

'I see him, Compass Zero. Carrying a suitcase.'

'Which way is he going?' Kessler asked urgently.

'North. Towards H Street. Do I follow?'

'No,' Kessler ordered. 'Stay where you are. He may double back.' The agent switched channels and called up Copeland. 'Compass Two, we have Little Fox coming your way.'

'Thank you, Compass Zero.'

'Where's he going?' asked Stone.

'Nowhere on foot,' Kessler answered. 'Closest Soviet address is the Maritime Attache, 21st and L.'

'A drop?'

'With a suitcase?' Kessler laughed.

'No, I guess not.' Stone grinned.

'Compass Zero, this is Compass Two. I have Little Fox getting into a capital taxi, heading West on H Street.'

'Smart boy,' Kessler said. 'He knows he's got Elder Brother on his tail, so instead of calling a cab he flags one down.'

'Where is Elder Brother?' Stone asked.

'He'll be around,' Kessler answered. He punched up Tobias and told him to come back to the safe house, then switched channels again and went back to Copeland. 'Anybody playing tag, Compass Two?'

'Two baggy suits in a Ford Escort,' Copeland answered, his voice rising and falling on a sea of static. 'They picked him up turning onto 18th. He's heading north now.'

'What did I tell you,' said Kessler.

Butting his cigarette, Stone stood up and crossed the room to the big map of DC pinned to the bare beige wall on Kessler's left. Red pins marked Soviet agencies and offices, black pins marked the BACK DOOR people, and a sprinkling of yellow pins marked Travkin's movements over the past few days. Stone's finger followed 18th Street up the map. Beyond Dupont Circle there were half a dozen potential destinations for Travkin. The most likely was the Soviet Military Office on Belmont Road. Ironically, the SMO was almost directly across from the safe house, separated only by the ravine and Rock Creek itself.

'It's the Military Office,' Stone said, turning to Kessler.

'My bet too.'

The two men listened as Copeland kept up a description of Travkin's taxi-ride. From 18th the taxi turned west onto S Street, then turned north again onto 24th. The taxi had entered the old Kalorama district, still an enclave of large detached houses dating back to the beaux-arts era.

'Now I know it's the SMO,' Stone said. 'There's nowhere else he could be going.'

'No evasive moves,' Kessler said. 'I guess he doesn't care about Elder Brother.'

'Maybe he's going to ground for a while,' Stone suggested. 'That would explain the suitcase.'

'Or maybe he's on his way back to Mother Russia,' Kessler said. There was a rush of static from the radio.

'Compass Zero, this is Compass Two. We've got a problem.'

'Go ahead, Compass Two.'

'Bit of a traffic screw up. The taxi turned onto Tracy Place and there's a truck blocking the street. Gateway Movers. If I get any closer I'm going to be sitting in the baggy suits' lap.' There was a pause. 'No, wait, the truck is backing up into a driveway – Shit!' The last word was a barking roar.

'Compass Two, this is Compass Zero. What's going on?' There was no reply. Kessler tried again, his voice urgent. 'Compass Two, this is Compass Zero, how do you read me?' Another pause.

'This is Compass Two, Compass Zero.' Copeland's voice, panting and angry.

'What the hell is going on, Compass Two?'

'It was a trap, Mort,' Copeland answered, breaking code procedure. 'The truck pulled back just enough to let the taxi through, then blocked the street again.'

'Little Fox?'

'Pinched,' Copeland managed, still trying to catch his breath. 'I tried going around on foot but it was all over. The cab-driver's unconscious, Little Fox is gone along with his suitcase and the baggy suits are going crazy.'

'Tell him to get the hell out of there,' ordered Stone. 'We don't want any involvement with the KGB or the local PDs. This one is going to stink bad.' He turned back to the map and stared at the intersection of Tracy and 24th.

Whoever was responsible for the kidnapping had pulled it off within two short blocks of the SMO and they'd done it in broad daylight. There was only one organisation with the facilities to work an operation like that. He pulled a drawing pin out of the map and jabbed it down on the intersection.

'Cooper,' he said, whispering harshly. 'It has to be!'

CHAPTER TWELVE

If Palm Beach is the last glitzy and overpriced refuge of America's not so nouveau riche, then the Breakers Hotel is her castle keep, an ornate fortress in polished, pink Tennessee granite, twin towers looking vigilantly out over the Atlantic, and also back across the narrow reaches of the intercoastal waterway to the uncultured horrors of West Palm Beach where McDonalds arches grow like golden weeds along the Dixie Highway and motel rooms are equipped with vibrating beds.

The Breakers had six hundred rooms, two swimming pools, tennis courts, and its own eighteen-hole golf course. The Italianesque hotel was based on Villa Medici in Rome, but almost ten times its size. Seventy-five European artisans created more than three and a half acres of ceiling frescoes, reflected in the highly polished pink marble floors and lit by scores of magnificent bronze and crystal chandeliers from Venice and Austria. The jutting east and west wings of the building formed an open courtyard, its centre punctuated by a gushing fountain, an exact replica of one in the Boboli Gardens of Florence.

Eric Rhinelander had no intention of staying at the Breakers, but preliminary reading in Jamaica indicated that the hotel would likely provide him with what he needed for the next step of his plan.

Rhinelander pulled in to a vacant spot between a silver Continental and a jet black Rolls-Royce Silver Spur. Dressed in a full set of crisp tennis whites purchased half an hour before in a West Palm sporting goods store and carrying an expensive racket, he was the quintessential Breakers guest: middle-aged, athletic and obviously wealthy.

Rhinelander began walking casually towards the main entrance, watching for the distinctive Capitol dome symbol that marked a DC licence plate. He found three without having to check out the main lot: a dark blue Cadillac Seville, a silver Porsche Targa and a Bentley from the mid seventies. Ignoring the Porsche he slid between the Bentley and the car beside it. The driver's side lock button was down. He continued on and stood watching the croquet players on the broad lawns beyond the palm trees. He let a minute or two pass, then turned and went back towards the south loggia, then around the fountain to the northern side of the court and the

Seville. The door was unlocked. Placing his racket on the hood of the car next to the Cadillac he bent down as though to tie the lace of his tennis shoe. Kneeling, he reached up and pulled open the door. Keeping his head well down he crawled into the car and pulled open the glove compartment. The title certificate was tucked into a clear plastic sleeve. Rhinelander pulled it out and scanned it quickly:

> JOHN HAMILTON GRAY
> 1949 CONNECTICUT AVE
> THE WYOMING APARTMENTS
> WASHINGTON DC 20009

Rhinelander returned the certificate to its sleeve, slid out of the car, eased the door closed and stood. The operation had taken less than thirty seconds. He gathered up his racket and headed for the main entrance of the hotel. Climbing the short flight of steps to the double-arched doorway he entered and crossed the cavernous lobby. He reached the main desk and spent a few seconds going through the motions of writing something on a sheet of hotel stationery. He folded the sheet of paper in four, then caught the desk clerk's attention.

'I'd like to leave a message for John Gray,' Rhinelander said quietly.

'Of course,' replied the reservations clerk. He was young, no more than twenty-one or so and very serious in a dark suit, white shirt and dark green bow tie. He tapped at the computer terminal below the counter and frowned. 'We have two J Grays staying with us at the moment.'

'John Gray from Washington,' Rhinelander offered. The clerk nodded.

'Ah yes, Mr and Mrs Gray.' He looked up and held out his hand for the message. Rhinelander gave it to him and watched carefully as the clerk put it in the appropriate box. Room 526. He thanked the clerk, then retraced his steps across the lobby, pausing at a bank of house telephones near the entrance to the loggia corridor. He dialled 526 and let it ring more than a dozen times. No answer. Fair enough.

Rhinelander went back through the main entrance and headed for his car. With the Cadillac parked in front of the hotel, Mr and Mrs Gray weren't far. The classic Breakers high tea he'd read about in the guide books wouldn't be served for another hour, which probably ruled out the dining room as well. The beach or tennis. Either way he didn't have much time.

Reaching his car he popped the trunk, tossed in his racket and leaned in, rummaging through the bag of things he'd purchased at the hardware store an hour or so before. Keeping his hands out of sight he took out a rectangle of sheet metal roughly the size of the paperback book he'd picked up at a local drugstore, which now lay beside his luggage on the floor of the trunk.

Working the sheet metal with a short-handled pair of tinsnips Rhine-lander cut out a semi-circle of metal on the long side of the rectangle, and then a smaller notch further back. He wrapped the small notch and the entire back half of the device in black electrical tape, leaving the half-moon cut and the rest of the metal bare. Reaching into the bag again, he took out one of the hacksaw blades he'd purchased and wrapped the last three inches in tape as well. When he'd completed the wrapping he slipped the sheet metal device and the hacksaw blade between the pages of the paperback, and closed the trunk.

Instead of going through the main entrance again he went through the southern loggia doors and followed the long lounge to a bank of elevators at the south end of the lobby. Paperback in hand he stepped into one of the elevators, punched five and waited. The doors closed, and he went up, alone.

The fifth floor corridor was empty. Rhinelander found 526 towards the end of the corridor about forty feet from the fire stairs. Getting in to the Grays' room wasn't imperative, and Rhinelander wasn't going to risk much for a glimpse of their possessions, but from a quick glance at the locks on the room doors it didn't look as though it was going to be too difficult.

The ornately cast, miniature lion's head escutcheons disguised simple latch-bolt mortice locks without latch guards or dead bolts. He wouldn't need the hacksaw blade. Glancing down the hall to make sure the way was clear Rhinelander removed the sheet metal 'key' from the book and eased it between the door and the frame of room 526, just above the lock. Poking it in so that the half moon was over the lock mechanism, he slowly pulled the device downward, pausing when he felt resistance. The half-moon notch was now over the latch bolt.

Rhinelander checked the hallway again, then curled his right index finger into the taped notch behind the half-moon cutout. Pulling gently towards himself, he began to 'walk' the sheet metal device forward. The metal caught the bevelled latch bolt and the door popped open. Rhinelander stepped into the room, closed the door behind him. He put the 'key' back into the book and the book into the back pocket of his tennis shorts, then began to count silently. At 300 he would be on his way out.

Rhinelander worked quickly, going through the cupboards first, followed by the bureaux and then the desk. He'd seen no bathing suits or bathrobes and there were no large towels in the bathroom. The chances were good they were at one of the two pools or the beach next door. As his count reached 150 he took his haul of personal effects and dumped them on the bed nearest the window.

Mrs Gray's purse, complete with wallet and credit cards, found hidden inside one of the extra pillows on the cupboard shelf. Mr Gray's wallet, hidden inside a pair of socks in his bureau. A set of keys from the side pocket of a tweed suit. Passports in the desk along with tickets, vouchers and a travel itinerary stuffed into a thick folder from Butterfield and Rosen, DC travel agents with an address on M Street in Georgetown.

He put the folder aside and opened Mrs Gray's purse. There was a set of keys inside the bulky leather bag. Rhinelander picked up the set of keys he'd found in Mr Gray's jacket and compared them. Both rings held a set of keys for the Cadillac and both had similar, but not identical safety deposit box keys. There were several small keys on Mr Gray's ring that looked like they might fit luggage, two well worn Medecos and a shiny single-pin key with the name Secor on the tab. Checking quickly Rhinelander saw that there were also two Medeco keys on Mrs Gray's ring. House keys. He took one from each ring as well as the Secor, slipping them into the pocket of his tennis shorts.

The contents of John Gray's wallet produced a brief history of the man's life. Sixty-two years old, grey haired with glasses, a semi-retired lawyer and senior partner in the firm of Gray, Gladstone and Taylor. Two children, both daughters, both married, both with children, one living in Texas, the other in Colorado. Rhinelander jotted down the man's licence number, then removed Gray's social security card from a back slot in the card holder, putting it into his pocket along with the keys. He went through the credit cards and removed the Diner's Club, slipping it into his pocket as well. His count was now at 200.

Opening the Butterfield and Rosen folder Rhinelander ignored the tickets and pulled out the computerised itinerary sheet. According to the print-out the Grays would remain at the Breakers for another ten days, then travel to Miami where they were booked overnight at the Hilton. The following day they were scheduled to board the *QE2* at Port Everglades for a round the world cruise. According to the schedule they would be gone for months.

The only other thing of interest in the folder was a folded carbon copy of a receipt from a Washington company called Housecalls Inc. According to the carbon Housecalls would have someone in to water the plants and collect the mail every third day for the duration of the Grays' extended vacation. Rhinelander frowned; a problem, certainly, but nothing serious. He took down the telephone number of the company, then replaced the carbon in the folder. His count was up to 250; time to be on his way.

He went around the room, returning everything to its proper place, finally reaching the hotel room door as his count reached three hundred. Rhinelander stayed a few seconds longer, his dark eyes scanning the room to make sure he hadn't overlooked anything. When he was satisfied he opened the door, checked the corridor and stepped outside.

Pleased with the way things had gone, Rhinelander left the hotel and returned to his car. A few moments later he was on his way back to the mainland. He'd been prepared to spend much more time developing his Washington position, but the Grays had given it to him in one neat package. At best he'd expected his sidetrip to produce an address in DC for a week or ten days; the three and a half month world cruise was an unexpected bonus. Even the Housecalls Inc. receipt was more of an asset than a liability; it would be easy enough to call them and cancel the service, and the fact that Mr and Mrs Gray had employed the company at all meant that they weren't on particularly intimate terms with their immediate neighbours.

Given his success at the Breakers, Rhinelander decided to move his plan up a day. Instead of booking in at the Holiday Inn as he'd originally intended, he drove to the Amtrak station. After a quick change of clothing in the parking lot he went into the station and purchased bedroom accommodation on the northbound Silver Star, paying passage all the way to New York. The train would reach Washington in the early afternoon of the following day.

Returning to the parking lot Rhinelander spent the next twenty-five minutes going over the rental car. He took the unused material from the hardware store to a dumpster beside the station, then added the tennis outfit, the racket and, finally, Gavin Holt's set of golf clubs. He kept the sheet metal key and the book, slipping them into the single suitcase he'd removed from the dead man's apartment in Miami. Chores done, he took the suitcase into the station, checked it with the baggage master, adding a five dollar tip to ensure that it reached his bedroom on the train in good order. He ate a mediocre meal at a greasy spoon on the other side of the street, returning to the station just as the train pulled in.

Later, naked, he lay on top of the crisp sheets, eyes wide-open and seeing nothing. Listening to the stuttering rocking of the train he allowed himself to think about tomorrow and Washington, and what he had been asked to do, and why, in the depths of some darkly shrouded well within his soul, he already knew he'd go through with it, no matter how great the risk of failure and its consequences, or how pitiful the odds of his success and its rewards. Finally, having reached no real conclusions, Rhinelander turned on his side, closed his eyes, and fell into a deep and dreamless sleep.

As Eric Rhinelander slept, Dimitri Alexandyr Travkin was slowly regaining consciousness and becoming aware of his surroundings. He groped his way out of absolute nothingness, following the trail of clues left by his awakening senses. The medicinal smell of a hospital, reassuring at first, then frightening. What was he doing in a hospital? Why couldn't he see or hear? Then the foul taste in his mouth he'd last experienced after having his appendix removed. General anaesthetic. Jesus Christ! They'd operated on him! Who?

Sight and sound at last. The faint whirring of an air conditioning unit, white acoustic tiles overhead and an inset fluorescent panel, dimmed. He lifted his head from the pillow, wincing as pain stabbed at his temples. Small room, pale green walls and a single, narrow window, uncurtained. Darkness beyond. Night.

Groaning, Travkin eased his legs out over the side of the bed and pushed himself into a sitting position. The pain in his temples was followed by a sweeping wave of nausea combined with dizzying vertigo. Gritting his teeth he swallowed hard, keeping the rising bile in his throat at bay. He waited out the nausea and after a minute or so it began to recede.

Definitely a hospital bed in a hospital room. He was wearing an open-backed hospital gown, tied once just above his buttocks. The floor was cool grey tiles. No intravenous, no catheters, no obvious pains. Surgery seemed unlikely. Why would they operate anyway?

Why would who operate? Splintered shards of memory began to form. He'd been in a cab on his way to the SMO. No more than a block or two from the Military Office the taxi-driver had turned down Tracy Place instead of continuing up to Kalorama Road. He'd started to say something, but there'd been a huge crashing noise and he had a vague recollection of a red white and blue postal van smashing into the side of the taxi. And that was it until now.

He forced himself to take a long series of deep breaths, trying to bring himself out of the threatening panic he was beginning to feel. He'd been snatched, that much was clear. His own people? Remotely possible, but highly unlikely. Why kidnap him when he was on his way in to the SMO anyway? That left Gurenko and Elder Brother, Central Intelligence, or Stephen Stone.

Pushing himself up off the bed with both arms, Travkin staggered over to the window. There were no bars on the outside, but the glass was embedded with steel mesh. He cupped his hands around his eyes and looked outside. He could just make out a open area like a playing field directly under the window, and the dark, shadowed shapes of a forest beyond. No lights twinkling, no reflected glow of a nearby city. He made his way back to the bed and sat down wearily. Gurenko and the KGB had nothing like this in the Washington area, and neither did Koslov.

Gently, using only the tips of his fingers, Travkin began massaging his temples, willing the terrible pain to go away so that he could think clearly. He closed his eyes and tried to concentrate, but opened them again almost instantly as the vertigo returned.

Not Gurenko, not Koslov. Stone or the CIA? Stone had neither the mandate nor the authority to organise a kidnapping and if it leaked to the press that the FBI was going around snatching foreign diplomats the Bureau's good guy public image would disintegrate. On top of that, his intuition from the beginning told him that Stone really *was* one of the good guys.

Which left Central Intelligence. Obviously the most probable, but still astounding, given the circumstances. For one thing the CIA was forbidden to operate domestically and, more importantly, the kidnapping violated the unwritten law that you didn't physically interfere with agents in each other's capital cities. Clandestines and illegals were fair game, but as a registered member of the Soviet embassy staff, Travkin should have had immunity. If that immunity had been violated, someone, almost certainly Hudson Cooper, was very worried.

Assuming the kidnapping had been a CIA operation, that meant he was in one of two places: Camp Peary – the Farm as it was known in the annals of spy fiction – or the less publicised Bowie Institute. The Farm was used to train potential agents in the basics of tradecraft and field operations, and it was more than a hundred miles from Washington, just outside of Williamsburg, Virginia, which would have involved a risky, long distance transport problem. The Institute, on the other hand, was less than forty miles from where he'd been snatched, occupying a small corner of the gigantic and absolutely secure National Agricultural Research Center just north of the town of Bowie, Maryland.

The Institute, built in the early thirties as the Maryland State Reformatory for Girls, had been taken over by William Donovan's OSS early on in the Second World War as a training centre for agents about to be sent overseas. It languished unused for a number of years after the war, its function usurped by the newly built facilities at Camp Peary. In the late fifties it was decided that the fledgling Central Intelligence Agency needed its own medical facilities close to Washington, and the interior of the old reform school was renovated.

During the sixties a number of the CIA's infamous MK Ultra LSD experiments were carried out at the Bowie Institute but by the seventies its role had become that of a rest and recuperation centre for agents in from the field, a discreet drug and alcohol detoxification clinic for selected Agency employees and their wives, and an occasional debriefing unit for high-ranking defectors like Vitaly Yurchenko.

It was Yurchenko who had provided most of what was known about the Institute, and even that had been sifted down through a number of GRU 'sympathetics' within Elder Brother. According to Yurchenko he'd been taken to the Institute on three different occasions, each session lasting several days. Perhaps owing to his high rank within the KGB they hadn't used drugs on him, but he reported seeing seeing several interrogation rooms equipped with drug-related paraphernalia, including gurneys fitted with leather restraints, pharmaceutical cabinets and intravenous equipment.

Travkin tried standing up again, one hand gripping the bedsheets. He edged slowly around to the end of the bed, then shuffled across the room to the door. It was locked, of course, and there was no knob on the inside. He kept moving around the edge of the room, propping himself up with one hand and ignoring the mild waves of dizziness. The closet was empty except for a pair of paper slippers and some extra bedding. No clothes. The bathroom was just as bleak.

Finishing his inspection Travkin guided himself back to the bed and sat down gratefully. Whatever drugs he'd been given were wearing off and he was slowly regaining control again. He pushed away the stabs of panic; long before becoming an officer within the GRU he had been *spetsialnoye nazhacheniye*, graduate of the Spetznaz training school at the Lenin Komsomol Higher Airborne Command Facility, southeast of Moscow. If he could survive the birch swamp horrors at the special forces unit in Ryazan he could survive anything, even the Bowie Institute.

Travkin hear a faint, electronic click and turned, frowning. The door to his room opened and he saw two men, both dressed in the loose-fitting white fatigues used by hospital orderlies. The men were of medium height, one more muscular-looking than the other, but both obviously fit. The muscular one was blond, while his slimmer companion was dark-haired and heavily bearded. The blond stood behind a wheelchair.

'*Preyezieu moy*,' ordered the dark-haired, slimmer man. The Russian was bland and unaccented – freeze-dried language from an American university.

'Why should I come with you?' Travkin asked, replying in English. 'I don't know who the hell you are, or where I've been taken.'

'You have no need to know,' the dark-haired man answered, still speaking Russian. 'I repeat: come with me.'

Travkin thought for a brief moment. To resist now, in his condition, would be foolish. He nodded, then stood up slowly. The dark-haired man stepped aside, allowing the blond to push the wheelchair into the room. He brought it around to the side of the bed and Travkin sat down. The blond man fastened heavy rubber restraints around Travkin's wrists, then turned the wheelchair around. The dark-haired man held the door open and Travkin was wheeled out into the hall.

They went down a long, brightly lit corridor, turned left, and took a shorter passage to a small elevator. They went down one floor, then followed a broad, marble-floored hall to what had once been the offices of the Bowie Reformatory's nurse. A full set of Travkin's clothing had been laid out across the old-fashioned leather examining table.

'Get dressed,' the dark-haired man ordered, speaking Russian. 'When you're ready go through that door.' He pointed to the other side of the room. The blond man undid Travkin's restraints and stepped back. A few seconds later they left, locking the hallway door behind them.

Travkin pushed himself towards the examining table and then stood up. The clothes had come from the suitcase in the taxi. Dark blue lightweight suit, pale grey shirt, underwear, socks, loafers and a blue and red striped silk tie, one of his favourites. He dressed, sitting down to put on the socks and shoes, then went to the connecting door.

Opening it, he paused, startled for a moment. The room beyond wasn't at all what he'd expected. Instead of a bleak interrogation chamber he found himself looking into a well furnished sitting-room. He stepped inside, closing the door behind him. A rattan sectional couch dominated the room. In front of it there was an ornate, marble-topped coffee table, its surface scattered with magazines.

Two upholstered chairs were arranged across from the couch, and behind them an antique writing desk stood against one wall. There was an art deco style fireplace, several logs burning cheerily in the hearth. The walls were painted a warm, oyster white and hung with a variety of well-framed, mid-nineteenth century oils.

A panelled door beside the writing desk opened and a man stepped into the room. He appeared to be in his late forties or early fifties, his grey hair thick and curly over a broad forehead and large hazel eyes. He was wearing suede desert boots, dark trousers and a brown tweed jacket over a light blue shirt. No tie. In his right hand he carried a clipboard and in his left a thick file folder.

'Mr Travkin?' the man asked, extending a hand. 'My name is David Cook.' Bemused, Travkin took the hand and shook it. Cook's grip was cool and dry. He gestured towards the couch and Travkin sat down. Cook followed suit, taking one of the chairs across from him. He opened the file folder on his lap and consulted the clipboard.

'Let's get the formalities out of the way first, shall we?' Cook began. 'Your name is Dimitri Alexandyr Travkin?'

'I'm not saying anything,' the GRU Major answered.

'You were born in Ljalovo, a small town on the outskirts of Moscow,' Cook went on blithely. 'Your father, Antonin Alexandyr Travkin, died of a heart attack six years ago. Your mother, Maria Fyedorova Travkin, presently lives at 26 Ulyanov Prospekt between Sokolniki Park and the Riga Station, is that correct?'

Travkin remained silent. He had always assumed that Central Intelligence had a complete dossier on him, but hearing his mother's address coming out of this man's mouth made his stomach twist. After a few moments he decided to go along with the odd interrogation and nodded.

'Yes, that is correct,' he said finally.

'Good, thank you.' Cook smiled, pleased. 'You presently hold the rank of Major in the GRU working under General Gennaddi Koslov, yes?'

'I am senior economic advisor to the Soviet Trade Mission in Washington and I have been illegally kidnapped by the Central Intelligence Agency,' Travkin replied. 'I am now making a formal request to contact the Soviet Ambassador immediately.'

'Of course.' Cook nodded, smiling again. 'I wonder if you could tell me at what point you decided to defect to the United States?'

'I have not defected,' Travkin answered calmly. 'As I just said, I was kidnapped by the CIA.'

'Would you say that your defection was politically motivated?' Cook asked, ignoring Travkin's interjection.

'I did not defect,' he repeated. Cook kept on smiling. He turned, looking back over his shoulder. The door beside the writing desk opened and the blond man who had guided Travkin's wheelchair appeared. He was now dressed in a white steward's jacket with small brass buttons. He was carrying a tray loaded down with a silver tea service and a platter of small pastries. He put the platter down on the table between Travkin and Cook, then retired.

'Refreshments!' Cook beamed. He closed the folder and leaned forward, putting it down on the table beside the platter. He set out two cups and poured. 'If I remember your file you take lemon and sugar, is that right?'

'Yes,' Travkin said. The whole thing was insane. It was the middle of the night and he was drinking tea! Cook handed him the cup and swept a hand over the tray of pastries.

'Help yourself,' the CIA man offered. Realising just how hungry he was, Travkin took two small meringues and placed them on the edge of his saucer. He stirred his tea and took a swallow of the hot, tart-sweet brew. He bit into one of the meringues, letting the piece dissolve on his tongue. The Institute apparently had an accomplished pastry chef on its staff. He took another bite and stared across the table at his interrogator. The questions continued.

Dressed in evening clothes and nursing a glass of scotch, Hollis Macintyre stood at the window in Hudson Cooper's Watergate apartment staring out into the darkness. It was well past midnight and he was tired. Earlier he'd spent several hours at his monthly gourmet society dinner in Georgetown, but his interest had been distracted by his need to know the progress of the Travkin operation, so the meal and the evening had been wasted.

The huge man turned away from the dark night outside, frowning as another stab of pain surged through his massive gut. On the far side of the room Hudson Cooper sat at the ornately carved desk, speaking softly into the telephone. Breathing heavily, Macintyre walked slowly across the large oriental carpet and sat down in a leather chair near the fireplace. He took a small sip of his drink, then set the heavy glass down on the table beside him. A few moments later Cooper joined him.

'Well?' Macintyre asked.

'Everything is going as planned,' Cooper answered, staring at the cold hearth.

'Your man at Bowie knows nothing?'

'No more than necessary,' Cooper sighed. 'I was careful to double blind the operation. The pick-up crew was from Covert Ops, Cook is a psych expert from the Office of Soviet Analysis. Tech services is handling the rest. It's set up to look like a variation on the honey trap. Travkin is taken by main force, but everything after that is set up to resemble a defection.'

'Will it work?' Macintyre asked.

'It should,' Cooper said. 'The debriefing suite at Bowie has half a dozen hidden cameras and microphones everywhere. By the time Cook is finished we'll have at least two hours of both video and audio tape to work with. The questions are set up to elicit responses that can be re-edited to suit our requirements. The end result will be a ten- or fifteen-minute segment that will make Travkin look like a grateful defector. We don't even have to make the defection public. A copy sent to Koslov or Gurenko will be more than adequate.'

'They'll believe it?' Macintyre asked sceptically.

Cooper shrugged. 'Perhaps not, but they'll have to accept it.'

'Repercussions?'

'Some harassment of our people in Moscow, possibly an expulsion, nothing more. If we don't try and make political points with the Travkin tape they may simply choose to ignore it. The present political climate requires us all to act like the best of friends, at least in the public eye. There may well be no repercussions at all.'

'You mentioned before that Travkin was trained as Spetznaz.' Macintyre said slowly. He picked up his glass and took a short swallow. 'Is there any chance of his escaping from Bowie?'

'Unlikely,' Cooper responded.

'But what if he does?' Macintyre pressed.

'We've learned our lessons,' Cooper said, smiling bleakly. 'Unlike the unfortunate affair with Comrade Yurchenko we will have proof that

Major Travkin was a willing defector to this country. No, Hollis,' Cooper continued, letting his head fall back against the chair, 'I think we've effectively defused Dimitri Alexandyr Travkin. Even if he did manage to get out of the Bowie Institute, he'd have nowhere to run. I can assure you that his own people have already written him off.'

'So the project continues,' Macintyre murmured softly, twirling the remnants of ice in his glass.

'It would seem that way,' Cooper answered.

'When do we hear from Mr Rhinelander?'

'Within the next two or three days if there aren't any difficulties. He'll contact Mallory and give him a yes or a no on the feasibility of the operation.'

'And if his answer is yes?' Macintyre asked quietly.

'Then presumably we call the committee together and make the final decision one way or the other,' Cooper answered.

Macintyre put his glass down onto the side table and stared thoughtfully at his host for a moment. 'You don't really approve of this, do you, Hudson?' he asked finally.

'The question of my approval is irrelevant,' the Deputy Director responded. 'I am a member of the Romulus Committee; that position holds inherent responsibilities, one of which is to ensure that this nation doesn't find itself with a lunatic at the helm of the ship of state.' Cooper paused for a moment, ducking his head and pinching the bridge of his nose with thumb and forefinger. He looked up again and continued. 'If you're asking me if I approve of the assassination of the President and the Vice-President of the United States, then the answer is no – I find the idea abhorrent. On the other hand I recognise the efficacy of such a plan and have no hesitation in recommending it.'

'That's clear enough,' the fat man answered, allowing himself a small smile. Grunting with effort he levered himself up out of the chair. 'I must be on my way,' he said, extending a hand to Cooper, who shook the proffered hand briefly, the led Macintyre to the front door of the apartment.

'I'll keep you advised about Rhinelander,' Cooper said, opening the door.

'I'd appreciate that,' Macintyre said. The two men shook hands again and then the fat man was gone. Cooper closed the door after him and let out a long breath. It was past one in the morning now and he was exhausted, but there was still more to do. His steps weary, he went back to his desk and picked up the telephone.

It was just after 9:00 a.m. in Moscow and the grey slate floors of Sheremetyevo Airport's Terminal 2 were awash in arriving and departing passengers. Small groups of militia were scattered here and there along the low ceilinged concourse and Sergei Kuryokhin also noticed a number of green-uniformed KGB border guards.

Carrying a single small bag the old man turned off the concourse down a narrow corridor leading to the VIP lounge, the fuming stump of a Lucky Strike clamped between his thin lips. He disliked long distance travel, especially by air, but the trip to Warsaw was unavoidable. His only consolation was that he would travel to the meeting on Aeroflot and not LOT, the Polish state airline.

A score of people were waiting in the lounge, luggage gathered around their feet, and all of them looked up as he came through the automatic doors. As quickly as they looked up they looked down again, intuitively sensing the aura of power that hung like an invisible mantle across the old man's stooped shoulders.

Kuryokhin frowned as one of the people stood up and approached him. It was Baklinov, the Washington Desk Controller from Tyeply Shtan. The burly, middle-aged man stopped a few feet from his senior officer and bowed stiffly.

'This is a surprise,' Kuryokhin said. He handed his overnight bag to Baklinov and let the younger man lead him to a pair of seats away from the rest of the waiting passengers. Kuryohkin sat down, pushing his cigarette into the sand-filled ashtray beside him. He adjusted his wire-rimmed glasses and stared at Baklinov. 'Well?'

'We've had a report from Gurenko in Washington,' he said hesitantly. 'It came in last night. I got here as quickly as I could.'

'Report on what?' Kuryokhin asked. He reached into the pocket of his thin, brown raincoat and took out a pack of cigarettes. He lit one and waited.

'Travkin, the GRU Major we were discussing.'

'What about him?' Kuryokhin asked, puffing out a cloud of blue smoke.

'It would appear that he has defected.'

'Explain,' Kuryokhin demanded, his voice soft.

'He has disappeared. Our surveillance was broken off. Apparently it was quite a sophisticated operation. Gurenko is positive that Travkin had help.'

'In other words it was preplanned,' Kuryokhin said.

'Yes.' Baklinov let out a long whistling breath. 'There may be some problem with Koslov. He insists that Travkin was kidnapped.'

'Foolishness. He is trying to save face. Travkin was his protégé and the lecherous old bastard used to be his mother's lover.'

'Whatever the case, Gurenko would like some direction.'

'Tell him to do nothing, at least for the moment,' Kuryokhin said after a moment's thought. 'If Travkin has defected the news will eventually leak out even if the Americans try to keep it quiet. Their security is like cheesecloth about such things. Gurenko should assume the worst.'

'And if Travkin reappears?'

'Tell Comrade Gurenko that from this moment on his Major Travkin no longer exists,' Kuryokhin said, smiling gently. 'If he surfaces again it only means that he has been turned by the CIA, or cut loose by them. In either event he is no longer of any use to us. His only value now is the embarrassment he is causing Gennaddi Koslov.'

A young and clearly nervous stewardess appeared bearing a tray of smoked salmon and squares of black bread. The tray also held a carafe of tea and two glasses. She placed the tray down on the small table in front of Kuryokhin and then vanished. Kuryokhin extinguished his cigarette, then took a piece of the salmon, placed it on a square of bread and put it into his mouth, chewing slowly. Baklinov ignored the food, knowing that if Kuryokhin wanted him to eat, he'd offer.

'Is there anything else?' the balding old man asked, peering up at Baklinov.

'No sir. I think Gurenko will be pleased. *Spasiba.*'

'*Nyeh probleme,*' Kuryokhin answered, startling Baklinov with his use of current slang. 'Now let me get on with my food.'

'Of course, sir.' Baklinov stood up, bowed again, and left the VIP lounge. Kuryokhin made himself another bite-sized sandwich, this time arranging a few pickled capers on the salmon. He popped it into his mouth, then poured himself a glass of tea.

Sipping the hot liquid he stared across the lounge at the mural on the far wall: broad-shouldered women gathering wheat to their expansive bosoms, muscular men sweating over forges. God, it was boring! He thought about Travkin and found himself wondering if there wasn't more going on in Washington than he'd first assumed. It was worth checking on when he returned from Warsaw.

CHAPTER THIRTEEN

In 1885 Henry Adams, novelist and historian, together with his close friend John Hay, statesman, built adjoining houses on the north side of Washington's Lafayette Square. Situated only three hundred yards or so from the front door of the 'President's House', the Hay-Adams residences became a focal point of capital society, with Theodore Roosevelt likely to drop in for afternoon tea, only to find that writer Henry James had already beaten him to the fresh biscuits.

The historic houses were demolished in 1927 to make way for a hotel, properly named the Hay-Adams in honour of the two famous men. The hotel's location guaranteed a certain cachet, but by the 1970s the Hay-Adams, although still a landmark, was certainly not on the 'A' list of Washington hotels: the rooms were shabby, and the service was arthritic. By the early eighties the hotel had become a ghostly old lady, maintaining a certain dignity because of her proximity to power, but sadly down at heel.

In 1983 the Hay-Adams was purchased by a Californian financier, and transformed. Within a year the hotel had regained her grandeur: rooms and suites brightened and refurbished, lobby lit with chandeliers, the exterior of the building cleaned, the brass polished.

Eric Rhinelander, although mildy curious about the illustrious building's past, was far more interested in the fact that south-facing rooms on the fifth, sixth and seventh floors had clear views of the north facade of the White House and the White House grounds. With his Nikon propped up on the small cherrywood breakfast table in his room, and using a 300mm telephoto lens, Rhinelander had been taking photographs since his wake-up call at 6:00 a.m.

To avoid arousing suspicion about his interest in the Presidential residence he was using Polachrome 35mm polaroid slide film which he would later develop himself using the inexpensive processing kit he had purchased the day before, soon after his arrival in Washington.

During a career as a professional killer Rhinelander had been presented with assignments offering varying degrees of difficulty ranging from hand to hand butchery in the jungles of Laos and Cambodia to surgically accurate removals on the platforms of the Paris Metro. He had killed KGB agents asleep in their beds, South American military leaders in the arms of their lovers, a British research scientist in his laboratory and a Turkish arms dealer in his private aircraft 19,000 feet above the Aegean.

But this, he knew, was very different. Any head of state, by the nature of his occupation, was a 'hard target' and the President of the United States was the hardest of all. Compounding that fact was Hudson Cooper's requirement that the assassination take place within the White House. At first glance it appeared not only fantastic, but insane.

Not once in the building's history had an assassination attempt taken place in the White House or on the grounds and since the killing of John Kennedy and the multitude of attempts on the Presidents who followed him, the White House had been steadily transformed into an impregnable fortress; there was even a rumour about a ground to air missile installation hidden on the roof of the Treasury Building.

On the other hand, he saw Hudson Cooper's point. To assassinate the President and the Vice-President in the White House would be to strike at the very core of American mythology. You might not approve of the man in power, but like the constitution, the flag and the Liberty Bell, the White House and the office it represented were symbols fundamentally sacred to the vast majority of Americans; tamper with them and you risked the rage of an entire nation.

Which, of course, was precisely what Cooper wanted. If the plan was successful and Nezar Assad, the terrorist, took the fall, Cooper and whoever he was fronting for would be able to completely change the focus of foreign policy in the Middle East. Qaddafi could be bled dry overnight and domestically, the spectre of international terrorism let loose in America would be the leverage and justification needed for enormous budget increases within the intelligence community.

Not that the political ramifications were any of Rhinelander's concern; he was here to find out if the plan was workable. He leaned forward and put his eye to the viewfinder of the camera again.

The north fence had two openings, the northeast gate and the northwest gate. Each gate had a small guardhouse manned by two uniformed Executive Protection Service officers. Every ten minutes or so the roving, plainclothes Secret Service agents patrolling the north lawn would use the guardhouses as rest stops. Scanning the expanse of lawn with the camera Rhinelander had counted an even dozen uniformed guards on patrol and six Secret Service agents.

Focusing on the White House itself Rhinelander could see two uniformed officers at the east wing gatehouse, two Secret Service agents walking the curving drive between the gate and the east wing portico entrance, two more uniformed officers walking back and forth along the length of the east wing, two more at the north portico entrance and six Secret Service agents around the west wing and the Press Office entrance.

In all he counted thirty-six people. Assuming that there were at least an equal number of agents and officers in the southern quadrant, it meant he was dealing with almost seventy people involved with external security.

There were also a considerable number of electronic countermeasures in place. Pushing the telephoto to its most extreme Rhinelander could make out the slowly moving turrets of closed circuit cameras hidden behind the louvres of the rooftop ventilating units, and there were still more cameras nestled under the eaves, their wide-angle lenses focused down on the grounds and driveways directly in front of the mansion.

Coming in tight on the fence close to the northwest gate he could also see the corner of a small grey box, partially hidden at the foot of one of the stone gate columns. A thick cable was just barely visible, snaking out from the box, down the gate column and into the ground; almost certainly the control box for a microwave security fence. A closer inspection would probably reveal half a dozen identical boxes in place around the perimeter of the grounds. Linked together, the buried cables would create an invisible barrier of ambient microwaves capable of detecting anyone climbing over the fence and walking across the grounds.

Rhinelander took another few exposures, then leaned back and lit a cigarette. At that sophisticated level of security he could also expect ground sensors in the lawn, infra-red capability from the closed-circuit cameras and possibly an intruder-radar setup. As well as all the manpower and electronics there were also the physical barriers. The big concrete obstacles put in place after the Beirut catastrophe had been removed long ago, but Rhinelander could see the tell-tale lines in the asphalt just inside the gates; try to make a high-speed entrance into the grounds and a spike-studded barrier would rear up out of the ground, puncturing your tires and ripping the belly out of any vehicle short of a tank.

The dark-haired man sighed, blowing out twin wisps of smoke through his nostrils. He picked up the three-ring binder from the small table in front of him and began jotting a few things down.

To a big game hunter this would be called a 'difficult lie', but to Rhinelander it was far from impossible. Even the most cursory examination of White House external security showed that the focus of their efforts was on the fence-climbing lunatic or the car-bombing fanatic. The implication seemed to be that no one in his right mind would want to kill the President of the United States.

To Rhinelander, who had seen the results of terrorist activity from Dublin to Dubrovnik, that kind of thinking was incredibly naive. He reached out and picked up the Fodor's guide to Washington he'd purchased in the train station. Turning to the section on the White House he used a yellow highlighting pen to underscore the visiting hours: 10 a.m. to noon, Tuesday through Saturday.

He tossed the book back onto the table. In an era of death squads, cassette player bombs in jumbo jets and the slaughterhouse politics of South America, the private residence of the President of the United States was open to the public five days out of seven.

Rhinelander shook his head, trying to imagine groups of tourists tramping through 10 Downing Street, or regiments of camera toting Japanese and Germans fanning out through the echoing corridors of the Elysée Palace in Paris. It was absurd, yet here in Washington it was accepted as the norm, as commonplace as a ride through the haunted house at Disneyland or a climb to the Statue of Liberty's crown.

He leaned forward and put his eye to the viewfinder again. The White House. Beyond the symbolism what was he actually seeing? A four-storey mansion, the ground floor almost invisible from this side because of a slope in the terrain, the top floor hidden behind the protective wall that ringed the roofline. From the east and west sides of the building, columned porticoes connecting the two storey annexes, the east and west wings. All of this in a parklike setting of trees, lawns and fountains. Impressive, perhaps, but there were bigger mansions on more lavish grounds within an hour's drive, and that was going to be the key to his approach; it was simply a question of degree. Every lock had a key, every problem a solution.

Taking his eye from the camera Rhinelander picked up his notebook again and carefully penned a series of headings and sub-headings, setting out areas of research which needed to be completed before he continued with the project at hand.

Schedules:
– Secret Service
– Executive Protection Service (uniforms)
– Services (Food?)
– Shift changes
– Lights? /Surveillance?/radio frequencies?

President/Vice-President
– daily routine/ is there one?
– kids/relatives
– vehicles/where?
– food again

Tucker/Teresi
– bios
– habits

Building/Grounds
– history
– floorplans?
– books/periodicals
– maps/plans
– accidental documentation

– Blair House/floorplans

Weapons
– silent
– probably non-metal (security/metal detectors?)
– lethal
– poison/flechette?
– CO_2?

Mallory
– shopping list

Rhinelander dropped the pen, massaged his eyes briefly with thumb and forefinger, then yawned. Enough for now; there was no point in getting too involved in the research until he was settled in John Gray's apartment at the Wyoming. He began packing away the photographic equipment; it was time to check out of the Hay-Adams.

By noon the assassin had left the luxurious hotel, taking his single suitcase by taxi to the more modest lodgings offered by the Connecticut Avenue Holiday Inn. He checked in using John Gray's name, offering the man's Diner's Club number as security against a proposed two-week stay at the hotel.

Rhinelander was not a man who placed much value on the concept of 'luck'. Finding the Grays at the Breakers and discovering that they would be gone from their apartment for such an extended period was a pleasant surprise, but no more than that. To treat it as a stroke of 'good luck' would be a mistake – depending on that sort of happenstance could be disastrous, hence the fall-back position at the Holiday Inn. If he had to bail out of the Wyoming quickly for some reason, the hotel was only a few hundred yards away.

Carrying his bag up to the room Rhinelander let himself in and locked the door behind him. The room was plain and functional with two single beds, a desk and a chest of drawers. Placing the suitcase on one of the beds Rhinelander went to the small, rectangular window and pulled back the heavy, pale green curtains; as he had requested, the room overlooked Connecticut Avenue.

Directly across from the window was the white gull-wing shape of the Washington Hilton. Facing the rear of the Hilton was the Wyoming. Rhinelander unpacked his camera, then returned to the window, using the Nikon's long lens for a closer inspection of the building. At a guess, he put the building's construction date around 1900 or slightly later. There were three sets of double doors, modern glass and steel, one set for each of the three connected blocks. With three main entrances it was unlikely that any one of them would have a doorman. The way things looked, getting into the building would be relatively easy.

And it was. Wearing jeans, a blue short-sleeved knit shirt and with the Nikon slung over his shoulder, Rhinelander left the hotel. He crossed Connecticut Avenue, pausing in front of the equestrian statue of a Civil War General to take a photograph. Walking casually he went up to the front door of the Wyoming's first block and pulled open the door. Making a show of fumbling for his keys, Rhinelander glanced around quickly. The foyer was a fairly recent addition, probably for security reasons. There was a buzz-board on the right and a double row of mailboxes on the left. Only fourteen names on the buzz-board, two apartments per floor with the Grays' listed as number 502. Directly ahead was a heavy glass door and beyond it the original lobby, complete with marble floor, and a curving staircase bracketed by old fashioned cage elevators on either side. No security desk.

Removing the keys from his pocket Rhinelander tried the first Medeco. It turned and the door opened. Moving quickly he crossed the lobby, pulled open the left-hand elevator door and stepped into the cage. He pressed the fifth floor button and the cage began to rise. A few moments later he reached the fifth floor and stepped out into a small public hall that mimicked the larger, main floor lobby. Using the second Medeco key and with the single pin Secor key ready in his hand, he let himself into the Grays' apartment.

The front door opened onto a small reception hall. At eye level on the right hand wall was a small grey alarm box with three pinlights, two green and one red. The two green lights were labelled 'monitor' and 'enable' while the red was labeled 'arm/disarm'. Below the lights was a lock switch. Rhinelander fitted the Secor key into the lock switch and turned. The arm/disarm light went from red to green. Pocketing the keys he closed the front door.

The apartment was enormous, and from the furnishings and accessories it was obvious that John Gray's career as a lawyer had been a lucrative one. To the left of the reception area a high, oak-trimmed archway led into a living room area at least forty feet long and twenty feet wide. Its lavish furnishings included a pair of tri-fold black laquer Chinese screens decorated elaborately with etched, gold leaf cranes and dragons, and a magnificent sixteenth-century English lady's writing table with intricate marquetry. On the left side of the hall was a den/office, one wall filled with books, while the one across from it held glass fronted display cabinets filled with golf trophies. A modern steel table held an Everex 386 computer with a large-screen colour monitor and a stand-alone Toshiba fax machine. On a shelf under the table there was a laser printer and on the desk there was a complex looking telephone console that appeared to be connected to the computer. The credenza was crammed with software boxes. Gray might have retired, but he hadn't put himself out to pasture.

Rhinelander took a small address book out of his jeans, sat down behind the desk and picked up the telephone receiver. He placed two calls. The first was to Housecalls, the apartment sitters. Posing as John Gray he told them that owing to illness their services would no longer be required and that he would be sending one of the lawyers from his firm to collect any accumulated mail and the key to the lobby mailbox. His second call was to the number given to him by Hudson Cooper in Barbados. On the third ring the connection was made, followed by the tone-beep of an answering machine. Speaking quickly but clearly, Rhinelander read off the number of a telephone booth in the National Visitors Center at Union Station, and a time – 10:30 the following morning. Mallory was to be there, waiting to be contacted.

The calls made, Rhinelander left the apartment and returned to his room at the Holiday Inn. It was 1:30; still time to do some shopping for a new wardrobe and pick up the mailbox key from Housecalls. After that the rest of his day would be spent browsing through some of Washington's better antiquarian bookstores doing preliminary research. By evening he would be settled in at the Wyoming.

Rhinelander smiled to himself, feeling the familiar tension gripping the pit of his stomach. Standing in the middle of the anonymous hotel room he closed his eyes briefly, visualising the White House as he'd seen it that morning through the lens of his camera. The stalking ground had been chosen, now the hunt could begin.

PART THREE

'A President has to expect these things.'

Harry Truman, commenting on the Blair House attempt

CHAPTER FOURTEEN

As Rhinelander prepared to set out on his shopping expedition Stephen Stone was finishing a late lunch at the Hotel Washington's rooftop restaurant, the Terrace. Seated across from him was Lyall Spencer, head of the Secret Service's White House detail. A light breeze was blowing, but both men had removed their suit jackets against the hazed heat of the early afternoon sun.

Spencer was in his late forties, a twenty-five-year man with Treasury, more than half of it spent as a Secret Service agent. He'd been promoted to head of the White House detail almost three years before and Stone knew he was just about ready for rotation to another field office, or to Secret Service Headquarters on G Street. He was a tall man, broad-shouldered and thick necked like a football player. His hair, or what there was left of it, was close-cropped and grizzle-grey. When he took off his standard-issue aviator sunglasses his eyes were a rich brown, the warm colour offset by the piercing, stone-faced gaze referred to as 'The Look' by Secret Service insiders.

Stone watched as Spencer stabbed his fork into the remains of his sachertorte. He'd come in contact with the man several times when Spencer was working out of the Washington Field Office and socially on two or three occasions, but knew little about him beyond the fact that he was divorced with two teenage children living in California.

Studying him as he attacked his dessert, Stone saw a man who lived a life of total, nerve-wracking concentration combined with numbing boredom. Personally responsible for the wellbeing of the most important man in the nation, he had to keep constantly alert and his day-to-day activities consisted of an endless series of drills and false alarms. An occupation tailor-made for heart-attacks, alcoholism and divorce. On the other hand, no one had drafted him – the choice of jobs had been his own.

As Spencer finished eating Stone hailed a waiter for coffee and when it had been served both men lit cigarettes and got down to the real business at hand.

'Discreet lunches at the Terrace aren't too common for the FBI and the Service,' Spencer said. 'From your phone call it sounds as though you're on a private fishing expedition.' His voice was a surprisingly cultured baritone. 'What's on your mind?'

'I'm just trying to cut some red tape,' Stone answered. 'A few quiet words early on could save us both a lot of paperwork in the future.'

'As long as both of us don't bother to mention the few quiet words to our respective bosses,' Spencer retorted.

'Well, it's not as though your guys and mine are on particularly good terms,' Stone said, shrugging.

Both men were well aware of the long-standing and ongoing difficulties between the Bureau and the Service. Partially due to the domestic security guidelines introduced in 1976 the FBI had placed most of its working emphasis on crimes which had already taken place, rather than accumulating information which might stop the events from happening. Given the curtailment of the FBI's domestic intelligence work, the quality of the information they actually did provide to the Secret Service had deteriorated simply because of its second drawer priority. Half a dozen Congressional hearings over the past decade hadn't done anything to solve the problem.

'All right. Screw procedure for the moment,' Spencer said. 'You ask your questions and I'll get my jollies at the irony of the Bureau coming to *us* for information.'

'Francisco Cabrera,' Stone said carefully, watching Spencer's expression. Nothing changed; the man was a cyborg in a grey flannel suit.

'What about him?' The Secret Service agent took a swallow of coffee and stared blankly across the table at Stone.

'I'm chasing down a few rumours about his visit.'

'Don't play games with me, Stone, I don't have the time,' Spencer answered. 'He's the President of Costa Rica, he's coming here next month to officially open the new embassy building. That's all public information. You're sniffing around my ass like a bitch in heat. Why?'

'Any threats against him?' Stone asked. 'Anything come up from OPI?' OPI was the Secret Service's Office of Protective Intelligence.

'This is pay to play,' Spencer replied. 'Why do you want to know?'

There was a long pause. Stone finally spoke. 'We've got a Russian who took a powder,' he said, juggling the facts slightly. 'A GRU high-end type. He's been making noises about Cabrera.'

'What kind of noises?' Spencer asked, suddenly interested.

'A possible assassination attempt,' Stone answered.

At the word 'assassination' Spencer's eyes flickered slightly and then the expression on his face hardened even more. 'How good is his information?'

'Very good,' Stone answered.

Spencer sat back in his seat. 'The obvious question then,' he said after a moment. 'Why isn't this going through normal channels?'

'I've been asked to back off,' Stone said quietly. 'I've been told the situation is outside the Bureau's mandate.' The implication was clear: if Stone was being muzzled the orders had come from an agency on a higher rung of the intelligence ladder, and if a Soviet defector was involved that meant the senior organisation was the CIA.

'Shit,' said Spencer. 'Just what I need, more political bullshit!'

'You really haven't heard anything?' Stone asked.

Spencer shook his head. 'Not a damn thing,' he said. 'How long did you have your pigeon before they took him off your hands?'

'Long enough to know that he was on to something,' Stone responded cautiously. Make the lie too complicated and he'd wind up tripping over it.

'Anything substantial?'

'No,' Stone answered, shaking his head. That was true enough. So far all he had was a trembling web of circumstantial evidence. Christ! If only Travkin had really defected to him!

'All right,' Spencer said. 'I'll check it out. Last time I looked we had about 40,000 potential freaks logged onto the computer. Maybe one of them is a Costa Rican expatriate with a bone to pick.'

'What about professionals?' Stone asked.

'Sure. Those too.' Spencer sighed. 'Where do I get in touch with you if something rings a bell?'

'Here,' Stone answered. He took a ballpoint out of his shirt pocket and jotted the safe house telephone number onto his napkin. He folded it once and handed it to Spencer. The Secret Service man stood and took the napkin, putting it into the pocket of his trousers.

'Thanks for the lunch,' he said, nodding. He put on his sunglasses, turned, and headed for the exit, threading his way between the empty tables. Stone watched him go, then leaned back in his chair, looking out across the city. Over the roof of the Treasury he could see the White House and beyond it to Blair House, the Presidential guest quarters. In a few weeks it would be used as Francisco Cabrera's residence while he was in Washington.

Resisting the urge to light another cigarette, Stephen Stone frowned. Glancing over the low wall beside him he watched the slowly moving traffic work its way up Pennsylvania Avenue towards the Capitol, a heat-rippled white dome a mile away, barely visible in the murky air.

'I must be nuts,' he whispered to himself. He'd put his career on the line by deliberately disobeying Ruppelt's orders, and now he'd compounded it by involving Spencer and the Secret Service. The worst thing was not having anybody to talk to about it. He felt a sudden tug of loneliness and realised that he was thinking about Debbie.

And that was a waste of time, of course, because she was still away at that conference in Paris. He shook his head, bemused, and allowed himself the cigarette. Somewhere along the line his life had come completely off the predictable rails of existence and now he was hurtling down some bizarre spur line populated by kidnapped Russians, Central American heads of state and a wife more desirable now that she was an ex.

With an irritated grimace Stone stood up abruptly and put on his jacket. That kind of thinking really *would* drive you nuts. The only cure was work, and one way or the other that meant Dimitri Alexandyr Travkin. The beleagured counterintelligence agent dipped into his wallet and pulled out a handful of bills. He slipped enough to cover the check under his water glass and followed Spencer's route out of the restaurant.

To Sergei Kuryokhin Prague represented everything that was wrong with Central Europe, past and present. Architecturally the dark city on the banks of the Vltava River was a paean of praise to the baroque sensibilities of the Hapsburgs, its steep, winding streets and looming hilltop fortresses acting as a constant reminder of its feudal origins.

As far as Kuryokhin was concerned the only good thing about Prague was the quality of its beer. Still, it had been part of his circuit of agent contacts for the better part of four decades and required his personal attention from time to time. His twice-yearly trips also served notice to the young turks of the KGB that he was still a force to be contended with and not simply an aging has-been. This trip, however, was more than just a public relations gesture; his agent in Prague was the access point of his pipeline to the West and a necessary element for setting up a contact with *Osin*.

The system had been in place almost from the time *Osin* had been activated. His Prague agent, part of an established KGB network, was linked to a secondary 'cut-out', supposedly an illegal run by the man in Prague. The cut-out in turn provided Kuryokhin with a connection to a freelancer in Amsterdam. The freelancer, a man named Tetar Van Elven, ran a wholesaling company and came to Prague regularly to purchase glassware.

The Prague agent knew nothing of Van Elven and Van Elven knew nothing of the Prague agent so the connection was clean. The complex system also ensured that *Osin*'s true identity was safe from a thousand and one prying eyes at Tyeply Shtan. The deep cover agent in the American intelligence establishment was the crowning achievement of Kuryokhin's career and he'd gone to great lengths to ensure that the identity of his most valuable asset would never be compromised.

At seven-thirty that evening, after a mediocre meal in the Hotel Ambassador's Pasaz Café, he stepped out onto Wencleslas Square and began walking south towards Opletalova Street and the looming equestrian statue of the square's namesake, King Wenceslas.

The square was actually a boulevard 800 yards long, its broad sidewalks shaded by trees, the tumbled skein of rococo buildings on either side containing restaurants, airline offices, clothing boutiques, antique stores and galleries. On summer nights such as this one the sidewalks were an obstacle course of ice cream vendors, sausage stands selling bloated *kolbasy* to anyone who dared purchase one, and wandering crowds of local citizenry, peasant women in dirndls from the outlying provinces and roving squads of German tourists.

Ignoring it all, Kuryokhin continued on his way to U Natrovski Alley, a narrow lane running off Wenceslas Square, its entrance almost invisible to the casual passerby. Kuryokhin turned up the deeply shadowed walkway, ignoring the darkened, grime-encrusted windows of the tiny shops on either side. Fifty yards down the alley he reached his objective: the dimly lit window of Antikvariât Masaryk.

The old man glanced at the meagre selection of volumes on display behind the dirty glass. A French language guide to Prague, long out of date, a fan of early Penguin editions of PG Wodehouse and two Stephen King novels in German. Peering beyond the stained felt of the display shelf Kuryokhin could see a cubicle no more than a few metres on a side, the walls filled with awkward-looking home-made bookshelves, the shelves themselves half empty. A middle-aged man with dark, slicked back hair sat behind a scarred desk at the rear of the cubicle, a curtained doorway at his back and an enormous marmalade cat asleep on the desk in front of him. The man was looking at a battered copy of *Penthouse* magazine: Masaryk at work, a moth eaten grey cardigan buttoned over his fat belly, studying the black market wares that kept him in business.

Kuryokhin pushed open the door of the tiny bookstore, pleased by the brief look of fear on the pornographer's face as he made his entrance. Seeing who it was, Masaryk settled back in his chair, exhaling loudly. Kuryokhin closed the door behind him and took three brief steps to the desk.

'I thought perhaps you might not be coming tonight,' the bookseller grumbled, looking up at Kuryokhin. He spoke in English, the only language common to them both. Masaryk was incapable of learning Russian and Kuryokhin refused to force his larynx around the impossible convolutions of Czech. The KGB man grimaced, his nose wrinkling. The smell of stale beer hung over Masaryk like a pall.

'I said I would be here,' Kuryokhin answered. 'I am here.'

Masaryk nodded dully and put down *Penthouse*. He pushed himself back in his chair and opened the centre drawer of the desk. Reaching into it he withdrew a thin manila envelope. He handed it to Kuryokhin and waited. The KGB man examined the package carefully. Inside was a single sheet of thin paper and a rail ticket stamped with the official seal of approval from CEDOK, the Czech state travel office. The ticket was dated for midnight the following day and would take him from Prague to Berlin and then on to Amsterdam. Turning his attention to the sheet of paper, Kuryokhin tilted his spectacles up on his nose, squinting in the dim light as he read the brief message:

'CANAL HOUSE 148 KEIZERSGRACHT. TEL 262–231 ON ARRIVAL.'

There was no signature but the addition of the figures in the telephone number ensured that both the train ticket and the hotel address had come from Tetar Van Elven. Kuryokhin slipped the sheet of paper and the railway ticket back into the envelope, then put the envelope into the inside breast pocket of his suit jacket. From the opposite pocket he withdrew another envelope, this one filled with well used German marks, Masaryk's standard currency of choice. He handed the money to the bookseller, who then placed it in the drawer of his desk. From the expression on his face Kuryokhin knew that Masaryk couldn't wait for him to leave so he could count it.

'Our business is concluded,' the KGB man said, making no effort to conceal his contempt.

The money in hand, Masaryk offered a thick-lipped smile. 'Until next time,' he said.

Kuryokhin made no reply; instead he turned away and left the bookstore. Walking back down the alley to Wenceslas Square he wondered how long it would be until one of the currency squads from the SNB raided Antikvariât Masaryk and dragged the oily little shit off to the cells at the Bartolomejska Police Headquarters. The old man shook his head slowly, mouth pulled down in a frown. He'd seen enough of the world to know that it didn't matter who ruled, Marxist, martinet or mushroom, every state, every city had its version of Lars Masaryk, and the trade which he enjoyed. The Eastern Bloc had no corner on the market in filth and depravity. Kuryokhin spat onto the pavement. In his youth such men would have been rooted out like vermin. Now it was the order of the day – he'd even seen such goods on the Metro back home. He shook his head again; he'd lived too long.

Reaching the boulevard he began trudging up the gentle slope, taking deep breaths of the cool night air. By the time he reached the main entrance to the Hotel Ambassador he'd managed to purge the sour stink of Masaryk's shop from his nostrils, his thoughts concentrated on the upcoming journey to Amsterdam. An hour later the white-haired old man had fallen into treasonous sleep, coiled, dark dreams of old battles won and lost rising from memory.

Dimitri Travkin lay on the bed in his room at the Bowie facility, leafing through a month-old copy of *Newsweek*, trying to ignore the constant itch of frustration caused by his enforced inactivity. Earlier that day they'd moved him out of the hospital wing, but his new quarters weren't much better. His room was small, with a narrow, mesh-glass window. The floor was hardwood, freshly sanded and glossy, the walls white over aging plaster. The room was furnished with a single bed, a straight-backed wooden chair and a nondescript chest of drawers. A closet on the left-hand wall had been converted into a tiny bathroom with a sink and toilet. The only decorative touch was a framed, government-issue official portrait of Richard Nixon.

Dropping the *Newsweek* onto his lap for the twentieth time in as many minutes, Travkin stared at the picture of the ex-President, wondering at the exigencies of fate which had made it his only companion. It was oddly fitting since both men had been trapped in a trembling, far-flung web of lies, counter lies, illusion and deceit, but there the similarity ended. Tricky Dick was making six-figure publishing advances while Dumb Dimitri was getting three bland meals a day and a monk's cell for his best efforts.

By now, he knew, Gennaddi Koslov would have written him off like a bad debt. Travkin didn't hold it against his boss; the old man wouldn't have any choice, no matter what his personal feelings were. The fact that he'd been kidnapped was irrelevant; once taken he was compromised, returning he would be suspect. It was the Yurchenko scenario in reverse and Travkin found himself wondering if his kidnapping by the CIA might be a delayed reprisal for the KGB man's infamous and highly embarrassing double defection in 1985.

The origins of his plight didn't really matter to Travkin one way or the other – his concerns were much more immediate. Following the preliminary interrogation he'd spent almost all of his time trying to formulate some sort of plan. So far he had identified his problem as having three stages: escape from the Bowie facility, somehow gathering evidence to prove that his kidnapping had been just that and not a defection, then finally, and most importantly, convincing Gennaddi Koslov of his innocence. For all his Western affectations and affections the thought of being marooned in the United States, unable ever to go home again, was unbearable.

His bitter train of thought was broken as the door opened. It was the Mutt and Jeff pair who'd escorted him to his previous interrogation, this time minus the wheelchair. Once again it was the slim, dark-haired man who spoke to him, this time in English.

'Come with us,' he said briefly. Travkin made no attempt at a reply. He simply nodded and stood up, allowing the two men to fall in on either side as they went down the maze of half-lit corridors to the pleasantly furnished room where he'd spoken with David Cook, his bland and strangely vague interrogator.

His two escorts opened the door to the room and allowed Travkin to enter. They withdrew, closing the door behind them, leaving the GRU man to himself. There was no sign of Cook, but there was an oddly familiar smell in the air. Cigarette smoke certainly, but neither the tart sweet odour of a blended American tobacco, nor the acrid fug of a European *tabac noir*. Travkin sniffed, frowning. A green raw scent, almost like a cigar.

There was a large, cut glass ashtray on the coffee table. Travkin picked it up, examining the half-dozen or so butts ground into the grey-brown ash. One of them was long enough to read the brand name: Coronado. Mexican? Cuban? Why here and now? A Latin American defector being debriefed? Silliness. Or . . . his mind did the necessary hop skip and jump to the obvious conclusion. Francisco Cabrera. Not a defector, but perhaps an assassin, or someone chosen to play an assassin's part.

He took the cigarette butt and dropped it carefully into the breast pocket of his jacket. There was still no sign of Cook. Putting the ashtray back on the table Travkin began to roam around the room, desperately trying to gather more information. Reaching the antique writing desk he paused, tilting his head towards the doorway beside it. Still no sound. He went through the drawers quickly. Pads, ballpoint pen, book of matches from a restaurant on H Street called Big Wong. Travkin knew it; basement dim sum all day long with an atmosphere like an opium den. He pocketed the matches and kept on going. Nothing, nothing, nothing. Wait.

The surface of the desk was protected by a large, buckskin coloured felt blotter in a leather frame. The telephone stood at the lower left hand corner and there was a Parker pen set in a marble base at the upper centre. For the most part the blotter was clean, but the area around the telephone was scored with a variety of doodles and scrawls. One in particular caught Travkin's eye. A single word in ballpoint, deeply inscribed and boxed, then struck out, with a telephone number beneath it.

LUPE

01–506–21 40 00

Lupe was Spanish for wolf. A code name, perhaps? The 01 prefix meant that the telephone number was international, but he had no idea what country the 506 number represented. Working as quickly as possible Travkin jotted down the name and number on a sheet of notepaper. Folding the slip of paper into a small square he bent down and slid it into his shoe, praying that it would be overlooked if there was a snap search.

He checked the desk to make sure everything was as it had been, then went back to the couch and sat down. Picking up a magazine from the coffee table he willed himself to relax, trying to slow the hammer rhythm of his heart. The name and number might mean nothing at all, but they could also represent the first faint crack in the door he'd been looking for.

'He took the dangle,' said David Cook, watching Travkin on the monitor screens. Beside him, Hudson Cooper nodded silently, lips pursed in concentration. Cook had given the evening observation room shift a dinner break and the two men were alone in the dim-lit surveillance suite. While Cook went back to the list of questions he'd been given for the next 'interrogation', Cooper kept his eyes locked on Travkin.

Taking the GRU Deputy Resident had been a calculated risk, but an unavoidable one. Now, it seemed, the risk was paying dividends. Initially the kidnapping had been a quickly devised solution to the unexpected problem of REDNET's snooping. Almost by accident Travkin had stumbled onto Rhinelander, and with Stephen Stone and his people keeping the Russian under surveillance the possibility of the real conspiracy being uncovered grew with each passing day.

The fact that both Travkin and Stone had misinterpreted the information and were following the red herring involving the Costa Rican situation was a bonus, but Cooper knew he couldn't depend on the cover story forever. Without some additional input by the Agency, either Stone or Travkin would have gone beyond it eventually, hence the kidnapping.

With Travkin removed as an element in the chess game Stone's source of information dried up overnight. Augmenting this was Cooper's thinly veiled intimation to Ruppelt that Travkin was an Agency asset, which in turn lent weight to the idea that the kidnapping had actually been a defection. To Ruppelt the Travkin case was out of his hands and good riddance. For Cooper, the required result had been obtained and the leak plugged.

The only remaining problem had concerned the GRU man's final disposition. At first Cooper had considered simply removing him like Dr Barron, but the kidnapping itself and the time spent at Bowie had exposed Travkin too broadly. Keeping him on at the facility indefinitely was also out of the question.

It was at this point in his thinking that the Deputy Director saw the opportunity for another improvisational stroke. If Travkin could be neither killed nor kept then he would have to be released. By now the GRU man was persona non grata both to his own people and to the KGB. Eventually Travkin would come to the obvious conclusion: to stay alive he would have to defect, and he would almost certainly defect to Stone at the FBI REDNET office. In the final analysis Cooper didn't really care if Travkin went over to Stone or was picked up by the KGB. Either way he would be debriefed and the 'dangle' information relating to the Cabrera scenario would come out, giving it even more credibility and building a false and winding trail away from Rhinelander.

According to Mallory the assassin had finally called the secure number earlier that day. The message had been straightforward and Mallory had been given access to the DDO's 'special account' at the Agency's proprietary bank in Miami which had electronically transferred the required amount to a dummy account in New York. Equipped with ID to match the dummy account, Mallory had left for New York on the shuttle earlier that evening and would be back in time for the contact call at the visitors' centre the following morning. The plan, it seemed, was unfolding as it should.

Watching Travkin on the screens in front of him, Cooper allowed himself a small bleak smile. With the knowledge of President Tucker's progressively destructive ailment and the possibility of Vice-President Teresi's assumption of power, the decision to develop an assassination plan had been necessary and inevitable. Even so it had depressed Cooper profoundly, leaving him with a cold sense of foreboding that ate at his bones like a winter wind. Travkin's intrusion had only made the feeling worse. But now, with the plan actually in motion, Travkin compromised and Stone effectively blocked, Cooper found himself beginning to believe that it might all work out after all. His smile broadened slightly as he tried to imagine which senior senator would be appointed to head the committee to investigate the assassinations.

'Mr Cooper?' David Cook's voice invaded his thoughts.

Cooper turned and looked at the man. 'Yes?'

'These questions. . . . from the looks of it I'm supposed to be homing in on what he knows about GRU activities in Central America, particularly Costa Rica, is that right?'

'Yes.'

'I was just wondering if we had something on down there. The questions are kind of vague.'

'Treat is as a fishing expedition, Mr Cook, nothing more,' Cooper answered. He stood up, taking a last look at Travkin, seated on the couch in the interrogation room. 'Get the transcript to me when it's done.'

'Of course.'

'I'll be in administration if you want me,' Cooper added. 'We're having Comrade Travkin transferred to the Farm tomorrow and I want to make sure the paperwork is in order.' He nodded towards Cook. 'Goodnight.'

'Goodnight, sir.'

The Deputy Director left the observation room and turned down the wide corridor leading past the old auditorium to the east wing of the facility. If Travkin was half the ex-Spetznaz commando his records indicated, he'd be safely sprung and wandering the streets of Washington DC by this time tomorrow night.

CHAPTER FIFTEEN

The night had cooled the baking, humid dome of air shrouding the capital, leaving long, ragged sheets of mist that lay close to the ground, clinging damply to every tree and lamp post, dew beading on each blade of grass for a few brief moments before the sun climbed above the pale stone monuments of the inner city, announcing the beginning of yet another day.

Eric Rhinelander, dressed in a dark blue Nike jogging outfit, pedalled the old fashioned three-speed bicycle down Connecticut Avenue towards Farragut Square, tyres hissing softly on the damp roadway as he piloted the machine through the thin, early morning traffic. The bicycle had been purchased second hand the day before from a sporting goods store on P Street off Dupont Circle along with the Paragon lock and the custom carrying case welded and bolted behind the seat.

Skirting Farragut Square, Rhinelander crosse H Street and coasted down Jackson Place to the intersection at Pennsylvania Avenue. He dismounted at the end of the street, then walked the bicycle into Lafayette Park, locking it securely to the bicycle rack almost directly across from Blair House on the corner. Fifty yards away on the far side of the street he could see the twin guardhouses and the heavy double gate that blocked off West Executive Avenue.

Using a key on a chain around his neck, Rhinelander opened the lock on the metal carry case and took out a small red nylon knapsack. At the same time he pushed the 'start' button on the Kyocera KD3030 video camera which had been hidden under the knapsack. With the camera running he closed and locked the box, opened the knapsack and withdrew a lightweight windbreaker to match his dark blue jogging outfit. He put on the windbreaker, slipped the straps of the empty knapsack over his shoulders and jogged across to the Rochambeau statue. He spent five minutes doing warm-up exercises, casually glancing across Pennsylvania Avenue from time to time as he went through his work-out.

His preliminary surveillance at the Hay-Adams and the reading he'd done the day before after making the rounds of Washington's bookstores had taught Rhinelander a number of things, the most important of which was timing. Even the few hours he'd spent at the Hay-Adams showed that everything at the White House was done on a fanatically tight schedule. Shifts changed right to the minute, patrols were made on a strict routine and people came and went to a time-clock's beat.

What he didn't know yet was the complexity of that rhythm – how the patterns of activity meshed together into an overall system. That was the reason for the video camera hidden in the bicycle's carry case. He'd chosen the Kyocera because of its time-lapse function, then added a tiny fibre-optic lens and battery powered light source, telling the salesman he was a teacher and wanted to record insect activity for his high school biology classes.

Later, in the basement parking garage of the Holiday Inn, after checking out the camera thoroughly, Rhinelander had used a metal punch to poke a small hole in the rear of the metal carry-case. He placed the camera and light source in the case, threaded the flexible lens cable into the freshly punched hole and secured it with a seam of clear nail polish.

Finally, in the early evening, Rhinelander had taken a taxicab down to Lafayette Square and spent some time trying to identify the best location for the bicycle the following day. From his time at the Hay-Adams he knew that virtually no one except visiting diplomats entered by way of the south portico, and that virtually all official traffic entered via the closed off West Executive Avenue, or the east and west entrances on Pennsylvania Avenue.

He eventually settled on the bike rack because he could leave the hidden camera there safely without arousing suspicion and also because it gave the best overall view. The nickel cadmium batteries for the camera and the light source pack had a record life of two hours, more than enough for Rhinelander's purposes. In the time-lapse mode the camera was only in operation for two seconds out of every minute, recording twenty-four 'frames' of video-tape every thirty seconds. Over a twelve-hour period the camera would take 1,440 individual images, catching any and all traffic going in and out of the two entrances, compressing it into twenty-four minutes of tape.

With his athletic bona fides firmly established in the minds of the Executive Protection Service guards on the far side of Pennsylvania Avenue, Rhinelander finished up his stationary exercises and began jogging, heading west past Blair House, then north towards Washington Circle. Turning up 19th Street he made his way to the Presidential Hotel, then caught a taxi back to the Wyoming.

He showered, changed, then spent two quiet hours going over more of the research material he'd gathered the previous day. By 9:00 a.m. he was having breakfast at the Holiday Inn and by 10:00 he was on his way to the visitors' centre at Union Station, the envelope containing his instructions to Cooper safely hidden in the inside pocket of his sports jacket.

*

Sweating in his wilted blue and white seersucker suit, Paul Mallory leaned against the telephone booth partition, the dead receiver to his ear. It was almost exactly ten-thirty and he'd kept the phone occupied for the last fifteen minutes, ensuring that he'd have possession of it for Rhinelander's call. The visitors' centre was thronged with tourists as well as the ebb and flow of traffic from Union Station and the metro.

He poked a finger under his glasses and swept the beads of stinging salt perspiration away from his eyes. He had a splitting headache, his stomach was hyperacidic and tied in a knot and his scalp itched. For the twentieth time since he'd climbed out of bed that morning he found himself wishing he'd gone into some other line of business.

The last few days with Cooper had been agonising. It took every ounce of concentration he had just to keep up the appearance that everything was normal, sending out budget memos, reminding the DDO of meetings and keeping the filing up to date. Thankfully Cooper had been spending most of his time dealing with another project involving a defector out at the Bowie facility, but even that didn't bring any relief from his tensions. For Mallory, given what he knew and what he surmised, imagination was his worst enemy. The day before, on the New York shuttle, he'd come up with a dozen different ways for Cooper to get rid of him and another dozen on the way back.

The more time that passed, the more Mallory's concerns about the Rhinelander operation solidified, especially considering his own close involvement. To someone with a mind as logical as his, the conclusions were inescapable. Assassination was an outlawed method within the Agency, by policy and by law, yet Rhinelander was a professional assassin. By definition, then, the operation planned by Cooper was out of office, so anyone close to it would be scrubbed.

'Shit,' he whispered, listening to the whispers and crackles emanating from the dead telephone reciever in his hand. His backup plan using the computer bulletin boards was fine and good, but to be effective as insurance Cooper would have to know that it existed and Mallory didn't have anything like enough courage to confront his boss with what he knew. Once again, logic came into play, because when you got right down to it he didn't really know anything at all; his suppositions were logical, but they were still just suppositions.

'Shit,' he repeated. Every involvement, every bit of contact and information just took him deeper down and there wasn't a damn thing he could do about it. He let out a long breath and tried to apply his logic and experience as a Threat Analyst in an optimistic light. The only thing he could come up with was the fact that he was still alive. He glanced at his watch. Ten-thirty on the button. He hung up the receiver, then wiped his palms on his pant legs. A few seconds later the phone rang and he picked it up. 'Mallory,' he said, trying to keep his voice firm.

'What's my name?' The tone was cool, unhurried. Rhinelander.

'QJ/RAIL,' Mallory replied.

'What's your slug?' Slug was the Agency word for a person's designated office and position.

'Operations,' said Mallory.

'516 10th Street Northwest,' Rhinelander instructed. 'Across from Ford's Theatre. There's a green refuse container with a swinging lid at the foot of the stairs. Drop what I want into the container. What you want will be stuck to the inside of the lid. Take the metro from Union Station to Metro Centre. Take the G and 11th exit. You have an outside limit of twenty minutes. Go.' Suddenly Mallory was listening to a dial tone.

It took Mallory fourteen minutes to reach the address on 10th Street, which turned out to be the residence where Lincoln was taken after being shot. It was a narrow brick building, sandwiched in between a grey office block and a nightclub. A curved staircase led up to the front door above the half-storey basement. True to Rhinelander's description there was a green metal refuse container at the foot of the steps.

Pausing at the stairway, one hand on the wrought iron railing, Mallory dropped his envelope into the garbage bin, then tipped up the swing lid and peeled away the envelope Rhinelander had left for him. There were a few people on the street but no one appeared to be paying any attention to him. If Rhinelander was anywhere close he was well hidden.

Mallory slid Rhinelander's envelope into his pocket, then headed down 10th towards E Street and Pennsylvania Avenue. He passed a payphone kiosk but ignored it, even though he knew he should be calling in to the office as soon as possible after the pick-up. Reaching the intersection at E Street he found his view overwhelmed by the massive fortress architecture of the J Edgar Hoover Building, which made him feel even worse. Here he was, surrounded by official Washington, contemplating an act of what amounted to treason.

At Pennsylvania Avenue he paused, seating himself uncomfortably on the edge of a large concrete pot containing a fountain of bushy flowering plants which were rapidly shrivelling under the hot, late-morning sun. Mallory reached into his pocket and took out the envelope. It appeared to be standard business size. There was no special seal that he could see except for the gummed flap, and the front of the envelope was blank. It had been stuck to the inside of the lid with loops of masking tape, leaving two one-inch square areas on the flap side which were still a little sticky.

Frowning, he slipped the envelope back into his jacket. He squinted across at the old National Revenue Building on the other side of Pennsylvania

Avenue, trying to figure out his best course of action. Cooper's only scheduled event for the day was a reception at Blair House for the Canadian Prime Minister, and that wasn't until 7:00 p.m. As far as Mallory knew the DDO was booked out to the Bowie facility for the day, which gave him some leeway. Even so, Cooper was well aware of the mid-morning contact and if he had any suspicions about Mallory's loyalties he could scan the computerised security log to find out when he'd checked in. At best Mallory assumed he had two hours, no more.

It was enough. Mallory nodded, making up his mind at last. The risk was worth the reward. Gangly, worried-looking, he climbed to his feet and went to the kerb. He hailed a cab, ducked into the battered vehicle and gave the driver his address in Alexandria.

Rhinelander, less than two minutes behind Mallory, picked up his envelope from the refuse container, then retraced his steps to Metro Centre and played subway tag for half an hour just to make sure that Cooper's man hadn't set him up with a tail. Finally, satisfied that he hadn't been followed, Rhinelander took a taxi back to the Holiday Inn, then walked across Connecticut to the Wyoming Apartments.

As requested, the envelope contained a Citibank passbook from a New York branch with a complete history of deposits and withdrawals and a current balance of $200,000. There was also a Citibank Visa, encoded to a James Smythe, a cashcard in the same name and a New York driver's licence with a fuzzy photograph that could have been Rhinelander or anyone else with the same colour hair.

Rhinelander went into the study, sat down and lit a cigarette. In front of him on the desk were stacks of books and magazines he'd picked up on his tour of Washington bookstores. Even for someone used to doing a great deal of research, Rhinelander had been amazed at the massive amount of information about the White House that was freely available. Putting the cigarette aside in Gray's crystal cut ashtray he flipped open his three-ring notebook, uncapped a felt pen and got down to work.

The White House, formally known as US Federal Reservation 1, was the first official building erected in Washington. The cornerstone of what was to become the quintessential American residence was laid in 1792. It had been designed by an Irish architect named James Hoban, and based on the plans for an English country home. Located on a slight ridge and overlooking a swamp that led down to what was then the Tiber River, the building was draughty, damp and uncomfortable.

Thomas Jefferson occupied the White House in 1801 and made the first major additions: the east and west wings, which concealed workshops, wine cellars and the Presidential stables. In 1812 the city was occupied by the

British and the White House was left a gutted ruin. It was reopened in 1818 by President Monroe, and in 1824 and 1829 respectively, the south and north porticoes were added. Over the next 120 years succeeding Presidents added, removed, altered and fiddled. Executive offices were tacked on to the west wing, bomb shelters were dug and tunnels were bored.

By Truman's time the building was on the verge of collapse, and the pragmatic little man convinced Congress that problems would arise if the ceiling of the diplomatic reception room collapsed on a visiting dignitary. Funds were allocated, the Trumans moved into Blair House, and the entire building was gutted. Two sub-basements and air conditioning vaults under the north lawn were added, then a steel framework was constructed to support the new floors and walls. The original woodwork had been carefully preserved, and when the renovations were complete, it was refitted. The project was finished in 1952 after four years' work and an expenditure of almost six million dollars.

There were other alterations made after Truman's, although none so complex. Roosevelt's swimming pool in the west wing annex was reopened by Kennedy, ignored by Johnson, then closed and transformed into a press conference room by Nixon. It had only recently been reopened by the Tucker administration. Kennedy also added a brand new and supposedly 'atomic hardened' bomb shelter which was now used as headquarters for the White House Communications Agency.

The Communications Agency was interesting in itself. According to the information Rhinelander had assembled, the WHCA was the largest and necessarily the most secret White House support group. Made up of a rotating elite unit of almost 800 military professionals, it operated the signal board, which connected the President to the nation's diplomatic and military communications nets all over the world.

On a smaller scale, but of more use to Rhinelander, was the knowledge that the WHCA central radio console also connected the White House staff car radios, and was in charge of supplying the Secret Service with its communications, including hand held 'voice secure' walkie talkies. The WHCA also operated the White House paging system which was capable of reaching any staff member in the DC area.

Finding accurate information about the Secret Service and other White House staff had been a little more difficult than tracing the building's history, but not impossible. After skimming a dozen or so books Rhinelander was beginning to build a reasonably complete profile of the executive residence and how it operated.

There were ninety-three actual staff members working within the White House, although none lived in the mansion. They included carpenters, plumbers, cooks, waiters and elevator operators, all under the supervision of the Chief Usher, who was effectively the White House manager. As well as the house staff there were thirty-six National Parks officers to maintain the grounds and manage the greenhouse and storage warehouse.

The Secret Service, Rhinelander discovered, had 1,800 agents within the DC area, 800 of which, in shifts, were assigned to the President and the Vice-President. At any given time of the day or night forty plain clothes agents were in position and immediately around the building. Their location, and the Chief Executive's, were constantly monitored by the White House communications centre located directly below the Oval Office in the west wing. There were also an additional 125 uniformed members of the Executive Protection Service on duty on the outer perimeter of the grounds and at the entrances. Both uniformed and plain clothes members were equipped with radios and were armed with a variety of weaponry that went from sidearms and automatic weapons to shoulder-fired Redeye anti-aircraft missiles.

As well as the Secret Service protective detail, there was a hundred-strong Technical Security Division, located in the White House area, which regularly 'swept' the White House looking for bugs, radioactive material or anything else that might harm the President and his family. The TSD was also responsible for the perimeter security system which included a buried microwave fence, just as Rhinelander had expected, as well as infra red cameras, motion detectors and antipersonnel radar within the building, and seismic sensors buried under the lawns to detect intruders. All of this was augmented in turn by a complex array of panic buttons, 'locator boxes', metal detectors and X-ray scanners as well as zoned identification procedures.

Using floor plans and exploded views from a *National Geographic* article as well as comparative plans from a *Life* magazine special on the presidency, Rhinelander began to sketch out a schematic diagram of the White House and grounds, detailing in the security with a set of coloured pens. At first glance it appeared to be an impregnable target, but from long experience Rhinelander knew it was just such a fortress mentality that led to oversight.

Castle walls and palace guards didn't stop an intruder from reaching Queen Elizabeth's bedroom and the most stringent security measures in existence hadn't prevented von Stauffenberg from placing a briefcase bomb within a yard of Adolf Hitler's knees. Glancing at the wealth of research material spread out on the desk before him, Rhinelander knew that within it and the steadily unreeling videotape he would find the logistical flaw, the chink in the armour, the single, simple error that would give him entry through the battlements of this particular Troy.

Paul Mallory held the envelope up to the glaring fluorescent light in the bathroom of his Alexandria apartment, trying to see if Rhinelander had taken any special precautions with his message to Hudson Cooper. He squinted up at the rectangle of cream coloured paper, checking the translucent interior with extreme care. After five minute, still nervous, Mallory took the envelope out into the living room, hesitated for a minute, then slipped the sharp end of his letter opener under the flap. Inside was a single sheet of lined paper. The message was brief and hand-printed in the terse, telegraphic style common to Agency reports.

IN MY ESTIMATION PROJECT IS FEASIBLE AND I WILL ACT ON THE ASSUMPTION THAT IT IS ONGOING UNLESS I AM OTHERWISE IN-FORMED.
TO EXPEDITE COMPLETION SUBJECTS MUST BE IN POSITION AS PER OUR DISCUSSION. FURTHER, INFORMATION REGARDING CROWN SECURE VOICE COMMUNICATIONS MUST BE RELAYED TO ME WITHIN 72 HOURS OF RECEIVING THIS MESSAGE.
YOU WILL BE INFORMED OF PROCEDURES FOR PRELIMINARY PAYMENT WITHIN THE NEXT SEVEN DAYS. IF PROCEDURES ARE NOT COMPLIED WITH THE PROJECT WILL BE TERMINATED.

The message was unsigned. Frowning, Mallory read through it again, trying to decipher its real meaning. Apparently Rhinelander had done enough preliminary work to conclude that he was capable of doing the job, whatever it was, but the use of the word 'subjects' indicated that there was more than one person involved. The line about 'Crown' and secure voice communications was also confusing.

One thing was certain – the use of the word 'subjects' almost certainly ruled out Cabrera as a target, as did the mention of 'preliminary payment'. While setting up the bank account for Rhinelander Mallory had assumed that the $200,000 Citibank deposit represented at least part of the assassin's fee, but according to this message, the preliminary payment was still to be paid. The largest CIA 'freelance' fee on record was $50,000 paid to the three-man team hired to assassinate Trujillo in May 1961, and even taking inflation into account any payment over and above a slush fund of almost a quarter million dollars would be wildly exorbitant, especially for the removal of a minor player like Cabrera.

But if not Cabrera, who? At least two people – the subjects – to be in a specific place at a specific time, and who rated a secure voice communications network with the code name Crown. Mallory shook his head; it had occurred to him that so far he'd been assuming that QJ/RAIL's targets would be killed inside the United States. What if that wasn't the case? Maybe Crown was Queen Elizabeth, or Prince Charles. It was no use; he simply didn't have enough information.

Mallory glanced at his wristwatch. With traffic it would take him at least an hour to get back to the office. He refolded the message carefully and slipped it back into the envelope. Shrugging on his wrinkled jacket he headed for the stairs. There was a quick-print shop at the corner where he could get the message photocopied, and probably pick up a new envelope as well. If he was lucky Hudson Haines Cooper would never find out that someone had been tampering with his mail.

Dressed in his jogging clothes once again, Eric Rhinelander retrieved his bicycle from the rack in Lafayette Square at almost exactly 6:00 p.m. Returning his windbreaker to the carry-case he switched off the camera, relocked the case and rode off. Half an hour later he reached the Holiday Inn on Connecticut Avenue, locked the bicycle to the rack in the basement parking lot and went up to his room.

He showered, changed into the clothes he'd set out on the bed an hour before, then returned to the basement parking lot. Making his way to the bicycle rack on the main level he unlocked the carry-case, took out the camera and left the garage through the main entrance. Carrying the camera by its hand grip he crossed Connecticut Avenue and entered the Wyoming.

It took another twenty minutes to cross-cable the VCR in John Gray's study to the 8mm format video camera, but finally Rhinelander found himself watching the comings and goings through the gates of West Executive Avenue. He ran through it quickly once, then replayed it, using the remote control to adjust the speed.

Most of the activity involved staff automobiles and the occasional limousine, but there were other vehicles as well including several delivery vans and a Parks Service truck. All but one were stopped and checked by the uniformed guards at the gate. The exception was a plain white 24-foot box cube van with government plates that arrived at 7:15 in the morning, according to the elapsed time counter in the corner of the frame. Rhinelander ran the sequence back and forth several times, picking up details including the fact that the front of the box above the cab appeared to be fitted with a refrigeration unit.

Smiling, Rhinelander stopped the tape at the point where the van was being waved through the gate by the guards without challenge. Lighting a self-congratulatory cigarette he began poking through neat stacks of research material in front of him. He found what he was looking for and leaned back in the chair behind John Gray's desk, flipping through the pages of the magazine he'd picked out of the pile.

He was reasonably sure he had it now: the secret of the way in was on the videotape across the room, his exit on page 486 of the April 1935 issue of *National Geographic* magazine.

CHAPTER SIXTEEN

Sergei Kuryokhin made his way carefully down to the main floor of the small hotel, one hand firmly on the railing. The Canal House had no elevator and the stairs were very steep. Still, alpine stairway aside, it had a wonderful little dining room which served a rijsttafel comparing favourably to that in some of the better-known Indonesian restaurants in the city.

The old man crossed the tiny lobby and stepped out into the cool night air. He buttoned his tweed jacket, then dipped one hand into his pocket, pulling out an almost empty pack of Lucky Strikes. He lit one, looking out over the dark slash of the Keizersgracht to the glittering lights of the narrow buildings on the far side. He smiled around the cigarette; to him Amsterdam was Venice without Italians and, outside of Moscow, his favourite city in Europe.

He turned south towards the Herenstraat, enjoying the sights and sounds, both on the cobbled street and the canal beyond. The street was alive with bicycles and cars, most heading in the direction he was going as the crowds of both tourists and locals converged on the *centrum*, or 'downtown' area of the city, its centre marked by Dam Square.

Just before the bridge spanning the canal at Herenstraat, Kuryokhin turned in to a small café. Choosing a table outside under the narrow awning, the KGB man ordered an Amstel and settled back in his chair. His objective lay less than fifty feet away – a houseboat moored to the canalside with the somewhat unappealing name of *d'Vijff Vlieghen – The Five Flies*.

Kuryokhin's beer arrived, head almost overflowing the sides of the large glass tankard. He sipped, then wiped the aromatic moustache away from his upper lip. From where he sat he could just make out the thin, insulated wire that snaked down from the slightly bowed roof of the houseboat, then found its way to a nearby utility pole onshore. Tetar Van Elven, Kuryokhin's agent in Amsterdam, was more than just an amateur spy, he was also a thief of electricity.

The white-haired man took another sip from the tankard, then lit a cigarette. For the next twenty minutes he sat calmly, smoking and drinking, his eyes roving over the café tables and people passing by on the sidewalk. Finally satisfied that there was no direct surveillance of the barge he drained the last of his beer and went inside the café to use the telephone.

'Hallo! Tetar Van Elven.' The voice was hale and hearty, filled with the casual bonhomie common to salesmen in any country.

'*Heeft u iets in zwart?*' Kuryokhin replied, using his identifying phrase.

'*Ya. In naylon.*'

'*Binnen tien minuten,*' the KGB man ordered. He went back to his seat under the awning, lit another Lucky Strike and waited. Well short of the ten minute limit, Tetar Van Elven appeared at the top of the cabin companionway on the *Five Flies*. He was in his late forties, and going to great lengths to look younger. His blond hair was too long, his thinly handsome face too tanned and his clothes just a little too up to the minute. Still, he knew his business and followed orders. Marxism might work for the masses, but after more than half a lifetime in intelligence Kuryokhin had learned that the better an agent was paid the more he produced; spying, it seemed, was fundamentally a capitalist affair.

Van Elven stepped over the low gunwale of the barge and crossed the sloping gangplank to dry land. He ran a long-fingered hand through his hair, then turned and headed towards the Herenstraat and the Dam. For Kuryokhin, Van Elven leaving the barge served two purposes; it gave him privacy, and if there was any surveillance, the Dutchman would draw it off.

The old man waited for another few minutes, then slipped a five guilder note under his empty beer glass and left the café. He crossed the narrow street, stepped onto the gangplank and cautiously edged his way aboard the *Five Flies*.

The barge was like a cross between a New York loft and an antique store. The interior of the cabin had been rebuilt into a single room, the floors highly polished, the open beamed ceiling fitted with four large skylights. The furniture was an eclectic mixture of everything from Bavarian woven-vine chairs to a Louis Quinze sideboard and dozens of shelves carried an astounding collection of glassware and crystal from every conceivable nationality and period.

In the centre of the room was a surprisingly simple dining table Van Elven used as his desk. On it, surrounded by stacks of papers, invoices and orders, was an IBM clone. There was a medium sized padded envelope balanced on the keyboard. Kuryokhin sat down at the desk and peeled open the envelope. Inside were a microcassette tape and a 3.5-inch floppy disk – not compatible with Van Elven's 5.25 disk drive.

The KGB man reached into the inside pocket of his jacket and took out a Phillips Memocorder microcassette machine, popped it open and inserted the cassette from *Osin*. He picked up the floppy disk and slipped it into his jacket, ignoring it for the time being. As usual the disk would contain various documents and reports of possible interest, scanned into the agent's computer and dumped onto the disk. The microcassette would hold the 'flash', or highly current information.

Kuryokhin inserted the tiny earphone from the recorder, adjusted the volume slightly and leaned back in his chair, eyes closed. There was a brief, hissing silence and then he heard the gravelly, mechanically altered voice of his prize agent.

> As you requested in your last transmission, the bulk of the material I've gathered for you on the computer disk relates to Agency studies regarding the installation at Ivanovo and transshipment of finished material to the new base at Kohtla-Jarve. Based on several conversations with Agency personnel at a high level I think we can safely assume that the initial cover story has been accepted by both Defence Intelligence and the Pentagon. Central Intelligence, however, is maintaining an on-off watch over Kohtla-Jarve utilising a one in three pass ratio with the KH11 satellite. With regard to this I would advise maintaining the camouflage routine until such time as even such limited surveillance is ended.
>
> I thought you might be interested to know that I was recently given a courier assignment by Hudson Cooper. As you are aware, I'm on the list as a regular messenger for the Agency as long as it doesn't conflict with my own work, so I wasn't entirely surprised when he called, but the substance of the assignment is odd and might bear investigation.
>
> For some reason Cooper wants me to purchase two million dollars, worth of gem quality emeralds and bring them to him at the Agency. Just as interesting is the fact that I'm to use funds drawn from the triple zero account at Credit Suisse. In case you're not aware of it, the three-oh account is a discretionary slush fund for the DDO's European operations, and using it isn't going to show up on the books for a long time, if ever.
>
> In terms of project budgets the two million isn't particularly large, but the gem purchase is suspect. It sounds like an attempt at making an untraceable payoff to some group. The other point of interest is the fact that I can't get any kind of line on this through regular channels. The only recent thing Cooper is devoting time to is a GRU defector named Travkin they've been holding at Bowie.
>
> If you want to look into this more deeply, the purchase is being made from Mouwes and Van Der Loon, number 8 Albert Cuypstraat. Cooper gave me identification as a representative of a Swiss-Dutch consortium called Ashengruppe Juwelen. I assumed that it was an Agency proprietary company but it's not listed anywhere. Frankly the whole thing stinks. Anyway, I thought you might want to pursue it. If you have any questions or instructions please transmit them in the usual way.

The cassette drifted into hissing silence. The KGB man pulled out the earpiece and stopped the tape. Once more the ubiquitous Dimitri Travkin made an appearance, this time in connection with the CIA's Deputy Director of Operations and a covert purchase of gemstones, probably for some kind of payoff, according to his tapeworm agent. There were no hard facts, but Kuryokhin had learned long ago that even the vaguest intelligence analysis by *Osin* was uncannily accurate. The old man made a small snorting sound. There was even a long-standing theory at Tyeply Shtan that the high-quality information provided by his mysterious agent of influence came about because *Osin* was actually a double agent working for the Americans.

Kuryokhin popped the tape out of the machine and put both into his pocket. He checked his watch. It was late – time for an old man with creaking bones to be in his bed. He pushed back the chair and stood up, sighing. One more day in Amsterdam and then home again. Much as he loved the Rodina, and Moscow in particular, the thought of returning to the Gordian knot of bureaucracy in the woods of Tyeply Shtan didn't encourage homesickness. Turning away he climbed the companionway to the deck of the *Five Flies*, then crossed the gangplank to the bank of the canal. With slow steps, lost in thought, he headed back to his hotel.

Like the four adjoining houses in the Beatles movie *A Hard Day's Night*, Blair House, the President's official guest quarters, is actually four separate addresses, two in Pennsylvania Avenue, and two around the corner on Jackson Place. Built in 1824, the Pennsylvania Avenue addresses became a favourite haunt of President Andrew Jackson and his cronies, eventually leading to the coining of the term 'kitchen cabinet' to describe their vital, but informal meetings.

In 1982, as badly in need of repair as the White House had been forty years previously, Blair House was given a complete overhaul at a cost of more than five million dollars. According to *Architectural Digest*, the net effect of the renovation, restoration and redecorating was 'stunning'. Hudson Cooper thought the whole thing was a waste of money.

Arriving at Blair House for the reception honouring the Canadian Prime Minister, he stepped out of the muggy late evening air into the air-conditioned coolness of the ornately wallpapered entrance hall. He endured the formal greeting from Maggie Scarfe, the Blair's official hostess, then followed the sound of chamber music and the smell of expensive perfume. It led him left through the drawing room to the much larger Dillon Room with its twin fireplaces and French doors opening onto the garden.

To Cooper the prettiness of the Dillon Room summed up his feelings about Blair House and his required attendance at so many of its official functions. For him, pale green, hand-painted Chinese wallpaper had no place in a room supposedly designed to represent the United States of America to foreign visitors. Neither did delicate porcelain and an obstacle course of rosewood occasional tables and silk upholstered chairs. In the first place it was like stepping into a furniture showroom and in the second place it was far too effeminate. Frowning, Cooper threaded his way through the chattering crowd of black ties and evening dresses. He nodded in the direction of a few people he vaguely recognised, then slipped out through the doorway into the courtyard garden.

It was just past eight o'clock. The reception had been underway since six. Fifteen or twenty minutes of well-considered mingling would guarantee that his presence had been noted and then he could go home to the Watergate and await the outcome of the Travkin business.

The courtyard was cool, shaded by the high, red brick walls of the new Executive Office building. Lines of magnolia trees softened the looming perimeter and a bed of flowers and shrubs gave colour to the centre of the garden. Guests meandered along the pathways, and here and there waiters cruised like white-jacketed pilot fish, palms loaded with trays holding drinks and canapés.

Cooper snagged a champagne flute from a passing tray and eased himself into the fray. At the far side of the courtyard he could see the lantern-jawed Canadian Prime Minister posing for an official photograph with his wife, the Canadian Ambassador and Vincent Teresi. Cooper turned away, keeping the stone wall of the flower bed between himself and the Vice-President.

Meandering slowly through the murmuring knots of Washington's elite, Cooper was aware that no more than half of the invited guests had any idea who he was, and the majority of those who did recognise him tended to turn away at his approach.

With the Director a semi-invalid for the past year and a half owing to a worsening heart condition, Cooper as his 'social designate' was required by protocol to attend most functions honouring a head of state, but he was a pariah because of the nature of his work. He was the grey man, keeper of the nation's nasty secrets and professional peeping Tom. Not your first choice for idle cocktail party chatter. The fact that he had the general appearance and demeanour of a slightly stooped mortician didn't help the situation either.

He chose a spot at the corner of the stone wall and watched the ebb and flow of elegantly dressed people, catching snippets of their conversations.

All of it was meaningless, words from another world. For Cooper there was nothing now but the terrible reality of Rhinelander's presence in the city.

It was like a slow motion film of frost growing on a wintery pane of glass – the razor edge of crystals joining, spreading and climbing in geometric shapes until the pattern was complete. It had been Hollis Macintyre's own cold breath that had begun the process and the senior members of the Romulus Committee who had approved it, but if Rhinelander failed Cooper knew it was his head that would roll.

'Mr Cooper.'

Startled, the CIA Deputy Director looked up and found himself staring into the media-perfect features of Vincent Teresi.

'Mr Vice-President.' Cooper nodded stiffly, ancient instincts asserting themselves as he placed his champagne glass on the retaining wall, keeping both hands free in the face of an enemy.

'Both doing our duties in the absence of our superiors, I see,' the Vice-President commented. The smile flashed but it had a wolfish edge. 'How is Director Maitland doing these days?'

'Not well,' Cooper answered, angered by the question. Both men knew that Maitland would almost certainly resign within the next few months, giving the Tucker/Teresi people an opportunity to place one of their own men in the key position. The CIA man couldn't resist an oblique dig of his own. 'How is the President?'

'Touch of the flu,' Teresi answered easily. 'He and the First Lady are spending a few days at Camp David while he gets his strength back.' The smile flashed again. 'Frankly, our friends from the north didn't really warrant interrupting his recuperation.'

'I see,' Cooper answered. He watched Teresi carefully, wondering how much, if anything, he knew about Tucker's real illness. Probably nothing; Teresi wouldn't be the first Vice-President to be in the dark about a serious illness in the White House. Lyndon Johnson assumed that Kennedy's back problems had to do with his naval exploits, and not JFK's long battle with Addison's disease.

'This may not be the time to bring it up,' Teresi said, still smiling,' but I'm concerned with your request for new satellite appropriations regarding the report you filed on activities at Kohtla-Jarve.'

'Oh?' Cooper replied calmly. It sounded as though Teresi had spent time memorising the proper pronunciation of the Russian naval installation on the Baltic coast.

'We're trying to ease relations with the Soviets,' the Vice-President explained, his tone chiding. 'The President and I agree that doubling up satellite surveillance of a base manufacturing a prototype coastal patrol boat radar system seems counterproductive.'

'The radar story is a cover,' said Cooper, trying to keep the irritation out of his voice. 'The fact that they left the appropriate equipment out in plain sight during a KH-11 pass wasn't an error, it was bait.'

'Presumably you have proof of this?' Teresi asked.

'The Soviets have been using a modified Mayakovsky class trawler called the *Odissey* as a chemical warfare factory ship,' Cooper answered coldly. 'Up until six months ago she was using Kiev as her home port, now she's coming in to Kohtla-Jarve.'

'That doesn't prove anything,' said Teresi. 'And I was under the impression that the ghost-ship scenario had been debunked.'

'You were under the wrong impression,' said Cooper. 'The *Odissey* is very real, unlike the Ivanovo installation.'

'Where the radar system is being manufactured,' interrupted Teresi.

'A major factory would leave an infra-red signature,' explained Cooper. 'The Ivanovo plant is almost cold. It's a warehouse for inventory coming out of Kohtla-Jarve, not into it. Given enough time on the KH-11 I'll prove it to you; all we need is a pass where the ship is in port and offloading.'

'I'm afraid that won't be possible,' said Teresi. He'd been keeping the best until last. This was the reason he'd instigated the conversation in the first place. The payoff. 'Your request for increased time has been denied, although you can bring it up at the next joint intelligence meeting if you wish.'

The CIA man shifted slightly, then picked up his half-empty champagne glass. He lifted it to his lips and drained the crystal flute. His face devoid of any expression, Cooper stared at the Vice-President without saying a word. He let a silent thirty seconds pass, then nodded, returned the empty glass to its place on the stone wall and walked away. There was no doubt in Hudson Cooper's mind that Vincenzo Salvatore Michaelangelo Teresi had paid his professional dues, but he lived in a world of politics and bright promises, while Cooper's world was one of much darker realities.

'Christ, I hope this works out,' Stephen Stone muttered. He sucked up the last dregs of shake from the McDonald's cup and stared moodily out into the darkness of the National Agricultural Research Centre. The car he sat in was parked on a narrow access road a little more than half a mile from the front gates of the Bowie Institute.

'Relax, Stef,' Mort Kessler said placatingly, seated behind the wheel. 'The plan's foolproof.'

'What time is it?' Stone asked, dropping the empty cup onto the floor.

'9:45,' Kessler answered. 'It's not due to go down for another fifteen minutes.'

'*If* it goes down,' Stone grunted. He reached out and pulled a Camel Light out of the pack on the dashboard. He lit it, closing his eyes as the the lighter flared, protecting his night-vision.

'Relax,' Kessler repeated. 'The information is good.' Tapping every available FBI source, which included one of the kitchen stewards at Bowie, he had learned that a 'unit' was being moved that evening at 10:00 p.m. Ferreting a little deeper he discovered that the Bowie Agricultural Research Institute had filed a flight plan out of the nearby Beltsville Airport for 10:30. The destination was logged as Patrick Henry International at Newport News but Kessler was fairly sure that the real objective was the restricted field at Camp Peary a few miles north on the York River.

'I should have my head examined for approving anything as harebrained as this,' Stone said. He dragged deeply on the cigarette, then exhaled, letting the smoke drift out the open window beside him. Outside there was nothing but the rich scent from the pines surrounding them, and the never ending rattle of crickets.

'It's not harebrained.' Kessler laughed. 'It's just tit for tat. You know as well as I do that all these so called high-level rumours about a defection are a crock of shit. Everything about the Travkin snatch was illegal. The CIA kidnapped a Soviet diplomat and are holding him against his will. That violates a whole bunch of established protocols, not to mention a few laws as well. How can the CIA complain when we just reverse the process?'

'Because we're not KGB, we're agents of the Federal Bureau of Investigation, no matter what your fancy licence plates say, and the Company is supposedly a brother organisation.'

'Horsepuckies,' Kessler snorted.

Within a few minutes of discovering that Travkin was about to be moved from the Bowie facility, Mort Kessler had jury-rigged an operation to get him away from the CIA. Harebrained or not, Stone had to admit that the plan was elegantly simple.

Using three pool vehicles from the Baltimore District Office and diplomatic plates liberated from the Special Services branch of the DC Department of Motor Vehicles the entire six man BACK DOOR contingent would box in Travkin and his keepers on the way to Beltsville Airport and benevolently re-kidnap the GRU officer.

In a best-case scenario the CIA would assume that the kidnappers really had been KGB retrieving one of their countrymen, while in a worst-case situation they might suspect Stone and his people but they'd have no way to prove it, and more importantly, they'd have no official way of doing anything about it.

Stone knew that Ruppelt would inevitably discover what had happened, but hopefully the material gained from debriefing Travkin would soften his anger. He was also sure that Travkin would co-operate, even if it was grudgingly. His own people would now assume that he was 'tainted' and the Russian would have no choice but to actually defect. Hudson Cooper was a powerful enemy, but the defection of a major player like Dimitri Alexandyr Travkin would provide a virtually unassailable bulwark against any attack mounted by the DDO.

Stone stubbed out his cigarette in the dashboard ashtray and stared out into the night, feeling the perspiration dampening the armpits of his windbreaker. The whole thing had sounded perfectly reasonable being discussed in the air-conditioned confines of the safe house overlooking Rock Creek Park, but out here in the hot, humid night he wasn't so sure. If they pulled it off they might be able to stop a political assassination and reel in a top grade intelligence coup into the bargain. If they failed, and he missed his grab at the ring, his career would be over.

He reached down on the seat and touched the walkie-talkie beside him. One wrong move, one man out of place, and the whole thing would go down hard. Stone had been on enough operations to know that things never went exactly according to plan and that something could easily go wrong. Christ on a crutch! Anything could go wrong. *Everything* could go wrong.

'If anyone's out of place it'll screw up,' Stone warned.

'No one's out of place, Stef. Sinclair's in the woods across from the front gates, Putnam has the spiked chain at the intersection, and Midbrook and Dofney do the block on the Springfield-Hillmeade Road. Fifteen seconds to pick up Sinclair will put us about a minute behind. We make up half that on the way to the intersection of Powder Mill and Springfield. Midbrook gives us the word as soon as he sees their lights and we close it up.'

Kessler reached out and popped open the oversize attache case that lay between them on the seat. It contained a Smith and Wesson anti-riot kit complete with 37 mm gas gun, Tru-flite penetrating projectiles, rubber ball gas grenades and half a dozen pepper-gas projectiles.

'Ka-boom!' The agent grinned.

Stone smiled back; the man's optimistic mood was infectious. 'Dimitri's going to be POed even if we do save him from the evil clutches of the Company,' he said and laughed. 'This stuff will have him crying for a week.'

'Better to shed tears than blood,' Kessler answered. There was a crackling sound from the walkie-talkie. The two men stiffened. Stone picked up the radio and Kessler leaned forward, turning on the ignition.

'*Es ist grün.*' Sinclair, giving the green code, spoke in German just in case anyone was listening in.

'*Ich verstehe,*' Stone answered crisply.

Beside him, Kessler was counting. 'Five, six, seven, eight . . .'

On nine he put the specially equipped hot pursuit vehicle in drive and began to move, headlights dark. Stone switched channels on the walkie-talkie and alerted the rest of the BACK DOOR crew.

'*Zündung.*' Ignition.

Dimitri Travkin sat between his two keepers in the front seat of the car and wondered if he was going for the proverbial last ride. If he was, Mutt and Jeff weren't telling him the final destination. Mutt, the blond with the biceps, was behind the wheel, guiding the dark green GMC van along the Bowie Institute's long curving drive while Jeff sat between Travkin and the door. The windows were wound up and cold air was blowing from the dashboard vents.

'Don't tell me,' the GRU officer said brightly, breaking the silence, 'you're taking me to the Eddie Murphy concert at Wolf Trap.'

'Shut the fuck up,' Jeff said coldly. They reached the end of the tree-lined drive and the high gates slid back on their rails, monitored by closed circuit video cameras from the main building.

'*Esvaynya,*' Travkin muttered. Pig. A humourless one to boot.

'What did you say?' snapped Jeff, the dark-haired one.

'Nothing,' Travkin answered, then lapsed into silence once again. Mutt, the blond driver, turned south onto Powder Mill Road. It was full night, the world collapsed to a narrow tunnel bored into the darkness by the van's headlights. Travkin had brief glimpses of ploughed fields and forests but nothing more.

The Russian eased back in his seat, wishing he had a cigarette but knowing that Mutt and Jeff were unlikely to give him one. He willed himself to relax and considered both his future and his options. At that moment, staring out through the windshield at the dark, unravelling road, neither seemed very promising. The interrogation by the bland Mr Cook had been superficial, no more than a fishing trip to find out how much he knew about the Costa Rican project. Now things would get nasty; hard questions and rough treatment, perhaps even drugs.

'Company,' said Mutt softly, eyes flicking to the van's side mirror.

'Where?' asked Jeff. The dark-haired man reached under his jacket and came up with a short-barrelled S&W .44 revolver.

'Behind us, two hundred yards and no lights.'

'Shit.' Jeff leaned forward and peered into the mirror on his side. 'Speed it up,' he instructed.

Mutt accelerated on command, the sudden increase in speed pushing Travkin back against the bench seat. The Russian sat stiffly between the two men, muscles tense; sudden movement with a nervous man beside you holding a gun was a definite no-no. His mind worked furiously, realising that he was being given an opportunity, but not sure how to take advantage of it. It all depended on who was coming up behind him. If it was one of Vladimir Gurenko's KGB goon squads intent on 'rescuing' him, he preferred to take his chances with the CIA; at least with them there was a possibility of coming out of the whole thing alive. With Gurenko there was not.

Mutt, tensed behind the wheel of the van, took the long curve at speed, coming into the intersection of Powder Mill Road and Springfield-Hillmeade at close to seventy miles an hour. Rocketing out of the T-crossing he was suddenly aware of two things: there was a vehicle approaching in the wrong lane with its headlights on, and all four of his tyres had blown out, the rubber cut to smoking shreds by the razor-sharp carbon steel of the spiked chain laid across the intersection only a few moments before. Mutt's driving was further encumbered by the fact that the forty-foot length of security chain had now entangled itself in both front axle and driveshaft, the flailing ends gutting the brakelines, fuel line and ignition system, while a two foot length sliced through the floor of the van, hacking through Mutt's right shoe, severing his Achilles tendon and turning his ankle into a pulped mass of bleeding flesh, bone chips and shredded shoe leather.

As Mutt began to scream and the van went into a long, broadside drift, the vehicle coming up from the south erupted in a retina-peeling blaze of light as its grill-mounted custom built halogen floodlights burst into life. Stone and Kessler, in the darkened vehicle following Travkin, speeded up at the last moment, the heavy-duty all steel police bumper slamming into the van broadside, pushing it into the shallow ditch on the right hand side of the road.

Travkin, blinded by the floodlights, was hurled against Jeff, now choking on his own blood, his right cheekbone smashed from its impact against the window. The CIA man's finger jerked spasmodically, firing the revolver into the seat beside him. The Russian grappled with his keeper, trying to turn the weapon away from himself, while on his left, Mutt was still screaming, coiled up on the seat, his hands desperately trying to reach the partially amputated remains of his right foot.

The GRU man was vaguely aware of a stuttering series of sharp, barking sounds, and then every window in the van was shattered as the BACK DOOR team began firing tear-gas penetrating projectiles, followed by a popping hail of number fifteen rubber ball tear gas grenades. Within a few seconds the van's interior was filled with a choking fog of chemical smoke. Before he passed out, larynx burning and eyes streaming, Travkin was sure he heard voices speaking in German, and not quite as certain of a goggle-eyed, rubber covered face peering at him through the shattered remains of the windshield. After that he didn't care, unconsciousness a blessed relief from the nightmare inside the van.

CHAPTER SEVENTEEN

For most people a city is a place of tall buildings, dense traffic and crowded sidewalks. Few urban dwellers realise that beneath their feet is a monstrously complex system of tunnels, conduits and chambers outstripping anything conceived of by Dante for his infernal underworld. Below the familiar surface lies a city in itself, a Hades of forgotten rivers, abandoned pipes and passages, sunken sewers, tubes, crypts and cellars.

After discovering his first clue hidden in the pages of the aging *National Geographic* magazine, Eric Rhinelander focused the next stage of his research on Washington DC's underground history. The information was readily available and after going to several municipal offices and making a return visit to one of Georgetown's antiquarian bookstores he had everything he needed.

The article in the 1935 issue of the *National Geographic* was entitled 'Wonders of the New Washington', and a portion of it described the newly built central heating plant at 12th and D Streets. A quick check assured Rhinelander that the heating plant, expanded and modernised, still existed. In 1935 the heating plant provided warmth to seventy-one buildings, including the White House. The giant steam pipes were carried through more than three miles of huge, concrete-lined tunnels.

A visit to the DC Planning Office and an hour spent at the Public Works Information Office gave the assassin a general history of the city's waste and storm sewer system and his trip back to the bookstore on M Street provided him with several arcane civil engineering textbooks relating to Washington. Collating the material back at the Wyoming, Rhinelander quickly built up an overview of the city's below ground environment.

Prior to its elevation to the status of national capital, Washington had been a malarial patch of swamp on the banks of the Potomac. During Washington's early years the various creeks flowing into the Potomac were used for both water and sewage, worsening conditions and giving Washington the reputation of being a highly unhealthy city to live in. Following the Civil War the first attempts were made to create a proper sewer and water system in Washington. The meandering branches of the Tiber Creek were covered over, and an aqueduct was built to bring fresh water from the north. For the next half century, as the city grew, so grew its underground system of water tunnels and sewers.

In 1897, as part of an enormous landfill operation, the Tidal Basin was created. While most people today view it is as a recreational area and a fitting backdrop for the Washington, Lincoln and Jefferson memorials, it is also a feat of hydraulic engineering. Using a system of locks and pumps, rising tidal water is captured in the Basin, then later flushed out into Washington Channel, thus ensuring its cleanliness.

From the civil engineering texts Rhinelander learned that the first sewers had been brick-lined and egg-shaped in cross-section, always following the slope of the land, no matter how convoluted the course. Later sewers and water conduits were constructed of clay or concrete pipe. Out of necessity the old and new systems were interconnected, and all were vented to the surface at intervals through manhole shafts and storm drains.

At 11:30 p.m., slightly more than twenty-four hours after Stephen Stone's BACK DOOR rescue of Dimitri Travkin, Eric Rhinelander parked his rented mini-van beneath the 12th Street Expressway overpass and slipped into the rear compartment to change clothes for his late night excursion. Peeling off his T-shirt and jeans he pulled on a black, one piece Lycra dive skin, then shrugged on a pair of DC Public Works coveralls he'd liberated from a truck in the heating plant parking lot earlier that day. Donning a battle-scarred hard-hat from the same source he added an equally battered doctor's valise and a clipboard.

Carrying the valise he crossed the Conrail tracks, then climbed the embankment to D Street. A few moments later he walked through the open gate of the heating plant parking lot, then boldly pulled open a service door and stepped into the main boiler room. The chamber was enormous, a broad central aisle lined on both sides with looming furnaces, several storeys high, each heavily insulated and joined together by a twisting, seemingly random web of heavy pipes and spidery catwalks.

The boiler room was brightly lit by scores of lights dangling from the girders overhead and empty except for two maintenance men working silently in the distance, ears covered by protective headsets against the constant, thunderous boom of the furnace blowers. Rhinelander walked casually across the central aisle, trying to visualise the design specifications for the plant he'd viewed on microfilm at the Planning Office.

He found the access door leading to the northern service tunnel, opened it, then took the winding metal stairway down to the heating plant's lower level. Once there he simply followed the directions stencilled in dark green against the pale yellow walls. Going down several more sets of echoing stairs he eventually found the tunnel entrance and went through a heavy, counterweighted door. The tunnel itself was slightly more than nine feet high and almost twenty feet across, lit by a string of caged lights that vanished into the distance. Bunches of pipes and cables were bracketed to the walls, snaking down the endless, gloomy passageway into infinity.

Keeping to the raised concrete walkway on the left of the tunnel, Rhinelander began to make his way northward. Here and there along the way the main steam pipes dipped below the level of the floor, allowing access to branch passages on the eastern side. Rhinelander also noted that there were heavy manholes set into the concrete floor at regular intervals, their code number and position stencilled on the wall: DCWW#234/12th /IND. JUNCT, PW#5/FREER SUB #3, PW#8/JEFF.

After walking for ten minutes he reached a niche carved into the western wall of the tunnel. Sealing it was a small grey-painted metal hatchway marked CONSTITUTION AVE INTERCEPTOR/WATER-GATE OUTFALL. From his reading Rhinelander knew that an interceptor was a main floodway providing emergency flood control in the event of a major storm.

Rhinelander put down the clipboard and valise, then looked both ways along the tunnel. Empty, and silent except for the steady sound of his own breathing. From the look of the old-fashioned lever and bar locking mechanism the door hadn't been opened in decades. Gripping the big locking lever in both hands he dragged downward. The sixty-year-old mechanism turned with surprising ease. Picking up the clipboard and bag he pulled open the door and stepped across the threshold.

Beyond there was nothing but darkness and before he closed the door he got out a compact diver's flashlight. He closed the door, pushing the inside lever to lock it, then turned on the light. In its brilliant beam he saw that he was standing in a small, semicircular chamber lined with damp, crumbling concrete. The room was no more than eight feet across and barely six feet high. In the centre of the floor was the opening of a shaft some thirty inches across.

Placing the light upright on the floor, Rhinelander unzipped the coveralls and removed the hard hat. Dressed now in nothing but the one-piece diver's skin and thick-soled sneakers, he sat himself on the edge of the narrow shaft, feet dangling over the side. Opening the valise again he took out his red nylon knapsack which contained a mask, insulated diver's gloves, utility belt, a strap-on Ikelite compass and half a dozen nine-inch Spare Air bottles, each one of the miniature emergency tanks giving five minutes' breathing time. The zippered compartment on the side of the bag also contained a spray can of glow-in-the-dark yellow paint, a short-handled ice axe, fifty feet of ultra thin nylon rope and an assortment of pitons.

Poised on the edge of the dark hole in the floor he wrapped the utility belt around his waist, then loaded it with the flashlight, still on, the Spare

Air bottles, the rope and the pick. He rolled up the coveralls, pushing them down into the bottom of the knapsack, then strapped the wrist compass onto his left arm, snapped on the diver's gloves, and finally threaded his arms into the knapsack harness. He stuffed the clipboard and the hard hat into the valise, closed it and dropped it down the hole between his dangling feet. There was a faint echoing thud as the bag reached bottom a few seconds later.

Rhinelander edged out over the hole, feeling for the ladder with his sneakered feet. Finding it, he reached out with one hand, the twisting light giving him a gyrating glimpse down into the yawning shaft. He descended, careful not to put too much weight on any rung before he'd tested it. A few minutes later, he reached another chamber identical to the one he'd just vacated. Dropping the bag a second time he descended once again, the air growing noticeably cooler, thick now with a deep, musky odour.

Suddenly he found himself in the main interceptor tunnel, a brick-walled crumbling vault at least thirty feet across and half as high. Rhinelander swung the light across the broad channel. It was a foul-smelling Styx, its flow the consistency of soup, its colour a putrescent brown so dark it seemed to swallow up the beam of light. Thin, dangling stalactites oozed from the mortar of the bricks in the curving roof and the walls were coated in a glistening film of subterranean mucosa. Rhinelander sneezed and the sound rebounded up and down the vault, the echo changed to a short, barking laugh.

Clipping the light back onto his belt he slipped off the knapsack and took out the spray can. He popped the top, shook the can briskly, then sprayed a large yellow X beside the shaft entrance. The paint ran slightly before it set, leaving a glowing twin track on the crumbling wall, like the cold leaked blood of some underground creature.

Rhinelander checked the dial of his compass, turning until he was facing west. Leaving the battered valise at the foot of the shaft he began to move, the light held before him, keeping to the centre of the walkway.

At intervals along the way the beam of his light picked out the openings of secondary sewers angling into the main stream. Because of the weather most were dry, but a few added small trickles to the main interceptor. Rhinelander also noted that some openings were much larger than others and fitted with dam-like weirs and counterbalanced gates to hold back all but the most serious flows. He could appreciate the engineering genius of a system entirely dependent on gravity for its operation.

Twenty minutes after reaching the base of the interceptor shaft Rhinelander found himself in a cavernous chamber at least thirty feet high, crowded with buttresses, pillars and cross-connected weirs. The water was deeper here. There were nine separate openings, angling off in all directions. Except for the roving beam of his light it was brutally dark and the air was foul, a rotted, choking stench that burned into his nostrils and set his stomach churning.

Resisting the urge to hold his breath Rhinelander consulted his wrist compass again and turned, following the needle until he was facing north. He was now directly beneath the Ellipse; according to his information the heating and air-conditioning vaults jutting out from the sub-basement below the north portico of the White House were exactly 2851 feet away.

Rhinelander shuffled forward along the slick walkway, bracing himself with one gloved hand against the sloping wall. Reaching the main weir that ran across the channel he stepped outward carefully, arms outstretched.

He reached the far side, then climbed a short, rust-covered iron ladder to the north side walkway. Arm muscles tensing he boosted himself up onto the lip of the tunnel he would now follow. He crouched, pausing for a few moments as he waited for his breathing to steady, then stood, head bent low under the low arched roof. Hunched over he began to move, his sodden sneakers making small sucking noises as he walked.

He paused again, dropping down to his knees, using his gloved hands to work the stiffening muscles of his neck and shoulders. He'd kept a rough count of his steps and by his reckoning he'd come almost 2500 feet. He treated himself to a few long breaths from one of the Spare Air bottles, then continued up the gently sloping tunnel.

A hundred yards further along the passage he saw the first evidence that he was nearing his objective: a patch in the left hand wall of the tunnel, the grey, pocked surface of the fifty-year-old slab of concrete showing its rusty, chicken wire skeleton. In the centre of the patch was the open end of a clay water pipe. It had been fitted during the Truman renovation of the White House. Thirty feet beyond that the beam of his light picked up a second and far more important clue overhead.

At some time in the past the arch of the tunnel roof had begun to fall in. Shining the light upward, he could clearly see the cause of the downward pressure. A section of the roof had collapsed completely, the broken bricks and mortar swept away by some long forgotten storm. The bright beam from Rhinelander's flashlight illuminated the resulting cavity and revealed a section of cast-iron steam pipe: a feeder branch from the main conduit in the heating plant tunnel. The pipe ran at right angles to the storm sewer, putting him directly opposite the north portico heating and air-conditioning vaults. The only question now was one of distance. How far was the tunnel from the vaults?

Rhinelander calculated that the vault wall was less than twenty feet from the sewer, but no matter what the plans he'd viewed showed or the biographies he'd read described, there was only one real way to find out his exact location. Slipping the pack off his shoulders he unzipped the side pocket and took out the ice axe. Choosing a spot where the mortar between the bricks looked particularly soft he began to dig.

The dark anvils of the thunderclouds had been building steadily since the late evening, rising over the hills above the Appalachian Trail, blotting out the stars. As the ominous mass of cloud slid towards the District of Columbia the first rain began to fall, fat droplets slapping the dusty rooftops. Within ten minutes the storm had broken completely, the pounding sheets of rain preceded by an advance guard of cracking thunder and jagged, blinding forks of lightning.

In Washington there had been no relief from the stupefying heat for almost three weeks and the ground was parched. Everywhere suburban gutters filled with foaming, racing streams. Within minutes the concrete trash traps in the first storm drains overflowed and water began to flood through the storm lines, scouring out a season's worth of silt, twigs, broken bottles and all the other garbage that finds its way into the sewers. Secondary lines filled, then spewed furiously into mains, spreading beneath the city, pressed forward by gravity and the force of new water from the continuing rain.

Eric Rhinelander had been working in the storm sewer tunnel for almost an hour and a half when he first realised that something was wrong. By then he'd opened a yard square hole in the brickwork of the sewer wall and dug another two feet into the heavy, clay-like soil beyond. So far there was no sign of the vault wall.

Dragging back yet another load of dirt into the already half-choked passage Rhinelander paused and looked northward up the tunnel. It took him a few seconds to identify what had caught his attention, but then he had it. The foetid, still air was moving, creating enough of a breeze to fan his cheek. He tensed, listening. The sound was faint, distant and echoing, but he recognised it immediately: rushing water, Niagara Falls through cotton wool.

He acted instantly, scooping up the knapsack and slinging it over his shoulders. He scrambled around the pile of dirt he'd created, unclipping one of the Spare Air bottles as he fled, hunched over, down the passage. He knew exactly what had happened and he cursed himself silently for not checking the weather reports.

The water struck when he was still a thousand feet from the interceptor chamber. Clamping the Spare Air mouthpiece between his teeth and hanging onto the bottle with one hand he curled himself into a ball and used the other arm to shield his face. Within an instant he was swallowed by the fuming water, then carried downstream with it. With a diver's instinct he tried his best to keep to the centre of the current, but even so he found himself being slammed back and forth against the tunnel walls.

Forty seconds later the hammering current reached the Constitution Avenue chamber and spewed Rhinelander out into the stinking pool at the foot of the weir. For a single, horrifying moment the struggling man was sure he'd be trapped in the foul quicksand of ooze, but with the foaming, trash-laden water rising quickly around him he managed to unclip the rubber-covered flashlight from his belt, then flailed his way to the opposite side of the tunnel and the iron ladder bolted to the slimy brick.

Reaching the walkway ledge he dropped down onto his hands and knees, panting. He was bleeding from a dozen scrapes and his dive-skin was torn to ribbons, but he knew he was lucky to be alive. He forced himself to stand up and then examined his position. Shining his light around the chamber he saw that the pool behind the weir was filling quickly, and the eastern channel, virtually dry a few hours before, was now filled almost to the level of the walkway. In another few minutes the dam would be topped and the lower interceptor would begin to fill as well.

Rhinelander quickly saw that any attempt to retrace his steps could easily end in disaster, and following the lower route was probably even more dangerous, especially if the rise in water level continued. His only choice was the overflow tunnel which lead down to the Tidal Basin. Wasting no time he walked unsteadily to the weir, then boosted himself up onto the lip of the southern passage. It was high enough for him to stand upright without any trouble. Because it was only used for emergency outflow the floor of the tunnel was perfectly dry and clear.

Rhinelander worked his way down the passage, one ear cocked for any sound of water coming from behind. Twenty uneventful minutes later he reached the tunnel exit. As he'd expected, the last few yards of the passage angled down sharply, ending in a smooth, slightly oily pool of water. For both safety and security, the open end of the outfall was located underwater, probably closed off by a grate.

After allowing himself a five-minute rest, Rhinelander took the still intact mask out of his knapsack, cracked another Spare Air bottle and slipped into the pool, using the flashlight to guide him. Breathing easily and ignoring the growing pain from his cuts and bruises he pulled himself down to the base of the outfall. The only trace of a grate covering the opening was the rusted remains of a linch-bolt. Unopposed he grasped the lip of the outfall pipe and pushed forward. A few seconds later he reached the surface, stripped off his mask and lifted his face into the pouring rain.

He treaded water, taking huge grateful gulps of the wonderfully fresh air, then swam the few strokes needed to take him to the quarried stone shore. Not surprisingly, given the hour and the weather conditions, the entire Tidal Basin area was deserted. Rhinelander lifted himself up onto the path at the edge of the basin. Shivering now, he quickly stripped off the tattered remains of the dive-skin, then put on the coveralls.

He put the utility belt, flashlight and clothing into the knapsack, weighted it with a few pieces of broken concrete from under the bridge, then dropped the tell-tale parcel into the water. Even with his wallet and ID safe in the coverall's zippered side pocket it would be difficult to explain what he was doing out before dawn in the middle of a downpour, but if a cop stopped him with the knapsack it would be impossible. There was nothing in it that couldn't be replaced anyway.

Rhinelander reached the mini-van half an hour later, changed into fresh clothes and drove to the underground lot at the Holiday Inn. Ten minutes after that, just before five a.m., he was stepping into the shower of John Gray's apartment at the Wyoming.

As he washed away the sweat and grime of his night's labours there was an unseen event taking place deep in the now sodden earth below the White House grounds, and although Rhinelander was no believer in fate, luck or coincidence, he would have seen the irony of it immediately.

The force of water thundering down the narrow storm tunnel had pushed away everything in its path, including more of the brickwork from Rhinelander's excavation. The continuing current began to erode the earth behind the sewer wall, eventually bringing down a section over fifteen feet long, including the ceiling. By dawn, with the rain over and the surface water beginning to recede, a new chamber had been created almost twenty feet long. In the southeastern corner of the low ceilinged cave there was an obviously man-made structure: it was the wall of the north portico vault.

CHAPTER EIGHTEEN

Dimitri Travkin used the remote control to switch off the VCR, then levered himself out of the comfortable upholstered chair. He'd watched the *Eddie Murphy: Raw* tape three times in the past forty-eight hours and he was getting sick of it. He'd also watched *Good Morning Vietnam*, *Robin Williams Live*, *Howie Mandel's Hawaiian Special* and eleven *Fawlty Towers* episodes. At first he'd been intrigued at this off-the-wall procedure for softening up a prisoner, but now he was simply bored by it. He was also bored with the endless succession of pizzas and fried chicken dinners he was being served and the bland, Holiday Inn decor of the two-room suite he was occupying.

Travkin went to the bathroom, urinated, flushed, then splashed cold water on his face. Drying himself off with a small, fluffy and very pink hand towel it struck the GRU man that his brief ablutions were undoubtedly going to be the high point of his day.

Sighing, Travkin left the bathroom and dropped down onto the bed, hands clasped behind his head. They'd taken away his watch, but by the colour of the sky he put it at early evening. Next would come the big question – pizza or chicken? Brought to him by the spooky, silent red-headed man with the almost invisible eyebrows. He'd unlock the door and enter the room, carrying a cloth-covered tray on one raised palm.

Placing the tray on the table in the sitting room he'd step back and give the Russian a brief half smile, then glance at the tray mysteriously. Travkin knew it was only a psych-move, but it worked every time. After the redhead left he'd lift the cloth on the tray, never quite sure if he was going to find food or a writhing mass of pit-vipers. Staring up at the ceiling he spoke out loud, doing his groaning imitation of an Uzbek comedian impersonating WC Fields.

'*Tovarich* Dimitri, you have the stepping made into ka-ka exceedingly deep.' It wouldn't get a laugh in the big room at the Rossiya, but under the circumstances it was the best he could do. 'Frankly, my friends, I'd rather be in Novosibirsk.' Better, but still not up to scratch.

Except for the bursting light, the tear gas and muffled German voices behind rubber masks he couldn't remember very much about his second abduction. In the last few seconds before he blacked out he remembered thinking that the Germans had probably been hired by Gurenko, but now he wasn't sure. Gurenko wouldn't have provided him with comedy tapes, and bland or not, the suite of rooms was far too decadent to be used as a KGB debriefing centre. Capture by Gurenko would have meant being doped, stuffed into a trunk and shipped back to Moscow on the next Ilyushin out of Dulles.

Travkin heard a faint knock on the door and frowned, swinging his legs off the bed. The redhead never knocked and the door was always locked anyway. He stood up and walked into the sitting room. The knock came again, louder this time. Travkin stepped forward and tentatively put his hand on the knob. He turned it and the door opened.

The man on the other side of the door was dark-haired, the temples flecked with grey, and good-looking in a craggy, rough cut way. He was wearing a wrinkled blue seersucker suit, light blue shirt and a dark blue tie. His penny loafers were scuffed and it looked as though he'd neither shaved nor slept in the past two or three days. Travkin recognised him immediately; it was Stephen Stone, his opposite number at REDNET.

'Mr Stone,' Travkin said, the pieces of his puzzle clicking into place. He stood aside and let the tired-looking man into the room. He closed the door behind Stone and gestured towards one of the flower print club chairs. 'Please sit down.' Travkin sat down on the couch and took a cigarette from the wooden box on the coffee table. He lit it and sat back against the cushions, staring at Stone with unabashed curiosity.

'I trust you're being treated well, Colonel Travkin?' Stone asked, speaking Russian stiffly and with obvious unease.

'Well enough.' Travkin smiled. 'And please speak in English. Your vocabulary is fine, but the accent makes my teeth ache.'

'Sorry,' Stone answered.

'I appreciate the effort,' Travkin responded. '*Spasibo.*'

The two men sat silently together for a long moment, watching each other and wondering who was going to make the first move. They'd been playing espionage hide and seek for the last year and a half, but sitting face to face was something different, especially under the present circumstances. Both Travkin and Stone had things to gain, and neither of them was about to give up something for nothing. In the end it was Travkin who broke the silence, and the ice.

'I gather it was you who snatched me from the gaping jaws of the Company. Many thanks.'

'Don't thank me yet, Comrade Colonel. Now that I've got you I'm not sure what I should do with you.'

'Call me Dimitri,' the Russian offered.

'All right, Dimitri. And you call me Stephen.' Stone paused, hesitated and finally reached out and took a cigarette from the box on the coffee table. They were unfiltered Chesterfields with as much tar and nicotine in one as there was in an entire pack of Camel Lights. Stone lit the cigarette and dragged happily.

'A question,' said the Russian.

Stone nodded. 'Shoot.'

'You rescued me from Central Intelligence. Why?'

'Kidnapping is a federal offence,' Stone answered glibly. 'That's what the FBI does.'

'Please,' said Travkin, frowning.

'All right,' said Stone wearily. 'In the first place, what they did was illegal. Kidnapping is a capital crime, and beyond that the CIA has no mandate for domestic covert action. In the second place, they were poaching in my territory, and last but not least, I want to know why they snatched you at all.'

'It was definitely a breach of protocol,' Travkin agreed, nodding. 'Can you imagine what it would be like if we went around plucking each other off the streets just for the hell of it?'

'So why take the risk?' Stone asked. 'What do you know that would make them do something like that?'

'I don't have the faintest idea.' Travkin shrugged.

'Bullshit,' said Stone. 'You must have an opinion.'

'Perhaps.'

'And you're going to keep it to yourself?'

'Perhaps.'

'Now who's playing games?' Stone retorted.

'Let's get something clear,' Travkin said, leaning forward. 'I can call you Stephen and you can call me Dimitri, but the fact remains that you're an FBI counterintelligence officer and I'm a Colonel in the GRU. I didn't defect to the Central Intelligence Agency and I haven't defected to you either. I am a registered agent of a foreign country being held against my will.' There was a long silence.

Stone stubbed out the half-smoked cigarette and sat back in his chair. 'Okay,' he said finally. 'Then go.' He glanced over his shoulder. 'The door's not locked. You can walk out. I'll even give you cab fare. You can be at Mount Alto in twenty minutes.' He cocked an eyebrow at the blond man seated across from him. 'I'm sure General Gurenko of the KGB will greet you with open arms.'

'Touché,' Travkin answered bleakly.

'Face it, Dimitri,' said Stone. 'You're screwed. After Cooper snatching you Koslov can't take you back, and Gurenko would like nothing better than to see you swinging in the wind. Step out that door and you'll have the GRU, the KGB and the CIA all over you.'

'So what do you suggest?' the Russian asked.

'Co-operate.'

'With the FBI?'

'With me. I pulled this off on my own.'

'I was wondering about that,' Travkin said, nodding thoughtfully. 'Stealing me from Cooper's people didn't seem like an operation your Mr Ruppelt would have sanctioned.'

'Ruppelt wouldn't sanction wiping his own ass unless he had a signed memo from someone higher up the ladder.'

'So this isn't a formal debriefing?' asked Travkin.

'No,' Stone answered, shaking his head emphatically. 'No tapes, no nothing.'

'Then why am I here? You didn't take me away from Cooper out of some Good Samaritan impulse.'

'Barron,' Stone replied. 'Cooper and Mallory going to Barbados. Cabrera. All of it.'

'Good grief!' Travkin said, affecting mock surprise. 'You've had me under surveillance.'

'No shit.' Stone laughed. 'You've been my main project for over a year now.'

'I'm flattered,' Travkin said and grinned.

'Cabrera,' Stone reminded him.

'Wait,' said Travkin, raising a hand, palm outward. 'We talk, but on one condition.'

'What condition?' Stone asked.

'We share information. I co-operate, you co-operate. The only way I'm going to get back into Gennaddi Koslov's good graces is by pulling some kind of diplomatic rabbit out of the hat. We work together. Agreed?' The Russian blew a long feather of smoke into the air.

Stone wasn't sure there was any rabbit in the world Travkin could produce that would ensure his reinstatement, but that was neither here nor there at the moment. After a reasonable interval he nodded. 'Agreed.'

It took almost two hours of back and forth conversation for the two men to complete their stories. Midway through the exchange they were joined by Mort Kessler and a large pizza from Armand's on Wisconsin Avenue. While the men talked and ate, Kessler used a thick pad of yellow paper to take notes.

'Okay,' said the redhead, seated to one side of the coffee table. 'This is what we have so far.' He cleared his throat dramatically and looked from

Stone to Travkin. The Russian took a slug of Pepsi from the can beside the open pizza box.

'Fire away,' Stone offered. 'Dimitri and I are all ears.'

'I'm doing this in chronological order, so jump in if I leave anything out.' He cleared his throat again and began. 'First we have Barron's telephone call. He makes it to Hudson Cooper, Deputy Director of Operations for the Central Intelligence Agency, and a little while later Cooper makes one to Hollis Macintyre, éminence grise of Capitol Hill and beyond. He, that is Dr Barron, has previously requested material from the library at Walter Reed which relates to a relatively obscure illness called Creuzfeldt-Jacob disease – apparently a nasty sort of Alzheimer's. It appears that any records of that request have now been scrubbed. Anyway, within a day or so of making his phone call to Cooper and Cooper making his call to Macintyre, Dr Barron winds up getting himself killed.'

'Murdered,' Stone interrupted. 'The autopsy was pretty clear about that. Given the time of death the water in his lungs should have had a higher salinity count since it was high tide when he died. He was drowned, but it was in low tide water. Took the ME a little while to figure it out.'

'Fine.' Kessler nodded. 'Anyway, Barron is murdered. Shortly thereafter Mr Cooper and his assistant, Mr Paul Mallory, take off for a very brief visit to Barbados. They meet a dark-haired, dark-eyed man of medium height calling himself John Duncan. Duncan appears again in Miami getting off a flight from Jamaica, and that's the last we see of him. Meanwhile, the word comes down from above that we're to red flag the surveillance of our man Dimitri here, and in fact, we're told to drop everything and anything that has to do with him. But we're doing some snooping around and we pick up on the Costa Rica thing. Then bam! Dimitri gets snatched. He spends time at Bowie, and during a preliminary interrogation a lot of the questions are about Central America. On top of that we have the Spanish cigarette butt clue and the Costa Rican telephone number. We rescue Dimitri from Cooper and that's the end of the story. Did I leave anything out?'

'What do you think?' Stone asked. Travkin was now lying down on the couch, his head propped up on a pillow. The Russian reached out and plucked a cigarette from the emptying box on the coffee table. He lit it and blew another expressive stream of smoke towards the ceiling. To Stone it appeared that the GRU man was incapable of thinking without a cigarette in his mouth.

'I think it has holes,' Travkin said after a few more thoughtful drags.

'Where?' asked Kessler, pencil poised over a fresh sheet.

'For one thing,' the Russian asked, 'why does Barron call Cooper?'

'You have a contact at Walter Reed, why shouldn't Cooper?' Stone answered.

'Okay,' said Travkin from the couch. 'Why does Cooper call Macintyre?'

'Maybe there's no connection,' offered Kessler, tapping the rubber end of the pencil against his chin.

'Let's assume there's a connection,' said Stone. 'Barron to Cooper, Cooper to Macintyre.'

'I don't know much about this Macintyre person,' said Travkin.

'Power behind the throne,' Kessler explained. 'He backed Tucker for the Presidential nomination, but not Teresi. He's been put out to pasture ever since the inauguration.'

'Forget about Macintyre for the moment,' said Stone. 'What about Cabrera?'

'It is all supposition,' said Travkin, swinging his legs around and sitting up.

'Explain,' said Stone.

'Thanks to Mr Cooper and yourself I've had a lot of time to stare at the ceiling,' the GRU man replied. 'The more I stare the less sense this all makes.'

'You mean Cabrera?' Stone asked.

'All of it. If this was a KGB operation I'd say we were being given *dizinformation*. We assume Cabrera is involved because of the visit to Barbados and because Barron was Morazan's attending physician at Walter Reed.'

'It makes sense.' Stone shrugged. 'If Morazan has Creuzfeldt-Jacob's then the CIA has to act quickly to get rid of Cabrera. Cooper hires Duncan to do the job.'

'Perhaps.' Travkin nodded. 'But what if it is all makeshift? A cover. Cooper is no fool, yet I have the Spanish cigarette and the telephone number in Costa Rica given to me on a platter.'

'Go on,' Stone prodded.

'Assume that Cooper has an operation in place, but also assume that he wasn't expecting my involvement,' the Russian continued. 'That would explain the kidnapping. He feeds me the cigarette and the telephone number to corroborate what you were already thinking – that Cabrera is the target – and then he lets me go, knowing that my only sanctuary lies with the FBI.'

'You think the whole rescue thing was a set-up?' asked Kessler.

'A fortuitous coincidence.' The Russian shrugged. 'Cooper has a file on me, he knows I was Spetznaz, yet he sends me off into the night with only two men in a van. Presumably I was being taken to Camp Peary for more intensive interrogation – proper procedure would call for a helicopter to take me from the Bowie facility directly there.'

'He's right,' Kessler agreed. 'Flying out of Beltsville was a little strange.'

'It all revolves around Cooper,' Stone mused. 'He's the focus.'

'Which brings us to the Barbados trip,' said Travkin. 'If we assume that the trip was to employ the services of Mr Duncan then he was acting outside of established procedure once again.'

'In other words, Deputy Directors of the CIA don't do their own field work,' said Kessler.

'That one's bothered me right from the start,' agreed Stone. 'Not only is Cooper doing his own field work, but he's also hiring a freelance, presumably out of Jamaica, if Duncan's flight into Miami is any indication.'

'Do you have anything at all on Duncan?' Travkin asked.

'No,' said Stone, shaking his head. 'He's a blank page.'

'*Chyorny*,' murmured Travkin. 'A black file.'

'What's that?' asked Kessler.

'An asset you keep to yourself,' explained the Russian. 'Duncan will be someone with no obvious connection to Cooper.'

'Why not a Costa Rican national?' Stone asked rhetorically. 'If you want Cabrera taken out without it coming back on you that would be the obvious way to go.'

'He is operating outside of normal channels,' said Travkin, 'and assuming a great deal of risk. This is what makes no sense.'

'So what are you saying?' Stone said.

'He's saying the result doesn't justify the risk,' Kessler answered. 'Cooper wouldn't put his career on the chopping block for a two-bit like Cabrera. We've been working on the Costa Rica angle because it's been made to look like the right one.'

'I agree,' Travkin nodded. 'It is like the aluminium foil dropped from bombers to obscure radar.'

'Okay,' Stone said, frustrated. 'If Cabrera isn't the target, then who is?'

'It all goes back to Dr Barron,' Kessler said, riffling through his notes. 'He knew something and it got him killed.'

'Then the real target is another one of the patients under his authority,' Stone added. 'Who?'

'I think I know,' Travkin answered quietly. He looked at the two men carefully. 'I think Cooper's target is the President of the United States.'

In Georgetown, less than a mile away from the FBI safe house, the four senior members of the Romulus Committee were meeting at Hudson Cooper's request. Cooper had arrived first, followed by Hollis Macintyre, then Joseph Swanbridge, the Secretary of State, and finally Stuart Shrenk, President Tucker's Attorney General. Shrenk, although new to the position of Attorney General, was a long time Washington lawyer and a close colleague of Swanbridge's. Given his authority as Attorney General and his relationship with Swanbridge it had been decided to tell Shrenk everything about the Tucker situation and the Romulus plan for its resolution. The Secretary of State had briefed him privately several days before.

Shrenk, Macintyre and Swanbridge were seated in the living room of the townhouse while Cooper stood in front of a wheeled stand containing a large video monitor and VCR. Cooper inserted a videocassette, reached behind him to turn off the lights in the room, then sat down. A few seconds later, colour bars appeared on the screen and the room was filled with the monotonous hum of an audio tone. Using a remote control, Hudson Cooper fast forwarded the tape.

'This is an edited tape made from a variety of sources,' Cooper explained, his voice hollow in the darkened room. 'Pieces of it are from security cameras in the White House, some of it is from broadcast sources, and there is also some material we've managed to appropriate from Mike Kaufmann.'

'The fellow doing the Tucker documentary?' asked Swanbridge out of the gloom.

'That's the one.' Cooper nodded. 'All the material on this tape was taken within the last ten days.'

The colour bars vanished and were replaced by a high angle shot of the state dining room. In the corner of the screen a digital counter began to move. The main table was set for twenty-five with the President seated at the north end of the table. The camera, discreetly located in the northwest corner of the ceiling, showed a half profile of the husky, balding man. To his right there was a somewhat doughy woman in her fifties wearing a dark blue evening dress, while on his left there was a young woman in her late teens, pretty, but with the same pudginess as the woman on Tucker's right. Clearly mother and daughter. Cooper hit the pause button on the remote control and the picture froze.

'The dinner was held in honour of the new German Chancellor, Johann Schiller,' Cooper explained. 'The woman beside the President is Annalise Schiller, the Chancellor's wife; the teenager is Angelika Schiller, his daughter. She's eighteen. Halfway down the table you can see Gail Tucker, the First Lady, directly opposite Secretary of State Swanbridge. The Chancellor is seated at the far end.'

'They barely spoke English,' commented Swanbridge, his cigar end glowing in the darkness. 'The whole evening was boring as hell.'

'Not for some people,' said Cooper. 'Watch.'

He fast forwarded again, and the dinner progressed in a Chaplinesque frenzy. White jacketed stewards came and went, heads bobbed back and forth, plates emptied and glasses filled. Cooper tapped the pause button again, followed by the zoom control. The screen filled with a grainy picture of the President's back and the space between his chair and the young woman beside him.

'State of the art video technology,' Cooper said. 'Japanese,' he added apologetically.

He hit the slow motion button and the three other men in the room watched, fascinated, as the President's arm snaked out of his own lap and into that of the Chancellor's daughter. The hand, showing just the right amount of starched white cuff at the wrist, moved up and down the young woman's thigh, then paused, fingers splayed, directly over her pubis.

'My god!' Shrenk whispered from the couch. 'What is he doing?'

'Just what it looks like,' said Cooper. 'It goes on for two or three minutes. Then he pulls his hand away as though he's been burned.'

'I never noticed a thing,' said Swanbridge.

Cooper sent the tape forward. The scene changed. This time the President and the First Lady were walking along a wooded pathway. In the background were two Secret Service men. Tucker was dressed in blue jeans and a dark green, cable knit sweater. Gail Tucker was wearing a denim skirt and a light brown suede jacket. A couple in late middle-age, out for an evening stroll.

'Camp David, the President recuperating from the flu,' Cooper narrated. 'This is footage from the Kaufmann documentary.'

The scene unfolded as the Chief Executive and his wife continued along the path. Just as they reached the camera position, Tucker paused. Cooper stopped the tape. The President's expression was one of childish bewilderment. The CIA man let the tape play again. Tucker turned and looked back at the Secret Service men, then spoke to his wife. She took him by the arm but he resisted, insisting on going forward. Tucker spoke again, and it didn't take a lip reader to make out the words: 'fucking bitch'. Tucker shook his wife off, then walked out of the frame, the expression on his face now one of furious anger.

'He's getting worse,' said Swanbridge.

'Indeed,' murmured Hollis Macintyre.

There was another twenty minutes of tape, each segment showing the deterioration of the President's condition. Most of the episodes were subtle but if you knew what to look for it was clear that the man's mental health was declining. When the tape ran out Cooper switched off the machine and turned on the lights in the room.

'Using a third party cut-out I had a blind prognosis done for a man of the President's age with Creuzfeldt-Jacob disease,' Cooper said. 'According to it, Tucker is in an advanced state. His next faux pas could be politically fatal.'

'Surely his wife must be getting suspicious,' said Shrenk. 'It isn't every day the President hauls off and calls the First Lady a "fucking bitch".'

'According to my information she's worried about exhaustion,' Cooper answered. 'I don't think she's taken it any further than that.'

'What about his doctor?' asked Swanbridge.

'Which one?' replied Cooper. 'The White House physician or the senior man at Walter Reed?'

'Either,' said the Secretary of State.

'Barron's replacement is a man named Eganthaler. He doesn't know anything and there's nothing in the files to alert him. As you're aware, the White House physician is Charlie Moorehead. A general practitioner, old friend of the family. He wouldn't know Creuzfeldt-Jacob disease if you struck him on the head with it.'

'Being made White House physician is a sinecure,' said Macintyre. 'We're all aware of that.'

'How long until the press catches wind of this?' asked Shrenk.

'It could be any time,' Cooper replied.

'This situation with the Russian,' Macintyre interjected. 'Has it been dealt with?'

Cooper nodded. 'He was picked up by the REDNET group. When Ruppelt is informed Stone will almost certainly be suspended. Travkin no longer has any credibility with his people. With Stone's protection removed he'll go to ground. Both of them are still operating on the Cabrera theory anyway; it doesn't present a problem.'

'I hope not,' said Macintyre.

'The question,' Swanbridge said calmly, 'is how do we proceed?'

'As planned,' Cooper replied. 'Nothing has changed appreciably. Frankly, we have very little choice in the matter, since communication with our man is a one way affair. At the last contact he said the operation was feasible. I've taken steps to see that the first payment is made.'

'Will there be further contact?' Macintyre asked.

'Yes.'

'He should be notified that speed is now of the essence,' ordered the huge, white-suited man.

'And if he asks for more money?' said Cooper.

'The question is irrelevant,' said Macintyre, 'since he'd have to be alive in order to collect it.' He turned to Shrenk. 'What about the succession?'

'As we discussed,' the Attorney General said, smoothing his tie under the lapels of his blazer. 'Both the Speaker and the President of the Senate have letters of disability on file due to their questionable health. Since the Twenty-Fifth Amendment doesn't cover the simultaneous deaths of both the President and the Vice-President I'll invoke the 1947 succession legislation. It was last ratified in 1979 so I don't see any trouble. Secretary Swanbridge could be sworn in immediately.'

'President Swanbridge,' intoned the florid-faced man. He'd obviously been drinking prior to his arrival at the meeting. 'That has a nice ring to it.'

'We won't let it go to your head, Joseph,' Macintyre said coolly. 'Rest assured.'

Hudson Cooper listened as the three men discussed the logistical problems resulting from the assassination, bemused by the bland ease of their conversation. Had Brutus and his conspirators been so calm in the last few days before the Ides of March? Had there been an evening like this before Kennedy's fateful visit to Dallas? This was a terrible moment in the history of the United States, unfolding in the well-appointed confines of a Georgetown home. It was insane, and the CIA man suddenly felt the desperate weight of his own history, decades lived in a phantom world where trusts were meant to be violated and truths turned into lies.

Once upon a time, or so they all believed, intelligence had been a game for gentlemen, played by gentlemen's rules. In his mind's eye Cooper saw the bronze statue of Nathan Hale standing guard at the front entrance to the CIA's Langley headquarters. The perfect gentleman spy, at least to Allen Dulles and the early espionage establishment in Washington, but to the British he was just another traitor, with no more honour than a Blunt, Philby, Burgess or Maclean.

And there is no pretence of honour here in this room tonight, he thought. None of us is Nathan Hale, regretting that he has but one life to give for his country, and Geoffrey Tucker is no tyrant to be deposed by men history would eventually deem heroes. He looked from one man to the other. Certainly not heroes, or even gentlemen, and definitely not a game. To Cooper that was the cold, dark terror of it: for these men the deaths of Geoffrey Tucker and Vincent Teresi were merely expedient, the rectification of a political error, a balancing of the nation's books. Business.

Five thousand miles and eight time zones away dawn was breaking over Moscow, its first pale rays putting a red-gold blush on the onion domes of the bell tower in the Kremlin. Across Red Square, a few blocks to the north on Zhadnova Street, Sergei Kuryokhin was already awake and preparing for another day.

Carrying his morning coffee to the main room of his apartment over the Sardine Café he noticed a new pain, this one running from his left shoulder down to his hand. He sat down at his scarred, ancient desk and used his right hand to massage the aching shoulder joint. The arthritis was getting worse and the cortisone treatments didn't seem to be having very much effect any more.

Kuryokhin lit a Lucky Strike, sipped the hot, sweet coffee and looked thoughtfully down at the folders spread out on his desk. They were all bright yellow, each bearing a crimson horizontal band and a firmly stamped notice in black: *SOVERSHENNO SEKRETNO* – completely secret. By rights the files should never have been removed from the central registry at Tyeply Shtan, but Kuryokhin's seniority and rank gave him special privileges.

He'd worked on the files until the early hours of the morning, taking notes and watching as a faint pattern slowly began to emerge. Gurenko, his Resident in Washington, had long ago infiltrated Koslov's GRU operation, and through that connection had come up with an overview of Dimitri Travkin's recent activities, including a copy of his computer logs. This in turn led to Barron, the Walter Reed doctor, his death, and Travkin's follow-up work.

Initially Kuryokhin had accepted the scenario involving Cabrera and Morazan, but the more he examined the possibility of Morazan's possible illness, the less likely it all seemed. Following his instincts and the odd titbit of information from *Osin*, he began working in another direction.

Hudson Cooper's telephone call to Hollis Macintyre and the Deputy Director's anomalous visit to Barbados intrigued him. From Gurenko's logs he'd followed the snakes and ladders course of Cooper's movements over the past two weeks. People of Cooper's stature were subjects of regular surveillance and tracing him wasn't particularly difficult. Interestingly, Hollis Macintyre's name kept on coming up, as did Joseph Swanbridge and, in the last few days, Stuart Shrenk, the Attorney General.

Meetings between Cooper, Swanbridge and Macintyre had taken place at Macintyre's country estate as well as a small townhouse on Cherry Hill Lane in Georgetown. The townhouse was owned by Delaware Real Estate Holdings, which turned out to be a CIA proprietary corporation. In other words, the Cherry Hill Lane address was a safe house.

According to the research information plucked from the fifteen million files on hand in the KGB Central Registry, Macintyre had figured in every administration since Roosevelt. A powerful figure certainly, but retired now and with no ties except social ones to Joseph Swanbridge and Stuart Shrenk and no connection at all to Hudson Cooper. There was also an unverified report that at one of the early meetings, the Deputy Head of the Joint Chiefs of Staff and the Secretary of the Treasury had also been in attendance.

Kuryokhin squinted, a trail of smoke drifting up under his glasses from the short end of his cigarette. He frowned, flipping through the pages of his note pad. A cabal of Washington's elite, a multi-million dollar purchase of gemstones presumably to be used as a payoff, Cooper's out of character trip to the Caribbean. Not for Cabrera or Morazan, that much was certain. If either one was a target for assassination men like Shrenk and Swanbridge would distance themselves from the operation, not embrace it.

The old man felt another bolt of pain in his arm and grunted with the fresh ache. Perhaps a visit to the pool on Volkhonka Street was in order. An hour in the *parilnya*, the steam room, instead of paperwork. He put out his cigarette and pushed himself up from the desk. Enough of this.

The pain was enormous, worse than anything he'd felt in his life, the razored talons of some enormous vile bird tearing into his chest. He knew immediately what it was – at last, his heart had failed, each blood pulse pounding through the frail organ wreaking the inevitable vengeance of time.

'*Ya umirayu*,' he whispered softly, amazed at the simple truth of his statement, 'I'm dying.' Turning, he took a single stumbling step towards the glass-doored cabinet on the far side of the room, his eyes fixed on the bottom shelf and a small, brightly painted wooden *matryoshka* doll. They would find it certainly, but would they see it, and seeing it, would they know what they had found? A good riddle to die with, and enough to make him smile, even with the terrible pain. The smile vanished then, the blood draining from his face.

'*Maht!*' he whispered, a child again, and Sergei Gregorovitch Kuryokhin, son of Zinaida Kuryokhin, took a final gasping breath and died.

Exhausted and mentally drained by the Travkin debriefing, Stephen Stone went down the short, dark hall and let himself into his ex-wife's apartment on South Capitol Street. He knew that Debbie wasn't due in from Paris until the following day, but he hadn't been able to bear the thought of his own bleak and un-air-conditioned bachelor. The conclusions they'd reached in the Rock Creek safe house were numbing and even the faint aura of Debbie's presence in the vacant rooms was better than facing those conclusions on his own.

The apartment took up the main floor of a gentrified brownstone tucked in behind the Rayburn Building just north of the Conrail tracks. It was an old-fashioned, high-ceilinged railway flat, the entrance hall opening onto a long corridor with the rooms all in a line to the right. The living room and dining room looked out onto the street while the bathroom, kitchen and bedroom faced a narrow alley. A rear doorway at the far end of the hall next to the bedroom led out to a tiny rear garden.

In what Stephen Stone knew was a deliberate attempt to separate her work and home lives, the entire apartment was done in Art Deco splendour. The living room was furnished with Frankl Chinese-style chairs, an ebony, gilt-wood and marble commode and a 1925 Paris Exposition rounded display cabinet inlaid with ivory in a floral motif. The dining room furniture looked as though it had been taken from an early twenties transatlantic liner and there was Fauré enamelled glassware everywhere.

Ignoring it all, Stone went down the short hall to the bathroom, stripped off his clothes and climbed into the shower. Standing under the noisy, lukewarm spray he let the water play over his face and body, faintly hoping that it would wash away his frustration and confusion.

Even if Travkin's assumption was wrong the FBI man knew there was enough circumstantial evidence to take action. The hiring of an assassin by Cooper was in direct contravention of a standing Presidential directive irrespective of the target. At the very least the Secret Service had to be notified so they could initiate an investigation, but the ramifications of that were enormous.

Cooper was almost certainly acting outside of normal CIA channels, but Travkin was right – his 'rescue' by the BACK DOOR group had been equally illegal and any information gained from it was tainted. If he went to Ruppelt the REDNET Director would have no choice but to suspend him and return Travkin to Cooper and the CIA. As it stood now Stone would be perceived as a frustrated FBI agent with a questionable Soviet asset as his only backup. Not even the *Washington Post* would go for a conspiracy story like the one he and Travkin had jigsawed together.

Stone stepped out of the shower, dried himself roughly and wrapped a towel around his waist. Standing in front of the medicine cabinet he wiped the condensation off the mirror and stared at himself. Whom was he trying to kid? Questions of belief were irrelevant. If Travkin was right and Cooper's target was the President of the United States, the CIA Deputy Director would use any means to keep the operation secret, including murder.

Frowning, Stone left the bathroom and padded barefoot down the hall to the bedroom, his rumpled clothes in his arms. He stopped in the doorway, open-mouthed. Debbie, his ex-wife, was sitting on the edge of the bed, peeling off her panty-hose. A black canvas suitcase lay open on the floor in front of her.

'Enjoy your shower?' she asked, smiling. He nodded from the doorway, suddenly embarrassed by the intimacy of the moment – he in a towel, she with her stockings down around her ankles. Bizarrely, he found himself becoming aroused. It was like getting a hard-on in your high-school math class.

'Yeah, thanks,' he muttered. She really was beautiful in a strange, plain way. She was close to his height with a model's legs but large, almost lush breasts. Her hair was cut shoulder length framing a wide, intelligent face.

Once upon a time the hair had been chestnut, but now it was faintly streaked with lines of grey she made no effort to conceal.

'I caught a late flight out of Paris,' she explained, yawning. She stood up, pulling the dark green dress up over her head. Beneath it she was wearing an almost sheer, cream-coloured bra and panties. The undergarments were as art deco as the furniture in the room. There was embroidery on the bra and a delicately curved see-through panel across the front of the panties showing the dark mass of her pubic hair. 'What are you doing here, by the way?' she asked, reaching up and unclipping the bra. She tossed it towards the suitcase.

'I needed someone to talk to,' he answered. 'I knew you wouldn't be here but . . .' He let it dangle, unsure of how to explain himself and trying not to look at her breasts.

'You sure you want to talk?' she asked, nodding towards the towel wrapped around his waist.

'Force of habit,' he said, smiling weakly.

'Bring your habit over here,' she said and laughed. He crossed the room, pausing in front of her.

'Look,' he began. 'You must be exhausted. I'll just put on my things and let you unpack.' Debbie Stone shook her head, then put her arms around his neck.

'I'm glad you're here,' she said quietly. 'It's a nice surprise even if you are trespassing.' She leaned forward slightly, taking his lower lip between her teeth and nipping gently. 'We may not be married any more but cohabitation isn't everything.' She slid her hand under the towel. He closed his eyes at the warm enclosing touch of her fingers, but instead of it arousing him further, he saw a vision of the Zapruder film from the Kennedy assassination, frame by frame, to the horrible image of the President's brains spraying upward and back over the trunk of the Lincoln in garish, 8 mm colour. He softened instantly.

'Sorry,' he said, opening his eyes and staring into hers.

She looked concerned. 'Problem?'

'Nothing I can talk about,' he sighed.

'Don't be silly,' she answered. 'This is your ex-wife, Deborah Basti Stone, Last of the Magyars.' Her hand milked him rhythmically and he began to thicken again. She paused, then used both hands to push him towards the bed.

'I think this goes beyond anything even the Last of the Magyars can handle,' he said, the towel falling away completely as he fell back onto the soft, down comforter.

'I wouldn't be so sure of that.' She laughed, dropping down on her knees between his outstretched legs.

*

An hour later Debbie Stone, nude, slipped out of bed, careful not to wake the sleeping man beside her. Despite his doubts she'd managed to handle both his physical and mental requirements, but while his gushing confession of the situation had allowed him to fall into an exhausted sleep it had left her stunned and wide awake.

The long-legged woman tiptoed to her closet, draped a pale green shantung robe over her shoulders and left the bedroom. Going to the kitchen she found a bottle of Riesling in the refrigerator, poured herself a glass and took it to the living room. She sat down in the floral print upholstered chair next to the telephone, took a few sips of wine, then took a cigarette from the zig-zag enamelled box on the side table. She lit it, then leaned back in the chair, staring up at the ceiling.

After a decade of work at the European Studies Institute Debbie Stone had analysed virtually every important intelligence operation mounted by both East and West since the end of World War Two. Her particular field focused on the Russians and the Eastern Bloc countries, but she was also an expert on the British, French, Italians and West Germans. Nothing in all she'd read and studied came close to the scenario Stephen had outlined to her.

Ironically, the only other piece of intelligence information with as much crucial importance as Stephen's was that of her own identity. She sat forward, took a last long drag on the cigarette, then crushed it into the ashtray on the side table. Deborah Stone, on file with the European Studies Institute and the Central Intelligence Agency as Deborah Basti, and in the files of the Hungarian *Allavedelmi Hatosag* or State Security Agency as Anna Danilla Rakozi, picked up the telephone, tapped out an almost forgotten number and waited. When her call was answered she spoke a single word.

'Autumn.'

PART FOUR

'I'm glad to be going . . . this is the loneliest place in the world.'
William Howard Taft, on leaving the White House
at the end of his term.

CHAPTER NINETEEN

During the course of his researches Eric Rhinelander had amassed an impressive library of books relating to the White House, including half a dozen formal histories, several architectural critiques and at least a score of tattle-tale biographies. He'd discovered detailed floor plans and cutaway drawings in both *Life* magazine and *National Geographic*, pieced together security information from several Secret Service exposés and built up a comprehensive photographic study of the Oval Office using various magazines and a number of books. Combined with personal observations and the minicam videotape he had been able to construct an accurate overview of White House personnel and their daily activities.

The working day at 1600 Pennsylvania Avenue began at 7:15 a.m. with the arrival of the food delivery truck. The vehicle was an unmarked, white refrigerated cube van on a Ford Econoline chassis and from his reading Rhinelander knew it was driven by a US Marine from the executive garage, with a Secret Service agent riding shotgun. Entering the White House grounds from Executive Avenue the truck stopped briefly while the driver's pass was checked by one of the gate guards. At the same time a second guard used a long-handled mirror to check the underside of the truck. After passing inspection the truck drove to the rear of the White House where the food was unloaded at the basement kitchen entrance.

Rhinelander knew that all food delivered to the White House was security-vetted on a regular basis – a high tech version of the royal food tasters employed by a variety of suspicious pharaohs, kings, queens and heads of state for thousands of years. In the case of the White House, foodstuffs from more than twenty different long-time suppliers were delivered to McCreery's Provisioners, a security-cleared catering company in Georgetown, where the various orders were consolidated into a single shipment. Under the Secret Service agent's supervision, the shipment, already on skids, was loaded onto the truck, then delivered to the executive mansion.

Following the van on three separate occasions, Rhinelander noted that on arriving at the rear entrance to McCreery's, both the driver and the Secret Service agent left the empty truck unattended for almost fifteen minutes each morning, presumably while they enjoyed a cup of coffee and a cigarette with the catering company staff. On his third visit to McCreery's Rhinelander crossed the narrow alley at the rear of the building and climbed up into the truck.

His thirty-second inspection confirmed his initial observations after viewing the minicam tape. The truck was brand new and equipped with a Thermo-King 9,000 BTU flush-mounted reefer unit. The refrigeration box was fitted over the cab, with nothing but a vent inside the Kemlite insulated cube. He'd been given a guided tour of an identical vehicle on a truck-leasing lot in Alexandria the day before and knew what to expect.

According to the salesman at the leasing company, the flush-mounted units worked well as long as the truck wasn't loaded tight to the rear wall; that would block the vent and let the frozen goods thaw. Enough air space had to be left all around to let the cold air circulate, hence, most trucks with flush-mounted units had a wooden baffle added on to the front wall of the box to prevent the skids being pushed up against the vent.

The Secret Service cube van was no exception. The plywood box was four feet high, eight feet long and jutted out approximately sixteen inches. Rapping it with his knuckles Rhinelander could tell that the baffle was hollow, fitted with a vertical brace in the centre. The end pieces, also plywood, were fastened down with six Phillips-head screws. Lots of room to hide, and more than enough time to remove the screws. Rhinelander took out a pocket tape, took some accurate measurements of the crate-like structure, then left the box unseen. He'd now dealt with the intial phase of his entry. The second phase was equally straightforward and took place the day after his last visit to the catering company.

Using the truck was one of three options Rhinelander had devised as a way of getting into the grounds, but getting in was only a small part of the battle. For the operation to succeed he needed to be able to remain within the White House undetected for roughly five minutes. To accomplish that he needed protective coloration – a disguise.

The simplest would be to impersonate a Secret Service agent, since they wore no uniform beyond the colour-coded pins in their jacket lapels, but the White House Detail was a relatively small group, the members of which knew each other well. Secret Service staff were occasionally called in from other field offices, but usually only for special events. A better choice was to dress as an Executive Protection officer.

His name was Paul Axworthy. At forty-four he had been with the EPB for seven years. For eleven years prior to that he had been a uniformed officer with the DC Metropolitan Police. His scores on the Sergeant's examination had been well above average over a four-year period, but eventually he realised that a combination of factors including ethnic quotas and internal politics were clouding his chances of advancement within the force, so he opted for the Executive Protection branch and was accepted.

During his time with the Washington police Axworthy had married, fathered three girls, and divorced. Most of his regular EPB paycheck and all of his overtime went to support his ex-wife and children in Fort Myer and what was left barely covered his personal living expenses and the rent on his one-bedroom apartment in Columbia Heights.

During his preliminary surveillance from the Hay-Adams Rhinelander was unaware of Axworthy's background, but he had marked him as being roughly the right physical type. Following the White House policeman home after shift end the assassin had discovered his address and name. The following evening, with Axworthy safely on duty, Rhinelander had let himself into the man's apartment.

It was tiny and immaculately clean. Framed photos on the white walls of Axworthy and his girls at Disney World, picture of Axworthy in his EPB uniform, class photo from the Washington PD Academy. There was a desk under the picture of his kids. Rhinelander went through the drawers quickly, building an image of Axworthy's past. Satisfied that he knew enough, he moved on to the large closet on the wall between the fold-out bed and the kitchen area. Like the rest of the apartment, the closet and its contents were a study in meticulous order.

Footwear was arranged by type and colour along the floor, while caps and hats were lined up on the shelf above the chrome hanger bar. The bar itself was completely filled: sport shirts on the far left followed by dress shirts in solid colours, then white uniform shirts. Suits and ties hung at the centre of the pole. The right side was filled with uniforms: five standard EPB uniforms, four of them in plastic dry-cleaning bags, a set of dress whites, two Washington Metropolitan Police uniforms, three US Marine uniforms, still fitted out with corporal's stripes, a Vietnam vintage set of tropicals, and a set of Marine dress whites.

From his research Rhinelander knew that the EPB uniform was much like that of the DC police. The only real differences were the gold stripe on the legs of the EPB trousers, the badge, and the shoulder flashes. He'd been prepared to simulate the uniform and its accessories, but Axworthy's wardrobe saved him the trouble.

From what he could see the White House policeman wore his uniforms in order, from right to left, probably at the rate of one a week. When he was down to the last one he would take the others in to be dry-cleaned. Given the narrowing time frame of his operation Rhinelander felt it was worth the small risk of the man noticing that one of the uniforms was missing. He took the uniform on the far left, then let himself out of the apartment.

The question of weaponry was next on his list. In works of fiction there was usually a brilliant gunsmith or weaponsmaster for the hero to visit but Rhinelander was well aware that in reality such men didn't exist, and if they once had, their clients had long ago removed them. Anyone involved in the business of professional murder would hardly put his identity and whereabouts into the hands of a stranger, and anyway, there was rarely the need. Forsyth's Jackal and Fleming's Bond aside, the real assassins tended towards cheap but efficient means of carrying out their assignments.

Hence, you had Stauffenberg's satchel of explosives for killing Hitler, Ramon Mercador's ice-pick for Leon Trotsky, Booth's Derringer, fired less than a foot from Lincoln's head.

In this instance, Rhinelander's weapon of choice would probably have been a hand grenade, but he knew that blood and brains smeared all over the walls of the Oval Office wasn't what Hudson Cooper was looking for. The CIA man and his ghostly conspirators were looking for something that would play on the evening news: murder most foul, but relatively palatable to the television audiences of the world.

A rifle would be ridiculous and using a shotgun at such close range was also out of the question, both technically and aesthetically. Some sort of handgun was an obvious choice, especially if he was wearing an EPB uniform, but being able to get off at least two accurate shots under the conditions he was envisaging was highly unlikely. After considering every aspect of his plan Rhinelander concluded that he needed a quiet, semi or fully automatic weapon capable of inflicting fatal injury at close range.

Ironically, the criteria he established for his weapon eventually led him to a real-life 'armourer'. Unlike the bow-tied 'Q' from the Bond books or Forsyth's dapper little Belgian, this weapons man was barely twenty, had shoulder length hair tied back in a pony tail, wore a Def Leppard T-shirt and operated openly out of a mall on the outskirts of Baltimore.

The young man's name was Willis Johnson and he managed a store called the Gasworks. The store supplied weapons, ammunition and designer clothing for something variously known as Paintball, the Survival Game and Action Pursuit. As far as Rhinelander could tell it was a high-tech and expensive version of cowboys and Indians. According to Willis Johnson the first paintball gun was designed to mark trees for logging companies. A forestry surveyor could choose a tree to be cut, and mark it from a distance with the CO_2-powered handgun. The 'bullet' was a gelatine ball filled with a mixture of paint and mineral oil.

Over time, the weaponry and its accessories had become highly sophisticated, as had the game itself. Instead of using old fashioned single-shot marking pistols and chasing after each other through the trees, organised teams now stalked each other on playing grounds complete with mock

Vietnamese villages, dummy tanks and palisaded forts, using 'constant air' machine guns with brand names like The Terminator. They wore full camo outfits, hand loaded their own paintballs and took their wives to national competitions all over the country.

On a range in the basement of the store, Willis Johnson demonstrated the technology with his own custom-designed weapon – a short-barrelled machine pistol fed by a small tank of CO_2 clipped to his belt and connected to the hard plastic butt of the Uzi-style weapon by a loop of rubber tubing. The air powered a spring, which in turn forced the paintballs along the barrel of the gun at about 600 feet per second. Not fatally rapid, but well below the speed of sound, which kept the gun quiet.

The range was made up of three fifty-foot lanes, each one separated by head high walls made of sheet plywood. At the end of each lane there was a black painted silhouette of a man. According to Willis the targets, also made of plywood, were hosed off at the end of each day.

'Just like a real weapon,' said the young black man, pulling on a pair of safety goggles and flipping a switch to light up the middle lane on the range. 'You got three settings: safety, that's the red dot on the lever, then single shot, then full auto.' Willis set the paintball gun on single shot and squeezed the trigger. There was a brief cracking sound and a blood-red stain three or four inches across appeared on the head of the silhouette. 'Sound comes from the ball smackin' into the wood,' Willis said. 'Quieter out in the bush.' He flipped the lever to full auto, adopted a pained Charles Bronson expression and squeezed the trigger again. There was a stuttering roar, ending abruptly as the twenty-round magazine emptied in under two seconds. Willis had stitched a line of red from the crotch of the target up to its neck.

'Impressive,' Rhinelander said. Willis handed him the weapon and pulled a fully loaded tube-like magazine from his fatigue jacket. He showed Rhinelander how to load the ball-bearing-sized paintballs, then stepped back. Rhinelander slipped the six-inch-long plastic air bottle into the pocket of his jacket, then settled himself into a firing position. He fired five rounds, left eye, right eye, heart, stomach and groin.

'You've used guns before,' said Willis, peering downrange at the stitched line of paint splatters.

'Now and again,' Rhinelander admitted. 'What would you say is the optimum range for a gun like this?'

'For real?' Willis asked.

Rhinelander nodded. 'Yes.'

'Fifty feet, sixty at the outside,' the young man answered. 'Trajectory's pretty flat, but the balls are light and the barrels are smooth bore.'

'I see,' said Rhinelander. He hefted the weapon is his hands. 'The CO_2 bottle is plastic and so is the gun. How much metal is involved in the manufacture?'

'Hardly any,' Willis answered. 'It sounds kind of silly, but one of the problems they used to have was cleaning these things, so now they're dishwasher safe. Most anything not plastic is made out of ceramic. The spring is probably the biggest piece of metal in the gun.'

They went back upstairs, and twenty minutes later, Rhinelander left the store, leaving Willis with a sketch of the weapon he wanted the young man to build for him. The gun, stripped down to barrel, trigger and frame, looked more like a fat-handled nightstick than a pistol. According to Willis it would take three days to create.

Rhinelander made two more stops before returning to Washington. Using the Yellow Pages he found a discount plumbing and heating store where he purchased two dozen second hand residential thermostats. Then he went to a hobby shop and bought three model-maker's syringes, normally used for putting glue in hard-to-reach areas. His out-of-town shopping complete, he returned to the capital, dropping his packages off at the Wyoming. Consulting his detailed notes on the upcoming operation he was pleased to see that there was only one thing left on his list.

Wearing a suit and tie Rhinelander crossed to the Holiday Inn and rented a car using the John Smythe Mastercard. He drove out of Washington, heading south on the Maryland side to the small town of Indian Head. There he found the marina mentioned in one of the guidebooks he'd purchased, and using the Smythe credit card he rented a twin-pontooned houseboat. The vessel was at least ten years old, painted a nondescript pale blue and offered only the barest essentials. At twenty-eight feet it had sleeping accommodation for six, a small galley and dining area and a head with shower stall. It was powered by twin inboards and according to the manager of the marina it was capable of six knots upstream and eight downstream if the tides were running in your favour. It suited Rhinelander perfectly. He took the boat for two weeks, put down a five hundred dollar deposit and told the manager he'd pick it up in the next day or so.

During the early planning stages Rhinelander had thought of something a lot faster than the houseboat, but the assassin knew he'd overstayed his welcome at the Wyoming, and the boxy vessel he'd rented was just the kind of anonymous living quarters he required for the last few days before the event. Satisfied with his progress, he drove back to Washington, dropped off the car at the Holiday Inn and returned to the Wyoming.

He spent the next few hours going over every detail of the operation, checking and rechecking each move and countermove. Access, exit and escape had all been dealt with, the question of weaponry and ammunition was in hand – he'd even chosen the date: Saturday, 12 August, with the Beach Boys performing on the floating barge at the Water Gate and the President of the United States celebrating his birthday at the White House. The only thing necessary now was his final telephone call to Mallory. Rhinelander glanced at his watch. The last few minutes of Wednesday, 9 August were ticking away. If all went well, seventy-two hours would see the operation to its conclusion. Rhinelander gathered his notes into a neat pile on the desk, turned out the light and went to bed.

CHAPTER TWENTY

Stephen Stone sat in the coffee shop of the Old Town Holiday Inn in Alexandria, drinking stomach-souring coffee, smoking Camel Filters in an unending chain and contemplating his future as a defrocked FBI agent with an out of date law degree and a fugitive Soviet spy on his hands. It didn't look promising, especially since Ruppelt was threatening criminal action unless he coughed up Travkin's wherabouts. So far Ruppelt had only put him on indefinite suspension but Stone knew it was only a matter of time. Cooper would pressure Ruppelt for Travkin's bolt-hole and Ruppelt would pass the pressure along.

A bored waitress filled Stone's cup for the fifth time that morning, then moved down the row of booths to the front of the coffee shop. The FBI man followed her with his eyes, then looked beyond her to the lobby, hoping for a glimpse of Mort Kessler. Kessler was his only link to the REDNET office now, and even that was tenuous; Stone had been under suspension for the last five days, and right from the start Kessler was sure that he was being tailed.

Stone sighed, added three cream capsules to the coffee, and lit yet another cigarette. Thanks to Debbie, Travkin was safe, at least for the moment. It had taken her a while to absorb the scenario he'd laid out for her that night in her apartment, but eventually she'd accepted it. They both knew she was putting her own career on the line by helping him, but she'd brushed aside his attempt at thanks and got down to the business at hand.

The following morning Debbie returned to work at the Institute and before lunchtime she'd organised a new safe house for Travkin. She'd spotted a typed advertisement for a summer-home rental on the bulletin board in the Administration Office and discovered that the owner was one of the Georgetown professors she'd done a research project for the previous year. She gave the woman a deposit and the professor gave her a set of a keys and a map. The cottage was on Lake Anna, a few miles west of Bowling Green on the Virginia side of the Potomac.

That evening, using Debbie's car and after making sure they weren't being followed, they drove Travkin to the cottage, pausing briefly in the little Civil War town of Spotsylvania to stock up on food. The cottage had turned out to be quite lavish – a four-bedroom log cabin with its own beach, dock and boathouse. The house was surrounded by trees, accessible only by a narrow winding drive leading down from the main, gravelled road. After settling Travkin in Stone and Debbie returned to Washington and parted company, Stone insisting that she have no more involvement in the affair. The next day he'd been suspended. He hadn't seen his ex-wife or Travkin since.

Mort Kessler appeared in the coffee shop just as Travkin was butting his cigarette. He slid into the booth across from Stone and frowned. 'You look like shit,' he offered. The waitress drifted by and Kessler ordered a large tomato juice.

'I feel like shit,' Stone answered. 'Anyone on your tail?'

'That's one of those dumb questions like, "Are you asleep?"' Kessler grinned. The tomato juice arrived and he took a sip. 'If I'd been followed I wouldn't be here, I'd still be dodging the tail.'

'Don't be irritating,' Stone sighed. 'Did anyone try to tail you?'

'Not today, not that I could see.' Kessler shrugged. That was good enough for Stone. Mort was a ghost when it came to surveillance and he knew every trick in the book.

'Okay,' Stone said. 'What's been happening?'

'You've got leprosy as far as the Bureau is concerned,' he began. 'Anybody working with you has been shit-listed.'

'You?' Stone asked.

'Bet your life,' Kessler snorted. 'I've got two weeks' leave, and then I'm off to the Seattle Field Office.'

'Cooper.' Stone grimaced.

'Some of it,' Kessler agreed. 'The Roop is pretty ticked all on his own, though. The big piss-off is that you won't tell him where you've got Dimitri stashed.'

'I told him I didn't know anything about Travkin,' Stone said. He lit another cigarette. 'I told him the last I knew about it, he'd been kidnapped by persons unknown.'

'He knows you're shitting him,' Kessler answered, sipping his juice. 'I think one of the guys we picked up in Baltimore must have talked. They tore up the Rock Creek place a couple of days ago.'

'Cooper again,' Stone murmured.

'I think so,' Kessler said. 'They've had two sniffers going through your office the past couple of days, loading everything into boxes and lugging them out.'

'Have they got anything on you?'

'Nothing but my association with you,' Kessler answered. 'No hard evidence about spiriting Dimitri away from the Company. I think the Roop is suspicious, though. He keeps on giving me these nasty looks when I run into him in the hall.' Kessler grinned. 'And to make it worse, I just told him I was taking my two week leave early.'

'To follow Mallory around?'

'That's the plan, isn't it?' Kessler asked. 'He's got to be the link to our killer.'

'If there really is a killer,' Stone grunted.

'What's the matter? Losing faith in comrade Dimitri's hypothesis?'

'No,' he responded wearily. 'But you have to admit the whole thing sounds pretty crazy. We're sitting on a conspiracy to assassinate the President of the United States, a Deputy Director of the CIA is deeply involved, and our best witness is a Russian Military Intelligence officer.'

'We've been over it a hundred times,' Kessler answered. 'Travkin's information is backed up by our own surveillance of him and it fits in with Cooper's visit to Barbados. So does the telephone call from Cooper to Hollis Macintyre. Those two have been thick as thieves for years and Macintyre was one of the back rooms boys who got Tucker elected in the first place. Now he's been put out to pasture.'

'It's still hard to imagine,' Stone sighed. He butted his cigarette and lit another. The coffee in front of him was mud brown and cold. He could feel his stomach beginning to protest. There was no antacid made that could take on indigestion brought on by an assassination.

'I don't have any trouble with it.' Kessler shrugged. 'You know as well as I do that this country was built on conspiracies and assassinations. And Cooper's not so far out of whack either; don't forget, he works for the same boys who tried to murder Castro with a poisoned cigar.'

'All right,' Stone said finally. 'How do we work it?'

'Like we said before. There has to be a link – Cooper's not going to expose himself if he doesn't have to. Mallory went with him to Barbados, so he's the most likely.'

'Did you manage to find anything on him?'

'Not a lot. Smart, our age. Heavy math background. Used to work in Threat Analysis. A computer whiz.'

'Doesn't sound like your average Company cut-out,' Stone offered.

'Maybe not, but he makes the perfect fall guy. When this is over Cooper could remove him without making any waves. His slate is so clean it squeaks; no immediate family, no close friends at the Agency, nothing on our files at all.'

'Presumably Cooper is working him blind,' Stone mused.

Kessler nodded. 'It's a good bet. All he knows is that he's servicing a covert agent for his boss.'

'He's got to realise it's an illegal operation,' said Kessler. 'Company agent operating within the country?'

'Don't be naive,' said Stone. He gave a dry laugh. 'You know as well as I do that the Company's got at least a dozen proprietary operations ongoing in Florida alone. Miami is one big recruiting station.'

'Still, maybe we can turn him.'

'On what grounds?' Stone snorted. 'Do we appeal to his patriotism?'

'Self-interest,' Kessler replied. 'If this really is a plot to kill Tucker, and if Mallory is running as a cut-out, you and I both know Cooper's going to off him as soon as the operation is over. Let him run *that* through his Threat Analysis computer.'

'Not yet,' Stone murmured. 'Let's watch him and see if we can get a lead on Travkin's man from Barbados.'

'What happens if we do find him?' Kessler asked. 'We can't go to the Roop, that's for sure.'

'If we have enough real evidence I can take it to Lyall Spenser at the Secret Service.'

'Okay,' Kessler said. 'We put a hot-watch on Mr Mallory.'

'All by yourself?' Stone asked.

Kessler shook his head. 'Putnam and Dofney are still in as long as I can let them take the after hours shifts. Where will you be if something comes up – home or uh . . .'

'Debbie's?' Stone smiled, filling in the slightly embarrassed blank. Mort Kessler was the only one of his co-workers at REDNET who was aware of the on-again off-again affair with his ex. He shook his head. 'No. I'll be at the safe house at Anna Lake with our Russian friend, at least for tonight. You've got the number.'

'Okay.' Kessler stood up. 'I'll call you if anything breaks.'

Stephen Stone watched his friend leave the coffee shop. He pushed the cup and the overflowing ashtray away and leaned back against the sticky vinyl upholstery of the booth. His stomach was churning, but that didn't account for the dull, deep ache in his guts. Somehow, perhaps bred by the instincts and paranoias of his profession, he knew they were running out of time.

General Vladimir Gurenko, KGB Resident in Washington, leaned back in his chair, eyes closed, hands clasped behind his neck. His deputy, Major Valentin Ivashutin, sat on a low couch on the far side of the room, browsing through the welter of teletype tearsheets and handwritten notes on the birchwood table in front of him. Behind Gurenko the large picture window was slashed with streaks of rain. It had begun early that afternoon and showed no signs of stopping. The rain was a false promise, though, and was doing nothing to offset the sweltering heat of the capital.

'Go through it again,' Gurenko murmured, his eyes still closed. 'As much as we have so far.'

'Our colleagues at Moscow Centre followed procedure when General Kuryokhin did not appear at his normally scheduled morning briefing,' Ivashutin began. 'A two-man unit was sent to his apartment. They entered and found the General dead, apparently of a heart attack.'

'There is no doubt of the cause of death?' Gurenko asked mildly. Within the ranks of the KGB 'heart attack' was a well-worn euphemism that covered a lot of ground.

'Not at this point,' Ivashutin responded, neatly avoiding a firm opinion. 'Once again following procedure the apartment was sealed after the body was removed and a team of janitors were brought in. In addition to the notes General Kuryokhin was making at the time of his death the janitors found a wooden key hidden inside one of the General's collection of *matryoshka* dolls. It took some time but they eventually discovered that the hand-made key opened up a small compartment behind one of the bookshelves in the room. The compartment contained a number of journals written in code.'

'Ignore the logistics of our intrepid comrades,' Gurenko ordered. 'Get to the meat of it.'

'The code was one that hadn't been used since the Great Patriotic War,' Ivashutin continued, his voice even. 'It was easy enough to break. At any rate, the journals have given us the identity of *Osin*, among other things.' Ivashutin leafed through the papers on the table and pulled out a stapled sheaf of hastily prepared notes. He hesitated for a moment, his small, bright eyes scanning over the rough dossier he'd prepared.

'Go on,' Gurenko ordered. He opened his eyes and sat forward in the chair, his small, long-fingered hands playing over the surface of the desk in front of him.

'She was born Anna Danilla Rakozi in Budapest, 17 August 1951. Her father was Dr Lutz Rakozi, a professor of history at the university. Her mother died in childbirth. In 1968 at the age of seventeen she obtained a scholarship in languages and history from the University of Moscow. We recruited her in 1970 and after her father's death in 1971 she returned to Budapest and continued her education while monitoring student activities for us at the same time.'

'What was Kuryokhin's interest in her?' Gurenko asked.

'After we lost Sasha in 1964 the General and other ranking members of the Foreign Directorate were looking for ways to reinfiltrate the Central Intelligence Agency. Given the CIA's own recruitment methods – generally utilising their so-called Ivy League universities – the General thought placing students within their educational system seemed a likely path. He left standing orders with the Secret Police in Budapest to alert him of any possible identity switches that could be made.

'According to the General's journals an opportunity presented itself late in 1973. A Hungarian couple who'd emigrated to the United States long before the '56 revolution returned to Budapest on holiday. They died in an unfortunate automobile accident.'

'Indeed,' Gurenko murmured softly. 'Automobile accident' was as much a euphemism as 'heart attack'.

'Yes,' Ivashutin answered. He paused, trying to find his place in the notes, then continued. 'The couple's name was Basti, Sandor and Danuta. He worked for a plumbing supply company in New York and she was a housewife. They had no children. Technical gave her a passport identifying her as their daughter and she accompanied their remains back to the United States. From what we understand there was no other family.'

'Of course not,' said Gurenko, smiling wanly. 'There wouldn't be.'

'Rakozi, now known as Deborah Basti, enrolled at Columbia University, obtaining a degree in European history and Russian. Considering her education at the University of Moscow and her language facility it isn't surprising that she was granted a postgraduate scholarship to the University of Georgetown. From there she was recruited by the European Studies Institute.'

'The CIA,' said Gurenko.

'Precisely,' Ivashutin agreed. 'In 1979 she was hand-picked by Hudson Cooper, Deputy Director of Operations. He's employed her as a strategic analyst and a high level courier ever since. She's been sitting in on every major project and debriefing for the last seven or eight years.'

'All the while being run by Kuryokhin,' breathed Gurenko, impressed despite himself.

'She is obviously the source of the General's so called magic touch,' said Ivashutin. 'According to his notes she was even hired as a consultant for their counterintelligence programme.'

'I'm intrigued by the connection to Stephen Stone, the REDNET man at the FBI.'

'A fortuitous twist of fate, by all appearances,' Ivashutin said, shrugging. 'They met at a conference and had an affair. One thing led to another. It's not too unreasonable when you think about it. They were both in the same field, a great deal in common. We don't have a psychological file on the woman, but one presumes there was some guilt on her part. It was a small bonus for the General; through her he could keep some kind of watch on the Bureau's counterintelligence activities.'

'A watch he saw fit not to share with us,' Gurenko responded. He tapped his fingers on the desk top. 'The General's conspiracy theory,' he prompted after a moment.

'It relates to the last notes he was making before he died,' Ivashutin answered, his tone hesitant again. Both men knew they were on dangerous political ground here. Kuryokhin was dead and there was no telling who his successor would be; by rights the man, whoever he was, would inherit *Osin* and the current, delicate situation.

'He made contact with the Rakozi/Basti woman in Amsterdam,' Gurenko said.

'Yes,' said Ivashutin. 'Not directly, but an information exchange was made. This fits with what we know of Deborah Basti's movements at the time. She was in Paris at a conference and took the last three days in Holland. They were there at the same time. According to the notes she was making a large gemstone purchase on behalf of Cooper, using an invisible Swiss account. It was her opinion that the gemstones, emeralds, I believe, were to be used as an agent payoff. The size of the purchase indicated a major operation.'

'That was as far as she took it?'

'Yes.' Ivashutin cleared his throat. 'General Kuryokhin developed the scenario further.'

'Using our logs.'

'According to our transmission records, yes. He connected Travkin's suspicions with information relating to Hollis Macintyre, Secretary of State Swanbridge, and Stuart Shrenk, the Attorney General. Apparently there were a number of meetings at a townhouse on Cherry Hill Lane. The house turned out to be owned by a CIA proprietary company.'

'Such men meet all the time,' Gurenko offered. He pursed his lips. 'You've checked the logs on this?'

'It's being done right now.'

'And the last meeting?'

'Macintyre, Swanbridge and Shrenk, also the Deputy Head of the Joint Chiefs and the Secretary of the Treasury. That was two days after *Osin* had given Cooper the gemstone consignment.'

'According to our own information and what I discussed with Koslov about Travkin's disappearance, the man had come up with a theory regarding Costa Rica.'

'Kuryokhin discounts it in his journal,' answered Ivashutin, leafing through his notes. 'A blind.'

'What do you think?'

'It isn't my place to offer opinions,' the Deputy answered calmly.

'Nor mine,' Gurenko parried, allowing himself a small, wolfish smile. 'Our duty requires that we deal in facts, not flights of fancy.'

'Yes.'

'So what are the facts?' Gurenko asked rhetorically, leaning back in his chair again. 'Travkin vanishes, but does not defect, at least according to Koslov. Cooper has an unprecedented meeting in Barbados. Cooper then requests Comrade Rakozi, Basti, Stone, *Osin*, or whatever you want to call her, to obtain a large gemstone consignment, presumably to pay off the man in Barbados for services to be rendered.' Gurenko paused. 'Just for the record, *tovaritch* Valentin, tell me again, what did General Kuryokhin conclude a few moments before his unfortunate and untimely demise?'

'The conclusion has no basis in operational information,' he replied uneasily.

'The conclusion is a documented fact,' Gurenko said softly. 'It amounts to being the General's last words.'

'It was Comrade General Kuryokhin's theory that such a group of men, such a large amount of money for an operation, and such an extraordinary juxtaposition of events indicated a major political assassination being planned.'

'And not the assassination of a Costa Rican police chief, or even a Costa Rican head of state.'

'No, Comrade General.'

'Who did Kuryokhin think the target was, Valentin?'

'The President of the United States.'

'The situation complicated by the fact that a senior member of the GRU and a deep cover illegal for the KGB are intimately involved in the plot.'

'Yes, sir,' Ivashutin answered, acutely aware that he had been outmanoeuvred by his superior. Any record, either his own testimony, or that of the hidden tape recorder undoubtedly spinning away somewhere in the room, would show that, technically, it had been he who had uttered the fateful conclusion. Glasnost or not, the bearer of bad tidings was still a universally unloved figure.

'We must develop some course of action,' Gurenko mused. He glanced at his deputy. 'Any suggestions?' he asked blandly.

'No, sir,' Ivashutin answered.

Gurenko smiled. 'You should show more initiative, Valentin,' he said, chuckling. 'You will go stale.'

'Yes, sir,' he replied coldly from across the room.

'I want *Osin* found, then followed. She is to have a 24-hour watch.'

'No action?' asked Valentin, obviously hoping his boss would overstep his bounds.

'Not yet,' Gurenko said, shaking his head. 'Not unless there is need. At this point we are dealing with a conspiracy, not an actual assassination. If it appears that she is directly involved with Cooper's plot then I will ask Moscow Centre for permission to eliminate her. In the meantime nothing but a day and night watch. The same goes for Cooper's little band. I want all of them put under surveillance, discreetly, and I want a permanent watch on the Cherry Hill Lane house.'

'That's a lot of manpower,' said Ivashutin.

'We have a lot of manpower,' Gurenko answered. He had two hundred legitimate agents to call on in the Washington area, and more could be brought up out of the Eastern Bloc embassies.

'Nevertheless. . . .' Ivashutin began, then let the thought dangle.

'Let us drop the pretence,' Gurenko said, breaking the silence, weary of the semantic dance which seemed to be part of his job. Beyond anything else he saw himself as a soldier, and for a soldier, problems were there to be solved, not evaded, while obstacles were to be surmounted, not avoided. 'We are both aware that General Kuryokhin's death will inevitably create a power struggle at Tyeply Shtan. So be it, and eventually that power struggle may impact on us both. For the moment we have a dangerous situation here which must be addressed. It is quite possible that there is a conspiracy underway by a group of high-ranking Americans to assassinate their own president. Two of our agents appear to be in some way involved. You realise, of course, that this is intolerable. We must in no way interfere with the Americans' internecine squabbles, but by the same token we must interfere enough to remove our own people.'

'Remove?' said Ivashutin, cocking an eyebrow. He began gathering up the papers on the table in front of him.

'Remove,' Gurenko repeated, his voice firm. 'One way or the other. Both Travkin and *Osin*. Before it is too late.'

'And if Stone or the CIA is in the way?'

'That will be their misfortune,' said Gurenko. 'The relationship between our two nations used to be very simple. We were each others' most feared enemies. Now we must pretend a friendship that is equally imaginary. The slightest hint that we were somehow involved in a plot to assassinate President Tucker would bring the world down around our ears. If he is to die, then so be it. We must remain like their symbol of justice – blind.' He swivelled around in his chair and stared out through the rain-etched window. Behind him Ivashutin pushed the papers into a single pile and gathered them up under his arm. A few moments later he left the office, shutting the door quietly behind him.

The full roster of Romulus Committee members began arriving at the Cherry Hill Lane house in Georgetown as dusk fell over Washington. The rain which had begun earlier in the day persisted, the slow, warm drizzle turning the entire city into a steam bath. By nine o'clock all the members had entered the townhouse, unaware that each of them had been photographed and videotaped by a team of damp and disgruntled KGB surveillance operatives on the roof of a house under renovation on Cecil Place, a few hundred feet away.

By nine-thirty the three stewards from the CIA catering department had set out coffee and water carafes around the long, burled walnut table in the dining room, and then withdrawn. The six members of the Romulus Committee then sat down and the meeting began.

As usual, Hollis Macintyre sat at the head of the table, with Hudson Cooper at the far end opposite him. To Macintyre's left sat General Marcus D Andrews, Deputy Head of the Joint Chiefs of Staff, and Elaine Goodhouse, the hard-nosed, honey-tongued Southern belle in her sixties who was Secretary of the Treasury. Across from Andrews and Goodhouse were Joseph Swanbridge, the Secretary of State, and Stuart Shrenk, Attorney General. The meeting began with Macintyre's request for an update from Hudson Cooper.

'It would seem that things are coming to a head,' Cooper said, speaking slowly. 'Our man has requested his payment and wants a final meeting before he proceeds.'

'Do we have a date?' Stuart Shrenk interrupted.

'Yes.' Cooper nodded. 'Some time during the President's birthday festivities.'

'That's the day after tomorrow,' drawled Elaine Goodhouse. She seemed surprised. 'This is all happening very quickly.' Goodhouse had been the last of the Committee to be told of the plan, and even then it had been over the objections of the others, mostly because few of the men at the table knew her. In the end, Hollis Macintyre had insisted; like Swanbridge and Shrenk, she was in direct line of succession and had to be informed.

'What about the Russian, Dimitri Travkin? At our last meeting you said the matter was well in hand.' Macintyre made a delicate bridge of his fingers, then touched it to the tip of his nose. Staring down the table, Hudson Cooper felt a small stab of revulsion at the gesture. Without the bulging file he had on Macintyre, the CIA man would have marked him as a raging homosexual long ago.

'As I informed you, Travkin was going to be released anyway. Initially I assumed he would be picked up by his own people. This was not the case: instead, he was "rescued" by Stephen Stone, Deputy Director of the FBI REDNET programme. Stone has since been suspended from duty because of the unauthorised operation.'

'Do we know where Travkin is hiding?' asked Shrenk, the Attorney General.

'Yes. A cabin on Lake Anna. We have the cabin under surveillance.'

'How did he find the place?' asked Andrews, the Army General.

'Through Stone's ex-wife. I suggested it to her, in fact.'

'I beg your pardon?' Swanbridge asked. 'You suggested it to her?'

'Mr Cooper is having his little joke with us,' mumured Hollis Macintyre.

'Deborah Stone works at the European Studies Institute. She is also in the employ of the Central Intelligence Agency.'

'I'll be damned,' laughed General Andrews. 'In other words you've got him all tied up with a ribbon and a bow.'

'Precisely,' Cooper said.

'And having him all wrapped up,' said Macintyre, 'it's now simply a question of to whom we give the package.'

'Frankly,' said Shrenk, 'from a legal position, the less we know about Comrade Travkin's eventual fate the better.'

'From a legal position all of us could be charged with conspiracy to commit murder, honey.' The Secretary of the Treasury smiled. 'But you're right. This Russian fellow is a detail I think we can leave to Mr Cooper. What we need to know is the procedure . . . umm, after the dirty deed is done, so to speak.'

'Indeed.' Swanbridge nodded. 'A smooth transition is necessary, we can't have any embarrassments like the Haig affair.' He turned slightly in his chair. 'Hollis?'

'There will be no embarrassments,' Macintyre soothed. 'With the exception of myself and General Andrews, all of you will be at the birthday party, is that correct?' There was a silent chorus of nods. Macintyre smiled. 'Good. Then it will be up to Joseph.' Macintyre tilted his huge, leonine head in Swanbridge's direction.

'As soon as we know that the President and Mr Teresi are no longer with us, I'll speak with Jack Reynolds and Charles Whittaker. Both of them will be at the party. Their letters of direction are already on file with Attorney General Shrenk, I believe.'

'That's right.' Shrenk nodded. 'After that succession is automatic. Joseph doesn't even need to be sworn in – he simply becomes the President of the United States by default.'

'I didn't know that,' drawled Elaine Goodhouse. 'What about LBJ being sworn in on Air Force One after the Kennedy assassination?'

'Window dressing,' grunted Hollis Macintyre. 'The old goat was doing some hard-core public relations and he knew it.'

'All right,' said General Andrews. 'Then what?'

'We bring out our own window dressing,' said Hudson Cooper. 'The media will want something to chew on – we'll give them our mythical terrorist.'

'We want to take the focus away from the actual assassination as quickly as possible,' put in Macintyre. 'Done properly, we can have the media and the public screaming for revenge against Libya instead of calling for a Senate investigation into the assassination itself.'

'And we certainly don't want that.' Elaine Goodhouse smiled.

'No, indeed,' Macintyre assented. 'At any rate, we will have Joseph installed as President within forty-five minutes to an hour after the event. From then on it should be relatively smooth sailing. With all the attention on our Libyan assassin, we should be able to clear up any loose ends.'

'Like a cabinet shuffle, Mr President?' asked the Attorney General.

'Among other things, Stuart.' Swanbridge laughed.

'A question for Mr Cooper,' said General Andrews.

'Yes?'

'For our man to accomplish his aims, both the President and Mr Teresi must be in the Oval Office at the same time. Granted, both President Tucker and the Vice-President will be in the White House for the birthday celebration, but how are you going to manage having them both in the Oval Office without arousing suspicion, either at the time or later?'

'That's been taken care of, General,' Cooper responded. 'I have already made the appointment through Rumsford and the Chief of Staff's Office. Nothing has been stated specifically, but the inference is that I will be using the opportunity to unofficially tender my resignation to the President. Teresi has wanted me out right from the beginning. With both myself and Maitland out of the picture he'll press for one of his own people to get the Director's slot. He won't pass up the opportunity to gloat. Rumsford is Teresi's man – he'll make sure the Vice-President knows.'

'What time is the appointment?' Swanbridge asked.

'Ten p.m.,' Cooper said.

'You'll be President of the United States by ten-fifteen,' decreed Hollis Macintyre.

'Unless something goes wrong,' the elderly, bespectacled man warned.

Macintyre waved a dismissing hand. 'Nothing will go wrong, Joseph,' he said firmly. 'I guarantee it.'

Deborah Stone sat in the silent living room of her Washington DC apartment and stared at the plain, grey-painted metal box on the coffee table in front of her. A combination lock was inset into the hinged top. All of her being was concentrated on it.

Her initial call to the long-sleeping cutout agent after learning about her ex-husband's hypothesis had led her to the shattering news of Sergei Kuryokhin's death, that news then culminating in the unearthing of the box now standing in front of her on the table. Stephen's incredible story and the savage irony of her own involvement through Hudson Cooper was difficult enough to deal with, but Kuryokhin's death was almost too much to bear.

She had only met her 'control' once, in Moscow, shortly after her recruitment into the KGB, but he had been a continuing presence in her life, and in a real sense he was the man responsible for the day to day identity she'd assumed for all these years. Somehow, she knew, he had also represented truth. Her own life, her marriage to Stephen, her friendships with co-workers at the European Studies Institute, her work for Central Intelligence – all of it was subterfuge, a tissue of lies. Kuryokhin had given her purpose, a reason for it all, and even if it was only done through tape-recorded messages, she could talk to him. Now that was gone, all that remained of her relationship with the old spymaster contained in the small metal box that lay before her.

She had known of the box's existence from the beginning, and its location, buried at a dead drop close to the mouth of the bypass tunnel at the National Zoological Park. Her cut-out, the man who'd informed her of Kuryokhin's death, knew the combination, but not the location. Finding and digging up the box had been easy enough, accomplished that evening after leaving Stephen and the Soviet defector at the Lake Anna cabin, but now she wasn't sure she wanted to know what it contained.

Debbie Stone, Kuryokhin's *Osin*, stood up, found her cigarettes and lit one. She moved nervously around the room, touching and shifting the art deco nicknacks she'd collected over the years. Lies, just like her name, her work, her world – icons to flesh out a character which didn't exist. She turned and stared at the box again, her thoughts feverishly trying to give her some kind of answer.

She sat down on the couch, puffing hard on the cigarette. There were three basic ways she could go, none of them without risk. She could follow official protocols on the death or removal of a control, reporting either to the Washington DC Resident or to Moscow Centre. But the Washington Resident was an unknown quantity – all she really knew about him was his name. Reporting to Moscow Centre was equally a shot in the dark. There was no way of knowing who would take over as head of the First Chief Directorate, or where that person's loyalties would lie.

Her second choice was to simply do nothing and become a sleeper. In many ways this seemed to be the most palatable, but she knew that eventually the strain of living in such a vacuum would become intolerable. The third option was to defect, but except for her own activities over the years she had little to offer in the way of KGB information. And whom would she defect to? Hudson Cooper or her ex-husband?

She ran a hand through her hair and shook her head; she'd be more valuable as an agent in place to both of them, but she had no stomach for it. She had allowed herself to be recruited by Kuryokhin because she sincerely believed that the Soviet way was inherently better than that of the West, and she still believed it: Soviet social democracy was a more equitable and humane philosophy than American monopoly capitalism – she'd seen the proof of that with her own eyes for more than a decade.

Balancing political philosophies was fine, but she had to deal with the harsh realities of both nations' intelligence organisations. The fact that she had operated virtually as Kuryokhin's private spy would be equally embarrassing to both the KGB and the CIA. The General's successor to the head of the First Chief Directorate would be unsure of her loyalties and Hudson Cooper would be the laughing stock of the American intelligence community if it became known that an advisor and special courier he'd chosen and vetted personally turned out to be a KGB illegal.

Finally, she opened the box, turning the stiff dial carefully through the combination. She pushed open the lid, leaning forward to see what was inside. A sealed envelope, two passports, one Canadian, the other Swiss, a bank passbook with the gold stamping of the Banque Credite Internationale de Genève, a small brass key on a leather thong, and a standard-sized tape cassette. There was no label on the cassette, but since all her communications with the General had been recorded, she assumed the cassette held a message from him.

Pulse pounding, she got to her feet, went to the bedroom, and took her Walkman from the top of her chest of drawers. She set it down on the coffee table, put on the headphones, then inserted the cassette from the box into the machine. She pressed the start button and waited. After a few moments' silence she heard Kuryokhin's firm measured voice, speaking in his Moscow-accented Russian. She blinked, startled, as she listened to the General use her real name:

My dear Anna Rakozi, the fact that you are listening to this recording means that I am either dead, or have finally run afoul of that octopus-like bureaucracy known as the KGB. One way or the other, the time has come for us to say farewell.

We have worked well together over the past years and I have taken every precaution to keep your identity a secret. However, if I am dead, or in the less than gentle hands of my colleagues at the Lubyanka, your identity will not remain a secret for long. In consideration of this fact, and I hasten to repeat that it is, or soon will be a fact, you are now faced with several decisions which must be made as quickly as possible.

First: there is the question of your work, and your loyalty to the organisation which employs us both. You have proved to be an outstanding intelligence asset and you have every reason to be very proud. On the other hand, as you are certainly aware, the KGB, like its counterparts in other countries, is an organisation much given to internal politics. An agent who was an unimpeachable asset to one man can be terrible liability to another.

Second: the question of your personal survival. If, for any reason, you doubt your welcome at Mount Alto in Washington, or at Moscow Centre, do not hesitate to remove yourself altogether. To facilitate this I have enclosed two passports as well as a passbook for a Swiss bank. The account there is in the name of Monique LeClerc, which is also the name on both the Canadian and Swiss passports. There is enough money for you to live comfortably for the rest of your life.

Third: the final disposition of my work as head of the First Chief Directorate. Over the last twenty-five years I have been making careful notes concerning my work. Initially I wrote them as an exercise in memory, and later with a possible eye to someday writing my memoirs. As time passed, however, I realised that the very act of writing the notes was dangerous and could easily be misconstrued by my superiors within the KGB and a number of enemies outside it. Rather than destroy the notes I chose to hide them, using my regular trips abroad to secrete them in a safety deposit box. Strangely, I found myself continuing to keep notes, perhaps out of wilful mischief, or perhaps to give myself some sort of immortality. I'm really not at all sure even now. At any rate, I continued to write, and continued to remove the complete notebooks. They are in box number 4979 at the St Mande branch of the Banque Nationale du Paris. The key to the box is on the leather thong. You may do whatever you wish with the notebooks – read them or not, distribute them or not, perhaps even use them as a bargaining chip of last resort if you need to. Their disposition is up to you, my dear.

Lastly: a final act for both of us if you choose to take on the role. There is an envelope with the passports, key and bankbook. Within it is a list of every illegal in the United States, Canada and the United Kingdom. It also includes a list of our assets in NATO. In all there are some 650 names, each with their recruitment dates and the initials of their recruiting officer. Some of them go back more than forty years, and some, obviously, are more highly placed than others.

Some time ago, after a thorough check of their status, I realised that the vast majority of these supposed 'agents of influence', each with his own dossier, case officer and interior budget, was in fact non-effective, at least in terms of intelligence. Some, like yourself and a few others, were and continue to be extremely valuable, but the rest could stand a good sweeping by an old broom like myself.

My suggestion is this: defect, choosing your 'guardian angel' with due care, and let them have the list, giving the names to them slowly, over a period of time, perhaps a year. At first glance this might seem to be a gigantic coup for the Americans, but in fact it might well deal their intelligence apparat a crushing blow in much the same way as the Philby/Burgess/Maclean defections. In that case, like this one, the agents concerned were either under suspicion, and therefore of limited value, or past their time of usefulness anyway. The result of their stories being made public was the complete disruption of British intelligence, to the point where their reputation has been forever stained. No other agencies trust them, no other agencies will give them access to sensitive material.

You are in a position to accomplish the same thing: a single agent bringing about the downfall of a country's entire intelligence establishment. It would guarantee your place in the history books, and mine, for that matter.

At any rate, my dear Anna, the decision is up to you. In closing I can say only that the choices should be made quickly, while they are still yours to make. *Dasvidanya*, my child, and may God go with you.

The General's voice fell silent, but listening, Debbie Stone could hear the faint creaking of his chair as he leaned forward to turn off the tape recorder. It sounded like a leather chair, old and worn, and the image of the old man in his chair made her shiver with a strange emotional force.

She pulled the earphones away and let them fall to the table. The General was right, her defection, coincidental with the revelations of his list of illegals, would rock the US intelligence establishment to its very foundations. She shook her head; it was as though her entire career had been leading to this culminating moment.

Lighting another cigarette she laughed, then reached for the sealed envelope in the box. Not only would she give them herself and the General's list, she would give them Dimitri Travkin and an internal conspiracy to kill their own President. For that they should give her a medal!

She tore open the envelope eagerly and pulled out the stapled pages which made up the list. She scanned the closely typed names slowly. Each was followed by his or her occupation and then by a date and the name and position of the recruiting officer. They were listed by the date of recruitment rather than alphabetically, the earliest going back to November 1945, the subject in question being an American Army Major stationed in Berlin. Debbie nodded to herself, recognising the name; the man had gone quite a long way since the end of the war.

She continued reading over the list, recognising some names and not others. From what she could tell the majority of the people on the list had been recruited shortly after graduation from university; almost all were professionals, and the bulk of them were men.

She made her way through the names, finally coming to the last page. Halfway down it her eyes fell across a name and she felt her mouth go suddenly dry. The date of recruitment was July 1969, and the place was Washington DC. Still not able to believe it, Debbie turned back to the beginning of the list. The date in the upper left hand corner was April 1986, the year in which the dead-drop box had been buried, seventeen years after the agent had been brought under the wing of the KGB. Hands shaking, she turned back to the last page, her eyes drawn to the name once again.

'He couldn't have known,' she whispered softly, and then realised that she was speaking Hungarian. It felt as though the familiar name on the list was being burned into her brain. 'He couldn't have known.'

CHAPTER TWENTY-ONE

Standing at the helm, Eric Rhinelander guided the squat, forty-foot houseboat up the Potomac Channel, keeping the throttles back and making little more than two or three knots against the steady current running down to the Chesapeake, fifty miles behind his back. It was early morning, the sky above a pale, steel grey, the river dark and cold. Wisps of fog hovered a few inches over the surface, torn and tattered like old cloth, dissolving into nothing as the blunt prow of the old C-Drifter slid almost silently upriver.

For the first time since leaving Jamaica he felt at ease and at peace with himself. The water, the boat, the silence and the solitude all contributed to his feeling, but he also knew that it was his subconscious at work, calming him, easing his mind into a narrow cone of concentration where there was no reality except for the job ahead.

With one hand on the small wheel he glanced at the chart spread out on the map table on his left. According to his calculations he was a little more than twenty-five miles below Washington, coming up on some place called Hogbow Island. It was owned by the National Parks Service, as were most of the dozens of Potomac islands.

He eased off on the twin throttles even more, barely making headway as he peered through the windscreen, searching for his landfall. In any other class of vessel he might have worried about running aground, given the treacherous convolutions of the channel and the hidden, constantly shifting sandbars on either side of it, but the C-Drifter had a draught of less than two and a half feet, and her twin 270 horsepower Chrysler engines were capable of pulling the hull off of anything but the biggest bar.

The island appeared suddenly as the last of the mist burned off with the first warming rays of the sun. Seen from half a mile downriver it looked like a small, tree-shrouded hump in the middle of the channel, but as Rhinelander swung the wheel a few points he saw that it was actually quite large, complete with two rocky projections guarding a narrow-necked bay almost a hundred yards across.

Keeping his eye on the little sonar screen perched on top of the console he pushed the C-Drifter across the unseen current, bullying his way across the surge until he was positioned just above the entrance to the bay. He cut the throttles almost to nothing, letting the vessel drift back down the river, then pushed both handles forward, the engines rumbling powerfully as he tucked the boat in between the two house-sized boulders and into the protected bay.

Once out of the current he idled the engines and let the boat's inertia carry it towards the narrow strip of gravel beach. The sonar screen was showing five feet of water almost to the shore. At the first wet crunching of the hull on the bottom he reversed the engines for a moment, backing off, then killed them entirely. The boat came to a full stop less than ten feet from the shore, and taking his time, Rhinelander went out onto the forward deck and dropped the single cleat anchor off the bow, warping it in tightly. Going to the stern he stepped off the boat carrying a line which he snugged around the broad trunk of a willow.

He fetched his binoculars and scanned the entrance to the bay and the river beyond. The opening to the small, hidden landfall was on the lee side of the channel, and even if there was boat traffic, the houseboat would be hidden from view, protected by the two large rocks at the entrance. Not that it mattered; he wasn't going to be here for long.

Rhinelander went back into the main cabin, ducking through the midships doorway. He gathered up the small KLM flight bag containing the custom-built paintball gun from the shop in Baltimore, and an empty knapsack. Carrying both bags he went forward to the galley. He opened the refrigerator and removed a large plastic sack from the vegetable crisper and a much smaller one from the freezer compartment. He put the plastic bags into the knapsack, slipped it over his shoulders and then went topside, the flight bag in his right hand. Going to the stern he dropped down onto the earthen bank, sidestepped the willow tree, then headed along a sloping path that led up through the trees.

According to his chart the entire island sloped upwards to a narrow ridge running along a north-south line. There were no buildings marked on the chart as navigation aids and from what Rhinelander could see as he made his way up the path, the bulk of the island was covered in a mixed forest of sycamore and sweetgum. The path itself seemed to be a dry streambed running down from the ridge, its gently sloping banks choked with fireweed and buttonbush. The leaves and branches were dark with rain from the night before, and Rhinelander found himself wondering if the area around the sewer junction and the north portico vaults had been eroded even more. He'd been through his subterranean escape route several times since his first visit, entering the system through an alleyway manhole off F Street and 13th rather than the longer walk from the 12th Street heating plant.

With the exception of a few small details and the package he'd ordered Mallory to bring to their next meeting, everything was in place for the event.

Rhinelander reached the open meadow marked on his chart and looked around. It was silent except for the angry hammering of an unseen woodpecker hard at work, and invisible from the river; ideal for what he had in mind. He spotted the rotted stump of an old tree on the far side of the small clearing and walked over to it, shrugging off the knapsack as he approached. Opening the pack he removed the large plastic bag and eased its contents out onto the stump. The bag contained a goat's head he'd purchased from a Greek butcher in Alexandria, kept cool in the houseboat refrigerator until it was needed.

He reached into the knapsack for the smaller bag, and then turned away from the stump, pacing off a large oval in the damp grass. For Rhinelander, worst case would put the President behind his desk in the Oval Office, offering the poorest target. The goat's head was lower than Tucker's position, but approximately at the maximum range from which he would be required to shoot.

Rhinelander positioned himself on the left side of the oval, roughly at the position of the entrance to the Oval Office from the Private Secretary's office and directly across from the bulletproof French doors leading out to the rose garden. From where he stood the goat's head was in profile – unlikely for Tucker at the actual moment, but a better test now of the ammunition he had created for the job.

The assassin squatted down, unzipped the flight bag and took out the custom-made weapon and a small, red-handled hatchet. Putting the hand axe aside, he examined the gun. With the exception of the trigger mechanism and spring, the pistol was made entirely out of flat black plastic and looked very much like a small sawed-off shotgun. The upper barrel was the magazine for the gelatine paintballs, while the lower barrel held the spring mechanism which powered the weapon. A 'constant-air' CO_2 tank was attached to the rear of the gun. When the trigger was pulled a brief burst of compressed gas was released, blowing a plunger down the barrel and forcing out the paintball at a rate of between 450 and 600 feet per second.

In the weapon Rhinelander had ordered, the mechanism had an automatic blowback cocking system which meant that it could be fired automatically, pumping out twenty of the ball-bearing-sized spheres in less than two seconds.

The barrel and cocking mechanism was eleven and a half inches long and the weapon fitted comfortably and invisibly along Rhinelander's arm from wrist to elbow, secured by two Velcro strips, beneath the stolen EPB uniform. The airfeed tube snaked back to his armpit and down to the CO_2 tank secured to his belt.

Opening the small plastic bag from the freezer compartment Rhinelander took out a dozen gelatine balls and fed them into the upper magazine of the weapon. Securing the magazine lock he flicked the toggle on the trigger mechanism, setting the weapon on single shot, then let it dangle loosely in his hand. He took several breaths, letting them out slowly, then lifted the weapon and fired in a single smooth motion.

There was a hard, coughing sound as the CO_2 charged the piston chamber and ejected the ball. A split second later the macabre target on the stump jerked slightly, the clouded, sightless eye of the severed head showing no reaction to the impact. Placing the weapon and the attached gas cartridge carefully on the empty knapsack, Rhinelander picked up the hatchet, walked across to the stump and examined the head.

Unlike his fictional counterparts in spy novels written over the years, he knew that a roast beef on a fencepost or a melon in a string bag was no test of a weapon's utility; the human body was more than meat, and the rind of a watermelon was no substitute for the hard bone of a man's skull – hence the goat's head.

Kneeling down, Rhinelander saw the impact point of the gelatine ball. It had struck half an inch below the left eye, creating a ragged hole an inch across. Using one hand, the assassin turned the head around on the stump. There was no sign of an exit and he smiled, pleased with his work. Lifting the hatchet he sighted along the centre of the skull and brought his hand down in a single hard stroke. The head split open neatly and Rhinelander examined the interior; he'd purposely told the butcher to leave the brain inside the head so he'd have an honest measure of the weapon's value.

The hatchet had sliced the brain into two pieces, revealing the damage done by Rhinelander's reconstructed ammunition. Using his index finger the assassin could follow the track of the 'bullet' as it chewed through the dark grey brain matter. Slamming through the cranium, the paintball had flattened out and broken apart, bits and pieces spinning at odd angles into the brain, slashing it into a stewlike, watery mass of tissue. He nodded, pleased once again; if it worked on a goat it would certainly work on the President of the United States.

The standard load for a paintball gun consists of a thick gelatine ball filled with a mixture of water-based paint, usually red, and cod liver oil. On impact the gelatine ball splits open and the oil and paint mixture splatters over a six to eight inch area of the target's clothing, thus 'killing' him.

Instead of the regular balls, Rhinelander had purchased several hundred empty gelatine 'bullets' which would normally have been filled with special paint, often fluorescent for use in night games. Using mercury from the surplus thermostats he'd purchased and the model-making syringes from the hobby store he had injected the empty gelatine capsules, using half mercury and half ordinary tap water. The water and liquid metal separated as cleanly as oil and water and after freezing for twenty-four hours gave him a projectile half ice and half solid metal. He had tested the balls once in the Wyoming apartment, putting a splintered hole in a quarter-inch-thick piece of plywood at twenty feet.

The ballistics were relatively simple. Fired almost silently from the airgun with a muzzle velocity of four or five hundred feet per second the ball spun with the heavier metal section ahead of the lighter half-sphere of ice. On impact the frozen metal would maintain the integrity of its shape briefly as it punched through plywood or bone, forced onward by the ice, which, like water, cannot be compressed at any velocity. With the impact-friction dissolving the gelatine skin, the brittle, frozen mercury would shatter, tiny splinters of it cartwheeling through the brain tissue like pellets from a shotgun. As the goat's head proved, the effect was violent, and clearly fatal. A secondary benefit was the neatness of the wound, since the relatively low velocity guaranteed that there would be no exit hole. Tucker and Teresi would lie in state with their coffins open and the walls of the Oval Office wouldn't have to be repainted.

Jamming the two pieces of the head back together, Rhinelander retrieved the paintball gun, then walked back across his firing range and took up a position some thirty-five feet from the target – the distance between the fireplace in the Oval Office and the President's desk. Setting the weapon on automatic he lifted the barrel a second time and squeezed the trigger. There was a dull, ripping cough as the machine pistol vomited a hail of frozen projectiles towards the remains of the severed head on the stump. All nineteen balls left in the magazine struck the target, smashing through jawbone, skull, nose and cheek. In a silent, bloody flurry, bone chips, brain matter, fur and fluid fountained into the air. Within three seconds of the trigger being squeezed, the goat's head had vanished, leaving little more than a thick dark stain on the low stump. At no time had there been a sound louder than the popping of a paper bag.

The woodpecker he'd heard before began its hammering again, some-where on the far side of the clearing, breaking the morning silence with much more force than Rhinelander's weapon. The assassin glanced at the gore on the stump, smiling.

'Excellent,' he said quietly.

There are a hundred different vantage points in Washington where tourists and other visitors can view the Capitol dome. The most famous is probably the postcard scene taken from The Mall, showing the dome and Congress in all their marble-white glory. The least known is almost undoubtedly the view over the cement works on the banks of the Anacostia River, in the wasteland between the Frederick Douglass bridge and the Washington Navy Yard Annex. Seen from the river, the dome rises, heat shimmered, above an apocalyptic assembly of rusting tanks, graffiti-decorated warehouses, flyblown shacks and piles of industrial rubble. There is constant truck traffic around the cement plant and once in a very long while a police car makes its way along the rutted dirt roads that meander through the trash tips and rubble, but for the most part it is a vast, weed and rat infested vacant lot.

Paul Mallory waited uneasily beside the nondescript blue Ford from the Langley pool, horribly aware of the small, flat pistol in the waistband holster beneath the idiotic Hawaiian print shirt he was wearing. Hudson Cooper had suggested arming himself for the meeting, supposedly to inspire confidence, and the armourer from Tech section had told him to wear something loose to cover the bulge of the gun and to give him quick access. Instead of confident he felt like something out of an old episode of *Hawaii 5-0* and the thought of drawing a weapon on someone like Rhinelander was nauseating. Grimacing, he pushed his glasses up onto the bridge of his nose and squinted over the wasteland surrounding him. If it came to that he could use the gun to kill himself, since pulling it on the assassin was tantamount to suicide anyway.

So where the hell was he? The telephone message from Rhinelander had been specific about time and place, but it was already half an hour past the appointed time and there was still no sign of him. There were no cars in sight and he hadn't seen a soul since arriving at the riverside rendezvous. He glanced into the open window of the Ford: two packages on the seat, both wrapped in brown paper, the smaller one containing a shoebox, which in turn contained Rhinelander's gemstone payoff, padded with wads of cotton batten. The larger held the specialised Motorola transceiver the assassin had requested, as well as the 2.5 kilogram warhead from an AT3 'Sagger' anti-tank round. The 'Sagger' was an obsolete Soviet weapon, now widely deployed in the Middle East.

'Mallory.' The voice came out of nowhere. No warning, no plume of dust from the dirt tracks criss-crossing the junkyard acreage. Nothing except the white, bright sun, and the voice. Rhinelander's.

'Yes?' Mallory answered. He let his hands reach back and touch the hot metal of the car door, wondering if the killer knew he was carrying a weapon. He blinked and then swallowed hard. The voice had come from somewhere directly ahead of him, close to the heap of reinforced concrete at the river's edge.

'You have what I want?' Definitely the riverbank. Shit! The son-of-a-bitch had come in off the water!

'Yes. Everything you asked for.' Mallory swallowed again, mouth dry.

'Good,' the ghost voice answered. 'Take it out of the car, bring it to the edge of the road, then leave.'

'Yes,' Mallory responded. He turned slowly, keeping his hands away from the pistol in his belt. Opening the door he reached in, picked the two parcels up off the seat and took them to the edge of the road. For an instant he thought he spotted something in the choke of weeds and garbage; a point of sun, splintered on what? The barrel of a gun? Lens of binoculars? Eyepiece of a telescopic sight? Cross-hairs like an invisible rune upon his chest. His fear took him back to Jamaica and the first split second after being discovered by Rhinelander. The dead cold eyes – dead and cold because of what they had seen. Frighteningly blue, capable of anything.

Mallory followed his instructions to the letter. He walked back across the road to the Ford, climbed in behind the wheel and drove away, his retreat marked with the dust flag thrown up by his wheels as he sped towards O Street. A few moments later he had gone, the two packages on the weedy verge of the road the only sign that he'd ever been there. The sun burned down and the dust of his passage drifted over the rubble and rubbish like the fading smokescreen on a battlefield.

'What the hell is going on?' Mort Kessler asked, peering through the binoculars. 'He waits for half an hour and then he drops the packages by the side of the road and rabbits.'

'We're missing something,' Stephen Stone answered, looking through his own powerful Zeiss glasses. Both men were discreetly hidden in a musty, abandoned warehouse two hundred yards from where Mallory had parked his car.

'There,' Kessler said, excitement in his voice. He leaned forward slightly. 'The right hand side of the road.'

Stephen Stone turned his binoculars slightly to the right. Through the lens he saw a lone figure clamber quickly over the pile of reinforced concrete that lay between the road and the river's edge. Beside him Mort Kessler dropped his binoculars and put his eye to the viewfinder of the Nikon on its tripod next to him. He focused quickly and hit the motorised shutter release, catching a dozen exposures of the man as he dropped down from the rubble and gathered up the parcels.

'Shit!' Stone muttered. 'He came up from the river – that means he has a boat. Why didn't we think of that?'

'Because we didn't have time,' Kessler grunted, snapping more photographs. 'We barely got to put the tap on Mallory's telephone.'

'Where would he get a boat?' Stone muttered, watching as the figure retreated back up onto the pile of rubble.

'Eastern Power Boat Club, or the Anacostia Boat Dock. Both of them are only five minutes upriver.'

'All right.' Stone nodded, stepping away from the grimy window. 'Get the pictures developed and then go sit on Mallory. I'm going to take a run at this guy and see what I can turn up.'

'Nothing heroic, I hope,' Kessler warned.

'Surveillance from a distance.' Stone grinned. He lifted a palm. 'Nothing more, I swear.'

'Contact?' Kessler slipped his binoculars back into their case.

Stone thought for a moment. Somewhere safe, with no chance of surveillance. 'The Key Bridge Marriot motel,' he said finally. 'The main entrance parking lot.'

'Good enough,' Kessler said.

General Arkady Vladimir Gurenko rode the elevator down from his office in the main building of the Mount Alto complex, contemplating his fate and planning his future. Brains, talent and drive had taken him to heights achieved by few without benefit of nomenklatura connections, but now circumstance threatened to take it all away. His career and perhaps even his life now depended on how he handled the situation with *Osin* and Dimitri Travkin, his every move scrutinised by the Weasel, Ivashutin.

Before his death, Kuryokhin had patched together a theory about a possible Presidential assassination, and both Debbie Stone, Kuryokhin's deep-cover illegal, and Travkin were directly involved. In the aftermath of such an assassination, the Soviet connection would almost certainly surface, mangling the concepts of glasnost and perestroika for a generation. Gurenko, like Kuryokhin and most senior KGB, thought Gorbachev's philosophies were madness, destined to bring the worst kind of *besporyadok* or social disorder to the Soviet Union, but the KGB was not the omnipotent power it once had been. The Politburo was unlikely to cast a benevolent eye on those involved in an American assassination plot.

By the same token, *Osin* was a valued agent and Travkin was a military officer; removing them, at least in political terms, would not be an easy feat. Koslov, Travkin's commanding officer in the GRU, was a fool, but a fool with friends in high places, and *Osin* had been Kuryokhin's sparrow. Even on the embalmer's table the old bastard still had power – power that would continue to be a force within the KGB even after he was buried in the Kremlin Wall. The janitors who'd gone through his effects in Moscow had come up with detailed operations journals going back over forty years and there was always the possibility that he'd made copies. Gurenko shook his head wearily – now there was a rumour that would circulate for decades!

The elevator reached the third sub-basement and Gurenko stepped out into a narrow corridor. The cinderblock was thickly painted in yellow and the floors were a dull brown linoleum. Gurenko was sure the decor had been chosen to remind the building's occupants of the Lubyanka, lest they become too enamoured of the glitz and glamour of Wisconsin Avenue, a few hundred yards to the east.

At the end of the corridor he pushed through a heavily padded door and his ears were instantly assaulted by an irregular madhouse roar of gunfire as he stepped onto the underground firing range. The Soviet diplomatic corps, and even embassy security personnel, weren't allowed to bring weapons of any kind into the United States, but that obstacle was easily surmounted simply by purchasing necessary armament at any of several dozen local sporting goods stores. The range also served as a testing laboratory for newly designed American armed forces ordnace which happened to come their way.

He found the man he was looking for in the stall at the front of the third firing lane. His name was Artyom Roginsky. He had dark hair shot with grey, and fists like hams, which were wrapped around a Swiss Rexim-Favor submachinegun. As Gurenko approached him, Roginsky tucked the wooden butt of the weapon into his hip and began triggering a series of short bursts down the firing line, his movements as studied and bored as if he were a worker hammering rivets into a sheet of steel.

'Roginsky,' Gurenko called, raising his voice over the booming echoes of the cavernous range. The large man turned, his expression blank. He recognised Gurenko, but showed no deference to his rank. On the US State Department files Roginsky was listed as a junior attache in the Cultural Services Division. In fact he was squad leader of a rarely used, ten-man Spetznaz commando, the only one of its kind in North America. In the previous two years they had only been used four times, on each occasion to track down missing embassy personnel. Two of the assignments had led to the police drunk tanks, one had involved a homosexual tryst and the last had been a bona-fide defection.

'Good afternoon, Comrade General Gurenko,' Roginsky said, putting the SMG down on the bench.

'The scenario given to you by Comrade Ivashutin is now operational,' Gurenko said crisply. 'Gather six of your men and meet me in the briefing room in an hour.'

'Certainly,' Roginsky answered. 'Is there anything else?'

'Nothing else,' Gurenko replied. He turned away and headed back to the padded door.

'Good,' said Roginsky. He picked up the Rexim-Favor, banged in a new magazine and stared at the dangling target fifty feet away. The target was man-shaped, silhouetted in black. Most of the chest was missing, a ragged hole blown through the target. The head was relatively free of 'wounds'. Roginsky pulled back the slide, toggled the safety off and slipped his right index finger over the trigger. He let out a short breath, lifted the weapon and squeezed. The head of the target vanished. The commando belched lightly. Time for a beer or two in his room before the briefing.

CHAPTER TWENTY-TWO

The three-man team moved through Paul Mallory's Alexandria apartment with methodical efficiency. All three wore dark blue windbreakers with 'Capitol Courier Service' printed on the back in white letters. Two of the three distributed the contents of two large suitcases throughout the rooms while a third worked at Mallory's computer. The project file on Mallory indicated the possibility of classified material being misappropriated and the man sitting at the terminal was a highly trained specialist in reprogramming and computer ciphers. So far he had located the embedded back-up signal containing Mallory's information on Rhinelander and he was now unravelling the time code that would broadcast the information over a nation-wide bulletin board network.

Ever since the James Agee and Victor Marchetti fiascoes of the late sixties and early seventies, followed by the advent of a federal Freedom of Information Act, the Agency decided that steps would have to be taken to guarantee the CIA's internal security. By the mid-seventies a ghost department within the Operations Division had been formed, blandly referred to in budgetary submissions as the 'Historical Analysis Group'. The HAGS, as they were called, supposedly worked out of a suite of offices in Georgetown, but were actually based at Camp Peary – the Farm.

Their mandate, far from analysing history, was to rewrite it. When an agent or an operation went sour, the HAGS went to work, removing or replacing public files, changing identities, and otherwise skewing events so that they conformed to approved agency policy. In a case like Mallory's, given to them by the DDO himself, their job was to cloud, corrupt and besmirch the subject's character, thus stripping him of any credibility. Although the DDO hadn't gone into detail, it was clear that Mallory was about to go public with material garnered while working as Cooper's Special Assistant.

To prevent him from doing this the team at work in his apartment was recreating the man's personal history, staging evidence that would mark him as a particularly nasty type of homosexual with definite leanings towards young boys. In addition they were also giving him a fully constructed background of love-letters and other correspondence graphically proving him to be untrustworthy, greedy, and potentially a threat to national security. Once in place the evidence was photographed, providing an evidence package that might eventually be handed over to the FBI for prosecution for espionage and treason unless the subject co-operated.

It took the HAG group two hours to complete the project. They left the apartment, carrying the two empty suitcases with them, climbed into an unmarked van and began the long drive back to Camp Peary. The apartment had been appropriately salted with damning evidence, the computer had been cleansed of damaging information, and all that remained was for a second and completely separate team to arrest Mallory and bring him in for interrogation.

Lyall Spencer, head of the Secret Service White House Detail, followed one of the paths that meandered around the north lawn, hands jammed into the pockets of his suit jacket, trying to ignore the sour pain in the pit of his stomach. After fourteen years in the service and three as head of the White House Detail he was seriously thinking of bailing out. He was forty-seven, divorced, verging on alcoholism and utterly jaded about government, the Presidency and any kind of public service.

In other words, he was burnt out and ready for rotation. On the other hand he was pretty sure that staying on in the Secret Service as a Field Director in Des Moines or some other godforsaken place wouldn't cut it after three years at the White House. The job was a pain in the ass most of the time, but it had its perks and it stroked your ego from time to time, not to mention other body parts. There were ladies in singles bars all over the world who'd do just about anything after you flashed your tin at them.

None of which was important right at the moment; he had the job to consider. And that was always the excuse – The Job. It covered everything from procrastinating about his future to catching up on his reading. The Job. Nothing in the world was more important than protecting the President of the United States, and he was the man responsible for doing just that. It was his favourite gripe to the other guys on the detail, and he'd harped on it so much they made him a T-shirt that said: 'The Buck Doesn't Stop There – It Stops Here.' Which was true, in a way; the President was responsible for the country, but he, Lyall Spencer, son of George Spencer, the New Jersey plumber, and Marie Spencer, apple crisp maker and part time bookkeeper, was responsible for the safety of the President.

He dropped down onto a bench beside the path and lit his fifty-first cigarette of the day. The rules said he wasn't really supposed to smoke on duty, but then again, the rules also said he was working the eight to four shift, which made it three hours into overtime. Spencer's personal rule about smoking on the grounds was simple: don't let the tourists see you, and pocket the butt once you're done.

It was the worst time of day for Spencer: the hours before dusk when shadows lied and the light flattened, throwing perspective off. In Vietnam they'd called it the Killing Hour, and even now it still made him nervous.

Which was ridiculous, of course, especially here. From the other side of the fence on Pennsylvania Avenue the White House was a symbol of American strength. Spencer knew better. The lawn where kids rolled eggs at Easter was actually a minefield of motion sensors. The fence itself was reinforced by buried microwave cables and the glass in the windows was armoured. The President might be at risk coming out of hotels or glad-handing crowds, but if he could be considered safe at all, it was here. Harry Truman had known the score when he referred to it as 'the big white jail'.

Spencer took a drag of the cigarette and let the smoke drift up into the still, humid air. Being nervous might be ridiculous, but it was part of the job. For all the motion sensors, metal detectors, interior radar and panic buttons, there was no real guarantee of safety for the Man, even here. You didn't need a high-powered rifle to take out a President – a loose brick or a paperweight could be just as deadly.

Tomorrow's birthday party for Tucker was a case in point. He and the other members of the detail had taken every possible precaution. The guests had all been screened, extra catering and cleaning staff vetted, even the cake batter checked for poison. None of it meant a thing. All it needed was a crazed guest who'd slipped through the psych profiles, and a carving knife. Still, they'd done the best they could.

The lunch he'd had with Stephen Stone still bothered him, though, and he frowned, recalling the conversation. If Cabrera was at risk, so was the Man. But even after checking he'd come up cold. He'd tried to call Stone, but the number he'd been given was dead, and when he called the FBI man's office number they cold-shouldered him until he dug around and discovered that he'd been suspended indefinitely.

Sighing, Spencer pinched out the glowing tip of the cigarette, grinding the hot ash into the gravel of the walkway. He dropped the butt into his jacket pocket, dusted his fingers off and stood up wearily. Stone had appeared to be a straight shooter, even though the Secret Service man didn't know him well. The suspension, coming on the heels of their conversation, was a weird coincidence, but there was nothing he could do about it now. Tin Pot El Presidente could wait until next month, right now he had a birthday party to organise.

Flipping back the tail of his jacket Spencer pulled the walkie-talkie out of its belt holster. He tapped the send button and checked in with the command centre in the east wing basement.

'Dungeon, this is Dragon One. What's our status?'

'Clean and clear, Dragon One,' replied the tinny voice of the duty watchman.

'Where's Diamond?' Spencer asked, using the President's radio call sign.

'Having dinner with Emerald in the family dining room.' Emerald was the First Lady.

'All right,' Spencer answered. 'Let me know if anyone goes for a walk.'

'Will do, Dragon One.'

Spencer returned the walkie-talkie to its holster, then continued down the gravel path, heading for the guard post at Pennsylvania and West Executive. He walked slowly, head bent, going over the security precautions for the following day, wondering if there was anything he'd overlooked and trying not to think about how good an ice cold beer would taste.

Returning to the Wyoming for the last time, Eric Rhinelander made himself a cup of tea, then took his packages to the den. Setting the box containing the gemstones aside for the moment, he slit open the heavier package with a penknife and carefully removed the contents. Placing the oblong anti-tank warhead on the desk he examined it carefully. The 2.5 kilogram charge was made up of ammonium picrate and was fitted with a spring-loaded contact percussion primer. Triggered by a simple clock-mechanism delay he'd already constructed, the warhead would provide a suitably loud explosion when the time came.

Rhinelander had already picked out the point where the main electrical and communications cables came into the vault and he would cut power from inside, but the detonation of the charge would serve as a distraction after the fact, and would also open up his escape route into the sewer system. The hollow charge, capable of blowing a hole in three-inch armour plate, was more than enough to open up the relatively thin concrete of the vault.

Next the assassin removed the Motorola walkie-talkie from the package, placing it beside the box of gemstones. The radio was the exact model used by the Secret Service in the grounds of the White House and set to their private frequency. He would have been able to find the secure frequency himself, using a modified scanner from Radio Shack or any other electronic supply house, but it seemed like a needless waste of energy and time when it could be just as easily provided by Cooper.

The last item in the package was a manila envelope. Rhinelander checked to make sure that Mallory hadn't tampered with the seal, then used his penknife again, slitting the upper edge of the flap. There were two documents inside. One contained a list of call signs used by the Secret Service White House Detail, complete with their designations, while the second gave a schedule of events for the Presidential birthday party. Rhinelander went over the call signs first, committing them to memory.

PRESIDENT—	DIAMOND
VICE-PRES. —	COBALT
1ST LADY —	EMERALD
SEC. STATE —	FLINT
SEC. DEF —	GARNET
HOUSE SPKR —	GOLD
NAT. SEC. ADVSR —	GRANITE
WH PHYSICIAN —	HELIOTROPE
PRES. SEC —	JADE
WHITE HOUSE —	CROWN
AIRFORCE ONE —	ANGEL
MARINE ONE —	BLADE
PRES. LIMO —	STAGECOACH
VP RESIDENCE —	SHIELD
US CAPITOL —	SWORD
ANDREWS AFB —	HELMET
CAMP DAVID —	CORRAL
SS DETAIL CHIEF —	DRAGON
SS COMM. HQ—	DUNGEON

Rhinelander turned his attention to the typed document for the party, complete with a list of invited guests, all seventy-five of them, as well as a full menu. It was a photocopy of an original produced on White House stationery. After quickly glancing over the list of guests he flipped to the page with the actual schedule on it.

6:30 p.m.

*

**GREETINGS IN THE DIPLOMATIC RECEPTION ROOM
SOUTH PORTICO ENTRANCE**

*

7:00 p.m.

*

**COCKTAILS IN THE EAST ROOM
'HAIL TO THE CHIEF'**

*

7:45 p.m.

*

DINNER IN THE STATE DINING ROOM

*

9:00 p.m.

*

CAKE AND COFFEE
THE LIBRARY
'RUFFLES AND FLOURISHES'
*

9:45 p.m.
*

FIREWORKS ON THE NORTH LAWN
*

There was a small notation on the schedule, printed neatly in pencil: 8:50/8:55. According to his research, dinners at the White House were invariably punctual. The meal would begin at 7:45 precisely, and end exactly an hour later. There would be a fifteen-minute break in the festivities while the guests made their way to the library, some discreetly making use of the toilet facilities on the way. During the quarter-hour break, the President and Vice-President would make a brief detour to the Oval Office at Hudson Cooper's insistence. The assassin unrolled his enlarged floor plans of the White House.

The state dining room was on the first floor of the mansion on the west side of the building. To go from there to the Oval Office meant that the President, Vice-President and Hudson Cooper would either use the back stairway leading off the main corridor or the private elevator. With two Secret Service agents in attendance the small elevator would be somewhat crowded, so it was more likely that they would use the stairs. From the stairway they would walk west along the corridor on the ground floor, passing the kitchen and the housekeeper's quarters.

If the weather was good they would probably then take the colonnaded walkway to the Oval Office via the rose garden, and if it was bad, they'd use the corridor that ran beside the newly reopened swimming pool. From the floor plans he knew the exact distances involved and had paced it off several times. At an average walk it would take four and a half minutes to reach the Oval Office.

There were four entrances to the Oval Office: a pair of French doors to the right of the President's desk, leading out to the colonnade and the rose garden, an almost invisible doorway set into the wall to the left of the desk, which led to the President's study, a doorway to the right of the fireplace at the north end of the room, leading to the secretary's office, and a doorway on the left of the fireplace, which was the 'formal' entrance to the room, leading out to a narrow hall.

The doors on either side of the fireplace were of heavy oak painted white. The doors swung in both directions, closed with vertical bolts, top and bottom. They were fitted with deadbolt locks with a knob turn on the inside and a key cylinder on the outside. The glass in the doors, like all the windows in the Oval Office, was bulletproof, and the drapes over the three tall windows behind the President's desk were lined with a bombproof synthetic fabric.

With the President and Vice-President in the office there would be two Secret Service agents on the outside, one at the French doors and another patrolling the area around the south windows. A third agent would be on guard at the hall doorway, and there would be a fourth on duty in the secretary's office.

For Rhinelander, the placement and number of people directly protecting the Oval Office and its occupants had been the project's major stumbling block. To get to the President, he would have to confront at least one Secret Service agent. After a great deal of thought he had eventually decided that access and egress to the Oval Office would be made through the cabinet room. The long narrow chamber adjoined the President's secretary's office as well as the colonnade and the hallway running along beside the swimming pool.

Approaching the west wing from the rarely used basement tunnel he would come up the stairs to the main floor in plain sight of the Secret Service agent at the outer door of the President's study, but he would then appear to be walking away from the Oval Office as he headed for the colonnade. He would then turn right into the colonnade hallway, and enter the cabinet room, using one of the two small doors flanking the chamber's fireplace. He would remain in the room until the appropriate moment, then enter the secretary's office through the connecting door. After eliminating the agent on duty he would proceed into the Oval Office. His work done he would then leave the same way he had entered.

At that point the explosion in the north portico physical plant vault would douse the lights in the mansion as well as the west and east wings. Since the vault also contained the mansion backup generator, the main house would remain dark. The entire security system for the White House and grounds had its own backup, but there would be a brief period while 'Dungeon', the west wing communications and security headquarters, was deaf, dumb and blind. It would be during this time that Rhinelander would make his way back to the north portico vault.

Standing orders required that when there was a potential Executive Threat, agents on the White House Detail would immediately cover their assigned people. With the President and Vice-President in the Oval Office, the entire detail, with the exception of the four-man group protecting the First Lady, would rush to the west wing, forming a tight, protective perimeter, both inside the building and outside.

Within ninety seconds of discovering the assassination every Secret

Service agent and EPS officer would be alerted, and the White House grounds would be locked up tight, making escape impossible. As the minutes ticked by, the perimeter would be expanded and the Metro Police and the FBI would be alerted. Bus stations, the railway station, Dulles, National and Baltimore airports would be secured. Eventually they might even resort to roadblocks.

And none of it would do any good at all.

The Key Bridge Marriott Motel is located on the Virginia side of the Francis Scott Key Bridge. Smoking, Stephen Stone stood by his car in the parking lot, watching as the lights blinked on at the Kennedy Centre, the dignified structure just visible over the trees on Theodore Roosevelt Island. Beyond the JFK Centre the rest of the city was lost in a dusky haze of heat and air pollution.

His search for the assassin had led to a frustrating dead end. It had taken him and Mort Kessler almost ten minutes to reach their cars and five more to reach the Power Boat Club on the far side of the Anacostia Bridge. Another ten minutes was lost while he established his bona fides with the club management, and by then it was too late. In the end all he had to show for his trouble was a list of boats rented and returned that afternoon. There were seventeen names, and because of his suspension he had no way of checking them quickly.

Waiting for Mort at the Marriott he'd tried Debbie's number at work and then at her apartment. No answer. There was no reply at the cabin either and that made him even more nervous; even if Debbie wasn't there, Travkin was. All he could think of was that the Russian was out of earshot, perhaps down by the dock.

He stubbed out his cigarette and lit another, ignoring the acid bite in his throat as he dragged deeply. If Travkin was right there was a plot to assassinate the President in progress, and by the looks of things, there wasn't a goddamn thing he could do about it. Both he and the Russian had been cut out of the system with surgical efficiency, robbed of their powers, stripped of their credibility. Christ! He didn't even have a weapon. He normally didn't carry one, and the Smith and Wesson automatic he'd been issued with was on the upper closet shelf in his apartment.

Mort Kessler's tan Ford turned into the lot. He found a spot, pulled into it and parked. He climbed wearily out of the vehicle and walked over to Stone. Boosting himself up onto the low retaining wall at the edge of the parking lot he looked expectantly at his colleague.

'Well?' he asked.

'Diddley shit,' Stone answered. 'A list of names for you to check out on the NCIC.'

'They took out Mallory,' Kessler replied baldly. 'I watched the whole thing go down from across the street.'

'Shit!'

'Right,' Kessler grunted. 'I guess they had a team inside. I followed Mallory back to Alexandria. He goes up to his apartment and ten minutes later an ambulance pulls up. Two guys in paramedic uniforms go up with a gurney and come back down with Mallory, sheet up to his chin, blood on his face. The ambulance splits and a couple of minutes later a trio of heavies comes down, all dressed in blue windbreakers and carrying suitcase-size briefcases. They climb into an unmarked van and disappear. All they needed were stencils on the back of the jackets that said CIA.'

'Cooper's got a clean-up going,' Stone responded, his voice dull. He flipped his cigarette butt into the growing darkness. 'He's closing all the doors.'

'You think it's getting close?' Kessler asked.

'Has to be.' Stone nodded. 'Duncan, or whatever his name is, wouldn't risk a meet like that unless it was almost time to make the play.'

'So what do we do about it? Go to Spencer?'

'With what? The suspended REDNET loonie with a defrocked Russian as his only evidence? I don't have a single fucking fact to give him, Mort. It's all conjecture and hypothesis. If I went to him the only person he'd arrest would be me.'

'So?' Kessler shrugged. 'We've only got one other option.'

'Such as?'

'Find Duncan. Take him down.'

'Easier said than done,' Stone answered. He reached into the inside pocket of his jacket and took out the folded sheet of paper with the Power Boat Club list on it. 'This isn't much to go on.'

'It's better than nothing,' Kessler said.

'While you're at it, see if you can get a rundown on what Tucker's going to be doing for the next few days. Any glad-handing, speeches, that kind of thing. If he's slated to be out of town, find out where he's going.'

'That should be easy enough.' Kessler nodded. 'The Protocol Office at State should have it. Anything else?'

'A weapon,' Stone replied. He paused, and gnawed his lower lip, a worried expression on his face. He thought about Travkin, alone up at the cabin, and of Debbie. Both of them were terribly vulnerable. 'Maybe you should get something for the Russian as well,' he said finally. Kessler looked sceptical, but nodded. He dropped down from the low wall, brushing dust off the seat of his pants.

'What's the obscure rendezvous this time?' Kessler asked, laughing.

'Here again. Say around seven-thirty tomorrow morning.'

'Okay,' Kessler agreed. 'Maybe we can do something civilised like have breakfast.'

'One more thing,' Stone asked. 'Take a run past Debbie's and see if she's around. I haven't been able to get in touch all day. She's probably up at the cabin with Travkin, but I'm starting to get a little worried. Her office said they hadn't heard a thing from her.' He looked at his colleague. 'And be careful, they might have the place watched.'

'Done,' Kessler said, and they parted company for the second time that day.

'I've always felt that you looked somewhat out of place in this decor,' Hollis Macintyre commented, glancing around Hudson Cooper's living room at the Watergate. The drapes were drawn over the picture window that looked out over the Potomac, and except for two tablelamps the large room lay in darkness.

'Miriam liked antiques,' Cooper answered softly, 'especially American Victoriana; she said it reminded her of her mother.' He nodded towards the large, ornately framed oil painting over the fireplace. The portrait showed a plain-faced woman, severely dressed in black from throat to toe. Below the painting, the mantel was choked with dozens of tiny metal picture frames, all filled with ageing photographs.

Macintyre bobbed his head in polite appreciation while Cooper climbed to his feet and made his way across the room to his desk. He gathered up half a dozen file folders and returned to his chair. Macintyre lowered his Wedgwood cup and saucer, placing them carefully on the glass-topped coffee table. He sat back against the sofa cushions, his expression blank, tiny pale pink hands crossed over the bulging vest of his suit.

'Presumably we're still on schedule,' he murmured.

'Yes,' Cooper nodded. He flipped open one of the folders and glanced at it briefly.

'From what you said on the telephone I gather that your feelings about Mr Mallory were not unfounded.'

'He fulfilled his role,' Cooper answered. 'He's been dealt with.'

'Good. No loose ends?'

'He came very close,' Cooper answered. 'He had some information embedded in a computer program as a safeguard. It's been removed and Mallory has been given a completely revamped legend for the official record. Closet pederast, depressed, potentially vulnerable.'

'Not entirely original,' Macintyre commented.

'Perhaps not,' Cooper responded, 'but safe enough. He has no family.'

'All right,' the fat man aquiesced. 'What about the rest of it?'

'The dinner begins at seven forty-five tomorrow evening. I haven't been invited, but I insisted that my appointment be scheduled for that night. Dinner ends at eight forty-five, coffee and cake will be served at nine. I'll have five minutes in the Oval Office – eight fifty to eight fifty-five.'

'At which point your man will strike.'

'Our man,' Cooper replied pointedly. 'Yes.'

'Grounds for suspicion there,' Macintyre murmured. 'We've already discussed the possibility of an assassination hearing after the fact. How would "our" killer know you were going to be in the Oval Office with the President?'

'Mallory will have told him,' Cooper answered coolly.

'I'm afraid I don't see.'

'Nezar Assad,' Cooper answered. 'Our terrorist from the Abu Nidal group.'

'Explain.'

'The legend that was developed has Assad co-opting Mallory through sexual favours; doctored photographs can be produced if necessary. Using Mallory as a pipeline to me, Assad develops his assassination plot.'

'And how does a terrorist get into the White House?'

'A Secret Service oversight, using Mallory again. An extra notation in their security file. Assad will be logged as part of the service staff at the dinner.'

'It sounds vague,' Macintyre interjected.

'It's meant to,' Cooper answered. 'A back story that's too complete is suspicious in itself. Fewer facts and more hypothesis leads to even greater confusion.'

'I see,' Macintyre said, nodding thoughtfully. 'The grassy knoll.'

'Precisely,' Cooper replied. 'The Kennedy affair is a perfect example. The knoll, extra gunshots, the motorcycle policeman's exchange, the doctored photos of Oswald, even Ruby's connection with the Dallas police. All we need are a few pivot points; public opinion will take care of the rest.'

'What about our people?' Macintyre asked.

'That's been taken care of as well,' answered Cooper. He leaned forward and fanned out the file folders across the coffee table. 'Just as you requested – complete dossiers on everyone in Romulus, including Swanbridge. They should be enough to quell any sudden pangs of conscience.'

'And is there a file on me?' Macintyre asked, smiling lightly.

'We're each other's best defence,' Cooper answered, returning the fat man's look with a smile of his own. 'We know enough to hang each other ten times over.' He gathered up the files, pushing them into a neat pile. He picked them up and dropped them in front of the huge, white-haired man. 'My last act for Romulus. After tomorrow I'm finished, Hollis. I really will be handing my resignation to Tucker.'

'That's absurd.' Macintyre frowned. 'Leave the Agency if you wish – you've certainly earned your retirement – but you know perfectly well that you must remain with Romulus. Even if you're inactive.'

'Don't threaten me,' Cooper answered, weariness in his voice. 'I'm too old and too tired.'

'It's not a threat, it's a fact,' said Macintyre. He grunted as he sat forward on the sofa. 'On three occasions over the past forty years, people have tried to take information about Romulus to the public. Two were members of the committee and one was a journalist with connections to a third member. All four individuals were eradicated before they could do any damage beyond promulgating the odd rumour or two.'

Cooper leaned over and opened the carved box on the coffee table. He took out a cigarette and lit it with his dead wife's silver lighter. For a moment Macintyre looked surprised – for Cooper, smoking was a rarely practised vice. The thin, hawk-nosed man took a careful drag on the cigarette, staring at the huge-bellied man seated across from him.

'Listen to me, Hollis,' he said finally, his aging voice flat and deathly cold. 'I've spent virtually my entire adult life working in the field of intelligence. I've made the art and craft of deception my profession. I've seen the smallest, most inoffensive of white lies turned into a towering conspiracy, I know things about this country and its recent history that would make your soul shrivel and turn black. So don't give me any lectures on the consequences of remorse.' He stabbed out the cigarette and looked back at Macintyre. 'Right here, Hollis, in this room, you and I are discussing treason and blandly planning the aftermath of assassination.'

'Do I detect a note of guilt?' asked the fat man, unmoved.

Cooper let out a short, barking laugh. 'Guilt?' he asked, eyes widening behind his spectacles. 'Guilt is for people who have consciences, Hollis, something you and I dispensed with many, many years ago.'

'That may well be true, but it doesn't alter the fact that I have no intention of spending the last few years of my life in prison. I merely wish to make sure that nothing has been left to chance, including the confessional urges of the people involved.'

'Then you have nothing to worry about,' Cooper answered. 'At least on my account. My sins are my responsibility and if I feel the need to atone for them I will do so alone.'

'Good enough, then,' Macintyre said, smiling pleasantly. He eased himself upright, using the arm of the sofa for support. He tugged down his waistcoat, then brushed away an imaginary crumb. 'One last thing,' he said, as Cooper stood.

'Yes?'

'The Russian and our friend from the FBI. Still a problem?'

'Travkin has gone to ground,' Cooper answered. 'Stone has been suspended. He's powerless. If he presents a problem he'll be removed.'

'Good.' Macintyre headed for the foyer of the apartment and Cooper followed. The fat man paused, one hand on the doorknob. 'If all goes well we won't be seeing each other for some time.'

'No,' Cooper answered, 'except for normal day to day meetings all the members have been advised not to see each other. Not that there will be much time for socialising in the near future.'

'True enough,' Macintyre agreed, his voice sombre. 'A few dark days ahead, I suppose.' He opened the door and stepped into the hall. 'I'll be at Stoneacres if I'm needed.'

Cooper nodded goodbye and closed the door, locking it securely. He walked back to the living room, glancing at the heavily shadowed portrait over the fireplace, and then at the cold hearth itself. He'd burned no fire there since Miriam died. 'Dark days indeed,' he said quietly.

After leaving Mort Kessler, Stephen Stone drove south through the last of the evening traffic. Night had fallen and the road ahead was almost empty as he drove towards Lake Anna and the cabin safe-house Debbie had provided.

Staring through the windshield down the long, twin cones of brightness cast by his headlights, he seemed caught within a single cycle of thought. A chance piece of information given to a Russian spy had led them link by link down a chain of events designed to culminate in the murder of a President. Stone had played the game of plot and counterplot for years, but for all its seriousness he knew it was just that; he and Travkin and all the others were players on a board with well-defined boundaries and rigid rules. Some days you won, on others you lost, but the game went forward. This was different and he knew that he was travelling uncharted ground; dark as the road ahead, and much more dangerous.

He reached the Lake Anna exit and turned onto the narrow gravel road that led down to the water. The cabin Debbie had borrowed was at the far end of the lake, screened from its neighbours by almost ten acres of pine and bracken. According to Debbie it had been built in the late twenties by the parents of her professor friend from Georgetown University.

Ten minutes after turning off the highway Stone's headlights picked up the cabin mailbox, the name Sleeman on its side in reflective tape. Slowing, he turned down the narrow drive, pine boughs slapping at the windows and brushing against the sides of the car. He tapped the horn three times to announce his arrival – the signal they'd worked out to separate the good guys from the bad. A few moments later he reached the end of the narrow lane, his lights flashing across the cabin. There was no sign of Debbie's late model Subaru wagon, and there were no lights on in the cabin. Stone killed his engine, switched off the headlights and climbed out of the car. Once again he found himself wishing he had a weapon.

He stood by the car, waiting for his eyes to adjust to the darkness. The cabin was at the top of a gentle slope which led down to the water. There were two entrances, the one facing him on the side of the cabin, and the main entrance through the screen porch facing the lake. A winding set of flagstones went from the bottom of the porch steps to the dock and the boathouse fifty yards away. Peering into the darkness Stone could hear the lake, but he couldn't see it. He sniffed: pine gum, grass in the small clearing, woodsmoke. There was a fire going in the cabin stove. He could hear nothing but ordinary night sounds and the ticking of his engine as it cooled. Lots of stars in a pure black sky, but no moon. Safe?

Maybe. But where was Travkin?

'Here,' said a voice, reading his mind. Stone whirled, dropping into a crouch, heart pounding. Dimitri Travkin stepped out of the darkness, palms up to show that he was unarmed. 'I heard the horn but I didn't want to take any chances.'

'You scared the living shit out of me!'

'My apologies.' Travkin smiled.

'Any sign of my ex-wife?' Stone asked, rising out of his crouch.

'She brought some supplies yesterday. Nothing since,' the Russian answered politely. He hadn't shaved since his abduction by Cooper and was now sporting a reddish-blonde beard. Either the beard or the circumstances had aged him.

'Let's go inside,' Stone said.

Travkin nodded and the two men walked to the front of the cabin, climbed the steps to the screened porch and went through a doorway into the main room.

It was a living memory for anyone who'd ever spent summers in a cottage by a lake. Couch made from the rear seat of a Model T, wind-up Victrola, scarred table, children's watercolours roughly framed and hanging from the wall, silhouettes of fish caught during some long lost July, their imprints outlined in pinholes through shelf paper. A small fire was crackling in the wood stove, taking off the chill, casting flickering shadows over honey-coloured floors glazed by ten thousand barefoot passages. Stone dropped down onto the automobile-seat couch and let his head fall back against the cracked, ancient leather. Travkin sat down on a straight chair, closer to the stove. Beyond him, stairs rose to dark bedrooms above.

'Bad?' Travkin asked.

'Worse,' Stone grunted. He sat forward, rummaging around in his pockets for a cigarette. Travkin tossed him one from a pack of Marlboro on the table to his right, followed by a box of wooden matches.

'How so?' the Russian queried, lighting a cigarette of his own.

'Cooper's taken out Mallory.'

'His assistant?'

'Yes. Just after he made a drop to our Mr Duncan. I tried to follow him but I lost him. Kessler followed Mallory and watched him get picked up by one of Cooper's teams.'

'So what are our options?' Travkin asked, scratching at the new beard along his jaw.

'Kessler's following up some leads on Duncan. I'm going to meet with him tomorrow.'

'I wish to come with you,' Travkin said slowly.

'Out of the question,' Stone answered firmly, shaking his head. 'Set one foot in DC and you're a dead man, you know that.'

'I must talk to Koslov, explain the situation. Perhaps . . .'

'What?' Stone asked coldly. 'Koslov's an old man. You know it's almost certainly out of his hands now. Gurenko's people will be looking for you everywhere.'

'Still . . .'

'Still nothing!' Stone barked. 'Right now you're the only piece of hard evidence that I've got. So you sit tight.' He took a deep breath, then let it out slowly. 'Sorry,' he said after a long moment. 'I'm going a little crazy, I guess.'

'Understandable.' Travkin shrugged. 'Neither of us is in the most comfortable of positions.'

'Quite the understatement,' Stone answered, laughing bleakly. Outside there was the faint sound of a horn. Three beeps. 'Debbie,' he said, standing up, relief in his voice.

'Quiet,' Travkin murmured. He slid past Stone, motioning for him to follow. The Russian padded quickly into the kitchen, then out the side door. The FBI man went after him into the darkness. Together they crouched down by the side of the cabin, hidden in the deep shadows. In the distance Stone could hear the sound of a car engine. 'Keep your face down, look from the top of your eyes,' Travkin ordered. 'A white face is like the moon, reflecting any light available. When she parks, make sure that she is alone in the car. If there is someone with her, we leave. There will be no heroics. Understand?'

Stone simply nodded. The Russian was in full command and Travkin's Spetznaz training went far beyond anything Stone had learned at Quantico.

The car appeared finally and Stone smiled, recognising the utilitarian shape of the station wagon and catching a glimpse of Debbie's face behind the wheel as she swung past and parked beside his own vehicle. He began to stand up but Travkin's hand gripped his forearm painfully. Stone was five inches taller and fifty pounds heavier than his companion but the Russian's grip was like iron.

'Wait,' Travkin hissed. Stone did as he was told, watching as she climbed out of the car, slamming the door easily behind her. She took a few steps towards the cabin, then paused. She turned then, and went back to the Subaru. Opening the passenger side door she leaned down, then stood again, this time holding a briefcase. Gripping it tightly she made her way towards the cottage once more. Travkin let out a short, sharp whistle, then stood up and stepped out of the shadows. Stone followed suit, then brushed past Travkin, moving towards her at a trot.

'Stephen!' she called out, stopping halfway between the car and the screened porch. 'What are you doing out here in the dark?'

'Playing commando with Dimitri.' He grinned, looking back over his shoulder as the Russian came forward. He turned back to Debbie. She looked exhausted. She was pale and there were blue-grey shadows under her eyes. 'Here,' he said, reaching for the briefcase. 'Let me take that for you.'

'No!' she said, pulling back quickly. Stone jerked his hand back as though it had been burned.

'Relax,' he cautioned. 'I'm not going to steal anything.'

'I'm sorry,' she said, nodding towards Travkin as the Russian approached. 'I guess I'm just a little on – '

A single round from the Finnish-made Valmet assault rifle caught her at the base of the neck, exiting just below the jaw and finally coming to rest in one of the wooden porch supports. A split second later Stone and Travkin heard the sound of the weapon and watched, horrified, as Debbie Stone lurched forward, eyes bulging as a second round struck her in the back, blowing out most of her diaphragm in a gory fountain of cloth, blood and bone.

Screaming, Stephen Stone threw himself towards her. As a third round took off the upper portion of her skull, Travkin gripped him by the back of his collar, pitching him backwards, away from the line of fire. Stumbling Travkin managed to drag him back into the shadows, his other hand jerking him towards the ground at the base of the porch steps. He pushed Stone's face into the dirt as a ragged volley of shots struck the crumpled form of the woman ten feet away.

Travkin made a quick, intuitive analysis of the situation. Too many shots, too quickly, but with no rippling hammer of automatic fire. Several shooters, all firing from the left, hidden in the trees. A run for either of the two vehicles would be fatal; their best bet lay in the woods behind.

'Low,' he commanded in a whisper, his hand tight on the back of Stone's neck.

'Debbie . . .' Stone's voice was anguished, choked with tears.

'Dead,' Travkin said harshly. 'Unless you want to die as well you must follow my instructions.'

'Who are – '

'Quiet!' Travkin ordered. He listened. Silence, not even the snap of a twig. Very professional. Waiting for them to make a move. 'Keep with me,' he whispered. His hand still on Stone's neck he began to shuffle backwards, keeping the porch between himself and the vehicles. If they were lucky the cars and the porch would mask their movements. Hugging the ground they reached the corner of the cabin and Travkin paused, listening again, eyes and ears focused on the dark curtain of trees twenty feet away. If one or more of the killers had split from the main group and come this way he and Stone would make perfect targets as they tried to cross the open space.

Still crouching, his hand on Stone's shoulder now, Travkin crab-walked along the side wall of the cabin, stopping at the stacked pile of firewood on his right. His eyes were fully adjusted to the darkness and he could make out the hard-edged shape of a hatchet sticking up from one of the logs. He reached out and pried the tool loose, hefting it in his hand. Better than nothing.

'Stay here,' he whispered, turning to the man crouched on his left. 'Count to ten slowly, then follow. Straight into the trees.' Stone nodded and Travkin stood and began to run, his movements smooth and silent. Numb, the image of Debbie burning in his mind, Stone watched the Russian melt into the shadows along the line of trees. He began to count and on ten he lurched upward and ran, nerves wire-taut.

Halfway across the clearing he heard a blast of sound and was almost positive he felt the sharp passage of air as the bullet creased his shoulder, then smacked into the side wall of the cabin a few yards behind. Without thinking he dropped and rolled, then scrambled the last few feet into the trees. Travkin was there to meet him, a Valmet rifle hanging from one hand. He motioned with his free hand and then slipped further into the trees. Stone followed, stumbling over the body of one of their attackers. The man was on his knees, head bent forward like a Muslim at prayer. The hatchet from the woodpile was buried deeply in the flesh of the man's neck. It had half-severed his head. To the dead man's left was a small collapsible shovel, blade embedded in the soft earth, and further left a neatly dug firing position, twelve inches deep and just large enough for a man to lie prone.

'Jesus!' Stone whispered. He clenched his teeth, fighting off the overpowering urge to vomit.

'Listen to me,' Travkin said, his voice clipped. 'I spent my first day here walking the terrain. We are thirty metres from the beach – a hundred feet. From there the ground breaks at the beach. Ten metres to the right is the dock and the boathouse. There is a powerboat, a dinghy and a canoe. When we reach the edge of the beach we will be exposed to fire from the cabin. Therefore we will go into the water rather than move along the sand. Do you understand?'

Stone nodded. Fear had frozen out every other emotion. The universe had collapsed into a tiny frame of reality that included no one else but the Russian. Right now Travkin was squad leader, commanding general and God all rolled into one.

'Head for the boathouse. Go around to the end of the dock. Keep the boathouse between you and the cabin. We'll take the powerboat. You are familiar with outboard engines?'

'Yes.'

'Good. You will start the engine but not until I am in the boat. Try to leave me behind and I will kill you. When we come out of the boathouse turn left sharply and follow the waterline until we are out of range, then head for the far side of the lake. On the map I saw in the cabin, there is a town, yes.' The Russian's English was deteriorating and Stone had to concentrate.

'A town. Yes.' He tried to think of the name and couldn't. Finally, absurdly, he remembered. 'Cuckoo,' he said. 'The town is called Cuckoo.'

'Then it becomes our objective.' Travkin began moving off.

Stone took a last look at the hatcheted man and followed. The Russian slid through the forest like a wraith, his sneakered feet hardly seeming to touch the ground. Stone kept close behind him, heart slamming in his chest. Behind them and to the left he could hear voices now, the words unintelligible. There was a deep, coughing sound and a muted thump, followed almost instantly by a gouting flare of light. They were burning the cabin.

Travkin and Stone reached the lakeshore and paused. Stone watched as Travkin took off his shoes, tied the laces together and hung them around his neck. Stone was wearing slip-ons but he did his best, shoving them into the pockets of his jacket. While he was doing that the Russian vanished for a few moments, then returned, carrying a charred piece of wood. He rubbed his hands over the charcoal, then stroked the sooty ash first onto his own forehead and then Stone's.

'Like before,' Travkin instructed. 'Go into the water up to your neck with nothing but the eyes and bottom of nose above water. Do not look towards cabin. Yes?'

'Understood,' Stone said.

Travkin smiled and clapped his companion on the shoulder. 'Boy Scout shit.' He grinned, then turned and headed into the cool water of the lake.

It took them less than five minutes to reach the boathouse, with Travkin leading, the Valmet held rigidly in his hands, level with the water. He paused in the lee of the dock, motioning with his chin for Stone to join him. From the corner of his eye Stone could see the blooming cauldron of the cabin fire and for an instant he saw Debbie again, eyes wide and throat torn open as she died. Chilled and shivering, he swallowed hard, joining Travkin at the edge of the dock. The Russian handed him the Valmet.

'They may have someone posted here. Wait.'

Stone nodded, holding the weapon out of the water, and Travkin slithered off. He returned a few moments later.

'All clear.' He took the rifle from Stone, then urged him forward.

They entered the boathouse from the open lake side and Stone dragged himself up onto the narrow floating walkway. The dinghy was hanging on the wall, supported by half a dozen thick, wooden pegs, and the canoe was strung through the rafters overhead. The powerboat was nothing more than an aluminium rowboat fitted with a 25 hp Evinrude.

Dripping, Stone stepped down into the rear of the boat, settling himself at the transom. He gripped the pullrope and waited for Travkin to join him. The Russian took a few seconds to check the back window of the boathouse, then undid the bowline and dropped onto the forward seat. Holding the Valmet ready across his chest Travkin turned and nodded to Stone. Gritting his teeth he put all his strength into his shoulder, ripped the starter rope and twisted the throttle wide open. The engine caught instantly and they surged out of the boathouse, the sudden acceleration almost throwing Stone out of his seat. He hung on as they thundered forward, bow rising, then snapped his throttle arm hard to the right.

Engine howling, the small boat careened along the lakeshore. Stone prayed desperately that there were no deadheads of hidden rocks in his path and kept the throttle open. In front of him, Travkin turned in his seat and levelled the assault rifle. There was roaring stutter that rose above the engine noise and Stone saw the dazzling pulse of the weapon's muzzle flash. He was vaguely aware of dense trees looming up on his left and then saw Travkin toss the now empty rifle over the side. A minute went by as they tore along the foreshore and then Travkin motioned with his arm.

'Turn!' he bellowed, raising his voice over the screaming outboard. 'Cross the lake!'

Stone nodded, pulling the throttle lever towards him. The bow spun around and then he straightened, pointing them towards the invisible shore more than a mile away.

'Who where they?' Stone called out, his voice torn away by the wind. He squinted forward, spray pounding upward over the gunwales as they raced across the dark, unruffled water.

'My people!' Travkin answered, fury in his voice. 'They were damn fucking Spetznaz!'

'How can you be sure?' Stone yelled. 'Why not Cooper's men?'

'The little shovel for one,' Travkin explained, half turning on his seat to look back at Stone. 'It is a trademark. And also the fact that the man in the woods cursed me into eternity as he died. In Russian.'

'Jesus!' Stone moaned. He wiped the spray out of his eyes with the back of one hand. 'We've got everyone after us now!'

'It could be worse, *tovarich*!' Travkin answered, breaking into a death's head grin. 'At least we have each other.'

CHAPTER TWENTY-THREE

At six o'clock on the morning of President Geoffrey James Tucker's sixty-third birthday, Eric Rhinelander pedalled his bicycle through the dawn streets of Washington. He was wearing a blue and green lightweight wetsuit, cut down to look like a form-fitting cyclist's outfit, and carried a knapsack on his back. The pack contained some small tools, black, heavy-soled lace shoes, Axworthy's carefully folded Executive Protection Services uniform, and the broken down components of the CO_2-powered weapon built for him by the Baltimore paintball store. A side pocket of the knapsack held the small, short-range detonating mechanism for the explosive he'd installed on the sewer side of the north portico vault late the previous night and the dedicated-frequency radio that would be fitted onto the uniform web-belt.

At 6:15 he reached the silent, empty intersection of Wisconsin Avenue and M Street in Georgetown. He pedalled through the intersection and continued down towards the Chesapeake and Ohio Canal, then dismounted, pulling his bicycle up onto the sidewalk. Looking around casually he checked to make sure that he wasn't being observed, then turned down a narrow lane.

Walking the bicycle over the dew-damp cobblestones he went past the Blues Alley Jazz Club, crossed a small open square and turned up a second, even narrower lane that ran parallel to Wisconsin Avenue.

Overhead the pewter-coloured sky was lightening to blue. It was going to be another heat-wave day and Rhinelander was pleased that he'd be spending most of it within the air-conditioned confines of the White House.

He parked the bicycle behind a dumper at the rear of a Wisconsin Avenue delicatessen and slipped into the darkened rear service doorway. He'd checked their hours of business and knew that they didn't open until 10:00 each morning, by which time he'd be long gone.

Stripping off the knapsack he opened it and assembled the pieces of his weapon, screwing the airhose connector to the barrel, then used surgical tape to strap the barrel to his forearm. The frozen magazine and its contents, now wrapped in sportsman's insulating plastic, would be loaded into the upper tube of the barrel at the last minute.

With the weapon in place Rhinelander kicked off his Nikes and dressed himself in Axworthy's uniform. He put on the lace-up shoes, then tossed the runners into the dumper. Finally he removed the paintball magazine, a compact, battery-powered Bosch ratchet screwdriver and a two-inch, plastic-handled awl from the pack, putting the magazine into the left inside pocket of his uniform jacket, and the screwdriver and awl into the right pocket. He adjusted the broad strap of the Sam Browne belt and patted the holster. It was the final touch to the uniform; using the James Smythe identification provided by Cooper's people he'd legitimately purchased a standard issue Smith and Wesson .38 Police Special loaded with Hornady wadcutters. He threw the empty knapsack into the dumper as well.

Finally he unhooked the bunji-cords from the bicycle frame and removed the dummy end of the truck baffle he'd created. It was identical to the one he'd seen in the Secret Service refrigerated truck, complete with recessed screw heads. On the inside of the plywood board he'd screwed and glued a kitchen cabinet handle and four spring clips to hold the baffle end in place after he'd left the vehicle. With the board removed he set it aside and manhandled the bicycle up and into the dumper.

The first stage of the operation now completed Rhinelander took out a package of gum from the side pocket of the uniform jacket, removed a piece and put it into his mouth. Chewing slowly he stepped back into the recessed doorway of the delicatessen and pulled down his fly. He urinated against the scarred wooden doorframe.

For the last twenty-four hours he'd regulated his food and fluids carefully, restricting his intake that morning to a thick, high protein drink of yoghurt, raw egg, brewer's yeast and desiccated liver. It would have to last him well into the night, and the last thing he wanted was a judgement error brought on by nature's call. A small detail, perhaps, but potentially disastrous.

A brief, vivid image snapped into his mind: a Viet Cong, black pyjamas around his ankles as he squatted in the bush, smoking an early-morning cigarette and loosening his bowels. The wiry insurgent never even saw Rhinelander, or the bright flashing blade that slit his throat.

Rhinelander glanced at his watch: 6:35. He eased out of the doorway, removed the peaked cap and poked his head out around the corner of the dumper. Almost time. From where he stood he could see the rear entrance of McCreery's Provisioners. The lane was too narrow for the truck to back up against the loading dock, so it parked sideways.

There would be two Secret Service men and four workers on hand from McCreery's. Two of the McCreery's men would stand in the truck, while the other two loaded. One of the Secret Service agents would stand at the rear of the vehicle to supervise the loading while the second, usually the driver, handled the paperwork in the office.

Rhinelander had watched the proceedings on three separate occasions and knew the routine. The truck arrived between 6:40 and 6:45. The two Secret Service men left the truck and went into the rear of the McCreery's building. Between 6:55 and 7:00 they would reappear, this time with the McCreery's workers. The loading took roughly fifteen minutes and the truck left the lane between 7:15 and 7:20. By 7:30 the truck would be arriving at the West Executive Avenue entrance to the White House for its security check.

Rhinelander heard the heavy rumbling of an engine echoing along the upper laneway and ducked his head back behind the side of the dumper. He checked his watch again: 6:40, right on schedule. Listening, he heard the flatulent sigh of brakes as the truck stopped in front of the rear loading bay. A pause and then the sound of two slammed doors – the Secret Service agents leaving the vehicle. Staring at the sweep hand of his watch Rhinelander counted the two men down. Lead man pushes the buzzer to the left of the door. Fifteen seconds for the Frisco Bay surveillance camera tilted in the upper right of the doorframe to check the two men. The metal door swings open and . . . Rhinelander smiled to himself as the he heard the faint sound of the door closing behind the two agents.

Without hurrying he walked out from around the dumper and headed up the lane towards the truck, counting silently. He checked quickly. Loading bay door closed, the surveillance camera tilted far too steeply to pick up his approach. Nobody in the alley. A drunk, overlooked, dozing in a doorway could ruin it all now. Thirty seconds.

He reached the rear of the truck and paused again, holding his breath, letting his senses warn him if warnings were needed. Still nothing. Gently he gripped the rear latch on the door and lifted it slightly, just enough to disengage the hook. One minute. He eased the door up with one hand, then boosted himself up and into the refrigerated compartment, tossing the dummy baffle in ahead of him. Once inside he lowered the door, pushing hard for the last few inches so that the outer latch clicked back into place. Ninety seconds. Cold enough to see his breath if there had been any light.

He eased to the right and swept his palm over the Kemlite wall until he found the toggle for the overhead light. He switched it on, blinking in the sudden glare. He *could* see his breath, and he could also hear the steady hum of the Thermo King unit. Two minutes, ahead of schedule. He picked up the baffle and went to the front of the compartment. Leaning the baffle against the wall he went to work.

Using the battery-powered screw-driver he removed the side panel of the baffle, careful to put each screw into the pocket of his jacket. Four minutes now, and even in the cold of the truck compartment, sweat was beading lightly on his brow. Screws out he took the awl out of his pocket, slipped it into one of the screwholes and jimmied the side of the baffle out of its position. Turning the baffle on edge he slid it back into the now opened box, then peered inside himself. Ten inches wide, sixty long and fifty high. Enough room to slide in sideways, half-crouched, one hand on the dummy baffle handle, clips or no clips. Too long and he'd cramp, but it was an unavoidable risk. Six minutes. Quick check of the compartment to make sure there was nothing suspicious. Ratchet placed in the far end of the box. Finally the light. Out. Seven minutes. One minute left to his self-imposed limit. In the darkness he made his way back to the baffle, found the dummy, then eased himself into the box, making sure he was facing the rear of the truck, and that the awl was in his free hand.

Hat off and held between the side of the box and his chest, Rhinelander crabbed sideways, then pulled the baffle into place. The clips made a small noise as they locked into place, but he still kept his hand on the handle. He tried to ignore the mild claustrophobia he felt with the unseen wall of the baffle inches from his face. Eight minutes and he was in.

Closing his eyes Rhinelander forced his breathing to slow and his heartbeat to follow suit. Moment by moment he went over the details of the plan, searching for the smallest flaw, finding none. Ten minutes. Five more and they would begin to load. Thirty-five and he'd be through the gates. It was going to work.

'Jesus,' Mort Kessler whispered, staring at the two men standing in the hallway. 'You guys really do look like hell.' He stepped aside and let Stone and Travkin enter the recently rented hotel room at the Key Marriot. They'd called Kessler an hour and a half before from a roadside booth just outside the small town of King's Dominion and asked him to get the room as well as some fresh clothes. The room had been easy enough, but the clothes were a different matter. Kessler was shorter than either Travkin or Stone so his own clothes wouldn't do and he'd had to resort to a 24-hour K-Mart just south of the Pentagon. The result was twin sets of jeans, cheap running shoes and a pair of T-shirts. Travkin chose the Iron Maiden shirt, which left Stone no choice but to put on Cyndi Lauper.

Kessler ordered a room service breakfast while his disheveled guests washed and changed. The meal arrived and Kessler drank coffee as the other two men wolfed down the eggs, bacon, hashbrowns and toast, telling their story between bites.

'How'd you manage to get a car?' Kessler asked as Stone wiped up the last of his egg yolk with a sliver of toast.

'He stole it,' Stone answered, hooking a thumb at Travkin. 'From a fishing camp on the other side of the lake. A Suzuki Samurai. Hot-wired it.'

'They teach you that kind of thing at GRU school?' Kessler asked.

'No.' Travkin took a sip of coffee, shaking his head. 'The Suzuki is much like the Soviet Lada Niva, one of which I own in Moscow. During Russian winters you tend to become intimate with your ignition system. The wiring of a Lada is an education in itself.'

'Where is it now?' said Kessler.

'Downstairs in the parking lot,' the Russian answered blandly. He sat back and lit a cigarette from the fresh pack Kessler had ordered with breakfast. Stone joined him. There was a brief silence.

'You're sure the people who shot Debbie were Spetznaz?' Kessler asked cautiously, his eyes on Stone.

'Positive,' Travkin responded. 'One of them spoke in Russian.'

'It couldn't have been some sort of ruse?'

'It's a pretty good actor who keeps to his part with a hatchet buried in his back,' Stone answered wryly. 'Why do you ask?'

'You asked me to check her apartment. I got over there around nine last night and the whole place had been torn apart. I mean trashed, Stephen. It looked as though they went through the place with sledgehammers.'

'If they were Spetznaz, why were they after your wife?' Travkin asked, frowning.

'Ex-wife,' Stone answered, clearing his throat. His jaw tensed as he tried to keep the emotion back. There was no time for grief now. 'Uh . . . Oh shit, I don't know! She worked for the European Studies Institute at the university, everybody knows it's a CIA front. She's – she was an intelligence analyst.'

'It still does not explain it.' Travkin shrugged. 'They had three targets last night: you, me and your ex-wife. Logically, the primary target should have been me if it was a hit team sent out by Gurenko. Instead they chose her.'

'A mistake,' Stone muttered, making a sweeping gesture with his hand. 'And it's not important right now.' He turned to Kessler. 'Anything on the list I gave you? Or the President's schedule?'

'Both,' he answered. 'If you were a White House groupie you'd know that today was Tucker's birthday, complete with fireworks on the lawn. Then he spends three days at Camp David before flying out to that World War Two thing in France.'

'Nothing here? No speeches at the Hilton, dinners, tree plantings, that kind of thing?'

'Nope,' Kessler answered, shaking his head. 'Not a thing.'

'Shit!' Stone grunted, butting his cigarette. 'It doesn't make sense. Duncan is here, so the hit has to be made here, not Camp David or somewhere in France.'

'It's not Duncan any more,' Kessler interjected. 'It's Smythe. Travelling on a New York driver's licence that turns out to be a phony. I've got an address too, which doesn't match the name. According to our friends at the telephone company Mr Smythe of the phony licence is staying at the residence of a Mr and Mrs John Gray in the Wyoming apartments, just off Connecticut Avenue behind the Hilton.'

'I'll be damned,' said Stone, managing a small, tight smile. 'How'd you get all that so fast?'

'I ran the names on the list and Smythe turned out to be the only phony. The powerboat company needed a telephone number to confirm the speedboat rental for yesterday. Our man had to give them a number that worked, and that gave me the address.'

'So, what do we do with this information?' said Travkin.

'Normally we'd go to Ruppelt and request about fifty backups from the DC office and a SWAT team from Metro,' Kessler answered with a snort. 'I figure that option's out for the moment. Same as you trying to get help from Comrade General Koslov.'

'No,' Travkin agreed. 'Not a wise move.'

'We hit the address at the Wyoming,' Stone said firmly, lighting another cigarette. 'What we're looking for is hard evidence that someone is trying to off the President. Without that we don't have a leg to stand on and in the end we *will* have to go to Ruppelt, or someone like him.'

'Unless he happens to be there when we bust in,' said Kessler. 'In which case we'd have to defend ourselves.'

'With what?' Stone asked.

'This,' Kessler answered. He lifted his attache case from the floor beside the table and opened it. He took out a plastic-bodied Glock 9 mm automatic in a spring-clip holster and handed it across the table to Stone.

'It's my own backup gun,' Kessler explained. Seated on Kessler's right, Dimitri Travkin pursed his lips thoughtfully, then drew a clawed hand down the line of his bearded jaw.

'There is no weapon for me?' he asked finally.

Kessler glanced at Stone, who shrugged. 'I'm not used to this glasnost shit,' Kessler said, frowning.

'He saved my ass in the woods last night,' said Stone quietly. 'We're in this thing together, Mort. Not to mention the fact that he knows how to hotwire Suzukis.'

'Okay,' Kessler said finally. 'You're the boss. I've got a cut down Franchi shotgun in the trunk of the car. You can use that.'

'*Spasibo.*' Travkin smiled, glancing at the two men. 'As you Americans say, let's boogie.'

'Jesus!' Kessler muttered, shaking his head. 'Who'd have thought I'd ever wind up partnered with a jive Russkie?'

William Osler, thirty-eight and bored, sat in the east side security kiosk of the West Executive Avenue entrance to the White House. Osler, with only five months on the White House Detail, had drawn the midnight to eight shift on outside duty. This meant that he spent most of his time patrolling the grounds and regularly stepping in dog shit left around by Tucker's three scotties, Huey, Dewey and Louie. At 7:25 a.m., with thirty-five minutes left in the shift, Osler was having an illicit cigarette in the kiosk, tapping his ash into the partially filled Dr Pepper can kept in the booth for that purpose. Standing in the kiosk entrance was Corporal James Corcoran of the Executive Protection Service, crisply outfitted in a spanking clean uniform.

In addition to safeguarding the life of the President and anyone else who happened to be in the White House, Corcoran, three years into the service and ex-Marine, was also keeping his eyes peeled for Lyall Spencer, Osler's boss, or his own topkick, Sergeant Wayne Dillabaugh of the carrot-coloured hair and short temper. Neither man appeared to be in the general vicinity. Directly across from Corcoran on the west side of the avenue was an identical kiosk manned by Chuck Zimmerman, who'd been in the same class with Corcoran when they joined EPS. Looking across the road, Corcoran could have been staring into a mirror. Both he and Zimmerman fitted the EPS profile perfectly: tall, fit and young, every inch the picture postcard cop with the country's most famous residence for a backdrop. The only difference was hair colour. Zimm's hair was coal black and Corcoran's was dirty blond.

'What time is it?' Corcoran asked, glancing over his shoulder at Osler. The Secret Service man tipped his butt into the can and tucked it back under the shelf-like seat. He stood up, yawned and glanced at his watch.

'7:29 and change,' he answered, joining Corcoran in the doorway. 'The chow truck should be here any time now.'

'Then we can all go home,' Corcoran sighed. Like Osler, the uniformed Executive Protection officer was on the midnight to eight shift.

'Just be thankful we won't be on duty for the birthday bash,' Osler said. He reached out and plucked the duty clipboard off the inside wall of the kiosk. 'Dragon One is on the warpath from what I hear. Everything by the book and no slip-ups.'

'How many on the list?' Corcoran asked, more to make conversation than out of any real interest. The Orioles were playing an afternoon game and he and Zimm fully intended to be there.

'Sixty,' Osler answered. 'Full checks, metal detector at the door, magnetic stripe coding on the invitations, the works.'

'What's the beef?' Corcoran asked. The bells and whistles were usually reserved for state visits.

'I'm not sure.' Osler shrugged. 'Some kind of rumour about terrorists, I think.'

'Terrorists again?' Corcoran snorted. 'Shit, we've been waiting for those guys ever since they installed all that crap in the road.' He gestured with his chin at the barely visible crease in the asphalt. Drive through an invisible infra red beam too quickly and a saw-toothed steel barrier flipped up out of the ground. Get beyond that and a string of hydraulic rams came out of the road like gigantic fists, slamming into the underside of the errant vehicle.

Osler stepped out of the kiosk and looked beyond the sliding wrought iron fence that blocked off the street between the kiosks. He spotted the white, unmarked cube van and smiled. Right on the button. He walked onto the road, clipboard in hand, as the truck pulled up in front of the gate. He recognised Ted Loates, the driver, and his partner, Sandy Hansen; both men worked out of Transport Division. He turned and nodded to Corcoran back in the kiosk. The uniformed man hit the button that opened the gates and the truck drove through slowly. Corcoran hit the button and the gates closed. Yawning and thinking about breakfast at the 16th Street Burger King a few blocks away, Osler went up to the driver's side of the cab and did cursory check of Loates' ID and lapel badge. Today it was bright yellow, which checked out, and the Transport man's ID was in order. As he went through the paperwork with Loates, Zimmerman strolled out of his kiosk on the far side of the road with the long-handled mirror. The EPS guard dropped into a squat and ran the mirror under the truck, switching on the built in flashlight. Satisfied that no crazed killer was clinging to the transaxle he went around to the rear and checked the lead and wire seal the driver was supposed to crimp over the latch when he finished loading. Everything was intact and Zimmerman came around the truck and gave Osler the nod.

'Clean,' he said. Osler looked up at Loates, immutable behind his aviator's glasses.

'Happen to know the day's password phrase?' Osler asked.

'Bully pulpit,' Loates answered, quoting Teddy Roosevelt's description of the White House.

'Woolly bullshit?' Osler frowned, cupping one hand over his ear, then checked the clipboard. 'That's not it, I'm afraid.'

'Screw you,' Loates answered, grinning good-naturedly.

'And the horse you rode in on,' Osler shot back. Loates dropped the van into gear and Osler waved him forward with his clipboard. He watched the truck head down the road, then turn in at the west wing parking lot. He shook his head. Dragging his ass around the dew-damp grounds of the White House all night sucked the big one, but it was still better than driving a truck. He checked his watch again. 7:35. Twenty minutes of walking around, clock out at the main office in the west wing basement, then on to Burger King.

CHAPTER TWENTY-FOUR

Having used the awl to bore a tiny, eye-level hole in the baffle, Eric Rhinelander waited until the last pallet had been removed from the truck before he slipped out of his hiding place. Smoothing down his uniform and adjusting his cap he moved to the rear of the truck and dropped down over the tailgate. From the videotape he knew that the truck usually remained at the White House for forty-five minutes before being returned to the Executive Garage.

Directly in front of him was the large door leading into the kitchens. Keeping his pace casual, Rhinelander walked by the open doorway and continued on along the service pathway to the mansion entrance behind the main stairway. He opened the door and stepped into a narrow corridor that led between the stairway and the curator's office on the right. To his left, lit from above by a single bulb, was the set of stairs leading down to the upper-level basement.

Descending, he reached the bottom landing and paused, listening and trying to keep his breathing slow and even. He closed his eyes for a moment, visualising the layout both above and below. It was almost 8:00 a.m. and there would be some minor confusion as the Secret Service and Executive Protection Service shifts changed over. At this hour the new shift of Secret Service agents would be concentrating their energies on the west wing executive offices and the President's private quarters on the first floor. With the heavy influx of tourists the EPS men would have their attention focused on the east wing entrance and the six ground floor rooms included in the public tour.

Visitors to the White House on official business were required to wear plastic identification cards, their colour-coding based on a series of zones established within the mansion and the two wings. A visitor wearing a card good for the east wing offices set aside for the First Lady would be stopped by Secret Service or EPS personnel if they attempted to leave their area, but the various EPS and Secret Service people could cross zones at will. A man like Rhinelander, dressed in an EPS uniform, would not be challenged unless he made an obvious mistake like trying to invade the Oval Office or the Presidential living quarters. Down in the cavernous basements the assassin could reasonably assume that he was on safe ground.

The first level basement contained a maze of small offices used by junior assistants, storage areas, the carpenter's shop, the entrance to the rarely used west wing tunnel and several large storage rooms. A narrow, dimly lit corridor also led to the furniture and service vaults located under the north portico – this was Rhinelander's initial objective. Watching the videotape and observing the flow of traffic into the west wing parking lot he had noted that most people coming to work at the White House arrived between 8:00 and 8:30, so the first level basement would almost certainly be relatively empty now.

The second level basement was a different story. It contained the Signal Corps Communications Centre, a cafeteria directly below the ground floor kitchens, the main laundry, and the entrance to the new east wing bomb shelter. Since the Communications Centre was manned on a 24-hour basis, there was always one shift on hand, but there was little reason for anyone working on the second level basement to come up to the first.

Heartrate and breathing slowed, Rhinelander turned onto the short landing, went down another three stairs and walked past the men's and women's washrooms. Skirting the service elevator he turned right down the central corridor running from east to west. As he'd predicted to himself, the passage was empty. Forty-five feet further on the corridor widened slightly and he paused. On his left were the double doors leading into the furniture vaults and the heating and air-conditioning equipment.

The doors were metal-clad and fitted with push bars, the floor of the corridor done in a dark, speckled linoleum. He scanned the doorway quickly, checking for any signs of an alarm system. There was nothing, and no sign of any visual surveillance either. He wasn't surprised. Given the number of rooms, offices and hallways in the building, total surveillance and wiring would be impossible, requiring scores of camera positions and alarm points; at best the Secret Service and the EPS were capable of monitoring key routes and intersections used by the public and the First Family. The basement areas were obviously not a priority.

He stepped forward and pushed on the bar of the left hand door. It opened easily and he stepped inside, closing the door firmly behind him. The furniture vaults were lit from above by banks of fluorescents. There was a main alleyway between the floor-to-ceiling metal storage racks, and half a dozen side aisles running off to left and right. Each rack was filled to overflowing with furniture no longer in use, but still potentially valuable. Stuffed chairs, chests of drawers, sofas, side tables and lamps were all catalogued and in their proper place.

Rhinelander scanned the racks and walls, once again looking for surveillance cameras. Nothing. Nodding to himself he walked rapidly down the central aisle to the dark green door at the far end of the cavernous room. Opening the door he was instantly assaulted with a blurring array of sounds emanating from an assembly of compressors, fans, heat exchangers and refrigeration units, all of it joined by a snaking system of thick conduits and sheet metal ventilation pipes.

He stood quietly, orienting himself. With his back to the door he was facing due north towards Pennysylvania Avenue. The main sewer conduit was on his right. He turned in that direction, making his way between the banks of shrouded compressors, finally reaching the far wall of the large underground chamber.

The corner of the room was partially hidden by a loop of ventpipe, but pacing off from the corner he found his position between a tall, slightly oily transformer unit and the vent. Just to the right of the transformer he could see the gasket opening for the conduit feeding power into the vault from the outside. Taking the awl out of his pocket Rhinelander picked away at the gasket, watching as the old plaster fell away easily.

Part of the Truman renovation, the vault was set on a cement floor, with double brick walls sheathed in a two-inch thick unstressed concrete shell. The bricks, plastered and painted over a score of times since then, were badly spalled, the mortar crumbling. The concrete skin, eaten away by by the acidic, swampy soil, was in equally poor shape.

Rhinelander glanced around. He was almost forty feet from the door, and well hidden. In the unlikely event of anyone coming into the room, he'd have lots of warning. The killer glanced at his watch. 8:20. A fraction more than twelve hours left. He crouched down, measured up from the floor with his spread hand as guide, then settled down to work with the awl.

The three men stood on the roof of the Holiday Inn and looked across Connecticut Avenue to the Wyoming apartments. Stephen Stone was using Mort Kessler's binoculars, scanning the windows.

'Sixth floor on the side,' Kessler instructed. Stone moved the binoculars fractionally. Beside him, Dimitri Travkin waited, a box containing a dozen red roses in his hands. It also contained Mort Kessler's cut down Franchi shotgun.

'All the blinds are drawn,' Stone said, finally fixing on the right apartment.

'And no one is answering the telephone,' Kessler said.

'It means nothing,' said Travkin. 'He could still be there.'

'No shit, Sherlock,' Kessler grunted, 'which is why Stephen here wants the trick with the flower box. Myself, I'd prefer twenty guys with Kevlar vests and some sharpshooters up here.'

'The flowers will work,' Stone said, lowering the binoculars.

'They better,' Kessler snorted. 'Because if they don't, Comrade Travkin here is in the shitcan.'

'You have a wonderful way with words,' the Russian answered. 'In my country you could have been a poet.'

'Yeah, right,' Kessler said, frowning as he searched the Russian's face for some sign that he was being teased.

'Let's get to it,' Stone said quietly.

Ten minutes later the trio had assembled in the sixth floor foyer of the Wyoming. Travkin, holding the box, stood in front of the door, while Stone and Kessler were out of sight against the far wall of the elevator. Before entering the old-fashioned apartment complex Kessler had used his penknife to slit the end of the flower box, allowing Travking to reach in and get his hands around the trigger of the Franchi while he waited. If the assassin answered the door with a drawn weapon, Travkin would take the expedient course of action and blow the man's brains out.

After the third try at knocking on the door it was obvious that no one was going to answer and Kessler appeared from behind the elevator. He motioned Travkin to stand back while he knelt down and used his FBI-issue lockpicks to open the door. Less than a minute later they were inside the large, gloomy apartment, and four careful minutes after that they knew their quarry had gone.

While Kessler and Dimitri Travkin began working over the apartment room by room searching for anything that might be useful, Stephen Stone sat down at the telephone in the den and called the telephone company's security office. Using his FBI authority he requested a list of all incoming and outgoing trunk calls made to and from the Grays' number at the Wyoming. The supervisor informed Stone that it would take at least half an hour. He told the woman to call him when it was done.

Stone checked with his companions, neither of whom had turned up anything, then returned to the opulently furnished den. After going through the desk drawers, filing cabinets and waste paper basket he was satisfied that 'Duncan' had cleaned up after himself thoroughly, if in fact he'd ever used the apartment at all. Frustrated, he went to the bookcases built into the room and began scanning the titles, wondering what sort of things the real owner of the apartment found interesting. It wasn't until he reached the shelves closest to the desk that he realised what he was seeing.

'Son of a bitch!' he whispered, going back to the first shelf. He checked the other bookcases quickly, then yelled for Travkin and Kessler. He moved back and forth, eyes flashing over the bindings, pulling out book after book and piling them on the bare desktop. Travkin and Kessler appeared in the doorway and stopped, watching the feverish activity.

'What the hell are you doing?' Kessler asked.

'Check it out!' Stone boomed out. 'The books were scattered all over the place, so it took me a little while. He didn't want to take a chance throwing them out, so he salted them around the room.'

'Salted what?' Travkin asked.

'The books, man, read the fucking titles!'

The Russian began going through the books, stacking them in piles on the desk.

Kessler joined him, reading off the titles as he worked. '*The Living White House, Jacqueline Kennedy's White House Tour, L'Enfant's Washington, Confessions of a Secret Service Agent, Protecting the President, Ring of Power: The White House Staff and its Expanding Role in Government,* a 1935 *National Geographic* magazine with a story on Washington and the White House, *A Day in the Life of the President, Washington's First Ladies, Upstairs at the White House* . . . Jesus, there's even one here called *Murder in the Oval Office.*' Kessler stared at Stone. 'My God, Stef, it can't be!'

'Why not?' Travkin queried. 'It would be the ultimate act of terrorism. A Libyan, perhaps, or a Colombian . . . that would tie in with Cooper's visit to Barbados, would it not, and the little charade during my incarceration at the Bowie facility?'

'It's madness!' whispered Stephen Stone. He shook his head. 'Maybe it's just a coincidence, maybe the man who actually owns this place collects books on the White House.'

'I think we can dump that theory,' said Kessler, flipping through the pages of a black, hardcover book. 'The son of a bitch made notes in the margin and used one of those fluorescent highlighting pens.' He cleared his throat. 'This is one of the passages he underlined from *Ring of Power*: "*On the inner protective perimeter are the agents in civilian clothes; there are over a hundred on the White House Detail.*" A little later there's another bit . . . "*The Presidential protective command post is located directly under the Oval Office. Throughout the White House Establishment electronic locator boxes tell agents, including the chief of staff, where the principal protectees are at any given moment of the day or night. Red Teams practise penetration to make vulnerability assessments, fixed base ground to air missiles are reportedly in the White House area, and shoulder-fired Redeye missiles are stored for use.*" The bastard has done his homework.'

'Incredible,' Travkin murmured, turning the pages of another book. 'This is from a volume called *Upstairs at the White House*. "*. . . for every dinner we went to the vaults beneath the north portico and packed up the crystal, gold flatware and china.*" In the margin he has written the single word: *Basement*.' Travkin fluffed the pages of the paperback. 'There are dozens of entries like that; he has annotated the entire book.'

Stone stared at the pile of books on the desk. 'Shit, we can't go through all of this now.'

'Why bother?' Kessler shrugged. 'This is the evidence you wanted.'

'This is a bunch of books with notes in the margins and sentences underlined,' Stone answered. 'It still doesn't prove anything.'

'We're not going to have proof until our man blows away the President,' Kessler answered. 'We'll have to go with what we've got.'

'Stephen is right,' Travkin answered slowly. 'We have nothing, except now we know that Mr Duncan, or whatever he is calling himself now, intends to strike down President Tucker in the White House, perhaps even the Oval Office. I'm sure that we might be able to decipher his method of access if we went through all this material, but I'm afraid we don't have time for that now.'

'We're in a bad rush all of a sudden?' asked Kessler.

'I'm afraid so, *tovarich* Mort,' Travkin said. 'Think for a moment. Stephen assumes a tying up of loose ends by Mr Cooper, you yourself saw Mallory excised, yes? And now we are here. Mr Duncan is not. He too has cleaned up. That can only say he is ready to make his move in the very near future. Perhaps today.'

'Oh shit!' Kessler groaned. 'The birthday party!'

'I beg your pardon?' said Travkin.

'It's the President's birthday today,' Stone explained. 'They're having a big blow-out at the White House tonight.'

'He will strike then,' Travkin responded firmly. 'I'm sure of it.'

'We have to give this to someone,' Stone said, biting his lip. 'We can't go after him without help.'

'You said Ruppelt was out, so who do we go to?' Kessler asked.

'General Koslov would laugh in my face,' Travkin said. 'And then he would hand me over to Gurenko at the KGB and his assistant the Weasel.'

'Nice guys,' Kessler muttered.

The phone rang six inches from Stephen Stone's hand and he jerked nervously. He picked it up on the second ring, then tucked the receiver between his shoulder and ear as he fumbled in the desk for pen and paper. He listened for several minutes, taking down notes as he went, then hung up.

'Who?' Kessler asked.

'Phone company,' Stone answered tersely. He looked down at his notes. 'Well,' he said after a moment. 'We don't know how he's getting in, or how he's getting out, but I think we know how he's getting away.'

'Explain,' Travkin asked.

'What do you do when a major crime goes down and the roadblocks go up?' Stone asked. 'The train station is being watched, the bus station and the airports too.'

'Rent a balloon,' Kessler answered sourly.

'Close,' Stone replied. 'From the phone record it looks like Mr Duncan-Smythe has rented a houseboat from a charter place downriver on the Potomac.'

The first exchange took place at noon at the foot of the Key Bridge on the Georgetown side. A steel-grey Volkswagen van drove down Wisconsin Avenue, turned west onto K Street and puttered slowly along underneath the booming Whitehurst Freeway until it reached the bridge. The van then pulled off onto the dirt parking area beside the river bank and waited. The vehicle had a small refrigeration unit on the roof and a bumper sticker which read: 'Caution – Show Oysters On Board.' It had no windows and carried North Carolina plates.

Inside the van, securely packed in a wooden crate, was the chilled corpse of Nezar Assad, the Lebanese terrorist previously affiliated with the Abu Nidal group. Nezar had been dead for several days, shot through the right ear with a soft-nosed bullet from a Smith and Wesson .38 Special. Since that time he had been literally kept on ice. Also in the box with Nezar was a six-pound charge of plastic explosive connected to a timer, and a tape-activated switch which would detonate the charge when the box was opened. Prior to his murder Nezar had been dressed in an off the rack JC Penney suit and penny loafers from Kinney. The wallet in his jacket contained his own identification papers, and his passport showed that his last destination prior to arriving in North America had been France.

Included in his effects was a bogus address book which included Paul Mallory's home telephone number in Alexandria, a DC Post Office box number which had been purchased in Mallory's name, and the telephone number of a small hotel on the Left Bank in Paris.

The hotel was known to most intelligence organisations as headquarters for the FLI, the Front for the Liberation of Iran, an anti-ayatollah group financed by the Central Intelligence Agency since 1982. William Casey, Director of Central Intelligence at that time, never had great expectations for FLI, but felt they were useful as a front for other anti-Iran operations. Hudson Cooper had inherited the group through Covert Operations and had kept them on the payroll at the same rate as Casey – $100,000 per month. Now the investment was about to pay off.

A second van appeared, approaching from the boathouse on the other side of the bridge. It was dark blue with DC plates. The blue van pulled up so that its side door was parallel to the Volkswagen's. Both van drivers then opened their own doors, screening the exchange from prying eyes. A short rolling conveyor was placed between the two vehicles and the crate containing Nezar's body and the explosive booby-trap was transferred to the blue van. Exchange complete, one of the men in the Volkswagen dropped out of the open door and spray-glued a large, official looking decal onto the windowless side of the blue van. The decal said: GRIFFIN SECURITY SERVICES INC. Griffin Security was the company hired a number of years before to protect and occasionally patrol the empty confines of the Iranian Embassy, abandoned since the days of the hostage crisis.

With the decal in place the sliding doors of both vans were closed and the two vehicles went off in different directions. The blue vehicle headed for the Iranian Embassy. When it turned in at the gates the driver's companion, dressed in a dark blue Griffin uniform, climbed down from the vehicle and unlocked the heavy chain securing the high wrought iron gate. The van went down the narrow, litter-strewn laneway to an enclosed courtyard at the rear, while the uniformed man relocked the gate.

The two men, both members of the FLI, had clear and simple orders. After parking the van they were to return to their hotel and wait. If they had not recieved further instructions by 7:30 that evening they were to go back to the van and wait for a rendevous with their American FLI contact. At 9:30 they were to open the crate in preparation for handing over its contents. The two men had no idea what the crate contained, nor did they care; as one-time members of the Shah's Secret Police, SAVAK, they were used to following orders without question, and in this case they had been told that their mission was vitally important and would bring them one step closer to re-establishing the House of Pahlavi in Iran. That was enough. Locking the van securely they slipped out of the abandoned embassy compound and returned to their hotel.

CHAPTER TWENTY-FIVE

Eric Rhinelander had done his research well and his timing for the projected assassination could not have been more astute. Any social event at the White House invites logistical chaos that spreads from the State Department's Office of Protocol down to the Head of the Secret Service White House Detail, and eventually to the chief usher. Daily routines are set aside, extra staff is brought in and security procedures become nightmarish. The Presidential birthday party was no exception.

Normally, the White House residence staff numbers just under a hundred, not including social aides and the staff of the messroom in the west wing. For Tucker's birthday party the number quadrupled. A sit-down dinner for sixty, followed by a reception for three times that many required contract staff hiring for the kitchens, thirty social aides from the four-service military pool, twelve extra drivers from the White House garage for chauffeuring guests without vehicles, twenty-five valet parking attendants, also from the military pool, and almost a score of volunteers from the visitors' office who would be required to do anything from combing through the State Department briefing book to make sure that allergy concerns were taken care of to using blow-dryers to make sure the rosebuds at each place setting were sufficiently unfolded. On top of all this there was the entertainment staff and their entourages as well as a CBS television crew which had been invited to record the proceedings for posterity.

All of these people, staff, contract and volunteer, had to be provided with identification and security passes allowing them into a variety of areas within the mansion. Extra Secret Service staff from the district office and beyond, EPS and National Park Police as well as Metro Officers brought in to handle potential traffic snarls all had to be briefed on the evening's activities and procedures. In all, there were 178 new faces present at the White House, not including Eric Rhinelander, the uninvited 179th.

By 6:00 p.m. the White House was a swarming madhouse of pre-party activity, while deep in the vaults beneath the north portico, Rhinelander had completed his preparations and was sleeping lightly, hidden from view by the bulk of one of the air-conditioning compressors. He had removed several bricks from the inner skin of the vault, revealing the bundled electrical cables and planting the timer-detonator which would plunge the White House into darkness for the few moments he needed.

To a civilian, unaccustomed to the violent interludes which were Rhinelander's professional life, sleeping, however lightly, might have seemed an odd thing to do in the assassin's situation, but Rhinelander knew better. He'd seen it in Laos, Cambodia and Vietnam – a final clearing of the subconscious or perhaps a fleeting confrontation with personal demons before confronting death itself. From his own experience he knew that it was less sleep and more self-hypnosis.

Within some corner of his consciousness Eric Rhinelander knew that madness had stalked him as far back as he could remember, but, knowing that, he had lived a life where the potential for insanity was nothing more than an occupational hazard. It had occurred to him from the beginning that his acceptance of Hudson Cooper's assignment was suicidally dangerous, but at the same time he knew that it could also free him for ever.

Dozing, always on the edge of wakefulness, Rhinelander went over his plan, point by point, assessing his chances, and concluding, as he had a score of times before, that barring the unforeseen, the attempt, and the escape that followed, would be successful. He knew, though, that there was a flip side to that coin; the unforeseen could never be barred completely, and, historically, no attempt on the life of a head of state, successful or not, had resulted in the assassin's escape.

Yawning briefly, Rhinelander awoke fully and checked his wristwatch: 6:45. The first guests would be arriving in the diplomatic reception room. He smiled calmly in the semi-darkness. In a little more than two hours from now perhaps the thread of history would be broken.

Lyall Spencer sat beside the duty agent at the video console in the Secret Service Communications Office in the basement of the west wing and scanned the monitors carefully. The ventilating fans in the room were blowing hard, keeping back the oppressive heat from outside and also sucking out the steady cloud of cigarette smoke the Detail Chief was producing. The Duty Agent's name was Roy Donner and the smoke was driving him crazy. He'd quit two weeks previously and even the sight of someone smoking on an old movie made him twitchy.

'How do they handle smoking at these things?' Donner asked, nodding at the monitors and trying to throw Spencer an oblique hint. Donner had been on the White House Detail for a year and knew perfectly well that all White House social functions were non-smoking and had been that way since Jimmy Carter's time.

'I smoke a lot when I'm nervous, Donner,' Spencer answered sourly. 'And I'm always nervous when the Boss throws a party.' He glanced at the screens. Cars all over the parking lots, limousines at the portico, black tie and evening dresses milling around the diplomatic reception rooms. Thank God he didn't have to listen to the bad Gershwin being pumped out by the four piece band. 'By the way, where is he?'

'Toilet,' Donner answered, checking the digital map on the console directly in front of him in the semi-darkened room. 'Second floor north in the family quarters. He's been in there for about ten minutes. Lousy protocol; must be taking a dump with *Time* magazine or something.'

'Presidents don't take dumps,' Spencer answered. 'They defecate if they do anything at all.'

'They used to sell the Dalai Lama's shit, did you know that?' Donner said.

'No, Donner, I did not know that,' Spencer said, sighing.

'It's true,' he assured his boss. 'He used to crap down this long pipe on the top floor of his palace and they had guys down at the bottom who caught it. They dried it out and made good luck charms. Made a lot of money.'

'You wouldn't make a dime recycling Tucker's shit,' said Spencer. 'Now pay attention to the screens.'

The Detail Chief butted his cigarette and stared over Donner's shoulder. The Boss and his family all wore location beepers, but keeping track of the hordes of intruders which had now descended on the White House was impossible. He had cameras for all the rooms on the ground and first floors as well as the kitchens, main hallways and staircases, but the lighting was half-assed, the cameras kept on fading out and even with a perfect picture you could barely make out whom you were looking at.

Spencer shook his head. The average American watching the White House on the news probably assumed the Secret Service and the other agencies involved in protecting the President had the most up-to-date equipment. Sometimes that was true, especially when it came to perimeter surveillance, but by and large they had to stumble along with aging goods just like everyone else. The same held true for the White House itself. The floors, brand new in 1950, had already been replaced in some of the rooms, worn through under the feet of thirty-seven million tourists who'd tramped through the place since then.

A telephone built into the main console rang and Donner picked it up. He listened for a moment and then handed it to Spencer. 'It's for you. Some guy from the FBI named Stone.'

Daniel Waxman paced nervously back and forth in front of the guardrail surrounding the Great Falls lookout, the turbulent waters of the Potomac making him feel slightly queasy. Behind him, only yards away, was the peaceful basin of the Chesapeake and Ohio Canal with its locks and large canal house. He would have much rather waited on one of the benches close to the canal, but his instructions had been specific – the meeting was to take place overlooking the thrashing waters as they pounded over the tumbled granite falls.

Waxman, in his forties, was a short, slightly overweight, Columbia-educated career bureaucrat with the State Department. During the early stages of his career, and his marriage, Waxman had seen himself rising to great heights in the department, sometimes postcoitally confiding in his wife Brenda that he could see himself as an Assistant Secretary, and, when he was feeling particularly pleased with himself, he could actually envision the ultimate phone call from the White House asking him to become the Presidential Press Secretary.

Eighteen years, a vague connection with Oliver North and simple attrition had seen to those ambitions, and now he was content to keep a low profile, have sex with his wife once or twice a month and do his job as senior editor of the *Morning Summary*. The *Summary* was produced by a division of the department's Bureau of Intelligence and Research and was designed to inform the Secretary and his principal deputies of current events and current intelligence relating to US foreign policy. Once upon a time Waxman had made a few melodramatic comments at parties about being in intelligence, but he didn't bother any more. BIR was nothing more than a place to gather Washington gossip, and he was as far as you could get from being a spy.

Which was why the call that afternoon had been so confusing. With Brenda visiting her mother in New York Waxman had decided to spend the morning catching up on the latest Tom Clancy novel, and the afternoon down in the basement working out the board for the war game he was designing. Between the book and the basement he decided to make himself a sandwich, and that was when the call came. The man on the other end of the line actually had quite a thick accent, and for a few moments Waxman thought he was being made the butt of a joke by the guys down at the office. Eventually, though, the man, who said his name was Horst Richter, convinced Waxman that he was serious.

Richter told him that he was an East German journalist who had been asked to do a favour for a friend. The friend had some information he thought might be of interest to the State Department. Richter then asked if Waxman would care to pass the information on. When the bureaucrat hesitated Richter went on to say that the information was vitally important, and by helping Richter out, he could collect some of the glory for himself. Briefly, Waxman saw himself with a White House parking sticker on his car again and in that moment he agreed – after all, what did he have to lose?

Now he wasn't so sure. Here he was, twenty miles out of town with the sun going down, waiting for some East European with a package. Standing there, staring down into the rushing water and feeling mildly ill, he found himself wishing he hadn't been so rash.

Hearing a shuffling sound, his heart suddenly pounding, Waxman spun around. Two men, both wearing jogging suits and sneakers, had joined him on the raised concrete platform. The plump little man swallowed hard. They sure as hell didn't look like Russian spies, but who knew? The shorter of the two men was wearing a bright yellow knapsack across his shoulders.

Mr Waxman?' asked the taller man. No German accent, something else. Shit, they were spies. Waxman felt his bowels turn to water.

'Who are you?'

'You are Daniel Waxman?'

'Yes.' Oh God! If he didn't find a bathroom there was going to be an accident.

'Good.' The taller man cleared his throat. 'I am sorry to bring you out here on false pretences, but I can assure you that it is most necessary.'

'What false pretences?' asked Waxman, his mouth drying to alum almost instantly. Bizarrely all he could think about was the fact that his mouth always dried up like that when he smoked pot back at Columbia. If he didn't shit his pants first he was going to faint. Christ! Why hadn't he listened to Brenda and gone to work for her old man?

'There is no Horst Richter. There is no friend.'

'I don't get it,' Waxman answered weakly. The other man had stepped back, blocking the exit from the platform.

'You are here because of who and what you are,' the taller man explained. 'You work in the Department of State, but you have no real power, you work in intelligence, but have no control. You are neutral.'

'I'll go along with that,' Waxman agreed. He'd go along with just about anything at this point. Just so long as he got out of here. The tall man made a small gesture with his hand and the shorter man stripped off the knapsack and handed it over. The tall man in turn handed the knapsack to Waxman who looked down at it blankly. The tall man stepped forward and took Waxman by the elbow. He led the frightened man to the rail and pointed to the island splitting the river into two fuming channels. A footbridge connected the island to the Virginia side of the river.

'Now then,' the tall man said, 'on the island you will see a man in a bright blue sailing shell, yes?'

'Yes,' Waxman answered, squinting.

'He is using a professional quality video camera, colour of course. He has just recorded our little transaction.'

'I . . . I don't get it,' Waxman stuttered. 'Who the hell are you people?'

'My name is Vladimir Gurenko, Mr Waxman. I am a general in the KGB and Resident here in Washington. My companion is Major Valentin Ivashutin.'

'Jesus!' Waxman whispered, horrified. He'd read enough John Le Carré to know that KGB generals and their assistants didn't prey on middle-grade civil servants for nothing. 'What do you want from me?'

'Rest assured, very little,' Gurenko said, his voice soothing. 'As you were told on the telephone, we would like you to pass some information on to the Secretary, Mr Swanbridge.'

'I haven't got access to Swanbridge!' Waxman moaned. 'You've got the wrong guy for this job, General.'

'You are the perfect man,' Gurenko assured him. 'As I said, you are neutral.'

'But how do I get to Swanbridge?' asked Waxman plaintively.

'By invoking my name,' Gurenko answered simply.

'And when do you want this done?' Waxman asked.

'Immediately,' Gurenko ordered. 'Swanbridge is at a White House reception. You know the chain of command. Get to him.' The Russian's voice was horribly blank and emotionless. Waxman felt as though he was arguing with a machine.

'You want me to get to Swanbridge, in the White House, just by using your name?'

'Precisely.' Gurenko nodded.

'You're nuts,' said Waxman, summoning up a shred of courage from some unplumbed depth. 'And what will you do if I tell you that I won't do it?'

'I won't do anything,' Gurenko said, shrugging, 'although the tapes we've just recorded could be rather damning.' He shook his head. 'No, Mr Waxman, we won't do anything to you, but your countrymen almost certainly will.'

'Just what the hell is that supposed to mean?' Waxman asked.

'The information in that knapsack contains material relating to the possible assassination of Geoffrey James Tucker, President of the United States. Your President, Mr Waxman, not mine. The information contained in the bag is not conclusive, but it is accurate, and we came upon it accidentally while engaged in other intelligence pursuits.'

'I don't believe this is happening,' Waxman whispered. His complexion had become ashen and there were beads of sweat at his hairline.

'It is happening,' Gurenko assured him. 'Act with speed and with courage and you will perhaps save the life of your President. Hesitate, and go to your grave knowing that you could have prevented his death.'

The KGB file on Waxman was slim, but it did note that he seemed to enjoy melodrama. Gurenko's words had been designed to appeal to that weakness.

'Look, I can't guarantee anything . . .' Waxman said uneasily. Gurenko shrugged philosophically.

'You can only do your best,' he said. 'But you will reach Swanbridge.'

'At the White House?'

'If possible. If not, go to his home. You know where he lives, yes?'

'Bradley Hills Grove, out by the Burning Tree Golf Club.'

'Very good,' Gurenko said.

'Okay,' Waxman blurted. 'What if I do get to see him . . . what if he doesn't believe me?'

'He'll believe you.' Gurenko smiled. 'And if he shows any hesitation you can say a few things to him as verification of your sources.'

'Like what?' Waxman said.

'Mention Shrenk, Cooper and Macintyre. Mention the meetings they had in the house on Cherry Hill Lane.'

'Shrenk, Cooper and Macintyre,' Waxman repeated. It sounded like a law firm but the little man knew better. The only Shrenk he knew of was the Attorney General and he was willing to bet that Cooper was Hudson Cooper of the CIA. Waxman was feeling worse with each passing second, but he was also experiencing a thrill he'd never felt with Brenda, or down in the basement with his board game. Sick-making or not, this was the real thing. Screw reading Tom Clancy – he was living it!

'Do you have any questions?' Gurenko asked. From the look in Waxman's eyes the KGB Resident knew he'd taken the bait and set the hook. The wide-eyed State Department flunky would go through the fires of hell to get the material to Swanbridge, and get Gurenko off the hook. In addition to giving Swanbridge the assassination plot, and thus absolving his own people of having any connection to it, he was also handing *Osin* to the Secretary of State on a silver platter. He smiled to himself, wishing he could be on hand to see Swanbridge's reaction.

'No questions,' Waxman answered, clearing his throat dryly. Gurenko patted the smaller man on the shoulder.

'Excellent,' he said quietly. Then he turned Waxman around gently, once again pointing to the man with the camera. 'And remember, I will be sending these tapes to your immediate superior within forty-eight hours. They will either prove your patriotism, or damn you forever if you decide not to deliver the information to Swanbridge. You understand this?'

'I understand,' Waxman said, nodding. The weight of the knapsack in his hand seemed enormous. He looked across the rushing waters to the small tree-covered island and the man with the camera. James Bond receded, replaced by Mrs Waxman's little boy Daniel. He turned to ask Gurenko a question, but the tall Russian and his blond companion were gone, small figures on the path that led down to the locks and the canal house. He was on his own.

CHAPTER TWENTY-SIX

'I must be out of my fucking mind!' Lyall Spencer fumed. Behind him loomed the massive pinnacle of the Washington Monument, three sides now in dusky shadow, only the west facade still coloured by the setting sun. The parking lot to the north was almost empty and the state flags encircling the monument hung limply in the sullen, overheated air. It was 8:20 p.m.

'That's what I thought,' said Stephen Stone, leaning against the Secret Service Chief's unmarked car, smoking a cigarette. A few feet away Dimitri Travkin was pacing nervously, watching the parking lot and the service roads running up to the huge obelisk. 'But I'm convinced there's a conspiracy underway to assassinate Tucker; all the evidence points to it.'

'You don't have any goddamn evidence,' snapped Spencer. 'You've got a lot of bullshit and a Russian defector!'

'He does not believe you, Stephen,' said Travkin wearily, pausing in front of Stone. 'We might as well give up.'

'How can I believe you?' asked Spencer. 'You're telling me that I've got a fucking assassin inside the White House right now, and here I am, talking to you guys beside the Washington Monument! Christ, give me proof!'

'We can't give you proof,' said Stone. 'We told you what's been going on, and the only possible conclusion is that Hudson Cooper, Hollis Macintyre and God knows who else are planning to assassinate Tucker, probably because he's suffering from something called Creuzfeldt-Jacob syndrome, a disease that leads to psychotic behaviour. We've run down this man Duncan as far as we can go. He rented a houseboat from a marina downriver at Indian Head, complete with charts all the way up to Great Falls. The guy at the marina says he saw Duncan loading all sorts of scuba equipment on board, as well as a couple of steamer trunks. Then we checked with the Eastern Power Boat Club down by the Anacostia Bridge – close to where he made the exchange with Mallory. Duncan, or Smythe, had the houseboat there all right, but now it's gone.'

'So where is it now?' Spencer asked. He glanced at his watch, a worried expression on his face. He was off home base in the middle of a major social event and if Headquarters ever found out he'd be dead meat.

'The Beach Boys are playing on the Watergate Barge tonight. You know the way it gets out there when there's a big concert – boats crowd in from all over. I think he's dropped anchor out there and he's using the concert as camouflage.'

'And you think he's inside the White House?'

'All the research books were about the White House. The notes in the margins all relate to the building – history, construction, renovations, floor plans . . . everything.'

'Jesus!' muttered the Secret Service man. He stared at Stone and then glanced at Dimitri Travkin. 'What the hell am I supposed to do about him?'

'He's with me,' Stone answered firmly. 'He was the one who figured thing out in the first place, he saved my ass at Lake Anna, and if we abandon him now the KGB will burn him.'

'I've got to check all this information,' Spencer said. 'I can't just –'

'There's no fucking time for that!' stormed Stone. 'Mort's going to see if he can round up people to cover the Barge. We've got to stop Duncan . . . now!'

At 8:31 p.m. Eric Rhinelander went over the wiring bypass to the main electrical trunk for the last time, then set the timer. Standing, he brushed down his uniform, then turned on the Secret Service radio, feeding the earphone wire up through his web belt in exact imitation of an EPS officer on duty. He tuned the radio slightly, adjusting the volume, then listened to the backchat from the various Secret Service and EPS personnel. As far as he could tell everything was going smoothly with the exception of a guest who'd had a little too much to drink and was being discreetly escorted back to her limousine. It took him a few minutes to connect call sighs to locations but eventually he had it figured out. Dinner was almost over, with Diamond and Emerald still at the head table, along with Cobalt, the Vice-President, and Flint, the Secretary of State, also in attendance. Heliotrope, the White House physician, was in his ground floor offices attending to a member of the kitchen staff who'd suddenly developed a bleeding nose. Nothing out of the ordinary.

Then Rhinelander stiffened. There was a call from the West Executive Avenue security kiosk, requesting a double-check with Dungeon on a scheduled meeting between Diamond and Hudson Cooper, the DDO for Central Intelligence. The duty officer was querying the call list since it seemed like an unlikely time for a meeting. A few seconds later there was confirmation from Dungeon and Cooper's limousine was allowed entry.

The security desk at the west wing main entrance would give Cooper his pass. The assassin took a deep breath and let it out slowly. It was time to begin.

At 8:44 the digital screens in both the chief usher's office at the north foyer and Dungeon, directly below the Oval Office, showed that the President and Vice-President had left the state dining room and were now proceeding to the Oval Office. As Dungeon alerted the security staff that Diamond was moving along with Cobalt, two Secret Service agents patrolling the grounds peeled off and headed for their positions outside the rose garden windows. Another pair of agents went up the narrow stairway that led from the basement to the corridor beside the cabinet room.

The first agent, a woman named Beth Sheldrake, took up a position in the private secretary's office between the Oval Office and the cabinet room. The second agent, John Donnelly, stood beside the main entrance to the Oval Office, giving him a view along the cabinet room corridor to the foyer at the colonnade entrance to the west wing. Neither Sheldrake nor Donnelly was in a particular hurry; they knew it would take the better part of five minutes for The Man to reach the west wing and the Oval Office.

As the Secret Service agents took up their places around the Oval Office, Eric Rhinelander left the gloomy security of the vaults below the north portico and headed for the rarely used entrance to the west wing tunnel. He turned right along the main east–west corridor and continued west past the silent carpenter's shop. From above he could hear the faint, muffled sound of music as the band began playing in the library. The assassin glanced at his watch: 8:46 – dinner would be coming to an end and if things were going according to plan, Tucker and Teresi would now be on their way to the Oval Office.

Rhinelander reached the tunnel entrance and paused. From the empty metal bracket it was clear that there had been a surveillance camera over the door, but it had been either removed for servicing or simply deemed unnecessary. Ignoring the lucky lack of technology he pulled open the heavy door and entered the tunnel.

Two minutes earlier, Lyall Spencer had returned to the White House with his two ill-dressed companions sharing the rear seat. There had been a raised eyebrow or two from the security people at the West Executive gate, but Spencer's badge and ID got them through. The Secret Service Chief rolled the car around to the parking lot across from the west wing main entrance and escorted Stephen Stone and Dimitri Travkin past the

Marine guard at the doors. He took them to the correspondents' bullpen across from the Presidential Press Secretary's office and sat them down in the empty lounge.

'Now don't you fucking move!' he ordered in a harsh whisper. He shook his head, staring at the two men. 'Christ, jeans and T-Shirts. Cyndi Lauper yet!'

'What happens now?' Stone asked. He found a package of Larks on the littered desk in front of him and lit up.

'I go down to the basement and start checking through all the contract staff in the building.'

'You should be looking for Duncan directly,' Travkin insisted. 'There is no time to look through files.'

'So tell me,' he scowled. 'Who am I looking for?'

'A little over six feet tall, good looking, dark haired, mid to late forties,' said Stone, 'that's the description we've been able to put together.'

'It applies to half the men on my staff, for Christ sake!' Spencer shot back. 'Not to mention maybe twenty waiters serving dinner.'

'He will not be a waiter,' Travkin said slowly.

'Why not?' asked Spencer coldly. 'Sirhan Sirhan took out RFK in a hotel kitchen.'

'Tucker will not be inspecting the kitchen tonight,' the Russian answered. 'Look for someone who has access to all parts of the building.'

'No such animal except for Secret Service and some of the uniformed types,' Spencer answered, shaking his head.

'Uniforms?' Travkin asked.

'Executive Protection Service,' Stone explained.

'How many on duty?' Travkin asked quickly.

'Tonight?' Spencer said, arching his eyebrows. 'For something like this they've probably pulled out most of their staff. Make it a hundred and fifty. Most of them on the outer perimeter.'

'How many outside?'

'A hundred.'

'Fifty inside?'

'Something like that. It's hard to say during an event like this.'

'He will be one of those fifty,' Travkin said. 'They are the ones to check.'

'Your Russian sounds pretty sure of himself,' Spencer said, turning to Stephen Stone.

'My Russian, as you call him, is pretty goddamned smart, Spencer, and I think he knows what he's talking about.'

'What if he's wrong?' Spencer retorted.

'What if he's right?' Stone answered.

'All right, but just stay where you are,' said Spencer. He turned and left them, heading for the cabinet room stairs and the Secret Service office in the basement.

Eric Rhinelander reached the west wing exit from the tunnel at 8:49. He straightened his uniform jacket, adjusted his cap and opened the door, stepping through into the basement offices and walking briskly forward. To his right was a short, darkened corridor that led down to the photo office and the Presidential barbershop. Beyond that was the Secret Service Communications Centre.

The killer followed the passageway directly in front of him, mentally counting down, his mind's eye giving him the route forward. He turned right, then left, then right again, walking past the closed doors of half a dozen vacant offices, finally reaching the curving stairway that led up to the press room on the main floor. He checked his watch again, noted that he was slightly ahead of schedule, and climbed the stairs, his right hand gently brushing the highly polished leather holster on his hip. Five minutes left. Ignoring the cool film of sweat building up under the wet-suit he continued to climb the stairs, keeping up his silent count.

At the top of the stairs Rhinelander turned right, following the hallway past the open expanse of the correspondents' bullpen, empty now except for two men in jeans and T-shirts, taking a cigarette break at one of the desks in the centre of the semi-darkened room. Cleaning staff? A factor to consider on his way out. He ignored them for the moment and continued on, heading back towards the colonnade.

According to the floor plans he'd examined, the next hurdle was the corridor leading down to the Oval Office. From under the peak of his cap he could see the double surveillance cameras discreetly mounted in the ceiling, one pointing down the corridor, the other facing him. He walked under the camera mount, catching a brief glimpse of the Secret Service man at his post outside the Oval Office door. Ten steps beyond he reached the colonnade entrance to the cabinet room and stopped.

He opened the door a few inches, poking his head around it as though following a patrol routine. The room was empty, the drapes pulled across the line of tall windows that looked out onto the rose garden. Without pausing he slid into the room, closing, then latching the door.

The room was dark but he'd studied enough photographs to be able to orient himself. Fireplace to his left, long, oval conference table running down the centre, twenty leather armchairs arranged around the table. Door at the far end of the room leading directly into the private secretary's office.

Working swiftly in the darkness, Rhinelander stripped off the Executive Protection Services uniform, grateful for the cool breeze from the air conditioning unit. With the uniform off he gently pulled the tape from around his arm and assembled the airgun, checking the CO_2 feed line connection carefully. Laying the weapon gently on the smoothly burnished surface of the table he squatted down and dug the tubular magazine out of the EPS uniform jacket. He pulled off the layers of insulating plastic and felt the tube. Still cold.

He tipped the magazine up, catching one of the paintball capsules in his palm, then tested it with his thumb and forefinger; the contents were still frozen, the water barely liquid around the inside edges. Good enough. He loaded the magazine into the upper barrel of the weapon and then, barefooted, made his way down to the other end of the room. Finally, he checked the luminous dial on his watch. One minute. Concentrating on keeping his breathing steady, the assassin waited patiently for the clock to run down. It was 8:53 p.m.

Beth Sheldrake, one of the five woman Secret Service agents on the White House Detail, shifted in her chair and leafed through a battered copy of *US News and World Report* she'd found on the coffee table in the private secretary's office. She yawned, covering her open mouth with her palm, wondering how long the Boss and Teresi were going to be in the Oval Office. She knew they were having a meeting with Hudson Cooper, a CIA heavy, but that was all.

It seemed like a strange time for a meeting and she frowned, wondering if she wasn't witnessing the opening moves of a latter-day Cuban Missile Crisis. She'd been a kid back then, but those few days had scared the shit out of her anyway – for two weeks she and her classmates had done A-bomb drills, skulking under their desks while the sirens wailed and their teacher walked around with a transistor radio plugged into her ear.

To hell with that kind of thinking, she told herself. It was hard enough spending forty or fifty hours a week at the White House without worrying about what its occupants were doing, and she was suddenly glad that the private secretary's office was soundproof; she couldn't have eavesdropped if she'd wanted to.

At exactly 8:54 p.m. Eric Rhinelander pulled open the door leading from the cabinet room into the private secretary's office. His eyes swept across the relatively small room and found the figure of Beth Sheldrake. She was seated – a fatal error on her part – and seeing him she was trying to drag her own weapon from the spring-loaded shoulder holster dangling beneath her two-button blazer.

During regular practice sessions at the Secret Service Training Centre in Beltsville, Maryland, she consistently beat out most of her colleagues, her draw-aim-and-fire times always under two seconds. In real life, with a magazine in her hands, seated on a padded couch and completely unprepared, she took almost three and a half seconds to close her hands over the butt of the standard issue S&W .357 slung under her arm. It took Rhinelander less than two seconds to pick his target and fire his weapon, and a further fiftieth of a second for the frozen projectile to impact.

From a range of only twelve and a half feet the effect of the mercury and ice 'bullet' was devastating. The Secret Service agent's jaw had dropped in surprise as Rhinelander entered the room and the ball struck her open mouth, easily penetrating the soft palate of her tilted head, smashing up into the medulla, shattering and sending shards of frozen metal into her brain. She died at once, respiratory and motor functions wiped out in an instant. She slumped down onto the couch, brain matter and blood draining down into her mouth and throat. There had been no sound except for the paper-bag pop of the CO_2.

Barely pausing Rhinelander took three silent steps to his left, then gently twisted the deadbolt knob on the door leading from the office into the corridor. Ignoring the body of Beth Sheldrake he skirted the desk beside the hall door and stepped across to the door leading into the Oval Office. He took a deep breath, fixing the floor plan of the famous room in his mind.

Fireplace on his right, grandfather clock on his left. Directly ahead there were two couches, divided by a coffee table and a padded, spindle-back captain's chair facing the coffee table and the fireplace. From the photographs he'd examined he assumed that the captain's chair was reserved for the President. Fifteen feet behind the chair was the President's large oak desk, and beyond that the triple set of floor to ceiling windows facing due south. To the left of the desk, beyond the flagstaff, were the French doors leading out to the rose garden, and on the right, the door leading to the President's private office and bathroom.

The President would probably be seated in the captain's chair with Teresi on the couch to his right. Cooper would be seated with his back to Rhinelander. Range for the President would be twenty-three feet, and for Teresi twenty-five. The assassin checked his watch: 8:55:30. It would all be over within the next ninety seconds. Rhinelander flipped the rate of fire lever above the trigger from single shot to automatic and reached out for the brass doorknob.

'Where the hell is Spencer?' Stephen Stone asked angrily.

'Sweat,' Dimitri Travkin murmured, butting his cigarette into a half-empty styrofoam coffee cup that stood on the desk between him and Stephen Stone. The Russian stood up suddenly, turning to stare out towards the hallway behind them.

'What?'

'Sweat,' Travkin repeated. 'A few minutes ago I saw a uniformed man walk down the hallway . . . there.' He pointed.

'So?' .

'He was sweating,' Travkin said, anxiety in his tone. 'I noticed it. Sweat on his sideburns and jawline. There was a dark stain on the collar of his jacket, at the neck. Sweat.'

'What are you getting at?' Stone asked.

'The building is air-conditioned,' Travkin explained. 'I can feel it.'

'So why would he be sweating?' said Stone, completing the thought.

'Sick?' Travkin frowned.

Stone shook his head. 'Not on a night like this. You don't want the guards sneezing on the guests.'

'He was the right size and colouring.' Travkin mused. 'I only saw him for an instant but . . .'

'It's worth checking out,' Stone said. 'It beats sitting here doing nothing.' He reached out and picked up the telephone on the desk, punching up the main switchboard.

'Anything?' asked Lyall Spencer, staring over Roy Donner's shoulder, examining the computer screen.

'Nothing out of the ordinary,' the Duty Officer said, shrugging. 'Everyone assigned to duty tonight signed in properly. The only way to check for sure is to do a radio count, make sure everyone is where they should be.'

'How long will that take?' Spencer asked.

'Better part of an hour,' Donner answered.

'Shit!' Spencer swore. 'That's no damn good!' He looked up at the big IBM clock set above the surveillance monitors. There was a faint click as the minute hand jerked forward. It was 8:56.

Rhinelander burst into the Oval Office and gave himself a two beat count to get his bearings. Dark green drapes were drawn over all the windows and the French doors, and the room was brightly lit by hidden rows of fluorescents around the ceiling cornice, giving the office a glowing, almost theatrical look.

The three men were in almost exactly the positions he had envisioned, except that Teresi was a little further along the couch from Tucker's chair than he'd expected. Both the President and Vice-President were dressed in evening clothes. Cooper, with his back to Rhinelander, was less than ten feet away.

For a brief, frozen splinter of time everything remained as it was. Tucker slouched in the captain's chair, palm supporting his chin as he looked across at Cooper, a small smile masking obvious strain. Teresi, youthful, his clothes more stylish than the President's, his collar stud open and his bow tie askew as he leaned forward, tapping cigar ash into the cut glass receptacle in the centre of the table. Cooper's voice, ragged and worried.

Then everyone began to move. As the door crashed open Cooper turned, giving Rhinelander a brief look at his pale, lean face. Tucker gripped the arms of the captain's chair, eyes widening as he began to push himself upright, and Teresi, the most telling, rolled down across the couch, trying to duck beneath the coffee table as the searching muzzle of the assassin's weapon swept around the room.

Rhinelander fired three bursts, one directly at the President, one at the diving figure of Teresi and the last towards the figure of John Donnelly, the Secret Service agent posted at the formal hallway entrance to the office, who had rushed into the room at the sound of Tucker's frightened yell and the ripping, stuttering explosions of released CO_2 from the paintball gun. In all Rhinelander fired nineteen of the twenty rounds in the magazine, with at least a dozen hits. Then, right on schedule, the lights went out all over the White House as Rhinelander's 'mine' detonated deep underneath the north portico.

'Jesus Christ!' Spencer roared as every monitor screen went dark. Scores of alarm lights began to flash on the board in front of Donner. Although both the Signal Corps radio communications centre in the second level basement of the mansion and the Secret Service communications room were serviced by secure, dedicated electrical and fibre optic lines, the mansion and wings were serviced off a transformer vault on East Executive Avenue, which, although regularly inspected, was not immune to sabotage at the access point of its electrical duct in the north portico vaults. With no light in any of the rooms, all the Secret Service surveillance equipment was made useless with the exception of the panic buttons located throughout the entire building. The panic buttons were in turn connected to a system of bells and horns which alerted the Secret Service and everyone else within hearing that the President was in trouble.

'We've got a PB alert in the Oval Office!' Donner boomed. Faintly, Spencer could hear the sound of bells. He knew that the guests, most of them halfway between the state dining room and the library, would be panicking, but he couldn't have cared less.

'Go Hurricane! Now, goddammit!' Spencer yelled.

Blindly, Donner hit the transmit button on the console in front of him and then spoke firmly and clearly into the microphone headset that curved in front of his mouth.

'This is Dungeon. We have a Hurricane warning in the west wing. No response, all agents converge immediately.'

Hurricane warning was a scenario that Spencer had developed himself and had practised with every shift of men on the White House Detail. It was a three-stage intrusion alarm, based on the concept of a lunatic member of a tour somehow managing to gain access to the west wing and perhaps even the Oval Office. The initial response called for every Secret Service agent on building perimeter control to converge on the Oval Office while outer perimeter agents and EPS officers would seal every exit. During drills Spencer had worked it down to an art, with his inner perimeter agents reaching the west wing within two and a half minutes, with full outer perimeter security in place in two minutes fifteen seconds.

Those were drills, however, and did not take into account the possibility of total darkness within the building, or the complication of what amounted to a state dinner, with guests and staff suddenly plunged into blackness. In fact, it took Spencer's agents almost four minutes to ring the west wing offices, and even then, only a third of the agents actually made it. Outer perimeter security was somewhat better and was fully in place within three minutes. In both cases, however, it was definitely a case of closing the stable door after the horse had bolted.

'What the hell!' Stephen Stone rose out of his chair in the press room as the lights went out and the booming tremor of the vault explosion shuddered through the building.

'Bomb?' asked Travkin, peering into the gloom at his companion.

'No,' said Stone, shaking his head in the darkness. 'I think it's going down. I think it's Duncan!' Frantically he looked down at the dark outline of the desk, searching for a weapon. The best he could do was a memo-spike complete with half a dozen unanswered messages. Scooping it up, Stone pushed around the desk and joined the Russian, who was already heading for the open archway leading out to the hall.

'He went to the right,' said Travkin.

'That leads to the colonnade and the cabinet room, I think,' Stone answered, feeling his way along, one hand against the wall. The FBI man reared back suddenly, spotting the darkened figure of a man less than twenty feet ahead, running hard.

Stone didn't hesitate; dropping into a half crouch he tried to catch the running man in a waist grip tackle. Beside him, Travkin acted more directly, lunging forward, arms outstretched. Stone made contact, then felt a terrible pain in the side of his head, followed by a blinding flash and a deafening roar. He could feel consciousness fading but in a final moment of lucidity he drove his left arm up, the memo-spike against his palm. He had the brief satisfaction of feeling the spike connect with flesh and bone and then he passed out, assuming, logically enough, that he'd been shot in the head and was now in the process of dying.

At 11:45 that evening, almost three hours after the Oval Office attack, Hudson Cooper was returned to the Watergate with a full escort of Washington Metropolitan Police and four Secret Service agents. Immediately after the attack he had been taken from the White House to George Washington University Hospital for examination. Leaving the grounds of the Presidential mansion he had seen Marine One lift ponderously off the south lawn, presumably taking Tucker and Teresi to Walter Reed.

Cooper had allowed a short debriefing while he was examined, but then, pleading exhaustion, he had asked to be taken home. Arriving at his apartment he locked the front door, leaving two of his four-man Secret Service contingent in the hall outside. The other two agents were patrolling the main floor and half a dozen Metro Police had been attached to the Watergate until further notice, or until the assassin was found.

Numb with fatigue, the stooped, thin-faced man poured a drink and eased himself down in front of the television in his living room. He lit a cigarette from the box on the coffee table, nervously rubbing the cool metal of his late wife's lighter in his hand as the TV sprung to life. Using the remote control he flipped through the channels, all of which were still broadcasting news of the terrible event. He finally settled on WDVM, the local CBS station.

Ironically it was only then that he learned exactly what had transpired over the last hours. The attack had taken place so rapidly he never had time to think, and after being whisked away from the White House neither his escort, the doctor examining him, nor Spencer, the Secret Service man who debriefed him, had divulged any information at all.

It appeared that Tucker had been killed during the attack, struck twice in the head, once in the throat and once in the chest. There were confused reports regarding the Vice-President, but at that point he was known to be in critical condition, if not already dead. Cooper's presence in the Oval Office at the time of the assassination was not being reported yet, but he knew that it would only be a matter of time.

There was virtually no news at all about the killer. The Secret Service wasn't talking, but the Marine guard on duty at the main entrance to the west wing reported that an ambulance had removed at least two people from the west wing. According to the guard one of the men was an FBI agent, and the story being circulated was that he had injured and possibly managed to kill the President's assailant. There were no confirmed reports of this, however.

Searching for more news, Cooper flipped to NBC's Channel 4 and found a secondary story being reported: an audio tape, purportedly recorded by a man named Nezar Assad, had been dropped off at radio station WNTR. On the tape Assad took full responsibility for the assassination in the name of of his organisation, the All Islam Liberation Front.

The tape went on to say that rather than endure the possibility of capture and trial, he preferred to die a glorious death at his own hand. Shortly after the delivery of the tape there had been a large explosion at the vacant Iranian Embassy compound on Massachusetts Avenue, which was now under investigation by the FBI and Metropolitan Police. Initial reports stated than at least one person had been killed by the blast, and perhaps more.

The NBC channel was also now confirming reports that an FBI agent named Stone had managed to injure President Tucker's assassin. From what the on-site reporter understood the assassin, wounded, had made his escape through the sewer and service tunnels running beneath the White House, and had left a blood trail indicating that he had been seriously wounded by Stone. The FBI man and his unidentified companion had been taken to Doctor's Hospital on Eye Street. As yet, there was no word on their condition, or any information about the man with Stone at the time of the assassination.

Taking a swallow of his drink, Hudson Cooper, now utterly drained of all emotion except a deep, unspeakable depression, watched as all the news networks broadcast a brief taped segment showing a haggard Joseph Swanbridge at the podium of the newly designed press conference room in the east wing. The Secretary of State, flanked on either side by at least a dozen Secret Service agents, was describing the Succession Act and explaining his position.

With letters of intent long on file by both the President of the Senate and the Speaker of the House, and in the light of the 25th Amendment sections relating to Presidential and Vice-Presidential inability to govern, he, Joseph Swanbridge, as next in line, was assuming the role of Acting President until such time as Vincent Teresi, in writing, declared himself fit to take the office vacated by President Tucker on his death.

Sighing, Cooper dropped back against the padded cushion of his chair and used the remote control to turn the television off. He sat quietly for a few moments, sipping occasionally from his drink, the cigarette forgotten in the ashtray in front of him on the coffee table.

He closed his eyes and instantly he found himself relieving the horrifying events in the Oval Office. He remembered turning in his seat on the couch, knowing what was about to happen, and seeing the face of the man he'd hired to assassinate Tucker and Teresi. Somehow he would have felt better if it had been the face of a madman or fanatic, but the face he saw was only cold and methodical, handsome perhaps, except for those flat, empty, expressionless eyes.

And then he'd seen the long black barrel of the gun, heard the coughing, ripping sound, watched Tucker lift half out of his favourite chair, only to be slammed back into it and tipped backwards onto the huge carpet inlaid with the Presidential seal, dead certainly before he struck the ground.

The telephone trilled on the end table at his right hand. He lifted the receiver and listened, staring blankly out across the room to the drawn curtains over the living room window. The one-sided conversation continued for the better part of five minutes and then Cooper hung up the telephone softly, pausing for a moment to watch the slight tremor in his hand.

He stood up, then, and made his way through the apartment to the bedroom. Bringing down an ordinary shoebox from the shelf in his cupboard he removed a Springfield Armory 1911-A1 .45 calibre automatic pistol. He slipped a full magazine into the butt of the weapon and pulled back the slide, pushing one of the fat-nosed shells into the breech. Taking the gun he went to the kitchen where he poured himself a glass of cold water, then returned with gun and water to the living room. He stood in front of the fireplace, staring at the painting over the mantel, then turned away. He didn't want to make any mistakes and knew that liquid would increase the concussion effect tenfold, so he took a long drink of water, holding it in his mouth while he inserted the gun barrel between his lips. Eyes wide open, he squeezed the trigger without flinching, and blew his brains out all over the painting of his mother on the wall.

CHAPTER TWENTY-SEVEN

Seventeen days after the assassination of Geoffrey James Tucker and four days after the release of Vincent Teresi from Walter Reed Hospital, Stephen Stone drove down the winding, tree-lined drive to Stoneacres, Hollis Macintyre's estate on the Potomac, south of Washington. The sun was lowering, casting long, cool shadows over the rolling lawns of the estate, and Stone was tired after a day which had begun with a farewell breakfast at Dulles Airport, an hour before Dimitri Travkin stepped onto the Aeroflot jet waiting to take him back to Moscow.

After two weeks of testimony behind closed doors for the newly formed Morgentaler Assassination Committee, Dimitri was returning home in his new role as media darling, and sporting fresh shoulder boards on his GRU uniform marking his promotion to Major General. Stone was sorry to see his friend leave, and over breakfast he'd made one last and only partly serious attempt at getting him to defect.

Travkin appreciated the gesture but declined; if he defected the best he could expect was a book contract and some brief notoriety before he faded into obscurity. Back home, given his hero's role in helping to track down Tucker's assassin, it seemed that the sky was the limit. As a representative of a new era in East–West relations you couldn't beat tackling a President's killer, even if you did wind up being kneed in the groin and left stunned on the floor as the assassin escaped.

Stone brought the car to a halt in front of the imposing columned entrance and climbed out into the cool, early-evening air, a slim briefcase in one hand. He touched the small bandage covering the all but healed wound at his temple and took a deep breath, enjoying the scent of new mown hay and the lilacs massed against the stone walls of the house. He went up the short flight of steps leading to the door and rang the bell. A few seconds later an elderly black man, his hair grizzled, answered the door. Stone nodded. According to the dossier he had built up on Macintyre, this would be Benjamin, his butler-valet.

Benjamin led him into the foyer, then guided Stone around to the large, high-ceilinged library. Macintyre had left the drapes open, allowing Stone a fine view of the sloping grounds leading down to clumps of shadowed trees at the river's edge. Beyond the trees the Potomac flowed down to the sea, and beyond, he could just make out the eastern shore.

Benjamin left him at the doorway and Stone made his way across the pegged oak floors to the big coffee table in the centre of the room. Macintyre was waiting for him, bulk arranged on a love seat, one small hand holding a tiny crystal liqueur glass, half-filled with some gleaming amber liquid.

'Agent Stone,' Macintyre said, his voice as rich as the liquor in his glass. He inclined his huge, leonine head briefly. Stone watched the man's eyes. Wary and analytical. He was on his guard.

'Mr Stone will do,' Stone answered. 'As of ten days ago I was seconded from the Bureau as Special Investigator for the Morgentaler Committee.'

'I was aware of that,' Macintyre answered, nodding again. 'What I am not aware of is your reason for requesting this interview. As you know, President Tucker and I were only barely acquainted.'

'Yes, I know that,' Stone replied. He snapped open the briefcase in his lap and withdrew a sheaf of paper. 'As of this moment our interview is strictly off the record.'

'Really?' said Macintyre, raising an expressive eyebrow. 'I'm not sure I want any interview I have with your committee to be off the record.'

'I'm conducting the meeting at the express wish of Senator Morgentaler himself. In his own words he'd like you to have as many options available to you as possible. I'm not sure I agree.'

'Agree with what?' Macintyre asked politely.

'He's willing to let you off the hook, just to keep things on an even keel,' Stone answered. 'Personally I think you should be tried for treason and then executed.'

'Good lord!' said Macintyre, amused. 'You seem to be a man of strong convictions. What do you base this fervent animosity upon?'

'Facts,' Stone answered. 'According to the information I've been able to put together so far, on my own and with the help of Dimitri Travkin of Soviet Military Intelligence, you were part of a conspiracy to assassinate the President and the Vice-President of the United States. You and several others, including Hudson Cooper, Deputy Director of Operations for the Central Intelligence Agency, as well as Mr Shrenk, the Attorney General of the United States, became aware that President Tucker was suffering from an advanced form of a dementia known as Creuzfeldt-Jacob disease.

'Based on your knowledge of the disease, or rather Hudson Cooper's knowledge through his connection with Dr Barron at Walter Reed, you and the others of your group decided that the best course of action would be assassination. You included the Vice-President in your scenario, knowing that his policies were far from being in accordance with your own.'

'Poppycock!' Macintyre laughed, taking a sip of his drink. 'Babble. You have no proof of any of this.'

'I'm afraid we have a great deal of proof, Mr Macintyre, some of it provided by Gennaddi Koslov of the GRU, and even more from Vladimir Gurenko of the KGB. They have been most forthcoming, Mr Macintyre, and it appears that your meetings at Cherry Hill Lane were better attended than you knew.'

'You intend to swear information at a Senate Committee meeting from known Soviet agents?' scoffed Macintyre. 'Good luck, my friend.'

'We have more than that. We have Hudson Cooper.'

'Cooper is dead.'

'He sure is.' Stone nodded. 'He was very emphatic about cashing in his chips. He had good reason.'

'Indeed?' Macintyre asked.

'Yup,' Stone said. 'He was the one who hired Duncan. We still don't have a real name for the man.'

'Or the man himself. Much like Lee Oswald,' Macintyre added.

'They found a blood trail in the sewers all the way down to the main junction,' said Stone. 'My people also had the houseboat covered. Duncan never appeared. The odds are he drowned in the main sewer or got trapped in one of the muck catchments.'

'Perhaps.' Macintyre shrugged. 'But the truth of it is, you have no killer, you have no conspirator who hired the killer, good Lord, you don't even have his name.'

'No,' Stone answered. 'Not his name, but I do have a list of other names. Names even the committee doesn't know about. In fact the only one who's seen these names is Josh Morgentaler.'

'What names are these?' Macintyre responded coldly. Stone smiled to himself. Cold or not, he was getting to the son-of-a-bitch.

'These are names my ex-wife sent me,' Stone answered, trying to keep his voice steady. 'She sent them to me before she was murdered by a KGB Spetznaz group. I didn't find them until I got out of hospital.'

'Ah,' Macintyre said theatrically. 'Now I'm beginning to see your drift. You wish to give information from the KGB to the Morgentaler Committee, but you also say they murdered your ex-wife.'

'That's right. They were worried because they thought she was going to blow a huge net of agents who'd been in place for years, some of them for decades.'

'What does this have to do with Tucker's killing? From what you say it would appear that your ex-wife was working for the Russians.'

'That's right,' Stone said. 'She was part of the group of illegals and deep cover agents the KGB was trying to protect when they killed her. I've met with General Gurenko and he showed me her file. It doesn't do my ego much good, but presumably being married to me seemed like a good idea from an espionage point of view.'

'I still don't see what this has to do with Tucker's death,' said Macintyre, 'or what it has to do with me.' The fat man's tone was exasperated.

'She also worked for Hudson Cooper as a courier, and sometimes as an intelligence analyst. She was a CIA mole.'

'And you got this information from Gurenko at the KGB?' Macintyre asked coolly.

'You bet,' Stone answered. 'These guys have got strict orders from the top: any help we need, we get. They're willing to cooperate completely, just so long as we don't implicate them in an assassination plot.'

'And this list of names,' said Macintyre. 'They know you have it?'

'They don't even know it exists,' Stone answered, grinning. 'Debbie was being run by one of their top people at Moscow Centre, a man named Kuryokhin, an old-style spymaster. According to the material Debbie sent me, she was his personal asset within the CIA.'

'I still don't know what this has to do with me,' Macintyre said wearily. He glanced pointedly at his wristwatch, a thin gold Patek Phillippe. 'It's getting late, Mr Stone, and I'm an old man. I need my sleep.'

'I won't take much more of your time,' Stone said, 'and my reasons for showing you the list are personal. I know I'll never be able to tie you absolutely into this conspiracy, any more than Cooper, Shrenk or any of the others. Morgentaler knows it too. But we want you to know you're being watched. We want you to know that *we* know – that's all.'

'All right, you've come down here to see what rattles when my bones are shaken. Consider it done,' Macintyre said. 'And frankly, I don't really think I'm interested in your list. I think you should be on your way.'

'You want to see the list,' Stone answered. The room was almost dark now, the light in the room a blue glow. Macintyre made no move to turn on any lights. Stone pushed the Xeroxed list across the coffee table at the fat man. 'It's the name underlined on the third page.'

Macintyre leaned forward heavily and picked up the list. He turned to the third page, turning it towards the windows and holding it close to his face.

JOSEPH GEORGE SWANBRIDGE/enlisted-Yale University/Mar 24/1940/key as code MARYBELLE.

'You can't be serious!' said Macintyre, turning to look back at Stone.

'Keep reading.' Stone zipped up his briefcase and stood up, his jaw tight with anger. 'It's all there, Macintyre. Rich boy at Yale, father a doctor, mother a radical poet. It's 1939, 1940 and the world's going to hell. Europe's in flames and the US isn't far behind. Time for a new order. Your pal Swanbridge went for it all, and they kept him away from

any obvious demonstrations or groups. They had him pegged as someone who'd go a long, long way. And he did.'

'It's insane!' Macintyre whispered. Stone leaned forward and plucked the list out of the man's hand. He opened the briefcase far enough to slide it in and then stared down at the slack-jawed man on the love seat.

'You thought you knew it all, didn't you, Macintyre? You and your invisible friends, your government by secret committee.' Stone's voice was dry and hard. He bent closer, his face no more than a foot away from Macintyre's. 'Well, you screwed up badly, Hollis. If your killer had finished the job your man Swanbridge would have made it. Bad enough he became Secretary of State, Hollis, but you actually made him President of the United States, even if it was for only a few days.' He straightened and shook his head.

'Think about that,' Stone said softly in the gloomy half-light of the book-lined room. 'You almost put a KGB sleeper in the Oval Office.' He smiled grimly. 'And you know what, Hollis? Everyone who's anyone, every power-broker who counts is going to find out about what you almost did. Cooper was smart enough to kill himself because he knew what would happen to him when it all came to the surface. The Senator wanted to give you the chance and so did Teresi but I'm willing to bet you don't have the guts to do the same thing.'

Stone tucked the briefcase under his arm and walked away, heels tapping on the shiny wood floors. He paused in the doorway and turned back to the fat man, slumped silently in the love seat, his huge head silhouetted in the last light coming through the French doors behind him.

'Prove me wrong,' Stone said, staring at the huge old man. 'By all means prove me wrong.'

Macintyre waited until Stone had gone, and then stood up slowly. He opened the doors and stepped out onto the small patio, edged with a waist-high stone wall. The fat man crossed to the wall and put his palms down flat on the cold granite as he stared out over the river.

Stone was right, he had no stomach for suicide, but God only knew, the prospect of his name and reputation being fouled was equally horrific. Without power he was nothing, and if he was nothing he would die. Sighing, he turned away from the darkening view of the water and at that exact moment the bullet from the Marlin .44 hunting rifle struck him full in the chest, slicing through the fatty tissue below his collarbone and blowing through his heart like a copper-jacketed fist. It was a perfect shot.

Hidden in the trees beside the rushing river 250 yards away, Eric Rhinelander watched through the Tasco scope as his quarry fell. He lowered the rifle and nodded. As best he could, he'd completed the assignment and closed the last door. All that remained now was the future.

* * *